MW01503279

THE ISLAND OF
MACBETH

MIKE KOSTENSKY

DENVER, COLORADO

GRATITUDE:

With extreme gratitude, I would like to thank Shirley Mars for proofing this book. With me it seems the words and ideas flow faster than my spelling and grammar. After my four years at Walsh Jesuit High and college, I would have thought I had learned to master the English language better. Oh, well; we learn what we learn, and that is why I'm glad I have a friend who is the master of editing and baking great cookies. Thank you, Shirley!

DEDICATION:

I have no choice but to dedicate this book to my wife Debbie, for she is one of the people I care about the most in this world, yet she was stuck dealing with my emotions, anger, and confusion as I tried to control the gouging need inside of me to finish this book once and for all. She is a saint for putting up with me at times. I guess that's what love is really all about.

Secondly to my children, Hope, Heather, Cody, and Holly, who make all things in life worthwhile!

THE ISLAND OF MACBETH: 2/28/98

IN LIFE, ALL THINGS ARE INHERENTLY EQUAL
REGARDLESS OF THE VICTORS OF LOVE AND WAR.
AT THE END OF TIME, WE WILL ALL LONG AGO HAVE
TURNED TO DUST. WHILE LIFE CONTINUES, WHAT
WILL STILL SEPARATE US, THE LIVING AND THE DEAD,
ARE THOSE AMONG US WHO DARED TO RIPPLE THE
POND OF LIFE.
    - MITCH OF MACBETH

Contents

CHAPTER 1:
WE GO WHERE
WE ARE TOLD

It's been too many years since Mitch felt the need to write, but only he knew how time and memories had a way of distorting the real story.

Like 1987 was only yesterday, Mitch could still remember the smell of sizzling flesh, fresh glistening blood, and the crazy out-of-place smell of Old Spice cologne that still invaded his thoughts. Periodically these unique thoughts reinvaded his senses, and sent him hurling back to that defining portion of a once-simple excuse for life. All these years and too many unanswered questions later, Mitch realized the real story deserved to be told.

How could he start? Would they listen to his side of the nightmare? How could he ever try to explain a thought that led to a revolution that almost tore a part of this country in two, when to him, portions of his blurred reality were still a bad dream? He knew, alone with his thoughts, that the brave ideals, good or bad, would always have a home in his memories. Memories that remembered where a little bit of Camelot's goodness did survive in a modern era, and that there really was a fabled time and place that lived on in people's hearts.

It's still hard for Mitch to believe that there was a slower time and place when the old never seemed to get older and the young stayed innocent. That was how life and death always seemed to unfold on the island of Macbeth, off the coast of Massachusetts.

With many passing years, the days still got longer as the nights got shorter. Seasons passed like the rusting fishing boats coming and going from that quiet, almost forgotten harbor. Always the same names inhabited this treasured community: same family names, different faces, just another island generation. Always two goals: the survival of family, and the preservation of the community.

Macbeth, it was said, was a time-warped community, a culture protected from those unseen evils that plague modern countries: evils that the doomsday worshippers said were slowly unraveling the social structure that made one feel secure.

The islanders were tucked away in their little corner of the world, keenly aware of what was happening around them, all just trying to hold on to that little piece of life that made them feel so unique and safe.

The only immediate access to Macbeth was by boat, a geographical fact that limited the island's exposure to the seedier segment of an overactive society. Mitch felt out of place: give him the graffiti-covered walls, litter, and crime-filled streets. That was the reality he was used to. A distorted reality learned and earned from years of battling those common vices and reporting from the city streets.

Being a magazine reporter, he tended to drift toward the uglier segment of society for that award-winning story, and the notoriety that goes with shock journalism. How Mitch was lucky enough to be picked for this story, he would never know. As most young journalists really believed, there would always be one defining moment in their lives, when they were king and the world was theirs and their words became the mightiest army. Without any further ado, let Mitch's fifteen minutes begin...

On assignment again, he, with no questions, was sent to Macbeth by his overfed editor, Hazel Gertrude Schmidt. She was probably a former editor with the Hitler youth, he would often say. He was sent with firm intentions of doing a romantic and colorful story about a seaside community, its fishermen, and its interesting collection of 425 souls, give or take.

Mitch's editor was sure this was a town where stories walked the streets and were just waiting to be scooped up and processed into literary form. Hag Hazel, as Mitch referred to her always demanded new and marketable reading material. Mitch, who was just her underpaid slave for the ever-hungry population of the heartland, was just looking for that escapism from the everyday 9-to-5 grind.

"Colorful," his editor said, "lobster-stewing, crabs-screaming, mom-and-pop stores with children still allowed to buy real candy, and eat it! There was a culture of children never afraid of who was watching them, ready to steal their unchallenged innocence."

Yes, there was still a town, outside of many folks' memories, where people really did walk hand-in-hand down a street of unlocked doors. Plain folks, old and young who would stay out past dusk, not worried about who was hiding in the dark shadows, those looking for some easy unsuspecting prey to snatch and defeat.

Strange, it seemed to him, strange for one so used to the routine of alarms and deadbolt locks: frustrated sense of modern day security, a security that only would keep the non-criminals away. The constant sound of sirens wailing to and from a frequent crime or accident scene, such common sounds, that after a while they all just seemed so unnoticed. To regular city dwellers like Mitch, it became just another sound of his city nature. In his city, the piercing sirens were just another familiar city sound, common as the country bullfrog strutting and sounding off his oversexed stuff.

Mitch's crammed and chaotic world, he was sure, was what he wanted and deserved. Mitch had started writing for his high school paper, only because it got him out of class and down to the school newsroom. In their little room, they hid away from authority, no one breathing down their necks or trying to stuff some crazy foreign phrase in their overactive teenage brains.

Mitch was in high school for the adventure of finding a woman: nothing more, nothing less. Face it, most teenage boys have about one goal in life after elementary school, and he wasn't going to be any different. Anyhow, by this point in his life, he figured he knew it all.

With a little luck and a lot of scotch, his parents survived his school years, with little help from Mitch. With the passing of time, he realized he really did like writing, even though it seemed Mitch could always start a dozen stories and never finish one. There were too many distractions around him, or there was always a better story to write--and, on more than one occasion, there was a young girl to chase and be rejected by all over again. Mitch could always turn back to his faithful pen and escape away into the inner depth of his constantly reeling mind.

Mitch's college years came in fast, like an out-of-control Mack truck, and the real world was here. A strange new world of credit cards, tuition, student loans, bills, and all the stuff that made him realize he was really going to have to get a real paying job.

Still fighting what society expected of him, he surmised that bills were created just for jump-starting out-of-touch youth back into reality kicking and screaming. The end of youth was always tough, as time marched on for all of them regardless.

His early years were sneaking away, and as with his dad before him, the 9-to-5 grind was waiting. The end of his age of innocence was as brutal as his dad had warned him about. Mitch's dad always told him, "Straighten up and listen to your folks; they might really know what they're talking about!" But did any of us ever listen? Mitch wasn't the exception, until reality bit him hard in the ass.

Mitch unfortunately knew not to worry – the bill collectors would find him soon enough. These modern-day bloodhounds seemingly alone possessed the magic wands and crystal balls for tracking most deadbeats down. The summer of '65 lived on for such a short time, as its memories faded away like the sunset of a drifting youth.

Campus papers and college journalism were great for people like Mitch, all young writers trying to write on the social edge. Campus politics, what's showing, who's doing what in intramural, and the usual fill-in-the-blank stories. Journalism was where it was. Give him khaki shorts, a pen and a note pad, and he was off; he'd conquer the world by 5 and be home in time for dinner.

Five years too long in college and a big degree in journalism, and out to the big pond of life he was sent. What had he really learned in college that he didn't already know?

Mitch was always amazed at how writing could tweak the reader's secret emotions, how his inexpensive pencil and paper could become his mighty sword. His carefully picked words now would deliver hurt, hate, and love.

Alone with his words, in his intentional silence, a writer stood with the bankers, politicians, and the lawyers. His powerful words could become part of them if they were lucky enough to read what he had dreamed. His crafted lines became the reader's white or dark knights, good or bad. The crusaders of their inner soul, as they, the readers alone in their private spaces, became his disciples of words. The devoted would now follow him and his visions as his new pages marched on in their minds.

It had been years since college. Boy, did Mitch learn that the real world could eat you up, and it would if you slipped. Realizing all of us might be only a footstep away from the homeless guy on the street, he trained himself always to just listen for those cold footsteps. Mitch knew that in this brave new world, life on the street is only one brutal mistake away.

He often wondered…what if he really had listened to his parents. Would it have made his life any easier? Probably not, he surmised: growing up was one of the greatest lessons he learned in life.

Oh, he thought, to be young again and start over. Don't get him wrong, forty was not that old. He had a nice car, a good job, and he was on his way to Macbeth.

CHAPTER 2:

PEACE

It was a hell of a send-off Mitch received the night before – he didn't even remember her name. She must have been great, or maybe it was the half dozen or so Long Island iced teas. His throbbing head didn't think so; it seemed to be rocking more than the boat. It really didn't matter now: she was just using him, he kept telling himself. Mitch knew who was using whom: the truth was ugly. Maybe in Macbeth he could get some of the redemption he needed for this damned lifestyle he led.

Mitch was surprised to see his editor Hazel show up at his party, but she was just there spying on him. He was sure Hazel had him all figured out by now. She'd had his number since he started. Mitch hoped that little redhead he was with last night didn't. Mitch didn't tell her he loved her--or did he? The only thing he remembered loving on her was that tight body, but he was sure by the way she acted that she had heard that line before. What would those crazy nuns think of their little schoolboy now? Bend over and get ready for the divine yardstick, he thought, salvation Catholic-style.

Riding the bucking, ancient ferry over the next morning didn't help Mitch's head: hung over again. He really didn't feel much like talking, but some kid with short red hair next to him kept pestering him. Peace McClure was this island chap's name. His parents were probably from the '60s, high on who knows what, both probably watching the animated movie *Wizards* over and over again. One day, coming down off some psychedelic trip, they must have realized she was pregnant and soon, out popped Peace.

Rather nice kid he was, just like his name. For a former flower child, he wouldn't fit in: he wore no tie-dye or beads. The boy was so conservative and pressed he almost made Mitch feel like the radical from his days at Kent State.

The trip dragged on and Mitch, still hung over, was bored, and like his mother, talking was his way of passing the time. Too bad for Peace, who was now in his sights as he pursued his trade and forced himself to pass the time of day by talking to him. Relentlessly badgering Peace if he must, he grasped for a foothold to start his story, just hoping Peace might be carrying some magic aspirin to relieve Mitch's frustrated inner demons.

Peace was young and a bit disillusioned with the real world. A stockbroker from Long Island – how would you figure? Peace use to repair subs for the navy. His unique name probably drove the war-loving general nuts. Mitch, in a weird way, figured that this character would be a great introduction for his island story, a story that had to start somewhere.

Relentless in pursuing his vile trade, Mitch trapped Peace as he spilled what little dirt he held on Macbeth. Peace was sure Macbeth was safe from talk show host, as Mitch got the feeling this ferryboat ride over was about the most excitement he was going to see. Mentally, he tried to prepare himself for a recess of life in the slow lane.

The remote possibility of Mitch being sucked into a

timeless vacuum, trapping him in a Mayberry R.F.D scenario for life, didn't worry him. Mitch was doomed to just a couple week in a slow hell. At least he would get paid, he hoped. Were the checks good in hell, he wondered?

Mitch should have figured Peace wasn't into any kind of drugs, aspirin included. Mitch's crowd never quite looked at aspirin as a drug, more like an essential vitamin. His headache was shit out of luck. He chugged his bottle of Mountain Dew as they talked, hoping the caffeine and fizz would kick him at least into low gear.

A hesitant Peace told how he left the island to join the navy and see the real world. But he saw it, and all he could think about was coming home.

"It sort of grows on you when you're not looking," Peace said. "You think everybody knows your business, and you're probably right. But in the end, does it really matter who knows what about you? At least on Macbeth, you're somebody. Back on Long Island I was just another face in a big crowd. When I was away, it felt great to have a place to belong." Peace paused, looking out over the railing. "You know, everybody needs roots somewhere, Mitch--it's a natural kind of thing."

Thinking for a few moments, Mitch interrupted. "I be-longed once, and then my folks moved. Hell, I belonged the next time, and then they moved again. After the last move I stopped getting attached. It helped the hurt the next six times. I just sort of figured we were like gypsies, just without the tent."

Looking away at the wave, Mitch talked softly.

"I can't really blame my dad. He had to work to feed us. Times were tough and we all had to pitch in somehow. My contribution was keeping a stiff upper lip every time I had to say goodbye to my new best friend. I guess it made it easier on my mom and dad. Kids were tough, or so my parents figured. I guess I survived by myself--and as usual, most of the time alone."

"That is sad, Mitch, real sad. I thought I was the sheltered one. It took getting away and a real job to show me what was important."

"Hey, don't feel bad for me, Peace!" Mitch blurted out. "I'm a big boy. I bounced back and got even! Let's talk about you." Mitch wanted to change the subject as quickly as possible.

The two of them talked small talk a little longer, both enjoying the warm spring sun. Peace, never bashful, took off his shirt to catch the warming rays. Mitch, more secure with his shirt on, looked away. Maybe a little embarrassed, he felt people didn't need to be subjected to the sight of his flab. Peace, on the other hand, was still a prime example of youth, with a washboard stomach and a natural tan just multiplying his natural good looks. Next to Peace, Mitch felt like the old man with the gut, just standing and hiding in Peace's healthy shadow.

Interrupting the tranquil trance, the glossy white deck door to below opened with a loud creak. Two beautiful young women walked out into Mitch's absorbing vision. In awe at their simple beauty, he just stood there staring as they noticed Peace. Not a moment of hesitation for Peace to say anything, and the two women ran to his open arms. Two young girls standing within inches of his ever-young body, while all a jealous Mitch could do was gawk.

"Peace what are you doing here?" the young blonde screamed.

All smiles, Peace jumped up and let the girls fall again into his waiting arms. "I'm here for you, babe!" Peace exclaimed. All Mitch could do was drool as he, not wanting to be caught, checked both up and down. What was standing before him was serious *Sports Illustrated* swimsuit material. Mitch realized all of sudden that nasty hangover was gone. Standing a bit taller now, Mitch stood and with some extra muscle power, sucked in his extra girth.

One sweet young thing stopped hugging Peace just long enough to lift up her loose shirt, showing off her new tat. Mitch was trying like hell to control his lust, though his hormones were surely planning an attack. With Mitch's mouth wide open, Peace slapped him on the back and introduced him to his old friends Julie and Lynn from Macbeth High. Mitch, caught off-guard, lost in his world of lust, managed a timid "hi," as the two girls, not the least bit interested in him, turned away and pursued Peace's attention.

Mitch knew he meant nothing, since he was just an old drooling sack of flesh to them. Never one to give up, he studied Lynn and the way she curled her youthful lips while squinting her soft eyes just right. She was the all-American girl, and beautiful at that, and Mitch, in his demented way, could only pretend he was really noticed.

Catching his breath, Mitch tried to join in, while Peace, not pausing, told the girls what had really brought him back to the island.

Not much room for Mitch to join in; his unnoticed talk went nowhere. This moment was just for two island girls and their long-lost friend, catching up on the missing years between them. In his thoughts, Mitch half figured the two girls out. Lynn was young, sweet, and innocent. Julie seemed stuck-up, overly pampered, and of course, daddy's girl. Who knows how these two opposites ever got together? Their relationship had to be like sandpaper. Mitch hoped someday Julie would learn a hard lesson--but not today, and not from this dirty man. Lynn was another story. He mentally undressed her again and again, without even forgetting her name.

Staring at these visions of youthful beauty made the stale time fly. The two girls, in what seemed like short time, finished with Peace--or did he with them?

As neither girl had an iota of interest in Mitch, they turned to leave. Walking and wiggling away as quick as they came, they waved goodbye with a shake of their tiny hips. With only one lovely secured away in Mitch's memory, he drifted off in thought.

With the ferry horn blowing, Mitch popped back into reality and learned Peace was returning to live where he had been born. He had been hired to do a restoration project on some old World War II navy equipment. The week before Peace had walked out of his stock-brokering job, saying the stress of selling was going to kill him. Can't blame the guy he guessed, doing what you hate had to be a waste of time, and life, it seemed, was too short any more. Thank God: Mitch realized that he'd never had to get a real job.

It was amazing the pull Macbeth had on Peace. Mitch had never really experienced that kind of attraction--not sober, at least. Macbeth was starting to sound too good to be true, as hard and painful to believe as it was. Mitch thought maybe all small towns are alike that in a familiar way: people really caring about each other, practicing simple compassion for mankind.

You know, one neighbor helping the other.

Peace almost, Mayberry-like said, "Caring for each other was the biggest thing I missed." Quirky as it sounded, he missed the belonging.

Thinking about his job in Long Island, he said, "You can be ripped apart for only so long till you have to get out of that deep rut that's holding you down. Familiar people start becoming just another face in a big crowd."

Mitch said, "Crowds were where I came from. I didn't know one face from the other, and that was good. I was anonymous." Though now, unfortunately, he could relate to Peace in an envious sort of way--surely jealous at that.

Peace, being overly paranoid for someone so young, left the upper deck to check on some tools he had brought on board. Mitch figured he probably was just tired of hearing him rattle on. Alone again, he drifted back into his thoughts of Lynn, and then to his new assignment, as he tried to mentally prepare himself for what Hazel had gotten him into. Somehow, Lynn needed to be involved, even if it was only tucked away in his mind.

Listening to the chugging of that old diesel motor of the ferry, Mitch couldn't come close to focusing on his assignment. Once the man with nerves of steel, now again reflecting on his once-solid future, Mitch was nervous.

The rusting ferry, jerking as it crept along, was enough to give anyone second thoughts about the probability of arriving safely. Mitch realized he had seen less rust on the cars from the salt-strewn streets of the North Coast. At least this ferry seemed to be moving forward, sort of graceful in its ignorance, as it cut through the waves shooting back at the old boat. With the wind and salty spray in his face, Mitch realized he was not quite the sailor he dreamt he was. As the saltwater irritated his hangover-induced, no shaving lotion shave, he once again was that wild and free gypsy his dreams were made up of.

Mitch had always been told that first impressions were important. *Well, folks,* he thought, *these days you've got to understand the rough life of a starving journalist (most of them lazy and confused), and all going three directions at once for a story that no one really reads.* Luckily for him, today held only one direction. "Land ho!" one of the passengers shouted as the island peered out from the once-vast horizon.

Macbeth, in its simple majesty, looked rather imposing for a big tree-covered rock. The island was four and a half miles long, sitting alone in the beginning of this big churning sea. As a sentry, she stood wrapped tightly with massive stone cliffs hugging most of the island's pitted shores. Solid rock cliffs, topped with a frosting of thick green pine trees, beckoning the true island dweller in all of them.

Why was it he always seemed to see a church steeple first, instead of the romantic lighthouses? Maybe it was God's way of telling him that He was watching over him. Lord knew, he needed all the watching-over he could get. Hope He wasn't watching over Mitch last night!

Tourism and fishing were Macbeth's biggest industries. During the summer and fall, Macbeth's tourists swelled the island's population, especially compared to the isolationism of winter. Upper-class vacationers, singles, tightwads, and families, all trying to find their little niche in this tight-lipped community that for six months the visitors thought they controlled. Vacationers were searching for that little sense of belonging that their real world couldn't deliver, and that only the frigid Atlantic winters could instill and baptize into the true islander. Mitch later learned that winter on the island was a rite of passage for the dedicated believers of surf and solitude.

Being early spring, there wasn't much of a big tourist rush off the boat, just Peace, Mitch, the girls, and a group of young teenagers, mostly kids who were most likely escaping their youthful responsibilities, jobs, or parents for the weekend. It was maybe their unsupervised turn at freedom and new independence, all on their quest for adulthood--still just kids too eager to leave the boundaries of youth. Yet they violated the spirit of the ages while they could, as once achieved, they would be destined never to return to youth again.

Peace and Mitch said goodbye and made plans to go out one night soon for a few brews. A beer buzz always sounded good to Mitch, though that day Mitch couldn't wait, and he needed a brew now to temper his returned hangover. In his life, something about the ocean, boats, and ice-cold brews with a lime had always worked for him. Mitch always had an excuse for the dedicated drinker, as he waited for his turn to get off the boat.

As he walked down the moving gangplank, the romantic whitewashed community opened up before him. Alone in New England again, he scanned the quaint town. Antique homes and storefronts, all weathered by the old Atlantic, bearing the look of years of battling and losing from the sea.

Touching down on the wooden dock, Mitch was one step closer to real land. His legs wobbled as if they were still at sea. In a hurry, he walked on past the cigar-smoking fishermen hacking off a few fish heads with the glassy shocked eyes of that day's catch. Weathered fishermen, with a swift firm stroke, returned their catch's waste to the swimming marine cannibals below, waiting for their next free meal.

The smells of fish innards drifted through the air, and fish pieces and parts coated the old wooden dock. *Romantic, all right*, he thought, *if you're a hungry seal*. Mitch, moving on much quicker now, was just trying to escape that fish smell and the penetrating look from an unforgiving death in a net.

From past experiences, Mitch knew that if you ever wanted the real pulse of a community, you had to hit the local tavern or coffee counter. A few drinks with a local, and the gossip was usually yours. Gossip sells magazines and stories, and magazines and stories keep Mitch employed. (Mitch had always liked being employed; it was just the work part of employment that he had a problem with.) He had always known he could never have been a good bum: he talked too much. Mitch would have driven the other bums nuts, as they probably would have knocked him off some cold, dark night in his sleep.

Intently and with a distinct purpose, Mitch walked the wet cobblestone street. Throwing his white duffel bag over his shoulder, he whistled the only sailor song he knew. He envisioned himself as the salty sailor from one of the countless Old Spice commercials of his youth, stretching his sea legs to the tune of "Popeye the Sailor Man." Still, in the distance he could hear the retreating ferry blowing her deep horn. One lone ferry chugged through the choppy stretch of sea that separated the island of Macbeth from the ever-forbidding coastland.

CHAPTER 3:

IN BEER WE TRUST

The island air was still damp, with the sun barely poking through the rushing clouds. Mitch walked down Main Street, keeping his eyes peeled for a local watering hole, just thinking about some refreshing frosty madness.

Slowing his poignant quest, trying with what little coordination he had, he navigated through the slippery, mist-covered streets. In an instant he realized how badly he missed the rough security of asphalt, covered with city-generated trash.

Something about sea towns and the smell of fish: *Is that a good smell or a bad smell?* he wondered. His nose said bad, but the locals said fresh, but how did you figure? Fresh was foul? He had smelled day-old casualties on the battlefield of war that smelled better than that. The life and times of a fishing community – the nose knows.

Walking the street, Mitch couldn't get over the many types of old porcelain signs. He had seen many signs like these before, but they had been retired to the many antique shops he had been forced to cruise with a few of his eccentric girlfriends.

Buster Browns Shoes sold here--must be a time warp, he surmised. He hadn't seen these shoes in a while. An old-time barbershop with a two-dollar haircut was next door. There had to be a catch. This was all too familiar, bringing back forgotten visions from one of his many childhoods.

Small towns seemed to have it all, plus the innocence all lost when communities outgrew themselves. At times he thought it would be nice to walk down a street and really know your neighbors again. What a change--a friendly greeting, instead of a grunt from an annoyed businessman in a hurry to catch his train to his little corner of suburbia. Times had changed, as Mitch knew too well, when he glanced at his reflection in the storefront window.

That day, feeling a bit cocky, almost better than these islanders, Mitch continued up the street looking in storefront windows as he went. In a satirical way he felt for these backward folks, refugees from a modern society, destined to live life on the back burner of a world passing them by.

Approaching the general store, Mitch saw its unofficial welcoming committee sitting lazily outside on a long-ago-retired church pew. The three would-be greeters, seemingly enjoying the day, munched on peanuts and whittled away on their pieces of wood.

Crunching up to them upon their carpet of nutshells and wood scraps, Mitch called out: "Excuse me gentleman, where could I get a good espresso around here?" He did not want to ask for what he really needed, which he knew was to rid himself of his persistent hangover.

With puzzled stares, the three old men replied with a chorus of "What?" so Mitch repeated his question.

"I'm looking for an espresso, or even a strong java!" With the sudden realization that these men were clueless, Mitch translated, "Just looking for some coffee, please."

Interrupting, Jay – the one with many hairs coming out

of too many of the wrong places — looked up from his feeding frenzy, and with peanuts still in his mouth blurted out, "What's your problem, long hair?"

Taken aback at his ignorance, Mitch fumbled for a come-back. Realizing he was on their turf, he restrained his response.

"Sorry I bothered you all. Anyhow, I'll just keep passing on through." Mitch nodded his head goodbye, understanding his ponytail was more than those elders were ready to handle. He knew in his outside way he had just invaded their perfect world. He walked away as the smell of unwashed old men and Old Spice sealed Mitch's decision — his nose strongly urged him to move on.

"Try Fanny's for some coffee!" one of the old men said with a laugh. Mitch turned and thanked the old farts.

"Yeah, she serves all kinds!" another of the old guys chuckled.

It was strange for a city guy like Mitch to be in a small town. Towns like Macbeth on the mainland had been retired from real civic duty, most destined to survive the remainder of their use fullness in the shadow of some large mall or big shopping center. Small town main streets usually became store after store of antique shops or book stores, not everyday busi-nesses like Macbeth's storefronts that remained.

Walking on, Mitch realized daydreaming wasn't going to get him a story, but he was sure the Flying Daisy would. His coffee would have to wait. *What a name for a bar*, he thought--if he could just figure how it tied in with the sea. It was probably the name of some fast schooner, or maybe an unlucky fishing boat that got marooned on this large rock.

The Flying Daisy stood out. A two-story structure, she

was; an old-style Victorian building of red brick, nothing like you would expect to find in an old fishing town. For a tavern she was almost forbidding, until Mitch caught the sight of the familiar Budweiser sign, his universal welcome. Taking his cue from Bud, he prepared to enter the dimly lit structure.

For Mitch, walking into a strange bar was always a rush. Upon entering, you have invaded the locals' territory. It was an area that had been marked by years of bad stories and boring jokes. Salty gossip flowed much freer when accompanied by a shot and an ice-cold brew.

Most neighborhood bars were filled with the old and young just whiling their empty time away--comrades in spirits till they walked away, until their next designated hour, to return again and assume their rightful position on their favorite bar stool, hoping to spin another fabled yarn, or just hear the calming sound of another live human voice. Loneliness and alcohol are hard habits to break; seems most seldom want to try.

It was 11:30 a.m. beer time, and his coffee would have to wait. If Mitch wanted a story, he would have to bite the bullet and enter the den of lions. Pushing the huge oak door open, it squeaked an awful sound as its well-worn hinges complained. With a sound that obvious, everybody in the bar turned and stared at him as he stood tall, trying to hide his renewed uncertainty.

How could you figure--a full bar so early in the day, with only one open stool, he thought...and that one stool was next to the biggest guy in the bar. When he walked in, every eye seemed focused on him as they sized him up. Do you stay or go? Seconds seem like minutes, while they check you over. Do they smell fear? It's all in the eyes as one by one, turned back to their drinks and resumed their passion.

Every once in a while you strike gold, even if it means sitting next to the town blowhard, and old Jack seemed to be Macbeths answer to that. Jack thought himself to be the town's authority on everything; Mitch gathered this after sitting by him for the longest five minutes of his life.

Jack was a big ugly man; years of working the sea could do that to a guy. He was one who seemed to be respected out fear rather than an earned regard. Mitch couldn't like everybody, and he prayed Jack didn't notice him listening.

Jack's kingdom that particular day was the walls of this bar, and his subjects consisted of the lonely drunks taking up the nearby bar stools. His crusade was achieving the right buzz to carry him through the rest of the day. His cohorts in drink seemed all too eager to follow whoever would buy their next round.

It seemed to Mitch that these souls all followed two masters: Jack, and their other unseen master whose presence was always felt. This master was every bit as strong—stronger, maybe--though he never would lift a finger to defend his willing subjects in their habitual defense. His control was over their minds and bodies, though most would never admit it. The mighty bottle had a hold on each of them, all just believers of this ruthless villain, and top shelf or house choice, the spirits controlled this den.

Mitch didn't really care to hear the mighty Jack boast, but Mitch knew Jack could kill him with one swoop of his half-empty bottle. Listening to his banter, he guessed when you have the common sense of a jackass, you can bully people for only so long, until they wake up and realize that what you say doesn't amount to a hill of beans. Those sitting around him seemed to be in some self-induced time out, just sitting, half listening, half not, as the time of day slowly ticked by.

"Pour me a Bud, please," Mitch said with a nervous smile, his voice cracking. The bartender looked up, as he polished his glass, and with a slight twinkle in his eyes, he poured the refreshing suds.

"That'll be 50 cents, mister."

Mitch threw down a crisp one. "Keep the change, my good man," he said, still not believing his good fortune for such an inexpensive glass of brew.

With a feeling of relief, Mitch guzzled the golden liquid down as quickly as his parched throat would accept it. Slapping the empty glass down, Mitch burped and nodded at the bartender for another.

"Thirsty, are you?" the bartender asked as he filled Mitch's next brew.

Jack nodded to the bartender as he laid the next foaming beer in front of him. Mitch laid down another crisp dollar, but the bartender pushed it back, informing him that this one was on the house.

"Who do I thank?" Mitch asked, while all the bartender could do was wink and shrug his shoulders.

"Thank you, all!" Mitch yelled, though no one seemed to notice.

Jack, as Mitch later learned, was one of the town's trustees. He figured Jack thought himself almost a king, even though all a trustee is, is one of three who spends and manages your tax dollars. Mitch figured votes must make you feel powerful, and here was a prime example sitting right next to him. A big ugly man with too much testosterone--probably the reason there was an empty bar stool next to him in the first place. He could only wonder the real reason, as the cheap talk he sought seemed to avoid him.

Sitting quietly, Mitch felt a cold stare consuming his spirit. Turning his head ever so slowly, he saw the toothless smile of a thin lady who looked much older than her real age. The years of loneliness and alcohol had done their deed. On the mainland, he probably would have blown her off. Today, feeling much softer, Mitch in his judgmental pity for this soft creature turned to talk.

Judith McGuff was her name, and alcohol was her game. Mitch's once-brave heart broke as he learned the reality behind this toothless face. Her life could have been so much different, if her two sons and husband had never gone fishing that cold November day. Never a trace of the boat or bodies was ever found. These victims were just another statistic for the Atlantic, and an abrupt end to Judith's former life.

Pity and sympathy are usually so easy to find in the bars and taverns across the nation. Just like the churches draw the faithful, the beer joints have a similar pull, their patrons just worshipping a different god.

He learned that somewhere buried in Judith's imperfections was the former model she used to be, only now her Paris runway was replaced by the cold oak bar; her flashing camera lights were now the one too many lighted beer sign reflections from the shot glasses raised in unanswered toast. Mitch pitied the stranger, or pitied himself for being so judgmental about looks, judging before he learned the true identity of the creatures behind the human mask.

As if asking silent forgiveness for his intentional judging, Mitch laid some cash on the bar and paid for Judith's fix. Wallowing mentally in his insensitive pity, his self-induced trance was broken by Jack screaming, just as the cold beer seemed to be breaking the hold on his hangover. The bellowing let out Jack's raunchy breath, nearly blinding Mitch, but at the instant Jack's hidden words revealed some truth.

Somewhere deep in Jack's raving, he made a point to Mitch, who was just a focused listener. Feeling a bit buzzed, Mitch bought Jack a beer, hopefully sparing his shallow life as the next potential sacrifice to Jack's beer gods. With head bowed in respect for his size, Mitch prayed for his menial life. Lifting his head slowly, he realized Jack wasn't totally full of shit, as he heard a note of caring and concern arise from his tiny heart.

"Hey, you all, I'm doing this for you!" Jack screamed. "I'm old and my time is limited. I could sit around on my fat ass for years, and not shed a damn tear. It's not today you got to worry about--it's your future, your kids' future. So you stare at your half-empty bottle and see in the long run who is going to help you more, you stupid drunks!" Nobody flinched, they just stared deeper into their noonday drinks and tried to ponder the meaning of Jack's short-lived words.

Tuning in to Jack's rage while trying to block out the normal bar bullshit, Mitch realized something was up. A little skinny guy named Norm started ranting about how unfair the state government had been to the pressing needs of his family, how he was a drunk because of them--because, of course, it was never his fault.

"It ain't fair!" he yelled as he stood bravely for support beside his bolted- down bar stool.

"I got a fishing boat, and I can't even fish enough to pay for it! Hell, Massachusetts can't even control the crime on Boston's own streets and they're going to tell me when to fish and when not to? They are all self serving idiots!" Norm was on a roll now. "Who's going to pay my bills and feed my family?"

Joining in the bar room rebellion, another brave alcohol-flavored patron jumped in, banging his full, now-foaming bottle of brew on the bar, all the while yelling, "Tea party, tea party now!" in between the splashing golden froth and his drunken babbling slur.

Jack was getting revved up when his veins began to pop out as his face reddened. "Norm," he said firmly, "we don't talk about this here! Slim, sit your bony ass down! There's a time and place, and this isn't either." Jack turned and apologized to Mitch, "Sorry, mister."

No sooner had Jack shut Norm and Slim up than Charlie Piper started in about the IRS seizing his home and savings accounts. Charlie was dead drunk and was just spitting his words out. Through his spit, there was an air of honesty to his yelling. Just maybe, he had a reason for drinking. The guy sitting on Charlie's other side said the governor was his reason, and would be his target if he just had the chance.

Somewhat stunned at what he was hearing, and in a silent moment, Mitch attempted to speak.

"Name's Mitch," he said, trying to introduce himself. Jack brushed him aside and blared in.

"Folks, I said this isn't the time or the place, let it go, let it go now!" Mitch was no stranger to bar talk. He got his best stories from drunks. *Please don't shut up around me*, he wished silently.

The old lion had spoken, and his bar mates calmed down. Mitch was sure he had heard all they were going to let him hear today. Nobody seemed ready to talk anymore. They sank back down to their level and nursed the drinks in front of them as a Johnny Cash song played over the speakers.

Mitch finished his brew and decided it was best to move on and leave this little hotbed of dissent. He bid Judith good day when she grabbed for his hand and squeezed caringly with a soft thank you. The softness of her former life still dwelled in her long thin fingers, fingers that all too quickly let go and grabbed for the security of her martini glass. With a wink and a nod, he knew he had helped someone by just being there to listen.

Once again, a lonely little tavern wouldn't let Mitch down. His quest had begun, as he made ready to leave with more questions than answers. All in a day's work for a struggling journalist.

CHAPTER 4:

MAIN STREET MITCH

Little did anyone in Macbeth know or even care who this snooping journalist was. This man was Mitch Marshal, a former Walsh Jesuit Warrior: this was his only claim to a limited local fame. What a high school football team that they were! They had guts and glory, and an obscene dedication to the ball of leather and all the rewards it could bring to a life off the field. A lot of good it did Mitch: just another deflated dream.

Mitch: what a name. Who were his parents getting back at? He figured he surely could have been a Tom or a Rob, but his cards were dealt at birth…what could he do? Mitch's parents must have known something he didn't. Oh well, what's in a name anyhow?

Maybe Jack didn't like his name. Mitch should have talked football. Maybe the big guy would have talked to him then. Who knows? He probably was a disillusioned Browns fan and the talk would go nowhere, as all one fan could do was wait for their Super Bowl chance that seemed to never come.

The time to scoot had come. Mitch bid good day to whoever would listen, put his tip on the bar, and was out on the road again. The Cash song was stuck racing through his mind. Why did this seaside bar play country? Joking to himself he thought of a possible tabloid story with headlines declaring, "Island Bar Doesn't Play Buffet!"

He stepped out, now hangover-free, onto Main Street, and was immediately blinded by the bright sun. A flurry of activity was taking place before him, as his barroom eyes adjusted from the dimness of the tavern. He just observed all of the town people walking, talking, passing the local gossip, and going about their daily business. They were happy and content as life passed by; no rat race here, just another beautiful, breezy spring day.

Totally amused at the town's attitude, he started down the wooden sidewalk, just absorbing the flavor of this quaint town. A bit stumped and confused on the weak directions to the room he would have for the next few weeks, he stopped. He looked about for some help, searching for someplace harmless for his inquiry. Mitch knew Paxton's Corner Drug store surely held the answer for some quick directions, as a pharmacist had to know everybody and everything in any little town.

Pushing the "Drink Dr Pepper" door handle, with the bell ringing atop the glass door, she swung open. It was a step back in time for him: a full-sized shiny coffee and soda counter. This was a store like the memories of Mitch's lost childhood, still equipped with gleaming stainless steel fountainheads and vinyl-covered counter stools atop a checkered red and white tile floor. Scooping some ice cream, a counter monkey was still serving chocolate Cokes and real malted milkshakes. The door behind him closed and he was surrounded by the sound of sizzling burgers and chipped chopped ham cooking atop a large flattop griddle, and of course Elvis, still, "All Shook Up" playing in the background.

Mitch, being a retired counter junkie, had no choice but to sit down, a wee bit buzzed. He knew he had to go in for the munchies fix: a vanilla shake with double malt, whipped cream, and two cherries. If that still worked, he would top it off with a greasy double cheeseburger with ketchup, mayo, pickle, mustard, and a thick slice of sweet onion, add an order of crisp French fries, and wash the whole mess down with a big cherry Coke. Then, stuffed and satisfied, he would waddle off, a better man after his fat-filled caloric counter redemption.

It seemed that no sooner had Mitch started attacking his feast than two young boys, Billy and Liam, joined him. Racing each other to the counter, they were in for their weekend ritual: throw a dart at the balloon-filled corkboard, and whatever price was taped underneath your busted balloon was the price you paid for one of Paxton's big and legendary sundaes. With no sundae over 50 cents, you couldn't lose. What a sweet deal, the boys figured. Between sundaes and greasy French fries, life was great at the ripe age of eleven. With a pocketful of your mom or dad's change, how could life ever get any better?

"Hey mister, could you please move down one?" Billy belted out. Mitch was more than happy to help out and moved down a seat, as he eavesdropped on the unspoiled minds of the boys.

The boy did call him "mister," which always struck a bad chord with him. *Isn't that a term for an old guy?* he thought. In his mind he was still in the prime of his youth, though he was sure that in their eyes he was on his way out. Regardless, Mitch could listen and learn.

In that store, for some reason he wasn't afraid to talk to these kids. He didn't feel the suspicion of guilt you're under when you talk to a strange kid at home. In time, Mitch was cutting it up with the two kids as they let him into their little world. It was forgotten world that Mitch once again was invited in to explore, but it could be seen only through the eyes of a kid.

The two boys were going to hike to Lookout Hill, a grand hill that gave an unspoiled view of the island. Mitch was curious and asked if they would mind if he followed them. The boys, in their adolescent vigor, agreed--but only as long as the old man could keep up. Mitch paid the kids' bill with his, and they were off on his first great adventure since escaping the bar.

Picking their steps wisely, they walked up the rocky trail. Looking down at the harbor, Mitch spotted an old WWII sub tethered to the dock. Being a closet war buff, he couldn't believe he had had missed this treasure coming in. The tied- up sub, her black recon tower reaching for the sky, with yards of faded canvas that covered her deck guns, was old and silent, almost waiting to be exposed and used once again. The dull and flat black paint attested to her years in the sun, as the sub slightly bobbed to the incoming tide.

The boys told him her name was the *Flying Daisy*, which answered one of his earlier questions. She had been bought and brought here by the local VFW as a tribute to the boys from Macbeth who had served in that Great War. She was bought cheap after she tired of the hunt and could no longer keep up with the modern fleets.

The once-feared sub now floated, guarding the harbor, slowly rusting into her future, and probably reminding the town elder folks of their ultimate human sacrifices. Mitch watched her flag as the cross and skull flapped in the strong sea winds. Her big deck guns pointed out to the sea, almost as a warning for the unthinkable future to stay away, at least away from this town.

Billy and Liam thought it was neat, putting this old guy through the physical challenges of keeping up with two little lunatics with too much energy for their own good. Mitch was equally sure that they, on their spiffy mountain bikes, only multiplied the untapped energy of their youth.

He tried to save face and keep up, but rather than risking his first heart attack on them, he slowed down to a gentler forty-year-old pace. Mitch could only watch, eating their dust as the two raced up the trail. Lucky for him, it was a well-worn path, and even a city boy like Mitch could follow it.

Tall and full pine trees towered over his head, all giving off that fragrant smell of sap and old needles, a smell that gave him back that forgotten warm feeling he felt in his slower days. Abandoned by his guides, Mitch pressed forward, enjoying nature's peaceful tranquility, realizing a crowded city could never look this good.

The trail was short and wound its way around a tall hill, emptying into a broad valley. Just like the immaturity of youth, the two boys jumped Mitch as he rounded the bend. They figured they could pull one over on this old guy, and they were right. Startled but amused from this childish prank, Mitch checked his still- dry pants. He walked on, plotting how he could return their generous favor.

Together again, the two boys left their two abused bikes and walked on, talking only as best friends did. Mitch must've passed their test, since he was now accepted as an equal, and, for a fleeting instant, was a kid again.

"Hey mister, ever kissed a girl before?" Billy blurted out.

Not knowing what to say, Mitch pretended he was deaf, since it went right along with being older, he figured. Billy didn't want deafness and ignorance as an answer, so he yelled it again, just louder this time.

Mitch had to answer, so with a question he said, "Have you, you little twerp?"

"Sure, mister," Billy said, knowing Liam was soaking it all in.

"I kissed Hope in second grade, she was a babe-a-rama, and I didn't catch anything like my big brother said I would. Heck, I don't even see why it's such a big deal anyway."

"Aghhhhhh, cut it out, you liar!" Liam laughed as Billy took a fun swing at his buddy. With that, Mitch hoped Billy had had enough of this subject, knowing they would have plenty of time to understand sex in the future. Hell, Mitch still never understood the opposite sex, and didn't expect that he ever would. But Mitch had wished too soon, as Liam broke the comfortable silence.

"My mom never kissed my dad and then one day my dad left. I think it probably was about the kissing. Then she met Jethro Whipple and we moved to the island. I know it's gross, but he kisses her all the time now, and they aren't even married! Should be, with all the kissing they do--it's really gross, man. All she tells me is stop being so nosy and go to bed," Liam shouted out.

Oh, if they only knew, Mitch thought. *Childhood is good enough without any distractions like sex. Save the mysteries for a later age, after childhood has been laid to rest.*

When he was their age, Mitch never thought about sex. He was more interested in playing baseball in the street, and "combat" in one of his little yards. He and his friends could play all day long, until their annoyed parents screamed for the fifteenth time to get their little butts in the house or be grounded for the rest of their young lives.

As an adolescent, baseball and combat were on Mitch's mind day in and day out, and girls were just a nuisance. Too bad his parents didn't agree. They tried to make peace by including girls in games meant for boys, but it never worked out. Some girl always went home crying, and one of the boys was always blamed and grounded again for life, even though a life sentence was always a matter of a day or two, a sentence usually enforced only until their parents got so sick of them asking when life was up that they sent them back out to the battlefield. He was a little braver now for surviving an adult's wrath and punishment. They were He-men women haters, and they were and proud of it at that. They were men on the move up--or so they all thought.

Coming out of the protective shroud of the forest, Mitch was in awe at the sight of the ruins of a great castle. It was striking, the way it gripped the crest of the highest hill, nobly keeping guard over the lush green valley below. A limestone tower soared over the solid limestone wall and its back to the sea.

The castle looked old, almost ancient, yet stood proud even after countless generations had passed. No drawbridge or moat, as he had always dreamed castles should have--just massive stone walls guarding them from the ghost of the past, or itself from the ghost of its future.

The boys informed Mitch that they were the guardians of the fortress. It was up to him to ask these young kings for permission to enter their treasured halls. He was amused at their beliefs, but knew better than to argue with two kings.

Mitch could only wonder what these ruins were doing here. He surely could have pictured these ruins in Ireland or Scotland, but here? Who could have envisioned this cultural monstrosity on such a small island? The castle looked like it was built to protect, but to protect what?

Getting straight answers from two eleven-year-olds was a story in itself. Their story, Mitch was sure, was much more colorful than the real story. Dragons, ancient people, and island trolls, he was told. The castle was going to be used again, the boys informed him. Mitch played along, asking when that would be.

"When the governor comes to take the fishing boats and the island away," Billy said with an air of seriousness. The truth from the mouth of a child! The truth of what his parents must have been worrying about back home. Through their worries, it all seemed so clear, as if maybe his story was about to be born.

Now anointed by Liam as the three musketeers, the trio stood under the shadow of the huge tower. Mitch was informed that a hole big enough for a small dog or a big rat was the only way in. Liam assured him he would fit. Should he trust an eleven-year-old, or look around for another way in? Mitch gave in and ignored his better judgment, dropping to his knees and crawling in behind the overeager children in front of him.

Cobwebs slime, and gooey things all smashed under his soft hands. This was just another roll in the mud for Mitch as he tried in vain to keep clean. It was a good thing he didn't have to face a parent's wrath and try to explain the condition of his clothes. Mitch hoped the kids' parents understood their children's burrowing habits.

In denial, Mitch slithered and crawled through places he wouldn't have dared to go as a kid. There was no turning back for this overweight adventurer. It was either move forward, or rot in here. The thought of all the slithering things was enough to keep him going. Once again, he tasted the kids' dust as they sprinted through the hole, while all he could muster was a slow slither.

He had always had a phobia about dark holes and caves— he didn't like them now, and likely never would. Gasping forward, looking for any signs of life, he spotted the beautiful brightness of daylight. Crawling with a renewed vigor, he busted out of the rodent highway to the laughter of his new buddies.

"Pay up," Liam said. "I told you he wouldn't get stuck."

Great! Apparently Mitch was just a bet to these two young bookies, but he was glad Billy lost.

Standing up, every muscle in Mitch's wimpy legs were throbbing. He stood amazed at the massive room before him. A forgotten room, he surmised--still grand in its rubble, yet noble in its mess. All he could think about was the lost history within these walls. What nobles and dignitaries had visited here in the castle's days of glory? Time must have taken its toll; for better or for worse, only the silent moss-covered stones knew the real stories.

The three of them spent the next hour roaming where they could. The castle had so many rooms, fewer answers. They crawled and climbed through many years of neglect.

Full-sized trees now grew out of what once was probably the ballroom, their pointed tops pushing through what little rotten roof was left.

Wall after wall of quarry stone seemed to have toppled by their own   weight. Regardless of her ruined state, this was still the ultimate children's playground, and Mitch could see why the two boys felt it was rightfully theirs.

His working mind told him this castle had something to do with the name of the town. The boys told Mitch that was nonsense, that Vikings had built it a long time ago, and that they would never call it Macbeth.

"It was protection from the awful dragons that used to roam these hills," Billy said.

Yeah, sure, Mitch thought. Dragons, maidens, vestal virgins, and a man called Macbeth, probably the Harrison Ford of the 1700s, he surmised. The boys were now the keepers of the key and the weavers of the tales; Mitch was just a willing guest in their domain. The real story, he decided, would have to come from the big people some other time.

The three plodded through the ruins and into a grand room, when the two boys bolted out a front door. Mitch heard his two betting buddies laughing as they ran down the hill toward the trail. *No entrance?* he thought. *Revenge is so sweet, even if it's only against a couple of kids.*

Mitch was refreshed by the innocence and curiosity of youth, tricks and all. Life to kids was always so new and fresh. It seemed behind every bend or tree was a new world ready to bite at their unbridled curiosity. Together again, the three marched away from the ruins toward the community of Macbeth, where the real world awaited them.

God, did he miss his youth, when friends were true and best friendships were measured in lifelong commitments, even if "lifelong" to a child meant hours or days. *Life back then was good*, Mitch thought, while his years now seemed to trickle away faster with every year that past.

CHAPTER 5:

MY KATE

Saying goodbye to his new best friends, Mitch brushed off the dust and gathered his bag. Stopping an old-timer for the directions he should've gotten at the corner drug store, he headed down Main Street with purpose. A mile up the street he spotted his temporary home: the Outta Years Bed & Breakfast, established 1897. *What a strange name*, he thought, hoping it wasn't owned and operated by the Grim Reaper.

Gazing up at its simple island elegance, Mitch saw the curtain in the second-floor window move. The sign said "Enter, friends," though he still felt the need to at least knock. He entered cautiously through the Edwardian-style doors. Taken aback by the old-style simplicity of the large eerie room mixed with the distinct odor of a cat, he waited. Mitch never was fond of the four-legged beast, as his eyes peered cautiously around looking for it. Wondering where the rodent could be hiding, he scanned the room; maybe those 35-buck hotel rooms weren't so bad after all.

"Hello," a soft voice said, her delicate sound breaking the silence. A quick glance and he was a man in love again. Too shocked at her beauty to talk, Mitch just stood in the doorway absorbing it as he searched for the right words and muscles to speak.

She was slender, young, and beautiful, with the looks of the untouchable girl next door. Maybe she liked writers, with the hurt-puppy-type look, he hoped. *Forever dreaming--it couldn't hurt*, he thought. In a quick reality check at this girl's hometown purity, Mitch just gawked for a few seconds more, until his perfect bubble was broken by the sound of purring.

"Hello... can I help you?"

Oh lady, if you only knew how you could help me, his brain answered silently while his early cat warning system went into overdrive.

"Yes, of course," Mitch said nervously. He felt his face grow flushed with embarrassment.

"There should be a reservation for me today. It should be under Hazel and that's not my name."

Babbling on he continued, "My name's Mitch, Mitch the underpaid writer." Not knowing what to say next, he just stood there for what seemed an eternity with his mouth open. He, the blundering fool, was sure she wasn't impressed, or hopefully at least amused, with this fool attempt at trying to find the inner energy to talk to this woman of his dreams. Thankfully again she broke the embarrassing silence.

"My name's Kate, and I've been expecting you," she said as she put her young, hand out toward Mitch. "Not much goes on in Macbeth this time of year, so it'll be nice having someone around the house again besides Amadeus. How long will you be staying?"

Shaking of his case of nerves, Mitch grabbed for the warmth of her hand, felt its softness as he shook it gently, and wondered silently about Amadeus: a husband, or a lover?

"I'll be hanging around a couple of weeks at least," he said while his brain kept telling him maybe he would be hanging around here forever.

Kate gently pulled her hand back from Mitch's grip. Breaking into a cold sweat, Mitch, felt a ball of fur rubbing against his legs, then peered down to see the fattest ball of golden-red fur he had ever seen. This cat was like the cat of his wildest nightmares, a cat lover's fantasy that would waddle around and be treated like a human for all the lonely souls that needed the ball of fur to complete their lives.

"Whoa, please could you get that cat away from me!" Mitch said.

"Amadeus won't hurt you! He loves everybody," Kate injected, and all the while the finicky feline started using Mitch's leg as a claw sharpener.

In imagined pain, Mitch was ready to drop-kick that ball of fur into kingdom come, when his better judgment and Kate's shapely body steered his decision in the right direction as he moved his leg quickly away.

"Mitch, come on in; he won't bother you. Let me show you to your room so you can get settled in and cleaned up, then I'll show you around the rest of the house," she said as she stood in the doorway with her hands on her hips, the sunlight wrapped caringly around her body.

"That sure must have been a fun ride over on that boat, with all that dirt and dust on you. I ought to march you out back, strip you down, and hose you off first!" Kate joked.

She would get no argument from Mitch if she wanted to strip him down. He would do as he was told for the love of her flesh; he was her puppy.

Hoping she hadn't got a whiff of his own un-showered stench, Mitch melted away as he followed behind her, though he knew regardless of his condition, he would follow this cute little thing wherever she wanted to take this bad Dawg.

Always trying to be macho, Mitch rifled through his duffel bag looking for some allergy meds to ease his oncoming reaction to that damn cat. Starting to sneeze uncontrollably, he dived for a torn open box of Kleenex sitting suspiciously on the floor. Grabbing a handful, he flung them to his face in a blinding flash, just hoping to curtail that impending river of snot.

Not realizing what he was up against, Kate let out a screaming, "No!!!" but it was too late. Mitch had wiped cat crap and Kleenex all over his face, realizing too late what Kate's frantic wail was all about.

"Sorry, Mitch…Amadeus doesn't always use a litter box," Kate said with a humiliated smile.

Mitch, embarrassed and contaminated, wiped the cat's revenge off his face, as the beast again continued to rub against his leg with that satisfied smile, confident in knowing that his territory had been marked.

Mitch's bedroom was small, but Kate informed him of the great view of the harbor and its fishing boats. It was a unique room with a tall, looming ceiling that seemed to vanish into the darkness, and huge old-fashioned windows that would be great for any scene in some horror flick. Peering out the window, Mitch could see the faint outline of the mainland across the channel, silently reminding him of the real world.

Easily, Kate broke into his thoughts, not realizing she was at the forefront of his mind. She told him how she loved to sit on this overstuffed bed at night after a warm bath, just air-drying in the warm summer air. Alone and naked, just staring at the mainland, she wondered about the many lives and stories unfolding behind the walls of the distant lights. Was she doing this on purpose to Mitch? Did she realize his thoughts were only getting dirtier?

Kate went out to grab Mitch some clean sheets. Amadeus, feeling his territory had been invaded, snarled as he glanced in Mitch's direction. Not one to take crap from a cat, he saw his window of opportunity, and gently booted that blubbery ball of fur in the direction of the closest wall. This was his room now!

"Meowwwwww!" Amadeus screamed out as his body thunked against the wall. More than a bit ruffled, the cat picked up its huge bum and ran away from this two-legged devil. Satisfied with his revenge, Mitch smiled as he sat slowly down onto the bed and placed his hand on a warm wet spot: Amadeus had won the first battle.

"What happened to Amadeus?" Kate asked as she flew back into the room.

Holding back his almost hidden smile Mitch replied, "I'm real sorry, I accidentally stepped on him. I'll really have to be more careful and look out for that cute little thing." All's fair in love and war, and Mitch's mind plotted his next simple revenge.

"Kate, I think Amadeus had an accident," he said pointing at the expanding wet spot on the bed.

Embarrassed by Amadeus' lack of respect for Mitch's bed, Kate quickly cleaned it up as she filled him in on her bed and breakfast business. He loved listening to how she talked, but could only think of how she sat naked at night alone on his bed. Any more of these thoughts and he would have to know where the cold shower was.

It hadn't been that long for him. Mitch was thinking and dreaming like a sex-starved sixteen-year-old. He realized maybe lust was his fountain of youth. Amazed at his reawakened feelings, a breath of fresh air had seemingly blasted into his stale life.

"Am I talking too much?" Kate asked wondering about his silence.

"Yes, I mean no, I'm sorry. I was just thinking. Don't mind me; it was a long day and an even longer last night."

Puzzled by his response, Kate spoke: "Just to let you know, we have to share a bathroom here. There's only one in this old house, it is right down the hall. Make sure you jiggle the toilet. Old plumbing, you know? Never seems to work right."

"Don't you worry, I'll jiggle away--and I'll even put the seat down!"

With a wink and a wiggle, Kate tossed Mitch the house key.

"Here's your key. We don't use them much here, but just in case. And breakfast is at 8 a.m. sharp. I'm just down the hall if you need anything."

His mind sped into fast-forward as he ordered his brain to stop lusting. He reminded himself that it was just the unused male hormones taking over.

"Mitch," Kate said playfully, "you can aim, right? Just kidding," she said with a cute giggle as she skipped down the hall, picking up her ball of fur, to his overwhelming relief.

With that, Kate vanished while a determined man mentally undressed her and did things in his mind that he couldn't write about. He was a demented soul in her midst. Was she ready for him?

Quickly, he unpacked his wrinkled clothing from his used duffel bag and headed down the hall for a very necessary shower. Mitch felt like a kid again, just discovering a new pleasure. While focusing his limited energy, he raced to spend some time with the new object of his awakened desire.

Almost running down the stairs after that cold shower, all fresh and clean, Mitch busted out of the stairwell door. She was amused at his spunk and speed, as he changed the subject from his stupidity and reminded her of the tour she had promised around the house. Kate led him by the hand, and into each and every room they went as she explained the history that went with it, though Mitch heard only a few of her words.

Her parents had left the house to her, both of them dying at an early age. Kate, out of necessity, grew up quickly, and this probably explained her fierce independence and drive. The house was Kate's life and love. No boyfriend, she said--he didn't believe it. All he could think of was if it was true, what a waste of a great body!

Kate's room was the last room they visited, of course. Maybe she planned it that way. She was single and all alone, so maybe she dreamed of this moment with him, or whoever else was lucky enough to show up. Her soft bed with the sheets all thrown around only invited the two of them for some mattress magic. Mitch couldn't see that in his cards tonight; she just didn't have the look of those dance club sluts he knew so well. This wasn't his territory, he thought to himself as he sat his self back down. There's always a first time for everything, Mitch had learned.

The two of them sat on her bed and talked for a quick hour. Time meant nothing as the minutes flew by, while Mitch absorbed the sights and soft smells of Kate. He couldn't even have told anyone what they talked about; he just loved watching the way she formed her words with her Hollywood lips. Kate was Mitch's idea of natural beauty, with those flowing locks of light golden-brown hair and that soft, tanned glow that seemed to emanate from her youthful skin. This was his heaven.

Kate was tired and softly told him good night, and that was his cue to part ways for the evening. Then, alone in Mitch's dreams, she walked with him to their imaginary room as tonight, in his world, they were one.

CHAPTER 6:

AND HER KNIGHT

Morning came not soon enough, with the sea gulls shouting at the rising sun. Mitch wondered why they blasted those damn horns going out to sea. Some would think horns were romantic and quaint, but he had a few other words for them, pulling his quilt tightly over his head, and trying to drown out the island's morning sounds.

Thanks to the noise, Mitch was up by eight, a seldom-seen time of day for him. Grabbing someone's leftover bottle of Aqua Velva after shave, he took a man-sized splash as a quick substitute for a shower. Ten minutes and he was ready for Kate. He sprinted down the stairs, watching out for a potential ambush from Amadeus and his meeting with his future.

"Good morning, Mitch. Did you sleep well in that bed?"

"Morning, all right--I slept great, although I missed the soothing sounds of sirens and the city. What's for breakfast? I'm a starving," he replied, still a tad groggy from his sound sleep.

"I'm taking you out for the best short stack this side of the Atlantic," she said with a cute smile, sipping her cup of steaming black tea.

"I lay awake half the night dreaming about your cooking. Oh well, I guess it'll have to wait. Let's go. Where's your cat-- uh, I mean car?" A Freudian slip he knew he better be careful.

"You mean bike, Mitch. We ride or walk on this island. Less pollution, you know, and better for you. Why, most folks around here don't even own a car!" Looking around the room, she looked for her friend.

"Amadeus...here baby." Kate called for him and wondered why she didn't hear the familiar purr of her feline.

"That's real strange; he usually runs for his breakfast, especially when I'm cooking. I'll leave the food out anyway. He must be in one of his jealous moods, you know--with another man in his house!" she said with a seductive giggle as she nudged Mitch in the ribs.

He wondered if he had kicked that beast too hard, or maybe it was that sudden impact with the wall. In his mind, all was fair and good until he heard the sound of a heavy thumping sound coming down the stairs. Amadeus was alive and well, and Mitch was sure he saw a smirk on his face as he passed by, making sure his fur touched Mitch's leg just briefly.

The two of them escaping out the back door Mitch knew he had bigger problems than a cat. Out of shape, Mitch hadn't ridden a bike in years, but that morning he was her puppy of love and would follow her wherever.

There was something to be said about following a beautiful woman on a bike--what that was, though, Mitch pretended he hadn't a clue, even though deep down he knew that it was those toned leg muscles combined with those skin-tight riding shorts. Was it the way she was perched on that seat? Who was he fooling? He would be all over that, if he had the chance. It was one of the most scenic rides Mitch ever remembered, at least until his muscles started to mutiny on him. First the legs, then the back, and then he had only his male hormones and pride to push him on.

Rounding the bend after ten minutes of muscular hell, Mitch saw the town before him as they slowly drifted to a stop in front of Fanny's Flapjack Heaven; life was good all over again. Not wanting to be a wimp in front of Kate, his mind screamed for water, lots of ice-cold water, while he coaxed his aching body off the hard seat of that bike. With his butt muscles protesting his every move, Mitch hoped Kate wasn't into the buff, athletic type, because he realized that his rapid breathing and panting had just blown his cover.

"You need some help there?" Kate asked, as she looked into Mitch's red and sweating face.

"No way, I think I just need to adjust the seat next time. It's not like I'm used to on my bike back in the city." Lying, he pretended to study the bike seat, buying some needed seconds so he could regain his breath and maybe a little composure.

Moving a bit slower than normal, the two entered the storefront. Fanny's looked just like the old waffle houses he remembered as a kid. A big lollipop tree with king-sized multi-colored suckers greeted every kid (or kid wannabe) as they walked in through the jingling door. Avoiding the sugary temptation, Mitch got the strange feeling he was interrupting a private meeting.

The two of them stood waiting to be greeted, but he felt like the new kid on the block, with everybody just staring. Mitch had seen this happen on TV, but seldom had he experienced it in real life. *What gives?* he wondered. *First it happened at the bar, now here?* He knew these crazy townsfolk surely had seen tourists before. Maybe city folk like him looked strange, or maybe saltwater and seaweed did weird things to people's vision. What was in the coffee, and where could he get some?

Not one for cold stares, Kate piped up, "What's with you all? He's a guest with me, wants to do a story on us all. His name's Mitch; he's a writer. Welcome him!" With that gentle warning the invisible curtain seemingly opened and people greeted Mitch as they would any other neighbor.

Following Kate back to a booth, Mitch saw the familiar old face of Jack and a group of about ten men filing out of the back room. The exiting group looked all too serious for breakfast – must not have had their coffee. Mitch, still a questioning journalist, asked Kate about the solemn group.

"Those fine men run our community and take good care of us all. They are God-fearing, decent men, all of them." End of subject, as she cut Mitch off without going any further with his line of questioning.

The two of them sat sipping the richest coffee Mitch had ever tasted, while he squirmed and tried to comfort his irritated hemorrhoid. Sipping his coffee black, he looked up just as Kate's friend Lynn came over and introduced herself. Mitch didn't need a second introduction: he would never forget her windblown look from the ferry ride over. Lynn was younger and unsure about herself, but that only intensified her beauty in his eyes. Innocence and vulnerability: two traits Mitch loved, but at times didn't quite know how to handle.

Lynn spoke about how she and some of her girlfriends weren't sure about the future direction of Macbeth and wanted to get together and talk. Kate said it wasn't a good time today, but to call her later and she would find time. Lynn nodded okay, tilted her head and shrugged her cute shoulders, then hugged Kate goodbye. Young and free, she slipped out into the spring sun.

What are these people afraid of? Mitch wondered. He felt a lot of tension in the air. He never worried about the future in Ohio, let alone a small, safe community like Macbeth. If these islanders only knew what the real world was like. He hoped for a hot refill of coffee; nothing worse than a half-empty cup.

Midge seemed to have more on her mind than coffee as she shuffled slowly back and forth with the coffee pot, just tempting him. Not waiting for her next pass, Mitch jumped up with his cup and chased her down, all for the love of another cup of java.

"Hold it, bucko. I bring the coffee around here!" Midge exclaimed.

"I'm real Sorry, ma'am. It was a long night. My name's Mitch--how do you do?"

"I do fine, when people don't rush me." Mitch took the hint as he sat down and waited for Midge to shuffle on by.

Lynn ran back in, escorted by a whiff of her cheap French perfume. Grabbing her two slow friends, Lynn said goodbye again as Mitch noticed the slightest smile when she glanced at him with a giddy look. He and a half dozen of the other men watched the young ladies parade out the front door. All the three girls were keenly aware of the stares their bodies were commanding. What if they had been only a little older, or Mitch a little younger? Bad Mitch--he scolded himself for his dastardly thought for the day.

After finishing a truly great breakfast, Kate and Mitch got on their bikes for a short tour the island. The island itself was not very big. At its widest point, it wasn't much wider than a country mile.

For a large rock, the island seemed to have a natural,

undisturbed beauty. Anywhere the two rode, they could hear the soothing sound of the ocean hitting the rugged shores. Pine trees were colored in a vibrant, refreshing green. Trees, everywhere they glanced, sprouted wherever a fissure in the rocky soil would yield the treasures of Mother Earth. It was a patch of earth that willingly accepted a rich carpet of pine needles, as they covered every inch around the countless trees waiting to welcome one tired and weary biker.

With a butt aching from the road (a road better covered in a car), Mitch persuaded Kate to take a rest. At this point in time his rear end didn't care where they parked it, as long as it was parked. Coming to a clumsy stop, he flipped off his bike like a senior citizen. In sore humility, he rolled off his feet as he crashed to the ground. Kate gracefully sat down next to him.

Sitting so close to Kate made this big city boy nervous; it was like a first date all over again. Should he kiss her? Should he hold her hand? What do you do? Mitch hadn't been in this predicament in years. Normally he would just go for it--what's another slap? But something wasn't right here. He thought maybe he really liked this girl, so much a woman. Mitch had been burned before and just didn't want to be stupid and throw away any chance he might have with her. *Move slowly*, he told himself. A second day on the island, and he was already a blithering idiot about a woman he hardly knew.

The two talked for hours, even though it felt like only minutes. He didn't want this feeling or connection between them to end. Through the dark clouds it started sprinkling, so Kate jumped on her bike and he followed to a spot she knew, out of the rain. A gentle rain seemed to be turning into a torrential island storm as they sped for any kind of cover.

Macbeth's road system wasn't much different from when they had settled the island some 150 years ago. The mud was still as nasty as when they first set foot on this big rock. By car, horse, or bike, the mud just plain drove you nuts. Pedaling became almost impossible. The torrential rain didn't bother Kate as she continued on with her history lesson about the island. Mitch, who was pretending he was listening, couldn't stop thinking about her wet t-shirt.

Mitch unwillingly learned about how the early settlers had come to island for the salt. Before them, the Indians had always gathered their precious white dirt from their sacred island. Then mining became the profitable thing to do: white gold. The beginning of Macbeth's population boom signaled a change for the Indians, banned from the island, like most of the rest of their native lands. *Times change*, Mitch thought. It was nobody's fault, just a sick fact of life.

Over the years, Kate had learned quite a bit about the history of Macbeth. She told him about the miles of salt mines tucked under the island, and how much salt the islanders used to sell. Then a new breed of miners started digging under Lake Erie, and Macbeth's salt market dried up. It was easier and cheaper to ship salt out of Ohio to the growing markets around the great lakes. Economics: the great equalizer. Macbeth's ultimate dragon forced the islanders to turn their economic eyes toward the forgiving sea.

Winding down the country lane, Mitch saw what was left of the old salt mines. Not much there; just a big boarded-up hole in the side of a hill, surrounded by some remnants of old buildings and rusted equipment. The old shaft was surrounded by some shiny new gates, barbed wire, and razor fences, which didn't quite fit this natural scene of rust and ages of neglect. Kate assured him that the shiny new fences were for the good of the kids; they didn't want anyone getting lost below in the confusing tunnels.

One biker and another forced-to-be-biker were soaked through when they finally stopped in front of the abandoned office building. Dripping wet and cold, they hurried into the old, weathered building. The ransacked office would have to do for a temporary shelter. The rain was cold and the wind was wet, but here at least the two could escape the elements and sit back and wait. They had nothing to do but get warm.

Kate must have been a Girl Scout, because in no time at all she had a blazing fire going in the ancient cast iron stove. In an equally quick instant, she slipped off her wet clothes and stood in front of Mitch as she warmed herself by the stove. Thank goodness for him she kept her undergarments on.

"I hope you're not embarrassed," she said. "You'll catch cold if you stay in those wet clothes." Mitch wanted nothing more than to dry off, but if she saw the bulge in his wet pants, all his hope would have been lost.

Kate was everything he had ever dreamed about, all those nights alone in his empty bed. Mitch was sure she would be in his dreams again tonight. Quickly, while she wasn't looking, he stripped and sat down next to the glowing fire, trying to hide what God had given him.

Embarrassed he was, embarrassed that he just didn't grab her and make crazy love to her like no man had ever done before. But at this moment in time Mitch was just a boy again--not the suave lady-killer from the city he pictured himself as, but a nervous boy in a strange new land. Mitch had finally met his match.

The two talked till his mouth was dry. They sat so close that it was inevitable that he held her; it seemed only natural. It felt like a closeness Mitch had never experienced before. He never wanted to let her go, nuzzling her as the time drifted by. The rain stopped, but neither of them wanted to move. The smell of her rain-soaked hair and her drying body had him more aroused than any strip club or the countless, nameless women he had often entertained.

In time they had to go, because as it always is, when reality knocks on your door and reminds you of a job you have to do, you do it. At this moment in time his job really meant nothing to him, and only the woman dressing in front of him consumed his every thought and desire.

The two unwillingly left the safety of their hideaway feeling fulfilled, yet consumed with questioning thoughts about each other. Was it love, infatuation, or just two lonely people looking for help to escape their solitary lives?

Mounting the wet bikes again, Mitch couldn't help notice the deep muddy ruts now filled with water in the road that led to the abandoned mine.   Didn't quite make much sense to him, but at this moment he wasn't thinking straight anyhow. He had never let his personal feelings get in the way of a story before. He guessed there always had to be a first time, so why not here?

The ruts just didn't sit right with him, but when he asked Kate about them, she pleaded the fifth. Without any further questioning they rode off, with Mitch dreaming of the next time he and Kate would be alone.

CHAPTER 7:

A DAY IN THE LIFE

There are times when the real world comes crashing down and ruins your perfect day. Most never expect it, as the clouds of doom and frustration roll in invading your personnel horizon.

Kate's close friend, Lynn, had a father who was drug salesman who pushed "legally" the latest medicine, and he happened to be in New York City for a pharmaceutical convention. In a timeless moment, Jebb Larson became just another crime statistic in a violent city, but the news hit like a shockwave to the people of Macbeth. Held up, beaten and stabbed, a useful loving soul, his life bled away, all for the lousy 32 bucks in his wallet.

The malicious work of an addict high on some illegal drug, most likely in need of cash for his next fix, never once considering the impact his cowardly move would have on the family, let alone with kids growing up without a father. Lynn's family, with both parents under one roof, was an uncommon family for most outside of Macbeth, but the norm for the island. They were now the newest victims of a society gone wrong.

Mitch never saw a community react like they did. An event caused by a mad animal truly overshadowed the blue-sky day all longed for. A few boats still came and went that day, though nobody really noticed. Most residents focused on some troubled inner thoughts, and ignored the large freighter docked in the harbor, unloading a year's worth of supplies and food into a few big trucks, all with mud-covered tires. Things happen and you accept it--just an unlucky fate. Mitch had a feeling this town was the exception.

As reality set in, an impromptu town meeting was posted for that afternoon. Mitch informed by Kate that it would be best if he did not go. She told him the meeting was just for the community. In their grief, they needed each other, and a town meeting would be their way of dealing with their loss. Mitch, fighting his feeling, knew he had to cover this, because this was real life-- and good or bad, he had to be there. Mitch, after all, was a journalist first and foremost, and his story needed to feel what this community was feeling; a story needs to breathe.

He knew that if he went he would be the uninvited guest. Of course he had sneaked into tighter spots than a town meeting before, and wasn't concerned. As little as Mitch wanted to leave Kate's company, he knew who still paid his bills. Lying was never hard for him, but that day for some reason it just didn't feel right. Regardless of his feelings, he told Kate he needed some time to get some inspiration for his story anyhow. Saying goodbye, he stepped out to explore this new world.

Walking into town, he ran into a friend. Peace, with Lynn's family on his mind, needed a distraction, with out a second thought, he invited Mitch to come see his new project, and with time to kill and more than enough curiosity, he didn't need to be persuaded.

Down toward the harbor the two went, Peace trying to explain to Mitch how close this community was, and how afraid some seemed to be of the mainland, and their lack of concern for each other. Almost paranoia, Mitch felt, but not wanting to offend his guest, he kept his thoughts to himself.

Peace's little project turned out to be the old *Flying Daisy* herself. Tied up to the rotting dock, the sub rocked gently. Mitch, always fascinated by the war, couldn't believe he was on a sub from that era; it was a dream fulfilled. He could almost picture Jimmy Stewart commanding one of these beasts as it plowed through the cold Atlantic looking for the dreaded German U-boats, man against machine in the war to end all wars.

Inviting him aboard, he raced up before Peace could even get the words out. Following his host, he slithered down the damp ladder into the bowels of the cold sub. All at once his human senses were overwhelmed by the smell of the many types of oils and musty smells only a true sub fanatic could imagine. He took Mitch into the engine room where Peace had the main engine torn apart to rebuild. To Peace it was a labor of love, but to Mitch it would be a pain in the ass.

"This old lady would never sail again," Peace blurted out. "But what the hell--the engine needed work anyhow."

"Then why do it?" Mitch wondered aloud.

"It was just the thing to do, man. When this engine is done later today, the sub will be almost ninety percent complete, in nearly the same condition if not better then when she left duty forty years ago."

Mitch knew he was impressed, but all he wanted to do now was explore the lady and dream.

To the command center they went, where Peace switched her on. The batteries kicked to life and lights lit up her control boards as the electrical life drifted back into her old circuits.

If only she could move one more time, Mitch wished, that he too could experience the hunt. Someday, maybe again in one of his many fantasies, Mitch and that Nazi U-boat would be together again, the hunter and the hunted.

He could have hung out on her all day, but knew better as he thanked Peace many times for the memories and climbed out. Letting his eyes adjust to the bright sunshine, he walked across her freshly painted deck. Peace, with a smile and a sub commander's hat, saluted him as he piped him down the gangway. Returning the crisp salute, Mitch departed and moved on for the meeting he still had to attend.

He was enjoying the moment on his merry way through town, walking down the street and dreaming of the *Daisy*. Looking around, he was amused and puzzled at the lack of amenities he was accustomed to taking for granted. Where were the local McDonalds, Burger King, or Mike's Place? There was no Higbee's or Sears. Instead there was Hank's Handy Hardware and O'Grady's Office Supply, Thelma Lee's Antiques, and Paxton's Corner Drug Store, home of the local lunch counter and soda fountain, where you could still drink a cup of coffee or a soda while they filled your prescription – what a concept. Macbeth really had let time pass it by. It made Mitch remember a better time.

Paxton's so reminded Mitch of the old Woolworth from his childhood. Oversized sundaes: he could eat two and waddle home with the biggest bellyache, because no matter the pain, it was worth it. Just the price he paid for porker's perfection; he had been a full-fledged husky kid, and proud of it.

Daydreaming, he remembered his mother who would always buy his pants at Penny's, because of the variety of husky-sized kids' clothes, which was just a more politically correct term than "fat kids' apparel." His parents thought the name protected him from the daily taunts from other kids. It didn't, but it really never mattered much to him. They were only cruel words, and at ten or eleven, there were more important things to worry about, like your next sundae.

Stopping in front of Paxton's Drug Store, Mitch bought a Coke out of an old vending machine that still served ice-cold Cokes in a bottle. Reaching for eight ounces of Coca-Cola magic for only 25 cents, he was a kid again. It was as cold and refreshing as he remembered it. Coke was always better in chilled glass.

On the sly, he ripped down a notice; he now knew the town meeting was going to be held at the church hall. Mitch still had a few hours to scope it out. He might as well get there early and find out what he was up against.

Wasting no time, he walked on toward the church. Hopefully the Lord was on his side for this story, or just to watch over him in his ignorance. Once again a little less weary, he stopped by Kate's house and grabbed a bike, and set off, almost eager for his quest.

Not having a car wasn't as bad as he thought. Bikes were always his passion as a kid. His first taste of freedom came on his mighty cherry-red Murray--the kind with the big chrome fenders that kids ripped off immediately to make it look cool--and oversized balloon tires, great for traveling where roads never went and cars dared not travel. On his old bike, he was always a wild Indian upon his trusty steed, free to travel and explore. At eleven, the world was still a big and new place, just ripe enough for youth to learn.

Now, twenty-nine years later, Mitch again was upon a mighty steed: ten gears and two knobby off-the-road tires. What do you do with so many gears he could never figure out, as one speed was always good for him when he was a kid. Now, older, the world didn't seem so new anymore; it had lost its innocence somewhere during the passing time.

With the crumbling of the gravel under his tires, he wondered why sometimes in life knowing too much really did destroy the child in all of them. That day, the suppressed child in Mitch was awakened as he rode through town with the wind in his hair, on his way to an old church. Once again exploring this new space, this once-mighty Indian rode.

Seeing the world over handlebars makes you realize what you miss driving around town in a sealed car. Your vision is limited to the world ahead of you, not what is left or right. Riding down Main Street in the open air, a forgotten world opened up to him. The sounds of people talking, dogs barking, and smells you never smell. Your senses are refreshed and tested the moment you, your bike, and the fresh air are one again.

It wasn't hard to find the old church up the winding road. This was the town's only church, as well as the center of life in Macbeth. The church complex held the town meeting hall, offices for the town's limited government, the town's counseling center, cemetery, school, and chapel. All these elements of society were in two turn of the century buildings, both painted an angelic seaside white. The church had always been a constant refuge for the islanders in their times of need. Mitch had a gut feeling the church was needed again.

In this community, there existed no separation of church and state. The church was involved in many aspects of the day-to-day running of the community. Though the government office was housed off of the church meeting hall, there was never a conflict of interest, just a strong, combined faith and trust in the church and its people.

The congregation was made up of the community and backed up by the town's limited government--a government that consisted of three appointed trustees and the clerk. Midge, was the town's clerk for what seemed like forever, it was said, she knew more about the community than the three trustees put together. She was Macbeth's mother figure, and the unofficial conscience of the town.

The three trustees were known at times for their fence-walking. All three could walk the middle of the fence better than a prowling alley cat, seemingly never giving you a straight answer, no matter what you asked; Mitch guessed this was the sign of a good politician. What this town needed was a cross between John Wayne and Ronald Reagan: a tough and firm, kick-butt, take-names kind of guy. Everybody deserved to have somebody wholesome to look up to. Here in Macbeth there were plenty of good intentions, but lack of follow-through, he guessed...or so he thought.

With a swift kick of his leg, Mitch stopped and dismounted his trusty wheeled Japanese bike, wondering what had happened to all the Murray and Schwinn bicycles? Not wanting to draw any attention to himself or his snooping, he hid his bike behind a shed and moved quickly. Might as well act as if he knew what he was doing, so right through the front door of the meeting hall he went.

Not much was happening inside the old empty church. He headed for the community corkboard, great for idle time. He smelled the overwhelming scent of knotty pine--and damn, did it smell better than all the rooms he remembered. The notices on the board were interesting. "TOWN MEETING AND PRAY SERVICE TONIGHT, 6 P.M.," and "SATURDAY RIFLE PRACTICE"--just what most churches would be pushing, right? Discussion group topic for this Sunday: Life without electricity. Whoa! Religion sure had changed since Mitch was its captive.

"Excuse me!" an older voice rang out. "Can I help you?"

"Why, hello," Mitch said with a startled voice. "You scared the piss out of me."

"Sorry, but can I help you?" the old voice repeated.

"Not really. I'm in town for a while doing a story. I was just nosing around trying to get a feel for the island."

"Well, mister, not to be rude, but we are closed today, so you best be on your way. But we're open all day Sunday for services, and sure wouldn't mind having you at our celebration. I have to go get ready for a special town meeting. Best be on your way, and you have good day." The elderly gentlemen pointed the way to the door.

Mitch got the feeling the old guy meant it, even though he knew he could take him. Scrawny little old fart--just doing his job, at that.

Heading out down the stairs, he couldn't help but notice a closet door slightly ajar and chained. Peeking in, he thought he saw rows of guns lined up neatly on the racks. His curiosity was peaking when he heard the voice of his dreams.

"Mitch! What are you doing here?" Kate snapped.

"Hey there," Mitch said innocently enough. "I'm just snooping around. I've always loved old churches." *Just kidding--God, please just get me out of this mess.*

"Lucky I found you. I have some homemade crab cakes in the oven--would you want to join me?" she asked.

"I never turn down a free meal. Take me, I'm yours," he injected as the old man crept behind him and closed the closet door.

"Peace has been looking for you," Kate said. *Why?* he wondered, knowing he had just seen him earlier.

Together under the shade of many old trees, they walked down the path through the cemetery. Mitch wanted to stay and look around, but figured this wasn't the time to raise any more suspicions. With a renewed sore butt, Mitch grabbed his bike and rode off, following Kate down the road.

The two of them talked for a bit, lazily riding back to her place. Mitch gathered that small communities weren't what he had always dreamed about. A lot of real uncertainty about the future was on the minds of these townsfolk: a town focused on worrying over what was uncontrollable and a bleaker future for the children. Seemingly too many outside forces were pushing in on the once- impregnable boundaries of this old town. Drugs, gangs, corruption, and lack of family values--all seldom-seen problems to Macbeth, but now, thanks to computers and technology, these problems were causing their private world to shrink as the outside world's problems now seemed to be shared with Macbeth.

Guarding values wasn't as easy as it used to be on the island. Staring at Kate, Mitch couldn't quite grasp the deep internal devotion she held toward these values. *Yet why*, he wondered, *does it seem like you really know somebody when in reality you've just met.* Love must have set its spell on you and when it does, you just can't forget it. Something about her piercing eyes kept Mitch from thinking straight. Then again, why would a church, a harbor of life, be keeping rows of guns, the harbingers of death, locked away? Is that what he really saw? Life today took a turn toward confusion as Mitch, the once-great thinker, contemplated.

Kate led him back to her house with the promise of a truly original island dinner. His mouth was wishing, but it wasn't for dinner, although tonight dinner would have to do. He needed time to start his story, but what would he write? How could he write? Infatuation and curiosity had his mind blank. No story until he answered a few more questions for himself.

While waiting for dinner, it was time to stare at the beauty of the harbor. He sat on the porch watching town folk starting to head to the meeting.

Dinner for Mitch was great: crab cakes, Cajun-spiced rice, fresh collard greens, and some kind of original island seaweed and beer bread from a book called *Island Steve's Seaside Cooking*.

Kate wanted to talk. He knew he couldn't, as much as he wanted to – Kate not going to the meeting equaled no story. Any other time it would have taken a herd of draft horses to pull him away from her, but curiosity had gotten the better of his testosterone as he retreated with his hormones. Pretending to be tired, he excused himself to his room. Pacing upstairs, he waited for the chance to make his getaway.

There are times in your life when you get that raw feeling that you shouldn't be doing something, and this should have been one of those times; instead, Mitch had a feeling of invincibility that he couldn't shake. Hearing no noise downstairs, ever so carefully he snuck down the back staircase, stepping over the mound of fur Amadeus slept, and out into the crisp spring evening he went.

The bikes were put up and locked in the garage, which forced Mitch to hoof it. After this assignment, he was sure he wouldn't need his health club pass for a short while. Running through the backyard like a young warrior, for a good three minutes he kept pace and felt good until his brain said, "You fool, you are going to die, I need oxygen!" He would have to settle for a brisk walk or face a second mutiny from within.

To him, walking always signaled daydreaming mode. When you're young and forced to walk to and from school, you have a lot of time on your hands. One mile seemed like ten. Sidewalks became your rural American trails, filled with any make-believe adventure your daydreaming mind could come up with. Most neighborhood bullies were your enemy. Your friends and brothers were your army. Together you were invincible, but alone you were susceptible, and right now, he felt the need for a few good friends.

Catching his escaping breath, Mitch snuck in through the back of the cemetery. Coming up to the back door, he could hear the meeting already underway. There was a lot of yelling, as the now-familiar voice of old Jack was heard. Mitch was too far away to hear anything clearly. Up the back steps he crawled. If he could just get in to the broom closet, which he hoped wasn't locked, he knew all would be well for this spy.

With the exception of a few gents standing in the hall, his coast was clear. While he pondered his few options, the front door opened. In walked his new angel. Kate was late, and like a tornado she sucked the two men toward her with her natural charm. Together they walked her into the meeting. *Thanks,*

Kate, Mitch silently thought. Quietly, the warrior within returned, and thankfully into their jungle he slinked, and settling carefully into the closet, he hid among the mops and the garbage.

Making himself comfortable in the tightness of the closet, he sat back to listen. Through the lecturing, what he heard next shocked him, and for a moment he was at a loss for words.

"Secession is the only answer! You want Washington to notice you? Then you must demonstrate your resolve. You must make the whole nation hear you! We are but a small community, but so were the original colonies. They too demonstrated their resolve and their dedication to their ideals. Why should our ideals be any less important?" Jack thundered to the applause.

Was this the same man Mitch had listened to in the bar? With renewed force and emotion deep in his voice, Jack paused for a brief second until he loudly began again.

"How long will you people wait? Seceding from this state surely is a bold step, so how can it not get attention!"

A voice in the crowd yelled out: "Will they believe us, or just laugh and make us the headline of the week for some grocery store tabloid?"

"Friends, friends, I can't answer that, but I can tell you now with my heart that they aren't listening to us today and they won't listen to us tomorrow unless things change, and change in a big way. Our corrupt governor won't let things change for our betterment. He will wait and wait, till we abandon our way of life for his motives of progress. He has the time and money, and he can wait, but we don't have that luxury, as most of you, and I myself, am all too aware. Sure, the system has got some good politicians, and for the most part, a good system of government. But democracy in Massachusetts is old and in need of repair. We have crime taking hold of our streets, destroying through fear what was good and fair about us. Washington, the free world's capital, can't even police itself! Its streets are reduced to a war zone. Its drug policy is failing to keep drugs out of the White House, much less out of our schools. Our once-state-of-the-art criminal system is in disarray. We arrest them, the courts and lawyers free them to terrorize the streets again--and why? You all tell me! We all know we need a system with teeth, and men not afraid to use those teeth for the good of all. Just maybe, this act of courage and devotion we contemplate here today can bring some of those morals and values we cherish back to the front pages where they belong. Maybe then, as a whole country, we can enter into a national discussion. Then, together as one people united, we can create a binding resolution that solves some of the problems plaguing society as we know it.

"Folks, I am scared," Jack pleaded. "I am scared for my kids, for your kids, and for the future generations of Macbeth. I want our children to have what we all had growing up: faith, freedom, security, and family. But we have talked enough tonight. Go now and be with your families and friends--and talk. Talk, and listen to each other with open minds. Seceding will brand us as traitors by some, but heroes by others. Life will go on, but Macbeth will be changed forever, I guarantee that! Change is always hard, but what are our options? Let us all now bow our heads for a moment and pray in silence for Jebb and his family. He was a good man, and didn't deserve what he got. Remember, and help his family through this pain, as I know all of you will. Good night, my friends, and God bless you all. Pray for the answers!" Jack had delivered a stirring speech and the stage had been set.

Mitch was mystified by the message and charisma that was evoked by Jack's caring voice. With one speech, he was a borderline believer. Without even hearing it all, he was moved, and his hardened emotions were stirring. For a brief moment he wasn't concerned about what could be the biggest story of his life. For once in Mitch's selfish life, he was concerned about others and not himself.

Jack had spoken with a true conviction that few let surface. Here in this church was a man Mitch hardly knew, but with few doubts he was sure this man would give his life in an instant, defending his beliefs and his family. A man with such strong convictions could be a dangerous man, or a true leader. How could Mitch have been so wrong?

It was best that Mitch just sit and wait until the hall cleared out. The townsfolk emptied out, all in deep discussion over this fork in the road. In his solitude, Mitch had plenty of time to come up with an excuse for his mixed feelings, and maybe a reason for Kate, if she realized he was gone. Right now it was better that he was alone with his thoughts, as he tried to rationalize his terrified confusion.

What in life really is right, and what is really wrong? He knew what Jack preached was treason; he also knew some of what Jack said was true. How could a group of people be so paranoid, yet so on the brink of doing something so very drastic as this almost final step? The outside world was weighing heavily on many as they walked home that evening.

CHAPTER 8:

THE FINAL STRAW

Earlier that evening in town, nobody really paid much attention to the group of kids getting off the ferry. To Mitch, this different group would have just been part of that urban city culture that all citizens see running around in modern cities and suburbia--a generation of children with way too much time on their hands, trying to make a statement about their individual lives.

Mitch's time of rebellion was different: long hair, bell-bottoms, peace, love, and Cat Stevens. These kids were the culture of AC/DC, Guns N' Roses, and Poison. Same bit of youthful rebellion in them as all, just looking for their cut against the grain of a normal life. Another blooming era destined to buck their parents' traditional social values as the rebel reared its head. Rite of passage from youth to adulthood, most were sure.

Nobody could have ever put it together, but what if Lynn had only spotted her father's treasured watch on the wrist of one of those creeps, as infinite a possibility as that was? The newspapers said all the killer wanted was his wallet – how could so many have been so wrong?

Lynn's father was a drug salesman, and what did drug salesmen have that was more valuable than money? Lots of drug samples. What an easy target his home in a small town could be. A small town with only a few cops surely made it an easier job than a well-patrolled city battleground. Lots of legal loot for resale in the big city, with all the junkies starved for a piece of the illegal action.

Preparing for the hunt, the enemy silently lurked within the town itself, slowly and unknowingly preparing itself for its role in breaking the camel's back. In life there must always be a catalyst to start the ball rolling, and for now this gang was within the realm of its fifteen minutes of fame. An evil catalyst from another generation was destined to put Macbeth on its collision course with its inevitable destiny.

It wasn't hard to find where Lynn's family lived. When the gang rolled her bleeding father, they got all his identification they needed. Once on the island, they were on their way to the big easy, or so they wished. Too bad they had picked Macbeth for their fight.

Lynn's family home was off Main Street, just a few blocks down from Tom's. The gang figured they would wait until the family went to sleep to break in. This was a safe town. They probably didn't even lock their doors at night. No deadbolts to slow them down--in and out, get the loot, steal a boat, and make their escape.

The thugs were right about the deadbolts, but who would have figured on silent alarms; who would have figured all the buildings in Macbeth were tied into a joint security system? It's hard to figure what drives a community, but paranoia must have been driving Macbeth's.

The punks, high on pills, walked into Lynn's family home with no resistance. They silently looked around, though they were thugs and had no idea what to look for. Splitting up, one found Lynn, and he knew he had found what he was after. A knife pressed against her throat and she was his. As he ripped the soft white t-shirt off of her, she screamed. With one punch, she was silent. Better for her that she slept through what this vermin was up to. He was, after all, just a wild animal on the hunt, ready to make his mark on this family; she was his prey that day.

The other goons managed to find the office and ransack it. They found little to steal--mainly physician's samples. Not enough loot to pay for their trip here. Pissed off at their un-rewarded venture, they kicked and punched whatever they could find. In their unrelenting, drug-induced anger, the gang made enough noise to wake the rest of the family.

Lynn's brother, all of fifteen, awoke first. Being the male of the family now, he came running down the hall with his bat, swinging and screaming crazily at the thugs. One shot to his young gut took him down. Then his mother in utter panic and terror chased after her fallen son. Pistol-whipped from behind, she crumpled down beside him, blood trickling from the back of her gashed neck. She looked up glassy-eyed from her tears and pain as she motioned for the other kids to stay hidden. These animals needed no more prey to abuse than they already had.

Jack and his men awoke quickly to answer the silent alarm. Hearing the shot as they ran towards the house was all the invi-tation they needed. Bursting through the front and back doors, they ran in like a SWAT team.

The young gang was caught by bitter surprise. The gun-toting kid that had the balls to do the shooting was stupid enough to try it again. Despite his anger at their intrusion, he didn't get far this time. Jack was ready and willing with one shot between the kid's gleaming eyes. His pathetic life drifted away in an instant.

The other two captured creeps were just the next unfortunate victims of the start and end of the conflict. Jack and the men knew they had to be eliminated so their story could never be repeated.

Whimpering for forgiveness, they were forgiven right before they accepted unwillingly the two shots to the backs of their thick skulls. What this gang did to Macbeth was an act of war. What Macbeth did to these boys was an act of revenge—and, some islanders would say, of courage.

In the saviors' hate they found Lynn, as her intruder was just finishing his forced deed.

"For God's sake, there is nothing worse than a man forcing himself on someone!" Jack screamed. The stunned rapist was grabbed with his pants down, pulled out of her, and dragged half naked and screaming outside.

One of the old islanders, old Harold, a Korean War veteran, had seen how the Chinese had handled these crimes.

"Hang the bastard upside down from a strong tree," he said. "Then cut off what little God gave him, and let the sucker bleed to death. It will give him time to think about what he did before he meets his maker. That is--if he can think straight, with all the pain he'll be feeling. Lord knows it worked in Korea; I guarantee it'll work here."

It didn't take long to complete Harold's deed with more than enough eager volunteers. No one seemed to notice the moaning and crying coming from the tree. They were more concerned with the wounded family inside. No family should have to experience the pain this family had been put through. Strength and resolve can go only so far, until reality just doesn't seem so real any more. This family was pushing the envelope as it headed to the clinic for the help it needed so badly, but could not completely absorb.

By morning, life seemingly returned to normal, except for the lone fishing boat carrying four weighted-down bags to the outer reaches of the ocean shelf, set to cast them off with little regard. This was trial and punishment, Macbeth-style.

In the confusion of the night, Jack and the gang didn't realize there had been six that came ashore on the dock, and now there were two left and they were scared. When you're scared and witness what they had witnessed, you do stupid things, and they were no exception. They were stranded on the island from Hell, outnumbered and with no common sense between them. In their minds, they were now the hunted. The scared kids still had guns, which make folks with no common sense public enemy number one. It was time for the scum to take refuge, and the church would do for their time of need.

After a few cold ones and some concerned beer banter, Mitch had made his return to Kate's. Walking through the door, he felt like he was back at his parents' home all over again and he had been a really bad boy. Kate, standing in the simple moonlight in a short t-shirt subbing as a nightshirt, was waiting for him to return. Beautiful as she was, all Mitch could think as she eagerly called out was that she was acting like an upset girlfriend.

"Mitchell! I thought you went to bed--and I'm not questioning you, but you know people talk. You shouldn't be out at night just wandering around – people just don't know you yet."

Mitchell? She just called him Mitchell, and only his mom called him that. What was he getting himself into? He almost liked the way she called him that.

"I'm sorry," lied Mitch, "but I couldn't sleep, so I walked on over to the Flying Daisy. You know, one more visit there and I get my regular card!" he joked. For some reason, he could tell she didn't think he was cute and maybe didn't even believe him, but he knew this was her town and she was still his room and board, even though he thought maybe she was falling for him.

In a quick moment, his interrogation was cut short as Kate got a call about Lynn's family. Dropping the phone in near panic, all she could say was "No!" Lynn's family had always held a special place in her heart. With the loss of her own family, these special people were the closest thing to family she had left. She had just received a brutal lesson in the kind of evil that really did lurk beyond the shadow of hope.

It was hard enough accepting the senseless tragedy of the loss of Lynn's dad, and now this crazy attack on his family. That evening, the walls of so many of the islanders' own homes were no longer the refuge from the outside world that they had always been comforted with. The night before, Macbeth had been safe, but by morning the stranger was now well within. That evening, the people of Macbeth learned that they had locks on their doors for a reason once again.

CHAPTER 9:

LOVE POTION

This was Kate's hometown and Mitch always just a questioning journalist with torn feelings. He knew his heart said to come clean with Kate about his adventure, but now wasn't the time. He had learned more than he should have. She had more important things on her mind than him.

"I don't know what to say, Kate--sorry just doesn't seem strong enough, and I know you surely don't need me bothering you."

"Please, I wish you would bother me," Kate quickly replied. "I'm just fed up and sick of this island and all its problems and now Lynn's family...why?" she asked as she wiped the tears from her eyes. "Everything has changed now--how could they do this?" She broke down sobbing again. Lynn's family was her family, and Kate needed to help, but how? They had needed her help last night and she wasn't there. Shock and loss are tough emotions, and breaking their grip was a one-way street out of town.

He knew Kate was sincere--Lord knows why else would she want to be stuck here with him. Lacking a better penance for his lie, he sat up with her and tried to get her to open up her guarded thoughts to him, still so much a stranger. For some unknown reason, through her genuine sorrow, he felt a growing connection with her, a connection that he hadn't felt with anybody for years. Mitch, Mr. Stone Cold himself, was feeling the beginnings of love again. He had thought he was getting too old for that, but who cared? Kate was upset, and any shoulder to cry on was better than none at all as he handed her the box of tissues, under the suspicious green eyes of Amadeus eyeing his litter box.

Kate wanted to go down and sit with the family, but knew she would be in the way, it was best if she waited till later, and if they needed her sooner, she would go in a minutes notice.

It was that time, and Mitch figured Kate needed a pick-me-up...or was it him? Regardless, it was a good time for the spirits to flow. Searching through her refrigerator, all he found was Mad Dog 20/20, probably some forgotten brew surely left over by some crazy college renters with more than enough hangovers to spare.

A beggar never being picky, he eyed its alcohol content, while he carefully opened the chilled bottle. Fully knowing the dog's revenge, he poured and sipped the red blend, while Kate, not in the mood for some simple relief from reality, chugged to forget quickly, making the contents of the bottle dwindle.

In high school, watching her drink that potion down would have been his kind of date. Kate was chugging for all the wrong reasons. In a weird way he just wished she would let him in and really talk to him. Mitch needed to belong to someone more than he needed a story. What was wrong with that?

Many times in life you want to be alone with your thoughts, and this could have been one of those moments for her--but that evening, Kate needed someone and Mitch was it. Why would he complain? He had a buzzed, beautiful woman sitting next to him, and any ravenous, red-blooded male would jump at the chance to take Mitch's place, zipper in hand.

Who could figure what controls a male's mind. Brought up a staunch Catholic, he knew his place, even if his mind and hormones didn't. Drunk and depressed was never an honest way to bag women...more a means to an end. In that moment of compassion his suppressed morals were reborn, as Kate's angel guarded her this time.

With time, the potion worked its magic, as she started opening up with her fears, fears about how the mainland seemingly did not care whether Macbeth and its people lived or died. The state government was surely interested in the bigger picture and what the island could become without the town. Little towns and communities like Macbeth were on their own with everything but choosing their destiny. These people were indeed worried--if not paranoid--about the impact of crime and the state government on them. After that day's violent events, a point had been delivered home.

The two of them talked into the moonless evening. Kate sobered up ever so slightly. Mitch hoped what happened to both of them later that night was more than just the alcohol and depression, and that just maybe she liked him for him. With the two talking, Mitch realized maybe he had met his match in passion.

A cigarette would have been nice if either had smoked. He would have to settle for Kate's undivided passion--and it wasn't against the US or its people. It was only a reaction to the corruption of a state government, the crime and the uncertain future of the islanders. He could sense this was no longer just idle gossip, it was thought out, and it was the meat and potatoes of the soul.

The plans for what could happen had been prepared in time measured in years. Preparation for supplies and logistics had been going on for months. This town was on the verge of rebellion against big brother and all that was wrong with the state government. Mitch felt they had already mentally crossed the line between acceptable and unacceptable behavior and he didn't think it made a bit of difference to any one on the island. Kate had trusted Mitch with her flesh and now her secrets!

What could cause paranoia in a community like this? To go this far was perverse in itself. The blame did not rest on the community; it was too complicated for that. The blame rested on to many out of control forces in a society as uncontrollable as theirs had become. The future had become Macbeth's biggest threat and enemy while the years of worrying had taken its toll.

Back at the church, the two kids were getting nervous for a long drugless night ahead of them, too scared to search for an answer to their addiction. No plan to make for these fools- -only escaping from that crazy town to worry about. For once in their lives, they truly felt fear as the visions of their friend's justifiable violent end fluttered through their dreams. There were no inner-city graffiti- covered walls to protect them, as they thought they were being hunted to be disposed of like the vermin they were. Now, for once, justice was on the right side. That dark evening they felt a little of the panic Lynn's father went through before they finished him off.

Spring nights were always long, but that night would be the longest night of the two thugs' short lives. Feeling quite uneasy, all the two could do was stare out the front window and watch down the street for the imaginary posse that was sure to attack them in their dreams. Both were too afraid to sleep, because behind every shadow there was a ready and willing mob ready to seek the ultimate revenge.

Waking up the next morning to the sounds of opera was a change from his usual morning radio show. Finding Kate naked next to him made his simple day even better. Mitch's world always seemed more perfect with someone to share it with, even back then when he didn't remember her name. Would she remember last night? Would she remember all she told him? He could only guess?

In the warmth of passion he still learned even more than he should have. Damn, he was a journalist; he knew, and was forced to know more. He thirsted for the answers that he tried to ignore. Macbeth's riddle had to be solved, while many of the answers were being dumped in his lap.

Though he wrestled with his inner thoughts, could there be a true need for these free thinkers, those who dared to think past the status quo? What if Thomas Jefferson had been told to pipe down, or if George Washington had remained loyal to Britain? It took free thinkers to make what all had that day, and freedom was never free.

The system could not and would not always be perfect. When it wasn't, they needed people who were smart enough to realize the need for the change. For a fleeting moment, Mitch thought maybe Macbeth could possibly be part of the answer, maybe just the catalyst the Union needed to look itself in the mirror and repent.

Many a times in history there were those who did not believe in change. These betrayers of change were comfortable in the old, afraid to advance and face what inevitably is new. Such a small town...what could they really possibly do?

In the early morning, Mitch could feel the softness of Kate's breath sleeping off the muted effects of that cheap dime store wine. It was best to let her sleep as he was sure Lynn's family would be her focus this day. Getting up early to turn that damn music off, with a cup of instant coffee in hand, he headed for the comfort of the rocker on the porch. Picking up the wet newspaper, always a day behind, he sat back to relax, as his thoughts kept drifting back upstairs to the naked beauty he had left.

As the fog drifted silently off the still of the harbor, he listened to the comfortable sound of the seagulls. With a solid clink from behind, he turned around quick enough to watch Amadeus rubbing against the door, pushing it shut. Once again, Mitch swore he saw a smile as the cat, dry and warm, laughed like cats do when the whole world goes their way.

Mitch, locked out in Kate's bathrobe he wore, he sat contemplating the reason for a wet newspaper and a dry cat. His concentration was quickly broken by the early-morning sounds of more than seventy men in fatigues marching in odd steps through the seaside neighborhood. No Gestapo march, just a rag-tag assembly of big, little, fat, tall, young, and old men, all trying to march to some imaginary beat. It was still early, and most were probably half asleep as they broke off the road and headed toward the path in the brush.

Mitch knew he had time to kill, as she would be knocked out for a few more hours, so why not snoop for his story, even if he was only in Kate's robe? With the force of Maxwell House in his veins, he would transform himself in to the super spy he pictured himself to be as he raced out in pursuit the advancing troops. Easily following the scented trail of Old Spice cologne, Mitch raced through the brush after the assembly of the assorted militia.

He could hang back, since it wasn't hard following so many men. Following the muddy trail, he imagined the early Indians tracking a herd of overweight buffalo as they stampeded through a virgin field. Just follow the trail of smashed foliage, and Pop-Tart wrappers; this modern-day version of the Yellow Brick Road couldn't have been any easier to find.

"Practice to live, you women, all of you, and remember why we practice! What happened last night was the real deal--lock your doors!" the man in front yelled with hopes of inspiring them in the early-morning dew.

"Next time it might be real bullets. In the raw confusion of battle, it's your bald head on the line, hopefully not guarding mine."

The complaining dwindled down as the group approached a small valley. The men divided into two groups, both running for cover. Next thing Mitch knew, one group was running straight toward him. There was not much time to come up with a plan, as he dove into the brush to wait and watch.

What he witnessed next was the biggest game of capture the flag he had ever seen: organized paint ball warfare with a middle-aged flair...a game of fun, now used to hone these everyday citizens' combat skills. These were skills of battle most males had developed years before high school, transforming elementary school kids into warlords running through neighborhood backyards, killing the countless imaginary enemies they came up with in their dreams--imaginary countries and visions of intense heroic combat drifting through young impressionable minds. Maybe a game, maybe another life lesson learned.

In this split second, Mitch's mind wandered as his guard was let down. All it took was one quick movement of his pink bathrobe and he was a target of a multitude of paint guns, shooting paintballs to the left of him, paintballs to the right of him, paintballs in front of him. He was now an unarmed and wanted man, spotted in his cheap cover.

Defenseless and outgunned, he surrendered. He was busted, welted, painted, humiliated, and standing in a woman's pink bathrobe. Good thing the old neighborhood gang wasn't here to witness this cheap mistake; this once-young warrior must be getting old in his humiliating blunder.

Jumping out of his worthless cover, both hands held high in surrender, Mitch was defiant as any POW would be. "Name, rank, and serial number," he said, joking.

Reality set in as the troops failed to get his joke, judging by the dozen fresh paintballs he then encountered. Moaning in real pain, he now became the perfect prisoner in the hands of his interrogator. It was hard being macho, covered with as many colors of paint as he was. He was a psychedelic flower child, born again in the Land of Oz.

"Well hell's bells, it's that damn long-hair. What you doing in them bushes?" a bald man yelled.

"He's a spy--what else would this he be doing hiding alone?" another outspoken soldier figured.

"Hell, I'm no spy, I was locked out of the house by a damn cat," Mitch yelled as he backed slowly away from the advancing group.

"I was just bored and curious and saw you all march by. Say, are you people lit up?"

"Fucking lit up! I'll show you lit up, you little long-haired sucker!" another voice from the crowd yelled, joined by the cheers and jeers from other salivating comrades.

"Lynch him, lynch him!" a few teenagers screamed.

Mitch was getting worried as he backed up, until he realized he could back up no more. Fearing for his life, he flashed back to the movie *Deliverance*, while he looked into the faces of the crowd, just wishing he had some flapjacks and muffins to distract this hungry mob--it might have bought him some precious time so he could run for his pathetic life…he just hoped he didn't hear banjo music!

"What do you want from me?" Mitch pleaded, pausing to wipe the dripping paint from around his eyes. "I'm just a journalist. I'm paid to be nosy; you all know that."

Ignoring the laughter in the crowd, he realized he might have to make a run for it.

"He sure does look pretty!" the tubby guy yelled. Sizing up his opponents, he looked for the heaviest section, just hoping for the quick sprinting advantage, before his legs gave out.

"Let him go," Peace said as he pushed his way through the crowd. "He's okay. He's with me."

"Bullshit. He's spying, I tell you."

"Spying on what? Grown men in mask and pajama tops, playing war? Lester, you need bigger things to worry about, like your son, who keeps chasing my sister. Let him go, and go home, Lester!" Peace shouted.

Shot down in his moment of glory, Lester walked away cussing to himself while he wondered about his son and just maybe his over active hormones of a teenager learning to prowl.

It didn't take long for them to decide to release the captive. They figured he had more serious problems to deal with, judging by the paint-covered welts all over his body. The victors, in their ignorance, believed his almost-true excuse of being just plain nosy, and maybe just a bit weird in that bathrobe.

Like a defeated soldier, Mitch thanked Peace for his rescue, and trudged home alone, hoping for the sympathy of the lady waiting for him. Again, contemplating the seriousness of Macbeth's resolve, he walked down the path that would head home. What if this little island really did believe they were an army, and that if push came to shove, they could fight? Lucky for him, this time the battle was only with paintballs and a half-awake army.

Coming home to Kate, Mitch figured the sight of him covered with paint would make her day. Knocking loudly on the locked door, Mitch hoped the sight of him would send Amadeus screaming. Kate with swollen eyes from crying, was dressed in only a t-shirt, as she slowly opened the door, focusing on him with that hurt puppy dog look as she forbade him to enter, rather demanding him out back to be hosed off immediately.

"Nice bathrobe, Mitch, maybe you ought to shave those legs next time!" she said with a weak smile. "Maybe that'll teach you!"

Defeated and humiliated, he knew it was better he took care of himself alone. Breaking into a bigger smile, her world took a turn for the better even though it was at his expense. He was a big boy, and pride is an easy pill to swallow in the face of defeat. He knew he had been paid twice last evening, and the reruns of that night would continue paying.

Lots of soap and water, and Mitch was pink again and extra hungry. He wanted the big fat cakes, whole hog sausage, and fresh over easy eggs with salt and pepper: Fanny's was on his mind and his stomach. Knowing he had ruined Kate's robe, he bribed her with an even better robe if she accompanied him on his breakfast quest.

He knew the game all too well, and it was time to talk straight with Jack, so he needed to be focused on what was going on. Mitch, feeling reborn from his brush with humility, felt the untested desire to be a part of the community and their mission. His real story would come in time, especially if he could almost live it.

The two were ready as they walked to Fanny's that day; it was the best move, judging by the size of Kate's hangover. The cold morning air has a way of clearing one's abused senses, and sitting on a bicycle seat probably wasn't the best idea.

"Kate, I'm going to confront Jack about what's going on here. It's no longer just looking for a story--I'm starting to believe there is a case for some kind of change, and I could help!" He paused as he stopped her in her steps, peering into her bloodshot eyes while he grabbed for her warm hands.

"It's just that I don't want everyone thinking this is another kind of community cult thing. You know, religious lunatics just waiting for their big spiritual ark." Kate didn't respond much other than a hmmmm or two: she wasn't much of a fighter at this point. Mitch knew she sort of trusted him, but right now life was just a clouded blur. The Mad Dog 20/20 had gotten its sweet revenge as it always did, and the need to see Lynn's family was still first on her mind.

At 9:30 a.m., just like every morning, Elmer Peddle

walked slowly down to the weathered white-stained church to slowly open it up. Methodically, he almost waltzed through his daily routine, for he had been doing it for too many years. Elmer, in his golden years, still pretended to sweep the well-worn wooden floors he had swept over and over every Monday through Friday. Never much dirt; it was just the set routine, and at seventy-five, routine was good. That old community church was Elmer's drive. He treated these sacred buildings like his own. Most knew his job at the church gave back more to Elmer than he to it. His usefulness had left years ago, but all knew caretaking the church provided his need to be, and his shortcomings would be overlooked.

The church that day was different for Elmer. It wasn't the same knotty pine smell he had grown use to after so many years of being there. Everyone on the island knew they didn't smoke there. Elmer knew that strong smell too well; he had lived with unfiltered Camels for too many years to forget that sweetness.

It was too late by the time Elmer figured it out--one whack on the back of the old head with a chalice and Elmer was out and bleeding. The drug-starved boys were starting to lose their grip as their little space was invaded. Elmer was not quite the posse they expected, but they knew sooner or later their turn would come.

CHAPTER 10:

WHERE ART THOU, ELMER?

Arriving at Fanny's, Mitch nervously glimpsed at Jack sitting at his usual table in the back. Not sure what to say, Mitch kept glancing over, while he tried to get the nerve up to go talk to him. In a moment of mind time traveling he went back to his years in grade school. He had many evenings nervously sitting on the edge of his bed getting ready to show his dad another bad report card. Only this time his mother wasn't here to bail him out and stand guard against his father's rage and assure him that he would live another day and redeem his pitiful self. Mitch was alone against this tiger, and he prepared himself to enter his jungle.

Enjoying his steaming black magic laced with four creamers and sugar, Mitch contemplated his next move. One with his country sausage, Mitch sliced, diced, and digested, while his over easy eggs soaked into his cakes, all on their way to solving his hunger crisis. Forcing him to eat slower, the time drew near. He rethought his mission, and weighed its merits versus his level of fear.

His oversized He-Man breakfast was now history, while Kate nursed her third glass of ice water, which seemed to go nicely with her breakfast of aspirin. In a moment, he found that inner strength he needed; must have been the pancakes filling up that gnawing hole in his empty stomach. He lurched forward like a wild madman, and entered into the jaws of certain confrontation, as the caffeine ignited his turbo boosters.

Jack was sitting back with Tom, a big black handsome man and, too many, the unofficial mayor and welcome center of the town. The two were seemingly enjoying their breakfasts.

Tom was strong as an ox, gentle as a lamb, and was the man if you ever had a question about anything in Macbeth. He easily radiated a genuine trust out of his big brown eyes. Mitch was relieved to see Tom sitting alone with Jack – he knew now there was a chance he would live to see tomorrow.

"Excuse me," Mitch said, clearing his throat. Jack and Tom looked up. "I know I'm not supposed to know what's going on, but I'm a journalist and I'm usually paid to know. As much as I don't want to admit it, I happened to be at your meeting yesterday."

Jack looked harder now. Was he sizing up Mitch's body for the charge? Mitch knew it wouldn't take much--one good hit to the gut, and with all that breakfast still in his stomach, he would be history.

"You were, were you?" Jack said as he slammed his coffee cup to the table, spilling a little bit of it.

Oh, great--his veins are going to be popping out now, Mitch thought.

Tom, seemingly oblivious to the conversation, was fussing with his oversized cakes, when he looked up and said in a clear voice: "Jack, don't get worked up over this. Have another cup of decaf and let me handle this." Then Tom, pushing his chair back, stood up with his massive body towering over a much smaller Mitch.

"Mitch, let's take a short walk," Tom said, looking down at him like he was Jim Brown in *The Dirty Dozen*. Mitch didn't know if he should be grateful for Tom's invitation or if he should fear for his future on the island. He picked the lesser of two evils when he walked away Tom.

It was amazing the respect people got when they were with Tom. Townsfolk literally looked up to him, for he had earned the people's respect and trust for the years of thankless service to them all.

"Mitch, forget the snooping. You really aren't very good at it anyhow. You want answers? I'll give you answers, just stop snooping. And man, what was with the pink bathrobe?"

Humiliated, he just couldn't respond to that question again.

"God-fearing," Tom said as the two walked down the street, "all of us. We believe in mother, country, and apple pie. God has been good, amen! We pray for it every night, just counting on God for it to continue. It's that simple, Mitch: peace, prosperity, and home. Last couple years, things have been changing. Bureaucrats say change is good, and I imagine some is. But we like it the way it is here--we like our lives here. We all help each other. For the most part, I would say we all love each other. Sounds weird to you, Mitch, doesn't it? It's not like that in the big city--is it, Mitch?"

He had no chance to respond as he just took in Tom's words.

"Years ago, developers and the state started making noise about developing our island. We weren't into it then, and we're not now. After one too many proposals, we told the mainland to basically kiss our grits. Ever since, we've been feeling the extra heat. Our taxes started going up, unfair audits, petty little irritating things – just enough to ruin your day. When we looked for help, of course no help ever came from the state. Our little island was cast adrift in the big ocean of red tape, and all the state said was that we're paranoid, and the time will come when we have to make a change. Mitch, none of us have any problem paying taxes. We just want our fair share. We want our piece of the pie. Look at our school! Should it matter that we have only fifty-eight students? We want the same education the kids on the mainland get. Our children want the tools to succeed just like the mainlanders do. Heck, our schools are lucky if we can provide enough coal to heat the building through the winter, let alone new books and computer programs! The school is old--she's been an old gracious lady, but she needs repairing, bad. We all tried to help, but a lot of folks are just skimming by themselves. Then Washington and the state started limiting our commercial fishing, and we live on our fishing. Other than summer tourism, fishing built this community. You can't just take someone's job from them like that. Fishing's all a lot of us folks here know." Tom was on a roll; all Mitch could do was listen, as Tom had found his passion.

"I contacted the state government, but got no help. I went to the mainland to see the governor. I finally sat with him for ten minutes, after waiting six hours. All that arrogant excuse for a leader could do was continually look at his watch. He said he felt sorry for us. 'What your people need,' he said, 'is job retraining – move to the mainland. We, your state government, have plenty of government-assisted programs just for your kind.' The governor didn't get it. I was making him late for golf or something. I know how to tell when a man cares, and this governor didn't give a rat's ass about us--not enough votes to bother him or his political career. Politics shouldn't be about the next time you're up for election: it's about today. It's about helping those who voted for you and those who didn't vote for you, too. Get it, Mitch? I hope so. I trust you, man. We will need you, and we need your skill with words." Tom paused and grew silent for a moment. "A lot of bad went on last evening, I wish I could tell you more, we all just need some space!"

Mitch felt like a great leader had come down from his throne to speak to him, and now he was humbled and a bit confused. Tom began to walk away, but turned back toward Mitch.

"Mitch, I trust you. I know you'll do the right thing after you think this through, so let's get together again soon and do a little more talking. In the end, no matter what, do right always, man."

Mitch, a bit dumbfounded at his greatness, could only watch as this humble man walked back into Fanny's. How could one small island be blessed with two great leaders? Mitch wondered what would happen if only the state government could be so lucky.

Feeling as if he had been let into part of the story, he sprinted back to breakfast. Kate was now drinking tea, holding on to the precious cup with two hands when Midge realized Elmer Peddle never made it to breakfast.

"First time in twenty years Elmer hasn't showed up," Midge said as she wiped her hands in her dirty apron.

"Tommy! Something is terribly wrong!" Midge, figuring on the worst, called down to the church. No answer. Things on the island were still uneasy due to yesterday's incidents. Midge was getting more nervous as the seconds ticked by; putting her pot of coffee down, she went after Jack and Tom.

It was turning out to be a bad day for breakfast for the unlucky two. With mouthfuls, the two of them were destined to be interrupted again, as their cold breakfasts were going to get a bit colder.

This interruption was different; it was Midge, and when Midge talked, someone had to listen. Both Tom and Jack knew Elmer was old, and his routine had to change sometime.

"No point in jumping to quick conclusions," Jack said as Tom, with a mouthful of home fries, nodded in agreement.

"Give it some time, Midge. Elmer's not a spring chicken anymore," Tom added as he continued sipping his lukewarm cup of coffee.

Both replies were the wrong answers, as far as Midge was concerned; she started screaming about who made the pancakes in this town, and she wasn't going to be put off by two big guys.

Most men can take a high-pitched female yapping for only so long, before either walking away from the situation or satisfying the reason they were being yapped at in the first place.

"Calm down Midge, and please grab us a few guns!" Jack yelled while he shoveled hotcakes faster into his demanding mouth. Midge was less concerned about the boys' hunger as she grabbed their half-empty plates from the table and told them to go! It was her time, and the boys knew who poured their coffee. It was a matter of respect.

Swilling down the last of his of coffee, Jack rose up. Tom followed, stuffing the rest of the massive flapjack in his mouth, which he managed to grab off the retreating plate. Heading for the front door, both bent down to kiss Midge on the forehead, hoping for the good luck only a real lady could deliver. Midge, with her arms crossed, stood at the front porch and was pleased at the results of her outburst. One of the regulars passed out some of Macbeth's arsenal, hidden away in a closet of Fanny's for the rest of the willing posse.

The posse--a half dozen breakfast regulars and Mitch--followed Jack toward the church, leaving Tom in town just wishing for the rest of his pancakes.

Over the wet cobblestone road they walked, and for a fleeting moment, Mitch felt he was back among his brothers and friends. Just walking and bullshitting, the way guys and true friends usually do. It was unconditional acceptance, sort of like being in a gang, just one of the dogs in the pack. It had more to do with being a guy, more so than just being able to write your name in the snow without using hands. It was all about, bullshit, an early spring morning, salty air, and AK-47s.

Never one to bring up the rear, Mitch ran ahead and joined Jack, leaving the rest of the posse to follow. He was bolder after his talk with Tom. Feeling that limited sense of trust, he wanted to ask a few questions while they walked. He held his head high, feeling he was part of the posse as they trudged on with a spring to their steps. Comfortable now, since once again Mitch belonged!

"Mitchell, I never quite understood you long-hairs. Why do you want to look like a woman?" Jack asked as he shuffled his large body down the road.

"Look like a woman? Hell, length of hair has nothing to do with it, Jack! And let me tell you, women love it. It's like a babe magnet where I come from." But Mitch was a bit taken aback at the thought that he had a female side. His male feathers ruffled, he ran his hand through his long brown mane.

"Why does it seem you city folk all so different all the time?"

"Were different?" Mitch shot back.

"You all are. Your to pushy, thinking you got the world by the balls, just grabbing the poor victims nuts tighter and tighter until they're ready to pop like a zit, then your victims say what you want them to say, and you print it."

"You got me all wrong, Jack. My life mission sure isn't to screw every interesting character I cross. Being here now with all of you means more than you can ever imagine. Sure, I'm here because of a story, but I'm going to give the reader a true story; you got my word on that – that is, if my word means anything to you."

"Words mean nothing. I have more people give me snow jobs with words than I care to count. Actions speak louder than words--so show me long-hair."

"Just give me a chance!" Mitch pleaded.

As the group walked on, he realized he never told Kate goodbye, but he knew going to help Lynn and her family was on her mind, and he would have just gotten in the way anyhow.

Pestering on with more questions, Mitch learned the real story about how the guns in the church closet came to be. In fact they were shipped right into the town's hands and harbor. Macbeth's law confiscated them, shipped the drug runners and crew to the mainland for prosecution, and kept the ship.

The *Danny Boy*, now sitting in the harbor, was 382 feet of rusting metal-- barely a float, but now the town's property. The old, tired ship broke down at sea and made the mistake of asking Macbeth for help. The fisherman towed her in while her crew ran away in a small single-engine boat like rats abandoning a sinking ship. Didn't take the town's officials long to find out why the crew ran so quickly. Too much cannabis and cocaine stashed on board, the drug runner gold, which was confiscated along with the ship and her arsenal. The plunder was just unexpected gifts from one anonymous Mexican drug lord.

What the town had in store for the ship was still a mystery. Mitch hoped they were not going to use it for what it was built for. His vote was an artificial reef. The *Danny Boy* would do better sitting on the bottom of the ocean floor rather than sailing on its surface.

The guns and ammo were just frosting on the cake to the islanders. Because of this blunder, some drug lord was stewing, having made a critical mistake in the game for the illegal trade they dealt in. The search and seizure law was put to full use here. Mitch imagined that the guns were probably left off the ship's cargo list. Just a clerical mistake, he was sure.

While this eager group of gun-toting townsmen walked on toward the church, Mitch was deep in thought about Kate, after giving up explaining the rationality of long hair. Not often had Mitch ever really thought about somebody else besides himself. He knew he could almost picture himself with her-- something about that drunken innocent smile she had last night. Kate was vulnerable yet defiant, and he always got off on that rebellious characteristic in a woman. Along with her own independent mind, Kate was drop-dead gorgeous, which also helped to move love matters along.

Three days on the island and Mitch was ready to toss New York and Cleveland away for good. He could start his own chapter of the Browns Backers on this island. Then start his own island magazine: *Macho Mitch's Island Tips*, he would call it. Other than the relative security of a small paycheck and hospitalization, Mitch could chuck it all for the raw romantic lifestyle of the island. A beach bum at heart...hot dogs, margaritas, and bikinis--he wished. Scotty, please don't beam me back home, Mitch thought. He wondered if Paxton's carried his size in a Speedo he would need to start selling from his hot dog cart, serving only all beef dogs, and genuine stadium mustard to the starving tourists.

Writers tend to overanalyze situations and events. To Mitch, Macbeth brought back all the warm fuzzies he used to get as a kid. Years had changed, but his memories and thoughts were as vivid as when he was snot-nosed and growing up. Mitch had memories that he cherished and never wanted to give up, but as with all good things, most memories melt away into the back recesses of our busy minds, some forgotten events lucky enough to pop up now and then when triggered by some familiar situation.

The overweight, band of men finally turned the bend and followed the road straight for the church. Like an omen from the gods of the sky, the heavens blackened and opened up dropping hail the size of golf balls down upon the merry band. Off in the distance through the rain, a weak ray of sun appeared over the heavily shaded church. Not unusual for this island on the coast, subjected to the many different trade winds that often crossed its path.

With the skies opening up on them, all the wet and no-longer-so-merry men took off running toward the church like a band of escaped lunatics from some forgotten institution. All of their soaked bodies were pulverized by the pounding hail and rain as it drove them onward even faster, with hopes of escape from the storm.

CHAPTER 11:
THINGS JUST HAPPEN

Most in the group dreaded the rain and headed for the simple protection of the church and all her surrounding trees. Amidst all the confusion of trying to escape the storm, most never realized the two church windows had slowly opened. Through the openings, a couple of cold gun barrels were shoved out and aimed into the wide-open courtyard at the charging band of men.

In a split second a load crack pierced the still air, then another, followed by a dozen others. The young man next to Mitch lurched forward, then backward, screaming and grabbing his bloodied leg, falling in a crumpled mess on the ground. Mitch stopped dead in his tracks, not knowing what to do or where to go.

More loud rapid shots continued to ring out from behind the church walls. Caught off guard, men just stopped and stared, all bewildered, more than a bit surprised, and not yet ready for the heat of battle.

In a mind-numbing instant, Mitch felt a burning, stabbing sensation in his hand, followed by a second powerful punch to his now-throbbing shoulder. Smelling burning flesh, he grabbed his shoulder, feeling the warmth of fresh blood trickling through his shaking fingers. Mitch had been shot. This wasn't supposed to happen, at least not to him – this was only a job!

Never one to keep his cookies down, a frenzied dizziness settled over his violated body. Falling to the ground he tried to fight the urge to blow chunks while his little world started to spin rapidly out of control. His shoulder and hand screamed in agony at the warm pain he was feeling.

Shots continued to pour out from within the church walls. He could only watched in a pain-induced haze as the lofting gray gun smoke drifted lazily out of the stained glass windows and up through the weeping willows branches, aiming toward the final security of the heavens.

Jack had had enough of the snipers' random shooting. He and a couple other men collected their scattered thoughts and returned fire immediately shooting down one of the windows shutters as they tried to aim. In a blur, Mitch watched as their return fire danced through the old white wooden sides of the church, turning it into Swiss cheese. Through the bullets, heat, and passion, the AK-47s slowed the thugs' volley down, buying just enough time to give Macbeth's pinned-down citizens a chance to work out a retreat.

Still in stiff denial, Mitch felt like a visitor to someone else's dream. Drifting in and out of some type of alternate reality, he was at peace and unconcerned as the shots danced about the cemetery and cobblestones around him.

With an unexpected slap, Mitch was caught off guard and jerked back into the cold reality of the desperate situation. Two men, more concerned about Mitch's safety than their own, sprang to his rescue. Together with more resistance than help from him, the men dragged him into the relative safety of a large cemetery stone and the unyielding protection of the dead.

The pain didn't last as long as Mitch had always imagined it would after being shot, just that damn throbbing feeling that crowded his immediate reality. Nor was his wounded fall as dramatic as when he was shot playing combat in his youth. Mitch wasn't worried about his shortcomings in real battle. He was too busy trying to rest and avoid that sickening feeling while he stared up through the thick branches. He tried to be strong, but his world seemed to spin faster, and out of his limited control. Life and death meant little to Mitch, as his real world just became a faint blur.

Jack, concerned with sight of real blood, sent Tim running back to town. Extra help had to come from someone. Most there weren't quite sure who they needed help from, but knew they needed it.

They had planned for this day--they knew it was coming, they just didn't know when, and it was time for the stand to begin. Jack knew it, as did some of the others. Most of the men had a good hunch, after last night's demonstration of terror and then justice that the ball of change had indeed begun to roll.

As in any battle, the church cemetery took on a whole new look, as its peace and tranquility were replaced with a smoking field of fire, complete with bewildered and wounded men scattered and shooting violently at the threat.

Two other unlucky victims besides Mitch were wounded, as they too sought sanctuary behind the large granite headstones. Now the stones seemed a little more eerie as warm blood dripped over the inscription on one. Death had knocked on someone else's door that day, but it seemed to avoid Macbeth residents at this particular battlefield.

Cowering in fear behind the bullet holes and their fresh patterns on the church walls, the thugs had a bigger problem besides the few rays of a renewed sunshine penetrating the warm holes of the spent bullets. Elmer was cold--not the kind of cold a warm blanket would have taken care of, just a warm casket cold. No hostage now, just a stiff corpse and another victim.

Crazy thoughts went racing through the kids' tormented heads. Now both were looking head-on at the possibility of death, as its cold touch seemed to get a little closer to the two. Topping off their bad day, the two gang members were stranded on an island that didn't seem to believe in a modern justice system. It seemed that tough love always has to hurt someone, and their number was up.

Because they were addicts off the streets, being out of drugs wasn't helping their scrambled minds. During the long cold night the two caged animals realized they needed more help than the cold gun barrels between their legs. With a group somewhere outside who wanted nothing more than to write them off for good, one thug, grasping for straws in a rare moment of rational thought, found the office phone. Calling the mainland collect, he prayed to a fair god that his urgent phone call would go through.

Getting a hold of his fatherless ghetto home, he screamed to the only fair voice he ever knew. Waking his momma from her well-deserved slumber, he screamed to her to just listen and then about how her innocent boys were fighting for their unholy lives, penned-up and scared by a town out of control, a town hell-bent on an old-fashioned revenge. They pleaded for her help for their unearned justice before the lynching rope found them.

It didn't take long after their lines connected for their one line together to go dead, just long enough for the mother who believed in her lost son's innocence to get the terrifying message and call the local police, crying and demanding help.

Her boys were stranded on Macbeth with no hope of survival! They were good boys and they need help. The thought never crossed her mind that they were so far away, and that they weren't where they said they said they would be. She was clueless, but could still only see the good they all had when they were so young. Too many jobs supporting her family, which she knew was so important to her, but she just couldn't bring herself to admit it wasn't their fault.

It was spring; love was in the air. With love abounding, the crazies always come out. The cops had heard it all before. To these veterans of one too many street battles, these inner city folks were simply trash and most not worthy of their time. One precinct after another passed this ordinary call over, claiming it wasn't in their jurisdiction, until it had been passed on too long and someone had the responsibility to answer it.

It wasn't just her call; cops on the mainland weren't very eager to help most. Job stress and too many crimes had dulled the sense of responsibility. They tried to get off the hook by claiming a shortage of men, too many cases to handle, or something along those lines. The call wouldn't go through, but just maybe this lady had something that should be looked into.

Buford Justice (whose parents, in their moment of raw passion, named their bubbly ball of a son after a movie addict's crush on Jackie Gleason's famous part), was called in to size up the situation.

Buford, head of the county sheriff's department, was

teed-off while teeing up. Interrupted by his pager during his game of passion, he stomped off the course in his golf knickers and matching '70s-style green hat.

The pissed-off Buford placed a call to Macbeth's babysitter, Officer Leroy. Buford was always able to get a relatively clear picture from Leroy, even though no good blood ever flowed between the two.

The sketchy details trickled in, and if it was a hostage situation, Buford wanted nothing to do with it. "Let the governor's state patrol deal with it, they have jurisdiction and manpower! Hell, they get paid to look good--why bother me?"

Leroy, in his worn uniform, could only smile as he pictured poor Buford all prettied up for his game of chance, but now just about losing his cool. Leroy, just trying to get under Buford's skin, dangled a barb out there for him to take.

"Bue, I agree, this is much bigger than you want to handle, even with all the raw know-how you possess. Pass it on, big guy--save yourself the hassles and all that overtime for something that might just be out of your league."

Buford couldn't agree more in his restored jolliness, as his game of golf was awaiting and Macbeth as usual was the last on his list of worries.

"You know, Leroy, it's your call." Talking with an all-beef hot dog stuffed deep in his mouth, while stadium mustard oozed down his tight shirt, Buford continued in his southern drawl.

"It's not really my jurisdiction, I only back you up when I can, and let me remind you: with those size 52 pants, Leroy, you're a lot to back up," Buford said, burping into the phone. "Excuse me...that Dr Pepper does it to me every time.

Harvey! Would you grab me another bowl of that fine chili with extra crackers?" Buford screamed into the background. "Leroy, you're a big boy now; stop bothering me. Maybe call your elected official for some direction. Better yet, Leroy, I'll call the governor for you! We're tight, you know. You just keep an eye on that home front, big guy, and I'll make sure you get some real help."

Leroy could only smile as he pictured Buford in all his glory. Golf wasn't his passion, only his excuse to be away from work. Leroy knew the situation well as he planned his next move and hoped this would attract the attention of the ones who forced Macbeth into this corner.

Speculation on the mainland continued to grow with each call from Midge as she gracefully planted those seeds of doubt as to what was going on in Macbeth. The governor wasn't sure if this event even merited his attention, but knew he had to respond, even if it was only with a statement.

Rumors of armed militia were being mentioned--and if they were true, they were more than any small department on the island could handle. Who knew what the real situation was? Leroy could only chuckle to himself as all concerned parties seemed to work themselves into a worthless tizzy every time he would tell them something new over the phone.

Leroy, sounding like the martyr, said he would drive up and scope it out for big Buford, but it was best he get some heavy backup up here soon, since all Leroy said he could hear was the gunfire. For once Buford agreed, as he saw his way out of work fade away, as the weight of the situation was about to shift.

Buford, never really interested in solving the island's issue, called the governor and suggested the governor use his state patrol mobile anti-terror unit to assist the island. The governor couldn't have been happier to demonstrate the force of his new toy army; it was an election year, and shows of force (at least to this governor) translated into votes. The situation appeared to be a no-brainer and a great media opportunity, as the small press pool was alerted and sprung to action with hopes of a possible new story to cover.

Gene Hampton Roe never was much of a respected governor--more of a pretty boy that got his job with looks, family name, and money. How else would he have survived?

The governor had been advised by his chief of staff to get involved with Macbeth, and it could only make him look good for his next election. He knew all too well that tough on crime always looks good in the polls. The governor needed all the goodwill he could muster, which was hard to get from a symbolic office, and a reputation tainted with too many ex-wives and mistresses chasing his legend, all just trying to sell his bedroom dirt for whoever was willing to buy.

The aides, who constantly worked on repairing his damaged image, got Macbeth on the line for the Governor. Midge, all excited with the call, ran to Tom, who was just getting filled in on what was really going on at the other end of town. The governor, hoping he had another one up on the trustee, informed Tom that the anti-terror unit was coming to solve their little problem.

Tom had heard all the shooting, as did most of the townsfolk that were milling about comparing notes. How the governor found out so quickly about this situation bordered on amazing, but was planned. It was just all too new of a situation for Tom, who was putting pieces together as quickly as he could gather them.

The governor, ignorant as ever, reminded Tom that he knew all about his constituents and their problems. All too familiar with this governor's moves, Tom knew he was just blowing smoke over his confusion, as the game was about to be played out using the governor as Macbeth's newest pawn.

Overreacting was expected in a show of force for the media, and the governor authorized sending in his elite Massachusetts State Patrol to quell the town's hostage situation. Tom, acting his best, tried to reassure the governor that they could handle the confrontation and were still in control of the event, but the governor wanted no part of their help.

Tom backed down and agreed to the troops. With a wink of the eye to Midge, and a bigger smile, he quickly got off the phone. With no time to waste, Tom grabbed his gun and ran toward the direction of the dwindling shots.

Tom was satisfied, and those six hours he had waited to see the governor didn't matter anymore: revenge would be sweet.

Let him send all that military might over here; it's theirs today, ours tomorrow, he thought. Pausing in the middle of this thought, Tom watched a young family quickly pass by, and he imagined ahead to a brighter future for all if this plan would only work.

Elated as he slowly ran with anticipation of change and fear of the shooting at the church, and not knowing where he was really needed, he turned around and headed back to the sanity of Fanny's. He needed to talk to Jack soon, but was needed here more for the questioning town folk.

Midge worked the phones like the pro. She really was active as she sent the word out to the island that the state patrol was on their way. With no visible apprehension or dissent, the town began its well-rehearsed plan; with the visible activity picking up along with the anticipation for the moment, it seemed the island's hour of destiny and recognition was fast approaching.

Fanny's elder coffee crowd wondered aloud if this really the town's time to draw the line in the sand--or maybe it was time to talk again? Tom hated making the decision alone, because this town had always believed in a fair democracy. But time was limited now, and there wasn't enough of it for a town meeting. He knew deep down it was now or never. Most knew there would never be a better opportunity, and others had already made their decision.

"Midge, I've never been one to back away from a decision. But right now you know I'm scared as hell at the thought of what this choice could mean for us all." Scratching his bald head, Tom wondered, hoping for some compassion and understanding from Midge.

"Tommy, you don't fool me. You might be a big bear, but you've always been a softy to me--and most of the rest of the folks of this town for that matter. We all trust in you and Jack. Each one of us has all fought with our emotions over what is right and what is wrong. It's your time to do what you have to do. We believe in you, or we never would have let this go on so long, so get to it."

Still at a loss for the real answer, Tom stood watching the increasing activity of the town, fighting with his inner demons as he wrestled with what his ultimate response would be.

But it really didn't matter: the governor had his vision. To him, in a delusional state, he was the hero for any and every small town America. His simple mind was set. The state patrol was going in, and his army was ready for the show. He needed more media, as he wanted the whole world to witness his might.

Finally leaving Fanny's, Tom headed up the street to Paxton's as fast as his large legs could move his body. He had to talk to somebody, anybody. Bursting through the door, Tom saw Carl, a fellow trustee, with a good-sized group of the locals. All were gathered and talking around the soda fountain with an assortment of weapons in hand; drinking flavored soda, trying to find out what was really going on.

Tom, panting, explained the situation as best he could. It wasn't much of an explanation, with only limited facts as to what was going on up at the church. The group was past the stage of hemming and hawing; the next move had now been placed in the town's hands. It was time for the town to stop talking and show what it had planned and argued about for so many of the previous years.

In the following minutes, with the backing of Paxton's soda crowd, Tom ordered the town's rag-tag militia mobilized, sending a group up to stabilize and reinforce the group at the church.

A crying nervous woman, holding her children tight, made Tom wonder if the men's choice was the best course. *Stop second-guessing yourself*, he thought. The state patrol was going to land, and it would be safer if the women and children were evacuated to the safety of the salt mines--no telling what could happen.

The island's volunteer firefighters and the older children got busy filling bags of sand: the bags that would be used for setting up the gun nests that were spread throughout the town – the gun nests that most hoped would never have to be used. Just a futile excuse and symbol of determination for occupying troubled minds while working up a sweat as the sand flowed.

The elders, slower but just as involved, set off at their gentler paces to open the mine. Time had slowed their bodies down, but not their minds. In their many shades of grays, they felt needed as they prepared to awake the sleeping generators within the mine and prepare her for a reception for the recipients of the evacuation.

The town became like an organized hill of ants with Tom as the queen ant. Every citizen had his or her duty, as they all prepared for the worst; it was a hubbub of activity, with all working like there was no tomorrow. No time for nerves as a focused people reacted with determination and pride. No time for second-guessing, as all the guessing had gone past the point of discussion.

Tom was busy organizing the work crews when a low-flying news chopper came cruising down the coastline. Hovering over the rooftops of this small town, the pilot looked for a place to land, and on this island places like that were few and far between. The chopper's powerful rotors kicked up dust, paper, and anything else that wasn't attached. Seeing an opening in the town square, it settled closer to the agitated crowd. The townsfolk, reluctant at first, stepped back and let the hovering chopper land.

With little regard for the old town square, the former bird of prey landed. As the dust settled, its blades swirled to a stop, and the chopper door slid open. With cameras rolling, the eager news crew jumped out looking for the first angle for a story they hoped would make the evening news.

With "CNN Mobile News Unit" written in big letters across its sleek white fuselage, there was no doubt to these reporters that a crisis was at hand somewhere on the rock.

Macbeth's welcoming party stepped forward and met the visitors as they leaped with cameras in hand, out the fuselage door. They all were quickly welcomed, then detained at gunpoint, as their cameras and news equipment were confiscated. In denial of what had just happened, they protested about their right to freedom of speech as they were cuffed and detained for their own safety. Until that jail cell slammed shut, they never figured that they were the story!

Of course this flagrant abuse of human rights didn't sit well with the news team, but there were just too many of the islanders, and too few of them.

"Go with the flow, kids," the stunning anchorwoman said. In their no-win situation, all they could do was follow the captors' rules and relax. The news crew for now would be silent observers to this event, while nothing would stop the story from unfolding before them. All the news crew could do was sulk as they saw their first-hand headline slip away.

Turning the crisis up, the islanders were now guilty of kidnapping, as an innocent news crew became the first prisoners in the unfolding conflict.

A concerned editor, hundreds of miles away, worried about why he couldn't get any live feed or chatter from his mobile unit. In desperation, he notified the FAA and Coast Guard to check for a lost chopper and his news crew, calling yet another crew to grab a boat this time and head directly for Macbeth.

CHAPTER 12:

UTTER CONFUSION

Mitch, still groggy and confused, awoke to the stabbing pain of being shot and bandaged. He didn't know what hurt more: getting shot, or his wounds being treated by an old doc who should have retired years ago. After minutes that seemed like agonizing hours, his wounds had been abused, then cleaned, and would have to wait till later to be stitched up.

Whipped and then defeated, Mitch rose on his wobbly feet, shuffling out of the dimly lit marble tomb that substituted as a makeshift triage center. He looked for Kate's familiar face, apparently unaware that the two thugs were still capable of pointing their loaded barrels at anyone in their view.

In his pain-induced trance, he figured war scars had to be a turn-on to women. Visible scars--just what he needed to add to his repertoire of stories for possible future female conquest. Would there be any other conquest, or was it just Kate?

The adrenaline had been kicking through Mitch's system like supercharged caffeine. His aching body wanted to sleep, while his charged mind wanted action.

"Buddy! You can't go there," an old-timer yelled as Mitch walked toward the direction of the church. "It's not safe, so sit down, young man. You should be resting anyhow."

Ignorant of his own safety, he had but one thought on his

mind--and it was finding that familiar face.

Jack wasn't into any more casualties as he yelled for some men to get that fool down. With a thud, Mitch was dropped like a blindsided quarterback and dragged back to the relative safety of the stones. Too weak to fight, Mitch had no choice but to go where they dragged him.

"Get him out of here and move him around back past the bend in the road. Help should be coming soon for the damn fool!" Jack was frazzled. Gunfire and blood had ruined a good day. He didn't have to be reminded now; he knew in his heart that the beginning of the end was here.

Kate had stayed at Fannies, talking to Midge, the gunshots in the distance were making Kate pace nervously about as she impatiently waited for her boarder to return. The ticking minutes on the clock only made the wait harder. In a moment of cold panic, she grabbed a coat and raced out the front door, running for the answers she hoped the church could provide.

With the wind in her face, she ran like a track star as she worried about a man she hardly knew--a man who had easily captured the empty heart she vowed would always be hers.

Her former life had been so complete, until this man from the mainland had shown her how empty it was. Breaking into tears as her mind played tricks on her, she approached the bend in the road, and the distinct smell of a fresh battle.

"Hold it, missy," an old familiar voice yelled out. Stopping in her tracks, Kate saw the two men sitting on the side of the road.

"Mitchell!" She screamed in joy, knowing he was among the living. Realizing he was hurt, Kate told the old-timer that she would take him back home and watch him. Happy to be free of him, the old-timer left quickly without ever looking back to return to the standoff.

Standing up a bit slower, Mitch leaned into her warm arms like the wounded soldier he pictured he was. In her over-caring pity, she walked her solider home, as Mitch was now a consecrated hero for Macbeth's backyard revolution, a purely unintentional baptism by fire and lead.

Eager reinforcements reached Jack and the remaining men still hiding among the stones in the cemetery. Tom really needed Jack's help back in town: too many questions from the concerned townsfolk, and no one but Tom to give them the answers. In Macbeth, Tom and Jack had always worked problems out together. Today on this little island there were two situations, and for a time the two strong-willed minds were forced to work apart.

Macbeth's reinforcements wasted no time in setting up offensive positions around the church complex. Surrounding the hall, the men worked at trying to keep out of sight of the nervous trigger-happy captives inside.

All the men around the church were waiting, unaware that poor Elmer's rigor mortis was moving along smoothly. With the patrol fast approaching, Jack realized they had a more urgent need than rescuing poor Elmer – the main part of Macbeth's arsenal and ammo were locked away in the church hall closet. Time was ticking away, and without a show of force, the situation in the church wouldn't be resolved before the mainland's response.

After what seemed like only short nap, Mitch awoke to Kate caressing him gently as she rested his aching head on her soft breast. Feeling like a penniless kid in a candy store, Mitch could only dream of the time they could have had. He knew that regardless of his hormones, his injuries required rest. Knowing also he had a paycheck still to work for drove him on.

Kate pleaded with him for some common sense on his part, but in Mitch's mind there was just too much happening outside his bedroom. He was still a reporter at heart, and had to go to where the action was. He couldn't rest, as he was too worried about what he was missing outside.

Kate had other plans to make him rest as she continued to caress him. She was a woman with one thing on her mind, who would use her womanly charm just hoping to sway his confused mind.

If it had been any other time or place, Mitch was sure there would only be one naked thought on his ever-perverted mind, but even the firm softness of Kate's young breasts couldn't satisfy his questions. This was what reporting dreams were made of. All would have to wait until later, as his focused vision pushed him to go.

Mitch had to go, not realizing the pain he was in until he moved. It wasn't so much the pain, just the constant throbbing that hammered his reality. Give him drugs, he wished. He was, after all, a wimp at heart, while his body pleaded with him to stop. With a little arguing and no compromise, Kate and Mitch walked slowly from the bedroom and headed toward town.

With prayers to God, Jack decided that the crisis at the church needed to be resolved immediately. State patrol and prisoners at the front door and thugs in the back were more than the militia was ready to handle.

It wasn't a complicated plan--just distract them in front and rush in through the back. No big fancy assault; just outgun them and overwhelm them with excessive force, the supreme equalizer.

Mitch later learned that when the militia finally busted through the back door, the two thugs were so whacked out from not having their fix that the townsfolk could have walked in the front door wearing their Sunday best.

The two sides exchanged looks at each other for a few brief seconds, when the two kids realized their ultimate fate all too well. Two loud bursts of shots rang out from within the church hall. Guilty, case closed: two tickets to hell, please!

Elmer's body was found where they had ambushed him. Death was never pleasant, but in Elmer's old frail state it seemed easier to accept. Elmer died doing what he loved, hopefully never knowing the fear the townsfolk did. Jack, Elmer's breakfast buddy and coffee partner, bowed his head as he asked forgiveness and prayed for Elmer's deliverance. Breakfast was never going to feel the same for Jack, as the breakfast circle got a little smaller. Out of respect Jack pulled down the church's American flag and laid it over Elmer's thin frame as they laid him down below the altar: once a patriot, always a patriot.

Nothing else could be done for Elmer, so the men turned their attention to securing and passing out the guns and ammo. Macbeth's militia wouldn't get a lot of respect with shotguns and .22s against military weapons. They hoped the AR-15s and AK-47s they had would make the patrol think twice about starting something, because nobody on the island really wanted a fight: life was still good. Most knew you could have only one bully on the block, and Macbeth wanted to be their own bully. Hopefully in the hours to come there would still be clear minds making decisions, to prevent things from turning ugly too quickly.

Midge, never wanting to be standing on the sidelines, showed up at the church, still in tears because of Elmer knew it was best to empty the church and hall of all the island records and family histories, so she set about arranging the removal of all the valuables to the salt mines for safekeeping. Rabid paranoia seemed to be changing to a just cause as the town and its people had found what they needed.

The news about Elmer Piddle's death had traveled quickly. Many of the children knew, he was like the grandparent they never had, and to others, everyday folks, he was just a caring fixture of the town. Sadness and denial consumed every caring soul on the island. The grief was tempered only by the need to be prepared for what could lie ahead. That day, heads were bowed in prayer as most wished for Elmer's safe journey and remembered the life of a very simple man.

CHAPTER 13:

AN INVASION OF SORTS

It didn't take the governor long to bask in the publicity he received for ordering in the Massachusetts State Patrol. The governor, the man with the golden balls, took quick and decisive action against the perceived evil forces of a little town maybe gone berserk.

Listening to the state patrol concerns of not enough men--and for extra backup, he also authorized sending the state's finest weekend warriors—who were then committed to a landing in a possible battle zone, a fact neither the troops nor the governor had any inkling of.

All he knew or cared about was the fact that once again he was in the national spotlight. The spotlight demanded attention, and attention had always been good for his career. Very pleased with himself, he pictured himself as the savior of his subjects as he ruled all from his make-believe castle.

With a realization the church was too far to walk, Kate and Mitch slowly made it to the cliff overlooking a deep blue harbor, both of them intensely watching the small-scale invasion off in the distance. The two sitting for a spell were now a part of the amused spectators making light of a serious situation. They judged the landing crafts as they tried to maneuver against confusing currents. Like ships built of cork, they danced among the currents tossed out by the smashing waves. Back and forth, the flat-grey-colored boats rocked as their occupants could only roll, quickly grabbing their unsettled bellies in agony.

Mitch could only imagine the utter chaos developing in the stomachs of the poor individuals on board. Some so bravely tried to hold down their morning meal of greasy eggs, buttery home fries, sausage, and grits. All on board hoped they would not soon be joining some of the other unlucky souls, methodically chumming these once active fishing lanes. All wondered if that extra paycheck from the guard was really worth all the hassle they on board were then experiencing.

High atop the jagged cliff, with the sexy voice of an airbrushed angel, Kate asked Mitch, "How do you feel about things going so quickly?"

"What do you mean?" Pausing for a brief second, Mitch searched for the right words to get out of this tight spot. "Aren't we maybe soul mates? Could I be your knight in shining armor? You know, your Big Kahuna of love?" Mitch almost chuckled, but it hurt.

Kate looked at Mitch with a puzzled look.

"You know, Mitch, do you have a serious side? I need to know your feelings, and you joke about it. I just don't want to be used again. I guess I'm just tired of being a weekend fling?"

"Hold it, hold everything. Don't even go there, Kate!" Mitch responded. "I'm just kidding. Good God, give me a break! I've never been any good with emotions, especially out-of-control female ones." Pausing a moment to gather his thoughts that were now treading water, Mitch whipped a rock into the cold surf, stalling for time, realizing again he shouldn't have done that with his throbbing wound.

"You know, you might think I'm full of shit, like most of

the women I've dated, but I feel there's got to be something special between us. The first time I saw you peeking out that window, I knew my life was going to change for the better. Right now you occupy most of my thoughts, even the ones that aren't about sex. God, Kate, I'd love to commit to you, but we hardly know each other. Let's let it rest for the moment. I'm telling you, what's important is that you can count on me." He thought to himself, *Damn, I only slept with her once — what do I owe her?* Deep down he knew when he was shot she was the first thing on his mind.

"Yes Mitch, I really want to believe you, but I've heard it so many times before. Commitment--to men, it's like bowling minus the beer. In my life, time just moves too fast anymore; it has got to slow down. Last week I was alone and content. This week I'm with you and confused. I'm sorry--I shouldn't have bugged you, especially with you hurting. I just wondered... when does my life start to make sense?"

"Let's worry about us later. You're here and I'm here, and that's all that matters. If it's anything to you, you're what I think about! Did you happen to bring any pain meds?"

A smile returned to Kate's face as she snuggled a little closer to Mitch, realizing Mitch, the man, had given her as much as he could for the moment. Not wanting an argument, she looked in her bag for the pain killers she had brought.

Mitch could only wonder why any woman would ask a question like that at a moment like this.

Jack and Tom, the strategists, picked up the pace as the island prepared. With nature's help, the island couldn't have been designed any better; this big chunk of rock was any defender's dream.

The island had only one real entrance: a narrow break in the cliffs that revealed a small inner harbor, as jagged stone cliffs guarded two other sides. The third side was an oozing black swamp of muck, and all the decaying smells associated with it. In warfare muck, mud, and cliffs were still any army's nightmare.

To add to any invading army's miseries, there was no ground long enough or flat enough for a landing strip. A modern fortress couldn't have been planned any better. Jack and Tom knew Macbeth's ace, and had carved their meager defenses around it. The invading forces had to take the only way in: through the harbor. Surviving the waves, hours later they motored into the harbor and docked. The stiff commander, General Urbon, after tidying up, debarked while trying to look like he was a reincarnation of General Patton leading his troops.

Shiny black boots and gleaming ivory-handled revolvers hung to the sides of the general's pressed uniform. He stood there tall, trying to look proud, and it might have worked but for those wet spots, fresh on his uniform – the remnants of his recent puking escapade. It was amazing what a uniform and stripes could do for a union electrician's inflated ego.

As the ramp of the landing crafts opened, fifty nauseated souls raced up on the docks. Many sought the feeling only solid land can give, hoping to regain control of their stomachs. The guard reminded themselves that they were here just doing their duty, for that extra paycheck to supplement some from their meager hourly wages, and most hoped they would clean up this situation before Monday, so they could go back to their 9-to-5 jobs and tell their new war stories to their beer buddies, wives, and whoever else sat long enough to listen.

Considering so little had actually happened on the island, the rampant rumors must have scared them back on the mainland. The general, not one to be bashful with lack of equipment, brought with him few tanks, a couple troop carriers, a fuel truck, and a few anti-terrorist assault vehicles.

With the heavy equipment unloaded, the center of the town became a bustling command center of erratic behavior. All the troops and state patrol jockeyed with mixed emotions, trying to prepare themselves to save this backwards, deserted town from an unseen enemy.

The general and his state patrol counterpart were driven up to the center of town. Their driver, not quite used to the vehicle, slammed on the brakes, skidding to a bumpy stop. Screaming orders, he jumped boldly out, yelling abusively at the driver, while pointing his white-gloved hands at the next victims of his attention.

"You three soldiers there, set up my command tent over here! And somebody move that damn tank out of my vision. I need a clear line of sight, 360 degrees or more." Clicking his boots like some pompous SS Officer, he, for a brief instant, thought he was better than these local troops that he commanded.

"Who the hell's in charge of this little town? I want to see him now!" He screamed with hands on his hips like some shrewd desert fox. This disbelieving guard putting his tent up wondered--did he sound like this when he was just an electrician? They were learning quickly how titles and uniforms can bring out the best and worst in people.

With a painful step after the walk down from the cliff,

Mitch learned of his part as the town's word man. Tom, passing the buck for the other trustees, informed Mitch that he and Jack couldn't have picked anyone better-suited for this important job, and if he would, he could give the general all the ins and outs about the town that he could make up. Mitch figured most people thought writers were just good liars. It must be something to do with an overactive imagination. No time, then, to ponder why he was chosen. Mitch, with a mission, went in pain to meet the general and do his part in this grand charade.

"Good day, sirs! Name's Mitch. I'm here to assist you with any question you have about the island." Mitch wondered was he going to be a criminal now, lying to the authorities after he crossed the line between right and wrong.

"Good--it's about time you people responded," the general said as he looked down at Mitch and his long hair blowing in the breeze. "Nice hair, Betty," the general mumbled to himself. "You can show me to the disputed area! Then fill me in on this little situation you have here--and who the hell can get me a good cup of black coffee around here? It's bad enough I'm here wasting my weekend on this rock." Biting his tongue, Mitch quickly knew exactly what he wanted to do with that hot cup of coffee.

"I'll see to it you get some coffee. Cream and sugar, you asshole," Mitch mumbled quietly to himself.

"What, boy? I couldn't hear those last words!"

"Sir, I said cream and sugar!" Mitch shot back.

"No black would be fine, thank you." The general backed off, realizing he had found Mitch had a throttle.

"Forget the coffee, get in that lead truck and show us the

way. My time's a-wasting." Mitch restrained the middle finger his mind wanted so badly to thrust in the air at that fine general. Mitch was sure the general would get his in time. Trying like hell to ignore the pain from his wounds, Mitch climbed into the cab of the front truck, hearing the two guards in the cab laughing at their fine excuse for a leader.

"Pompous little arrogant asshole he is," the driver said while Mitch barely got into the truck. Moving over to make some room for Mitch, the other guard joined in.

"Sorry, man. He's not my general. He treats everyone like shit, except his wife. Heck, she knows the little secret he hides in his pants." Breaking into a big smile, the guard threw his spent cigarette out the window as the three began to laugh loudly together.

"Is there a problem in there, gentlemen?" the general said smugly, standing below their cab.

"No sir!" the driver said sharply, while his buddy jabbed his fingers into the driver's ribs, just hoping he could get him to break a smile in the asshole's direction.

"We've got a job to do, and I don't need a bunch of snot-nosed little boys playing games in the front of my column--do you understand, ladies?" Mitch bit his tongue hard as his little demons raced around his plotting mind, just wanting to lash out an equal verbal attack. Common sense and restraint on Mitch's part won out as he sat silently working on his revenge.

It would take a lot more than this general's antics to infuriate him. He had already infuriated the patrol ordering them to stay in town, while the big boys investigated the shooting. Doing as he was told, Mitch led the column on their way, the Pied Piper leading the children of the mainland to their first meeting with destiny. While he piped his imaginary tune, they drove on.

Mitch wondered if life could get any better. Only days ago, locked up alone in his one-bedroom apartment in a bustling city, swilling a Corona and lime, he stared out the window at a thousand empty blinking neon lights, planning his next hunt. Back then that was his focused passion—now, the leader of an armored column, he was part of the grand charade while the island family planned and played.

Before he left, the general had ordered his troops and patrol to set up a rear staging area. In this guarded area, he left about forty troops, plus the other less-important vehicles, and fuel of the state's rapid deployment force. Escorting the general went the tanks and troop vehicles, all convoying first down Main Street, with the same destination: the church. What a grand parade it could have been, had it only been a holiday with an excited crowd to watch it.

The general questioned out loud why so few people were lining the road to watch the heroes drive through town. His warriors had left their safe homes to come here to save this town. As far as the general was concerned, the townsfolk were still ungrateful peasants, a second-class backwoods people cowering behind their locked doors, out of touch with the real world. What a shame, he thought; how lucky for them this general had come to solve their insignificant problems. Better for them they stay hidden away and let the real men do the job.

The rear troops and patrol had nothing much to do but look down the road as their buddies in arms drove away. All the vehicles left were a trail of diesel smoke above the road as the column vanished into the interior of the island.

Like a ghost in the night, Tom Skinner and his battalion moved silently behind the Main Street buildings. He expected no bloodshed, just the troop's weapons, ammunition, and some new hostages. He was never one to be greedy; they needed the supplies to even up the score.

The second confrontation of the island saga was ready as the last man and beast got into position. Tom knew all too well the divine scent of battle, and his nerves and muscles tightened in burning anticipation. Tom had set many other traps in war before. Vietnam wasn't so long ago, in his mind. He also knew that in some minds the war had never ended. Tom was lucky enough to be one of the few that didn't have to relive it night after haunting night. The Vietnam conflict had sharpened his nerves and like an old tiger; he knew when to hunt and when to strike. Once again his blood boiled with an eager forbidden fear, as the hunt was about to begin.

The hardest part of the siege was making the green troops wait. All the men were ready to leap and attack, while warm adrenaline pumped feverishly through their veins, only fanning the mood to strike. Five minutes, ten minutes, then fifteen minutes, and Tom finally raised his hand. It was time. Tom the conductor let his mismatched orchestra begin. The other guard column by then was far enough ahead not to interfere, too far away to notice Macbeth's moment in history. Surprise and size would still be on the town's side, for the time being.

It seems some of the most important strategic conflicts are the shortest. This was to be one of them. Out of a nearby building Julie and Emma opened a storefront door and emerged dressed to attract attention, wearing tight jeans, high-heeled shoes, and skimpy tops. This little part of the male world stood still for a second in time to watch the girls on parade.

The girls, Macbeth's answer to runway angels, succeeded overwhelmingly in distracting the troops guarding command post. In a moment created by the girls' magical steps, the men fell in love with the illusion, as they hooted and howled in hot anticipation. For a short moment the men were back in the strip club of mainland, lusting and eager, away from the rules and shackles of their wives and girlfriends—a group of men all too willing to cross the thin line between commitment and the cheap and easy, as they forgot their mission for the moment.

While many of the troops followed the parade, a unit of mounted horses galloped out from the alleys behind the storefronts. It was an unexpected step back in time, as the confused troops hadn't the foggiest idea what to do with a foe they had no training for.

It was man and snorting beast once again reunited against the modern machine. The size and power of the almost mythical beasts caused widespread fear among the young guard and patrol. Columns of snarling beasts turned the organized camp into a circus of chaos. It was not the troops' fault, as they were just a group of confused men, many of whom had never been face to face with a live horse before, now being herded and controlled by their massive power and the men upon their backs controlling them.

Leading the thundering cavalry unit, Jeremiah, remarkably fit for his age, rode in on a Belgium draft horse. The size of this mount caused many of the troops to stand and stare in amazement at the size of the sweating beast. With the help of this great distraction, Tom and his neighbors on foot walked into the camp and surrounded the men, ordering them immediately to drop their weapons and surrender. Some of the surrounded men contemplated the value of fighting on for a few bucks as they stared down the barrels of Macbeth's weapons.

Other weekend warriors looked at the best Macbeth had to offer in dumbfounded amazement. Then, almost on cue, the surrounded men started laughing-- laughing at this strange collection of Macbeth's men surrounding them. From their point of view it was comical; how could any modern police force or army take this assortment of men seriously?

Fat men, bald men, young men, tall men, all wearing too many different shades of nail polish turned war paint. Some had feathers hanging from the leather straps around their bald or ball cap-covered heads. Beer bellies, no bellies, love handles--and all sitting atop their trusty four-legged sweating steeds of muscle. Grown men playing cowboys and Indians, surrounding a modern army--it was a joke!

Some of Macbeth's men saw their evil governor in these men, the same governor who also would not take the island-ers seriously. Their laughter called for specific action, as Tom would not see his troops humiliated for the cause. Drawing his machine gun, Tom released the safety and sprayed an ear-shat-tering volley of lead at the now-dancing feet of the shocked troops.

The troops didn't want a battle; all they wanted to do was go home, relax, and return to life in suburbia. This island's problems weren't worth their bloodshed or pain. Maybe if it had been their own backyard or family they would have un-derstood the resolve these people would fight with. Today, though, the part-time warriors and patrol were lucky; today they would not have to find out about their captors' unyielding determination and the will it breeds.

On Tom's command, the men started dropping their weapons as they stared down the barrels of many assault riffles and into the determined faces of the militia of Macbeth. Now stripped of their hardware of war, all they could do was watch and obey. This day more prisoners of war had been taken as the second conflict ended without a drop of blood. Oh, how sweet war could be if all battles could end this way, Tom prayed.

The captured troops were gathered up and relieved of all their useful accessories and marched single file to the salt mines. It was deemed in the town's best interest to keep the prisoners healthy and protected. Jack and Tom knew the world didn't need any flashing news shots streaming across the country and world of bloodied and bruised US soldiers. The evening news had turned up a nation's passion before, with pictures from old bloody conflicts, igniting people's emotion. Only the media wouldn't capitalize on the isle of Macbeth, if the islanders could help it.

Motoring on toward the church went the rest of troops. Hidden and silently waiting, the second half of Macbeth's painted militia waited: forty men and boys with the nerves to achieve what some people only had a chance to dream about. All those hiding stood covered in war paint like different generations before, symbolic of their holy struggle and a bond with America's native population that few outside of the island really understood.

Hidden among the pines, intently watching the rear of the marching column, a burly Willy Bo sat and waited nervously with his rifle and silencer. Hoping for a little West Virginia luck, Bo, trying not to hyperventilate, took aim at the last troop carrier in the column, and with a quick look he held his breath and shot a clean hole through its radiator.

In a steam-induced flash of hissing moisture, the wounded truck started belching steam, and the driver rolled it to an abrupt stop. The motionless truck's concerned driver jumped down and scratched his head as he watched the billowing steam escaping from his engine. Seeing the futility of holding up the whole column, the driver waved to the other trucks to keep on going ahead. The driver, wondering what had happened, would check out the problem and maybe catch up later.

The loud column continued on around the tree-covered bend, soon out of sight. Macbeth's men, seizing the moment, jumped out from the protection of the thick trees.

Racing down the hillsides, they attacked like drunken lunatics of the Cleveland Dawg Pound, charging for the remains of a defeated Pittsburgh team.

Acting as an almost well-trained unit, they surrounded the stranded truck. Without a shot fired, they apprehended the next eleven doubting prisoners. The sides were evening up, as the next batch of stunned men headed hands held high, single file for the security of the mine.

Few questions were asked by the new prisoners, just utter disbelief at the actions of these islanders. "Why are you guys doing this?" a guard asked, drawing only blank stares from the militia. "Hell, you fools can't possibly think you're going to get away with this. Are you all playing with a full deck?" another wondered, getting visibly annoyed at a lack of response from the captors.

Getting upset at the islander's apparent ignorance, an officer yelled out: "We are from the US of A, you assholes! Shit is going to hit the fan if you don't release us now!"

"Move on and shut up!" an islander yelled, clearly losing his nerve, as he slammed his rifle butt into a dragging prisoner's ass. Evoking a look that could kill, the guard hurried on as he felt a bit of Macbeth's resolve.

There was more work to be done as the rest of the column marched on ahead, oblivious to the actions taking place behind, while a communications officer wondered why he couldn't raise the command center back in town.

CHAPTER 14:

JUST WEEKEND WARRIORS

Taking a few troops prisoner is one thing, but facing full-sized tanks was another heavy story. The advancing column reached the church and wasted no time setting a textbook perimeter around it. The general started to wonder also why he couldn't raise the supply detachment back in town.

Mitch, always thinking, told him the island had always been tough on radio signals, Bermuda triangle kind of thing. Of course the general, using a shred of common sense, didn't believe his excuse, instead ordering two soldiers back to town to check it out. Mitch didn't have a chance to thank him; he wouldn't have understood anyhow. Mitch had a feeling the militia would be waiting for them with open arms--all in a day's work.

The men at the church had more than enough time to prepare a reception for the general. A half dozen of Macbeth's bravest were holed up within its sacred walls, all just playing their parts as unwilling thugs. Most were chomping at the bit for the time and moment to do their part in helping defend the island. The island was still vulnerable and its relative security was still compromised until all the tanks were neutralized and the remaining troops brought under civilian control.

As boys, most of the island men had all smoked out ground-hogs before, so to the men on the island, the tanks were just big moving groundhog holes. Silently crawling up their cold metal sides, the would-be warriors tossed homemade smoke bombs into the tanks open hatches. Running for cover, the men turned around in overly eager anticipation, waiting and watching, to witness the magic they had created with a little sulfur and a few other readily available chemicals.

Little by little, puffs of grayish-white smoke started burp-ing out the hatch openings, followed by billowing clouds of a putrid sulfur-smelling gas. In seconds, the tank crews scam-pered out, coughing and gulping for any fresh air their starved lungs could hold down. Mitch was amused, and sure the real Patton would have appreciated Macbeth's display of backyard pyrotechnics.

Macbeth's hidden men added more chaos to an already uncertain scenario, silently setting fire to the church's garden shack. Things were heating up for the general, as he felt him-self losing his grip on the real situation. That day, military text-books meant nothing to him, as he looked for a way to control this unique event.

Through the crackling and hissing of the burning wood, all those old tired and oil-covered rags the militia had stuffed in the shack sent clouds of the black smoke drifting quickly through the clear air. The situation went from clear to hazy as all present felt they were entering another dimension: smoke so thick you could cut it; the only way any one had any grasp of the situation was by yelling... yelling for someone to lead them home.

In his growing panic, the general had no idea that all his

tanks were being smoked out, only a growing fear that reinforced his gut feeling that he was somehow losing control. Little did he know his troops were being apprehended with the help of a legend of a battle from the ghost of tribes long gone. One by one through the cover of the nauseating smoke, Macbeth's men called on the spiritual help of the island's long-dead ancestors as they snuck in and out if their man made fog, all in the name of humanity, spare the bullet to save the man.

He was nearing desperation, the general screamed, "Pull everyone back now, it's a mother fucking trap!"

Running in circles, not knowing where to go or what to do, he wished someone was there to give him the answers he so needed.

Guessing he should scream louder, he yelled, "Circle the trucks--form a defensive perimeter--now!"

All his yelling didn't stop the retreating troops running in so many different directions; not one was willing to stop and listen to his orders in their own personal hours of need.

The general's doomed realization came too late, as Macbeth's men let go of their silence and started yelling and reverberating blood-curdling screams. The guard, shocked and disorganized, lost its glue and melted down.

With the situation spinning further out of control, one smoking tank broke rank and sped out of control, careening widely toward the whitewashed church. A shot rang out, then another, and soon, too many to count. Who was shooting? Nobody seemed to know, as many just threw themselves on the ground, covering their heads.

Blinded and out of control, the tank went blasting through the old church like a wrecking ball on treads. Teetering, then tottering, the old steeple leaned, then toppled into the smoke-covered mist, followed by a loud crashing sound of the old church bell. Splinters, shards of stained glass, and pages of church hymnals filled the void of the sanctuary, as the ruins settled into a jumbled mess.

The tank, seemingly enjoying its challenge with its rampage, came blasting out of the wrecked church, detouring to the left through the meeting hall, its Desert paint scheme now covered by the town's community billboard and the pink streamers left over from the mother-daughter banquet.

In this churchyard, the men were running every which way as the blinded tank careened widely out of control. Completed with its pillage of the church, the Godzilla of a tank raced methodically away down the narrow country lane. The blinded crew tried in vain to clear their eyes and lungs to control this out-of-control mechanical beast. Partially trapped inside by the smoke, the part-time tank crew worried about their folly, still unsure what had happened, more concerned about facing their general and his wrath.

A few dozen more widely scattered shots--then an annoying quiet returned to the disturbed area. With the advancing silence, Mitch looked over the destruction, feeling uneasy, and wondering what would be gained by the end of this fiasco.

With no time to waste a few of Macbeth's men, feeling brave, ventured carefully through the remains of the church, looking for the men who had played their part inside. Still a bit cautious with all the live ammo around, Mitch could feel the hairs on the back of his neck standing. He needed time to deal with mixed emotions, feeling out of check by the violence, while the smell of gun smoke and burning rubber filled air spaces, and reminded all how close that battle really had been.

In the ruins of the church, the groaning of the wounded men drifted eerily out of the collapsed chambers. The wounded voices that were able called for some unseen help they hoped was out there. The simple bloodshed had begun, as lives were changed in a blink of an eye and the situation on the island was turned up just another notch.

If the silence wasn't holy enough on this newly consecrated battlefield, the church began to smolder within its ruined walls. Those searching for the wounded could hear the distinct crackling of long-ago-dried wood beginning to ignite. Macbeth's regulars, thinking of the trapped islanders inside, jumped into the ruins of the church, quickly pulling and dragging the wounded they could find away with them. War drew no discrimination as the anguished cries emanated from both sides. Together in mercy both sides pitched in to help each other, while realizing what mistakes they had all just made.

Alone on a dock in the breached safety of the harbor, Peace and the pharmacist Carl Paxton had their own problems. The billowing black smoke from the church only egged the hungry media on as irritated news crews, adrift in their boats moved closer and closer to Macbeth's shore, hoping to satisfy their spiking curiosity.

In most conflicts nothing ever is really fair. The two men were stuck in town, worrying and wondering about the shooting and explosions from the church's direction. Alone, the two could only guess what the score on the island was. The only tool working in their favor was the live gunshots they shot over the heads of the media, hoping to persuade some of the fools to stay back for their own good.

Hearing live gunfire, some of the media got the hint and turned tail with their "Eye in the Sea" news boats and raced back out of the uncertainty of the harbor. These were the sensible few heading for the apparent safety of an open sea, while some sat back, waiting for their big chance and hoping to race back in and grab that once-in-a-lifetime picture or story. Life or the big buck--most knew what was more important to these dollar-driven paparazzi.

Overhead another chopper pilot buzzed the island, churning up what little air space the island had. Carl, being an overly nervous druggist, kept fiddling with his site as he aimed his rifle in the air, hoping to scare away the helicopter with the young cameraman hanging dangerously out of the fuselage. Not one to ever intentionally hurt anyone, he sited behind the moving fuselage when he accidentally released his bullet with his nervous finger.

With a splatter of blood, Carl's hot bullet punched a hole through the young newsman's hand, releasing his expensive news camera to the forces of gravity. Free-falling, the camera dove straight down, smashing into a thousand pieces as it impacted the hard ground.

In shock, with the screaming and bloodied cameraman in back, the chopper pilot retreated for the open sea, screaming, "Mayday, Mayday!" for whoever listened.

Carl's vision never had been very good. Today for once it helped, as Macbeth's airspace and harbor cleared in a quick instant, with the news of the eagle-eye sniper spreading like a brush fire across the airwaves.

"Holy shit, Carl! Why the heck did you do that?" Peace

yelled out.

Shrugging his shoulder and scratching his graying head, Carl answered, "I surely couldn't tell you--and I know I didn't do it on purpose, anyhow."

Pausing, he tried to catch his excited escaping breath. "God, I didn't mean it. Even if my life depended on it, I couldn't do it. Really, Peace, it was only an accident. I was only stroking the trigger."

"Had to be Elmer steadying your hand—right, Carl?"

"No way, no how. I never wanted to hurt anybody, even a newsman."

He was shook up about the accident, as he hung his head low, shaking it back and forth.

"Don't worry, man; you worry too much. I know it was only an accident. Anyhow, look at that chopper go! Mission accomplished! Big boy, you cooked their goose today." Peace, more excited than Carl, gave him a bear hug, as he continued to ramble on while celebrating Carl's big victory.

"Carl. I wouldn't have believed it if I hadn't seen it with my own two eyes!"

"Stop it, Peace. Shut up! I just hurt someone."

"No, Not on purpose you didn't Carl. That makes it almost legal. Life goes on, anyways—you're just part of the grand scheme of things."

Peace, amazed at Carl's luck, assured him of his important role in the defense of the island. Carl, more amazed at his luck or just maybe his hidden skill, eased up on himself for the moment and absorbed some of what had just happened.

Never one to showboat, Carl for once was caught up in this bit of a personal and unintended rush. For a minute in his normal life, Carl was a force to be dealt with, even if it was only accidental.

He almost hesitantly shrugged off the oncoming limelight, wondering how his shot could have been that far off. He wondered to himself if he should still be dispensing drugs, with his poor eyesight. Only he knew the answer. That afternoon he made the big play, and as a former nerd the big play let all forget his imperfections. The gathering crowd looked at old Carl as a warrior and no longer just as the town pharmacist. Carl, for once, felt whole.

The CNN reporter and camerawoman still detained back in the mine waited impatiently. Macbeth thinkers and would-be strategists felt it was best to get their story out as quick as possible. They did not want to be confused with some home-grown terrorists, cult, or religious fanatics. CNN would be their line to the world, while its news crew would unknowingly be Macbeth's pawns.

Tom had insisted the world see Macbeth's people as they really were. This was a town filled with law-abiding, struggling folks who loved their country. Most were deserving of a fair shake in a modern world, with the backing of the constitution to make a fair living, interested in protecting what was theirs and closest to their hearts.

Thanks to Carl's shot, the idea of a non-violent rebellion was quickly exiting most of the news vampires' thoughts. "Conflict at Macbeth," headlines would now say. Carl's lone shot seemed to be heading for that shot that was heard around the world. Back tracking was all Tom and Jack could do now. Blood had been drawn on national TV, and it was unarmed blood at that.

The encroaching news crews had been pushed back, but for any vulture, once was not enough. At an unnoticed moment, they were ready to pounce back on the carcass just to continue picking, waiting for their next opportunity to sneak in for that photo. The real story meant nothing to them; Macbeth's people were just a faceless culture and the media's ticket to another headline. With Carl's shot the whole story became juicier, and surely more lucrative for a starved news world hell-bent on finding some excitement.

Tom had lost his patience with encroaching media. In a rash decision, reacting to the heat of the moment, Tom saw the solution tied up rusting away in the harbor. Some how they would tow the town's confiscated drug freighter, the *Danny Boy*, out to entrance of the harbor, anchor it, and then sink it. With a lot of luck, plus a hole in the hull the size of Texas, the water would rush in and settle the rusting hulk right in the narrowest point of the harbor.

CHAPTER 15:

DAVY JONES WELCOMES ALL

It was probably a fitting fate turning that drug ship into an artificial reef that for once she would be on the right side of the law. Tom prayed in a rare moment for an ace in dealing with this pestering media nuisance.

Jebb--the self-appointed tow master just because he held the keys to the biggest boat--doubting the plan, tugged, cussed, pushed, and cussed some more as he nudged the *Danny Boy* into position. He knew fishing boats weren't tugs, as he waited for the old diesel engines to blow. With the old ropes straining, the boat fought to hold its position as the current played easily with the ship.

With hardly a moment to spare, Peace released the anchor on the *Danny Boy* for the last time. Looking around the empty bridge he bid this pirate lady good night. Her only remaining struggle was the currents in and out of the harbor.

Peace, never one to trust the judgment of Fanny's short order cook and his green tank crew, raced off the deck of the doomed ship, taking a leap of faith onto the waiting boat. With the smell of diesel fuel and burning engine oil, the tired fishing boat cast off the lines of the *Danny Boy* and headed for the docks.

Flipping eggs and making biscuits and sausage gravy didn't prepare them very well for operating the confiscated tank. It took more than a bit for them to drive it back into town. Dave and his crew comprised of a dishwasher and a short order cook, all had the answers to when it came to aiming and firing the tank's cannon. Arguing, they tried with ever-good intentions to aim the big gun. Heads or tails aside, they settled on dead reckoning and luckily one big target to shoot at.

Placing the first shell in the barrel, Dave kissed its rear end goodbye and slammed the metal door shut. Grabbing his ears in anticipation of its thunder, he pushed the trigger. With a roar, a flash and a pungent stink of gunpowder, the projectile hurled itself in the direction of the boat.

The first shot didn't help the struggling tank crew's thirst for respect. Way off its mark, the shell shot over the port bow of the ship. Arching, then slicing, the shell shot through a sail and rigging of one of the curious pleasure boats anchored not far enough away. Horrified, its crew and guest got the hint as the shell exploded off in the distance behind the schooner. Not waiting for the next shot, the captain about-faced and headed for the safety of the open sea. Maybe he should have listened to his daughter when she told him the island had probably gone mad.

With the temperature in the tank bordering on sweltering, the team feeling was rapidly fleeting as the unity of the moment before was replaced by blaming each other for the blunder.

"You're a big moron, Dave. How the hell could you miss the ship? You couldn't have asked for a bigger target, could you?"

"Bite my target, Pete! Maybe I should have let one of you women try. I'm sure you got a lot more experience than me--Lord knows, breaking the amount of dishes you do has to count toward something!"

"He's right, Dave," Jake said, "It's got to be the biggest damn target I've seen, except maybe your wife Midge's ass," he laughed.

A bit pissed off, or just maybe embarrassed, Dave shot back. "Bullshit, all of you--I didn't ask for this job, so stop bitching at me and help me figure out how to lower this damn barrel."

Jake, quite proud of his comeback, chuckled a bit as he loaded the next shell. In a moment of justice and humor he stopped laughing and spoke, looking straight at Dave.

"I know what would lower my big barrel." He paused for a moment before finishing his thought: "One look at your wife!"

The tank crew burst into laughter, as the tension in the tank eased a bit. Dave, dejected, thought of his homely wife back in the mine just waiting for her man and probably missing her weekly fried chicken.

Luckily for Macbeth that day, the boys had flipped and turned most of the levers and buttons in the tank, and one of them brought the barrel whirling to life. Peering and squinting through the site, the barrel lowered as the *Danny Boy* came into the crosshairs.

"Whatever you guys just did, hold it there. I mean don't even fart! I got this thing aimed right up its ass." Dave was sure if this had been a ten-point buck, the trophy rack would be hanging on his wall over his bed.

Easing back in his seat, Dave wiped the beads of sweat

gathering on his forehead. Tightening his dirty fingers, he pulled the trigger. Crossing his other fingers, he let out a Geronimo-sized yell as the barrel came flashing once again back to life.

In a rushed second and another deafening blast, the stillness of the evening air was shattered by a sudden swoosh and roar. In a gathering rumble of water, there was a major explosion below the ship's water line. The explosion was almost muffled at first until its unrestrained force ripped the rusting metal hull wide open, releasing the built-up pressure and noise as the detonated power reverberated through the shuddering ship and surrounding area.

The excited screams of the crowd gathered on the dock told the crew that the ship was indeed hit. The amazed crew popped the hatch open and climbed out to watch the wounded ship, wondering if it really was the last shot.

High-fiving each other in excited disbelief, they then were more than just Fanny's kitchen crew. All seemingly a bit taller, they got out and strutted their stuff, basking in the warm feeling of a job well done.

Few minutes later the ship listed heavily in the direction of her blast hole, with her bow quickly submerging. It didn't take long for this Bahamian freighter to sink, and sink she did. Like a ship built of lead, her final end came quick. Her hull slammed into the sand bottom, leaving two towering smoke stacks jutting out of the foaming debris-laden water.

The exposed black stacks seemed to issue a silent warning for those who would dare to try to cross her submerged hull. The ship's faded decks now were a twisted death trap of tangled wires and riggings. For once, in her demise, the *Danny*

Boy had served this part of humanity well.

The harbor itself was a bit more secure with that sacrifice. The news crews in a slow retreat were having a field day, moving away from the scene of the sinking, snapping picture after picture of the shooting and the sinking. The news crews were afraid yet excited in a greedy kind of way about what to expect next.

Atop a high cliff overlooking the harbor, a couple of boys with their bikes leaned up against a flagpole and slowly lowered the US flag, symbolic as it seemed. Grinding to a stop, a few of the retreating boats watched and realized the importance of the moment. While the photographers snapped the shots they hoped would make the *TIME* cover. Atop the hill, the two boys reverently folded Old Glory.

As quickly as the old flag came down, up went an even bigger US flag, just a bit different, with an extra large-big blue star sewn upon its field of stripes, clearly visible for all who cared to notice. Rising below it was the flag of the colonies "Don't Tread on Me!" Macbeth's line in the sand had been drawn. The national discussion was about to begin as a dozen wide-angle lenses kept snapping the unbelievable shot.

Jack tried the best he could to sort the battle out. The general was no help after he was easily caught hiding behind the old church outhouse, and it was said he wasn't shaking what he had in his pants. This small battle, to the general, was then more real that the textbooks had ever taught him. More afraid then he had ever imagined, the worn-down man gained the look of defeat. Staring face to face at the reality of death made the man of courage realize his humanity that day--hopefully for the future good of all he commanded.

The general's second-in-command should have been in charge, as he rallied his troops and tried to restore some kind of order to his gun-shy troops. Concerned about the fate of his command, he rattled off orders hoping to end the chaos of the battle.

Jack studied the man and watched his fair determination to help. He could almost bet the second-in-command hadn't kissed enough butts in his career to move all the way up the ladder. The guard wasn't really much different from the real world; merit and ability apparently to often took back seat to brown-nosing and who you knew...sad facts of life in a society of faceless people.

Later that day, the out-of-control tank was located. The inviting swamp on one side of the island had unwillingly joined in the battle, as its thick grasping muck trapped the tank and its crew like some unlucky wandering prehistoric beast.

The tank crew was relieved to see the search posse approach. Waving a flag of surrender, not knowing the difference between muck and quicksand, the men of the 9-to-5 grind had to much time to entertain visions of a horrible suffocating death. Trapped on their metal tomb, looking over the football field of muck to the temptations of solid ground, the men had recurring visions of countless jungle scenes of surfaces that sucked the life out of many unlucky souls as Tarzan stood by.

Coaxing the men off the tank became harder than finding them. With muck up to their waists, Macbeth's men waded in and helped the doubting crew off their perch. With the tank secured by nature, the islanders had their own version of a German pillbox, with its mighty gun guarding the lonely backside of the island.

The old church hall lay in a bed of dancing and smoldering embers, charred broken wood giving little crackling testimony to the many dreams and ideas born and lost here over the past years. In generations to come, Jack was sure, many would someday wonder how such an insignificant church could have given birth to such radical fears.

Covered with ashes from his beloved church, the pastor, gripping his own M-16 ever so softly, stood bravely beside his flock, and reminded all that had gathered that the church was more than just a building. His church was and always would be the individuals and families that made up its congregation. Wiping the tears of soot from his eyes, he felt a bit emotional over the destruction of such a beautiful building, but as sure as his solid faith, the church would always live on in each and every living soul of his church family.

Digging amongst the rubble, the rescuers found a bit charred and smoked Elmer. A young man, sensing the need to do more, climbed across the charred embers and carefully pulled Elmer out. The old man's gray locks of hair were reduced to almost unseen stubble, his worn clothes and the flag randomly burned away from his almost-naked thin frame. Out of an earned respect, they covered Elmer's body with a nearby altar cloth, while Pastor Berry, feeling the need to do something, prayed aloud for his old friend's certain redemption.

The coffee bunch, keenly aware of their task together, gently loaded Elmer "pass the cream" into an old garden cart for his last ride home. The two thugs surely would not get the same respectful treatment, as their bullet-riddled bodies were left in the smoldering rubble. The ensuing smoke and flames gave the burning dead a hint of their final judgment, as their mortal remains were consumed by the glowing embers of a strong faith, and what was left would surely give the gulls a treat.

Back in full control of the island, the local militia gathered the wounded and the prisoners of the battle and assembled all in a macabre kind of parade. The islanders all felt a bit justified with their victory as, with a little rhythm to their step, they marched, guarding the parade back into town. Marching to the beat of an old islander playing his bag pipe as his young son beat his band's high school drum, together they marched home for freedom.

The pastor had always practiced what he preached. Still, with a gun slung over his shoulder and a Bible in his hand, proudly and reverently with the limp of age he walked beside the body of his friend. He was sure that with Elmer's physical demise, that day up above Elmer watched and smiled at the islanders, casting blessings in all the directions they were needed.

For that last time, Elmer was going to town--only this time he was not the hobbled old man who knew too much of the worldly pain that they all remembered. The old garden cart creaked and rattled as it was pushed, as the burden was much more than it was used to.

With a stiff warning from their captors about fair coverage, the CNN news team was let out and escorted from the confines of the mine to report the story at the church. The excited news crew, with video cameras taping, witnessed the parade of soot-covered men, many still with shades of smudged war paint and blood on their faces, escorting the old man's remains and more prisoners home.

Reporting on the implications and results of what many assumed was the first battle of this generation on American soil, they ignored the countless battles that took place every day in the countries defeated cities. They were biased because they just couldn't make the connection. Maybe Macbeth's people were just too common, and that was why it was so significant. The news team was satisfied again with the possibility of such a scoop, and maybe the beginning of one of the biggest stories of their careers. Thanking their captors again and again, they knew what side they should be on if they wanted to stay informed.

With the continued reporting of all the shooting coming from the island, the governor's office was coming to life. His proud troops were being marched down Main Street as captives in defeated humiliation, and as POWs of a war. What kind of people could perpetrate this kind of sacrilege against his righteous administration, he wondered? As the CNN special report was allowed to air, the administration's phone lines lit up, while the governor, as usual, hadn't done his homework. Macbeth had been his responsibility, and yet it took this action to remind him it was more than a rocky, forgotten community. Just being a figurehead for the party machine, judgment isn't always your best trait, and equally important is common sense. The governor, reaching for a quick scotch, had little notion of what to do next as he looked nervously in the direction of his aides as they called out orders for whoever felt the need to listen.

Sipping his drink, he worried like never before that his platform of lies could come apart as his policies of attrition and humiliation would start to be noticed. Knowing he truly lacked the direction to manage the crisis, he quickly poured himself another shot.

He knew he had to be in control somehow, he screamed: "This is bullshit! We need get ahead of this situation now, or we are all done. No little island is going to destroy what I worked for, and what I deserve! You all like your lifestyle as much as I do, so get with it. I want our options!"

His secretary, just trying to do her job, interrupted with a handful of messages for the governor. Throwing them back at her, he yelled, "We are in a meeting for the rest of the day and I don't want to be disturbed." She knew he was losing his grip, as she wondered if this was all worth his continued abuse.

An aide, clearly pissed off at the man, yelled back. "Well, maybe now you see what the hell I was talking about. I warned you they were pissed off and wanted more than your arrogance. I know all too well you've told me so many times that I work for you, so you tell us what you want done. Remember, I'm just your employee!"

The governor, not believing this guy was talking back to him, shot back.

"I will not take that crap from you or anyone. You don't want to be part of this team, get the hell out of here! Remember--I lose, you lose. So boy, do your job or get out!" Finding a bit of a spine, the governor mumbled to himself. It was a bad time for a crisis, or was it? His next election was less than a year away, and credibility was already in retreat. All this guy could do was look for someone to blame, and that day it had to be the bumbling of his guard to take that fall.

Throwing unneeded fuel into the fire, the governor ordered in more fresh troops, which certainly would move the crisis up a notch, only this time the troop deployment would be different. The governor would control the situation unfolding by brute force. In his mind the island had declared war, and war would not be tolerated on his watch.

Like any handful of sly politicians before, the governor had higher offices he aimed for. The man had always desired to dip his hands in foreign policy, and that day he got his wish in his own backyard.

The national spotlight would focus on him and his split state. The wolf in the politician's clothes was afraid he could be discovered if he wasn't careful. He dreamed he was a military genius, with troops, war machines, and plenty of hungry madmen to go around. In his worst hour, this lunatic would lead the guard in their hour of need.

For the rest of the eventful day, life moved on around Macbeth. With a little time to mourn, a lone fishing bell tolled off in the distance as a somber funeral took place, a little different from the others, with the church and its altar just a blackened skeleton as a backdrop. Holy ground was no less sacred that day, and maybe just a little bit more holy. The stale parcel of earth had been consecrated with the fresh red blood of battle.

The reverend spoke to the crowd from his heart. Crafting his words, he made all realize the true person they had lost and heaven had received:

"Never feel sorrow. He has gone home. Elmer sits in a safe harbor and watches us now. Please just feel fortunate for knowing this simple man. Please grab your neighbor's hand and let us pray together for his soul and ours as we fight for what we know to be the truth! God and my dear friend Elmer, please watch over us and please grant our enemies the wisdom to see the real truth. Until we meet again dear friend, may God hold you in His arms, as you hold that toast of bitters, until we meet and drink together again. Good fishing, my friend. Amen."

It was good, as that little man who always fancied himself a son of Ireland became the leprechaun he was born to be.

CHAPTER: 16
SHE STILL WANTS ME?

The rumors of the island's rebellion went across thousands of TVs, radio waves, and computer screens. It was a story reported more out of an odd curiosity, rather than credibility.

It seemed in a world on the fast track, there were too many whacked-out groups crying wolf anymore. So many crises involving some troubled aspect of humanity made most folks just glance half-heartedly at the story, and then surf on to the next channel or page. Most viewers were almost bored or half-awake, more interested in the junk food they were munching on, blankly staring, waiting until the next recapitulation of an almost-real tabloid headline caught their wandering attention and occupied some fleeting time in their reality.

Most of the public knew that in this modern age, someone who would dare challenge a state government, let alone the world superpower, was a rare person indeed. Law-abiding citizens figured send in the SWAT team and have the mess cleaned up by dinner and ready for the evening news. Events had been rather dry lately--no meat and potatoes stories. Political scandals and the Middle East were old news. The few on the island had hoped the media would jump on their story, at least until the next big crisis or event unfolded. Macbeth's dilemma needed to be front page, or it would fizzle like a wet fuse.

In Mitch's real world, there were always bigger problems

to worry about, though his problems never seemed to amount to much compared to Macbeth's. To a public on news overdrive, there always would be the same old day-to-day problems that had always been around, just a new generation trying to deal with the shortcomings of the past. Most figured, why bother with a little town's mess when the big picture was what it always was about?

With the narrow vision this governor relished, the rabble-rousers locked away on their island didn't deserve ten seconds from his day. Acknowledging them was the last thing he wanted to do, figuring it would be history by the next day. For his administration, this was but another short-lived story for the media, and a little practice for his guard.

Spending the time on the island, Mitch was starting to understand what the administration on the mainland and his yes-men couldn't. The residents in all those little insignificant towns were what really made up the big picture. Macbeth's revolution in its infancy could be in danger of becoming grocery store tabloids, a flash-in-the-pan story.

He hated even to say what he deeply thought, but violence added attention and credibility to any action. Mitch, still throbbing from his wound, knew all too well again about conflict and sure didn't want it to happen here. In his short career he had seen enough of what violence and hate could accomplish for a dedicated people. Thinking back to Bosnia, Africa, Vietnam, and other forgotten places, he could still smell the stink of rotten and decaying flesh, the unforgettable death stares of so many victims.

Events seemed to be increasing on the island, while nature just did its thing. The governor, with his feeling of invincibility, thought he was in the driver's seat, and behind closed doors was pushing for a rock-solid solution for his falling poll numbers. It was his toy army and his sandbox – too bad for Macbeth!

It seems that in any conflict it's easy to order in the troops when you or your loved one isn't one you are ordering in. The governor was excited at the prospect of a violent, quick resolution. *Why be quiet at all?* he thought. What he was defending was a righteous cause, and he a noble man, defending his people and his vision of democracy. His advisor, with his pressed suit, manicured nails, and Gucci glasses saw the pot of gold at the end of this rainbow that was dumped in their lap. "We need a press briefing TODAY!" he suggested. This would be this administration battle and their answer to their needs, as the governor poured them both a triple-malt scotch.

With the noise of a second invasion organizing, in the harbor of the mainland, more troops, tanks, and trucks loaded with equipment waited to cast off and head to the island with their own version of excessive force. Guts they had, but paychecks were what they wanted. One powerful invasion force and this small crisis would be resolved before Washington would even get wind of it. Congress would talk about it in the halls as the take-action governor would be praised and mentioned in all his wisdom as maybe one of the next to join their ranks--at least, that was how the governor saw it.

Always covering up the real story and the fact that he knowingly tried to hide the crisis from Washington, the governor never had a clue that the FBI had been watching this event unfold. Some wanted them involved, while others had the big brother syndrome to worry about. Maybe this was just too small--but if it got bigger, the FBI and the ATF should be involved, yet the state was still in charge. With bombs mentioned, it caught everyone's ears. If things heated up, everyone would be jiving for a forward position. For now, the state was going to lead this dance.

Making this situation harder was the lack of credible information coming out of the crisis area. It seemed that whoever entered the island was just swallowed up. One by one an entire unit was held, but unfortunately the islanders seemed to be the only ones who knew about it.

It didn't take long for pieces of information to eventually start to trickle out, from the insane rumors of mass killings to the radio blackout by the troops as the island was being swept and controlled. Nobody really knew what to believe, as only the whiffs of the vanishing smoke on the island led some to believe that something had happened.

"Mitch!" Kate yelled as she walked in the mine toward him carrying her cat. Cringing at the sight of that beast, he reluctantly held his ground as the beauty and beast drew near.

"Please just keep that cat back for now; I'm really not feeling very good." He gave Kate his best cringing painful look.

Maybe a bit miffed at the thought of Mitch not caring for her feline friend, she replied, "Sure, Mitch!" with a sarcastic tone to her voice, doubting his real intent. "What's wrong? Is it me, am I asking too much?" she asked while stroking her purring cat, which seemed to only aggravate him more.

"Now come on, please don't start carrying on like other women--it's really nothing," he replied, sounding a bit ruffled, while he wondered if she was turning into one of those other women he had used. "It was more than just a crazy day, Kate! I still don't believing all that happened. I am a criminal now."

Hesitating just long enough to get his attention, she looked at him.

"Mitch, you are no more a criminal than I am. I know it's crazy, you really owe me nothing. I just met you, and I do care for you, but I get a feeling maybe you're trying to avoid me sometimes. Just remember you don't owe me anything other than your board--I'm okay with that." She turned and started walking away.

With his mind racing he wondered, *What? A woman who isn't going to put up with my shit?* Dumbfounded at how quick this relationship had moved forward, he felt maybe he cared more about her than she him. But what he had been through today how in God's name could she be asking him a stupid question like she did?

"Sometimes I just don't get it with women! One minute you're good with everything, and the next minute you're starting things. I'm just here doing a story, right?" He was struggling to gain control of the situation again.

With Amadeus tucked safely in her arms, she turned back toward him. "Mitchell, I'll be around when you feel like talking--and remember, we have to change your bandages sometime!" Mitch hadn't scored any points and he knew it, and if she called him Mitchell one more time, that cat was going down!

Outside the walls of the harbor, the media was pushing the envelope, with the earlier lesson apparently losing its appeal. As the waves kept edging into the harbor, so did the media's boats. This crisis had the potential to be a big story; whoever nabbed it first would reap the rewards. To so many on those bobbing boats, it really didn't matter if it was truly right or truly wrong; it just had to be sensational. A few of the true journalists knew in their hearts that there always would be two sides to a story, and one of them needed to get Macbeth's.

In the cold of the mine, little groups of folks were called to report to the lower levels. Most folks and families would gather what few belongings they bought with them and shuffle down below. It seemed that maybe they were planning for the worse as it appeared the road ahead might be a long one.

Mitch, watching all this happen, questioned what was going on. He was told this relocation was about survival and safety, plain and simple. He thought to himself, *how long is anyone going to stay in this inhospitable place?* Visions about the beauty of the sun, salty air above, and home were surely haunting these folks...they were haunting Mitch, and he really had no attachment to their world. He knew no matter how strong they appeared, it was only a matter of time before some would start cracking. Survival means nothing to anyone when your mind starts playing those dirty tricks on you as you hunker down in the darkness of the depths--he knew it and they knew it.

It must have been that paranoid doubt that the islanders had planned for. That mine and those rock walls would be near impenetrable. It would surely take a bunker buster to end this resistance; surely someone would step in before that would happen. Clear-thinking minds on the mainland would know that, right? Mitch hoped so, but in confusion the outcome could never be predictable.

Regardless, with the invasion theory so real in their minds, the three-foot cement and steel doors built to seal the mineshaft were real. The fresh air system and all its hidden intakes were meant to last the long haul, and tunnel after tunnel filled

with supplies and food let anyone know they were deadly serious, as the islanders had clearly made their choice months if
not years before.

She was back as fast as she left, as he saw Kate heading
towards him!

"Hey Mitch," Kate yelled out as if nothing had happened.
He wondered now what; didn't she just blow him off? It didn't
matter--she was back, and he was happy.

"Have you seen Lynn?" Quelling his perverted thoughts for
the moment, he pretended he didn't hear her as he quickly
said, "I'm sorry about earlier." A lot had happened so fast. How
much did she know? He had the feeling that he needed to talk
to someone, and that someone was Kate. He didn't have the
answers, just the questions as he searched for a way out of a
long explanation.

"Sorry, Kate; it's not you or your cat, it's me. You know I
want to be with you--in fact I've never gotten this close to any
woman this quick. But I've got to write something! Anything!
Just so much going on and I still don't have my head straight."

Pausing, he looked in her eyes. "I still live in the real world,
and I have obligations, I have bills, I'm just doing what I got
to do. You must understand, this is really hard for me." All he
needed was some violin music in the backdrop and it would
have been a perfect moment.

"Mitch," she replied in a sultry tone. "You don't need to
make excuses or apologize to me, I understand." She ran her
slender fingers through his hair as she arched her back; she
pushed herself closer to him, knowing all along what power
she had over him.

"Lynn and I were going to go outside and head into town

to pick up a few things. I'll catch up with you when we get back. Right now I have to find her. She worries me more than ever now. If you run into her, tell her I'm looking for her."

"I will Kate, but be careful out there--no telling what could happen around here!"

She wondered if Mitch ever could be ready for any kind of commitment to her...or anyone. Was he maybe just one of those guys just interested in an occasional romp? She was second-guessing her possible future, maybe realizing her knight in shining armor wasn't everything she had always dreamed about.

With a quick wave, Kate headed toward the exit of the tunnel, with Mitch not missing a single footstep.

Distractions gone, his mind drifted back to the miracle this mine seemed to be. A hole in the ground past its useful state--or so its old operators thought. Now this old space had been turned into a totally self-sufficient colony of hydroelectric power capable of putting out enough energy to power a small town. Hard to believe all this back-yard magic was so alive and well under the town.

As events seemed to unfold at a quicker pace, CNN started to interrupt their programming for the new headlines: "*Standoff at Macbeth.*" The reports the media chose to air were certainly scattered and vague. A lot was said about the attack on the church, burning buildings, and the runaway tank, but not much reliable information came out of the island. The real meat and potatoes stories had yet to emerge, as public started to thirst for real-time information.

Soon the other networks besides CNN were begging for news privileges that still hadn't come. Tom wanted no pictures taken of the islanders. Mitch didn't agree; a human face on the situation could add points to any cause, especially the innocent faces of youth. This wasn't only his show, and as hard as it was, he tried to keep the outside from snooping.

Next day most of the world was just beginning to understand that this was now a bigger hostage situation than before. How could they believe that Macbeth now held POWs captured on American soil? The governor was unknowingly helping the islanders as he demanded silence on the captured troops as he scrambled to control an out-of-control situation.

In the rolling waves outside the harbor, a frustrated media was losing their patience after being brushed aside. With stomachs beginning to rumble as wave after wave bobbled their boats, the crew and passengers were beginning to break. With no real alternatives, one by one the news media edged closer.

Jack knew that their homegrown militia was small enough without having to guard against another encroaching army. It had to be in the island's best interest to slow the media down again. Macbeth was no place for any media circus and the chaos it would surely breed.

Guessing that they could do only so much to prevent the media from invading, a quick decision was all it took to get the island to make its next calculated move.

Silently slipping into the cool water of the inner harbor, some of the island diver's made their move. One by one, each member of the team slid beneath the oil-soaked surf. They were armed with small packs of plastic explosives, just an island version of an underwater Molotov cocktail.

Swimming past the eerie wreck of the *Danny Boy*, the divers peered at her resting hull with a deeper respect, now in her death sensing her new cause. Aided by the power of youth, they swam hidden to where the media boats waited. Among the four of them, it didn't take long for them to attach and set each timer on all the ten bombs on the unsuspecting boats. The placement of each bomb was calculated to offer the most possible safety for those on board, for this act wasn't about blood; rather, it was a warning statement issued by explosives.

With their mission under their belt, the kids couldn't resist a few back yard pranks with a few of the other boats. Edging up under a couple of the bigger boats, it didn't take long to locate and pry open the drain plugs. *Surprise!* they figured as they swam toward the safety of the harbor. All was quite as it should have been above the water.

CHAPTER 17:

TWO OLD HENS

Not much time after the divers snuck out of the water, a group had assembled on the cliff. Curiosity was getting the better of them as many sat in their lawn chairs, some munching chips, others drinking a beverage from their coolers. The mine was surely getting on some folks' nerves, as many snuck out for any reason they could come up with.

Midge and some of the women from the knitting guild had a few words with the men about the coming assault on the media. It was a drastic move whenever explosives are involved, and this wasn't sitting right with any of them.

The men knew the women were right as they had the load speaker system brought up and set up on the cliff. All the women wanted was a fair warning issued--nobody would get hurt, except for the boats...and with that, the media would know how crucial it was that they stay away.

Elma, still with a bit of that spunk that made her famous, satisfied that the microphone would work, handed it to Jack. Not the rock star he knew he wasn't, he dropped the microphone with a loud thump that went ringing through the speakers, he was sure now the microphone worked. Clearing his throat a few times into the microphone didn't matter; what mattered then was his message.

While the boats grew silent with anticipation of what was

going to be said, Jack spoke into the microphone: "Testing, testing, one, two and three. I always liked doing that, you know!" he chuckled. Turning a bit serious, he spoke again.

"You folks out there on those boats, we have warned you to get back from the island! You haven't, and now I am warning all of you to put your life vests on and move to the front of the boat…we don't want anyone hurt."

The minutes ticked away and they just sat in the boats, no one being in any hurry to do what Jack asked.

This time, raising his voice, increasingly uneasy about his message, he told the boater in real terms that bombs had been planted under the boats. "I'm as serious as rats on a pile of cheese," he said. "We surely don't want to send any of you home in pieces--I mean the ones the sharks don't get first. The bombs are real. Some of your boats will sink. Move to the front, where you stand a chance. The choice has always been yours, but the time to react is now!"

The old man on the cliff sounded serious, and had planted enough doubt in their minds that they moved quickly to the front of the boats while fighting for a life preserver. Game or not, he was serious, and they had no alternatives at that point.

Not wanting to miss the fireworks, Mitch, with nothing to do, walked up to get a front row seat on the cliff. There wasn't a chance in hell he was going to miss this show. Scanning around, he looked for Kate, but she and Lynn didn't seem to be around. Maybe they didn't know…or too much real action for them, he figured.

Almost like an old Belushi film, he watched as Midge-- once a waitress, always a waitress--passed out ice-cold brew and iced tea to whoever asked. For just a quick flash in time, he felt like he was in Rome at the Coliseum, just waiting for the lions and Christians to battle. Barbaric and sick as it was, he knew his blood was running hot in anticipation of the show and the fury it would bring.

The wait seemed to drag on; the anticipating crowd on the cliff passed the time catching up with each other. Anticipation was turning into skepticism, as nothing seemed to be happening below. Focused minds were getting bored as many watched the seagulls battling the wind and surf in search of their next meal.

To some of the observers, a few of the boats seemed to be developing a noticeable list--most likely the reaction to the extra action of the divers. The show must have been starting.

The boats started listing quicker, as the flooding was happening for sure. The old man on the cliff was right, and by then his words had real meaning. Not sure what to do, a few of the boats started their engines, maybe hoping to leave, but sticking for the time being by land was probably the safer of their options.

As the few boats started slipping under the surf, with their occupants swimming toward other boats, the quiet crowd on the cliff broke into applause while some overeager islanders tossed their empty beer bottles into the surf. This was good news, as the media cameras shot footage of the events unfolding and the crazies on the cliffs.

The circus-like atmosphere of the evening was broken, as one by one, ten small explosions pierced the moment. Focused explosions sent smoke, fiberglass, and parts of boats hurling into the air. It was good they had moved forward, as some of the explosions were more than had been planned for.

It all seemed so surreal from the cliffs above. This orchestrated confusion had happened right in front of Mitch, and though probably it was one of his top potential stories, he couldn't even report on it. It was getting hard to believe that an act of this civil unrest could have gone this far in such a short time, and in such a modern era. Even in its forgotten innocence, Macbeth was still part of the real world, and things like that just didn't usually happen.

Too much Hollywood to him anymore, it seemed. His reality seemed like make-believe, and for the moment make-believe started feeling like reality – things just were not adding up. This event really hit home, as Mitch and his little bit of personal confusion realized that the thin line between sanity and insanity had finally been crossed in the waters below.

In the uncaring waves, big and little news folks, and boat pilots were now running around and jumping off perfectly good boats. Nobody knew what was going to blow and what wasn't. This hadn't been part of the plan, but if unorganized chaos was, it had certainly worked.

The spectators above were amused in a sick kind of way. "All in good fun," one on the cliff said, as Macbeth had flexed its puny muscle again.

"Sure beats quilting with the old hens, huh, Elma?" Midge yelled to a disbelieving Elma as she stood there wiping her hands on her apron, just shaking her head.

"Aghhhhhhh, Midge, you festering varmint, bite it!" A slightly intoxicated Midge thought in disbelief: *Did those words really come out of Elma?*

"Elma Lou! If your dead husband heard those words of hate out of that denture-filled mouth of yours, he'd start drinking again--not that he ever stopped, mind you."

"Midge, you old bat! Lloyd never drank after he met me, and surely not around a flabby hussy like you!"

"Sure he never drank, and that water down below isn't wet either. Elma, you have to get a grip on reality, girl – your husband was a closet drunk. He sure as hell wasn't buying fruit punch every other day down at the liquor store, either."

Those two old bats were getting ruffled, and the gloves were coming off, until Elma almost gave in.

"Stop it, stop it now! My husband is dead, God rest his soul. Have you no heart, Midge? Look at those unfortunates thrashing around below in that cold water...and you're only worried about getting under my skin. You are nothing more than an unfortunate, unsatisfied bitch, with an extinguished fire down below!"

"I'll old bitch you, you cranky old lunatic; I know what your husband drank. Lord knew as hard as he tried, his bottle of gin couldn't make you look any better."

Elma had enough as she grabbed one of her quilting needles and went after a chuckling Midge. Jack and Mitch just looked at each other in utter amazement. No one wanting to make the first move to stop that old cat fight, as in real time it played out.

Midge with her forward momentum was too much of a match for Elma. No matter how fast Elma tried, a quilting needle in one hand was not the answer to her fight. In utter frustration she whipped her needle like a javelin in Midge's direction. Arching nicely through the air, it hit granite, pinged once and flopped harmlessly to the surf below.

Elma, defeated, realized the show the two had put on.

Straightening her wig, Elma assumed the role she pretended so hard to be. Midge, out of reach, slapped skin with one of her coffee buddies as he handed her a fresh beer from his cooler. Her battle was over for now.

Below, a few still filmed the continuing mess of the burning and sinking boats from the safety of their rubber rafts. These true reporters knew the film in their cameras was their story, and that the world would need to see more than an abandoned boat with engines still running, headed on a roundabout path toward the rocky shores. It was only a matter of time--maybe minutes--before boat and rocks met. Boat owners and news folks could only watch as they thrashed loosely in the waters. Thanking God for insurance, life preservers and their lives.

Without a second thought about turning the engines off when the boats were abandoned, this circling medley of out-of-control powerboats would careen into each other's thin hulls. This had turned into a water-style demolition derby, which was great fun unless you were one of the wet few in the water, dodging the unmanned crafts. One by one, the damaged boats took on water and sank, neutralized and out of the picture. Mitch, a bit uneasy at the fiasco his brothers and sisters of the media were in, could only sit back and think how ironic it was; for once, the media was the story for the early-morning news.

Relative calm slowly returned to the outer harbor, with a few empty boats bobbing in the distance, more out of spite and an opportunity to make a point that the boats were to be silenced. The young tank crew jumped at the opportunity to prove their worth. With a little skill, and a whole lot of West Virginia luck, the crew took aim. A half-dozen shots later, the crew managed to sink both into the welcoming sea. The media's armada had been silenced, and all that remained was the oil slick and pieces and parts.

Getting their cue, the three rescue boats skipped out of the harbor to rescue the cold and wet. It was never hard to find the victims, as this bobbing group made more commotion than a group of hungry seals, making sure they were seen, with intentions of sparing themselves the fate that would occur from the jagged rocks of the shore. Skilled fisherman weaved in and out of the waves, trying not to mince anyone up before they hoisted in their catch of the day.

More cigarette-starved hostages were just what the islanders needed. Move them back to the island, dry them up, and get them ready for an awaiting news conference. Macbeth's new messengers they were. Tom's madness really did have meaning after all. Feed them mentally and physically and let them go home fulfilled and with the story--messengers hopefully on a mission of mercy.

Tom had always figured the truth could never hurt. A true story could do more damage in it truth than a well-oiled army. Macbeth's stories from the heart must be the island's redemption. The islanders needed the support of the mainland on their side. The final confrontation could be avoided, if the mainland could be convinced to carry Macbeth's silent shield of peace in their heart and assure the ultimate victory. It all seemed so right in discussion!

The ball was back in Mitch's court. The weight of his words had shifted again for once in his simple life, and he could feel it. Trying to hide his penned-up emotions, he felt an ever-greater need pushing him to complete his task. In his heart, for once, he felt justice fill up his being; he was a man on a mission, if he could only come up with the words to save an island and its people.

Hazel, back in the armpit of the nation, was in a tizzy; pulling all the strings she could, she managed to get a message to Mitch. She must have worked for the CIA or the devil in a previous life. How she got through to him, he would never know. He was sure someone had been paid dearly for this opportunity.

Her message, as usual, wasn't cordial, and he knew wherever he was, he was still her paid man, and did what she said. Hazel demanded her exclusive, and declining was not an option for Mitch.

Idle threats at one time would have petrified Mitch. She was a rather large, ugly woman and would literally throw her weight around. For once in his self-centered life, he felt in charge now as he realized his problems didn't amount to a hill of beans compared to the mountains Kate and the islanders had to cross. Unwittingly he was at a great crossroads of his life, but at the moment all he could do was stew and contemplate the direction his life was going to take. He hadn't asked for this, but in a individual moment he was forced to grow up once and for all.

Finding the answer to his problem usually consisted of never dwelling too long on the problem in the first place. Evading problems was easier for the spoiled hidden kid in Mitch--the kid who would tape tattered *Playboy* pictures to the door of the neighborhood creep's home just for kicks and blame it on someone else. It was easier to run from the answer than face the truth.

Knowing it wouldn't work this time, he left the cliff and

slipped down to an empty lobster boat as if it were his. Jumping on board, he switched on the CB, just hoping someone would answer his call…and luck was with him. He only wished he could have given his editor his exclusive in person.

In an almost apologetic voice for what he asked the man on the other end to do, he almost felt bad. Encouraging him to use a few select words, as the innocent messenger would tell Hazel to kiss Mitch's big "exclusive" rear end, and when she got done with his butt, she could take his little job and proceed to shove it where the sun never shone. He was done working for her, and that was for certain!

Thanking the man for his help, and satisfied for the moment, he sat back in the pilot's chair listening to the gulls and the small waves splashing up against the rocking boat. Even on the verge of chaos, life was good and it really only was a job, he kept telling himself, while wondering what beverages might be stowed below that could make this moment even more perfect!

Mitch had a bad feeling that the display of calculated force outside of the harbor was surely going to shift the situation into a different gear. Macbeth's militia had swiftly and decisively defeated another unsuspecting, unarmed army. Yet in victory the islanders still needed the avenue for unbiased news coverage, or else its true message would be lost to the gutters.

After the sabotage and bombing of the boats, Jack knew the time was right to put a face with their fight. The fresh media POWs needed the opportunity to sit down one on one with the women, the old, and the children of Macbeth. Time, which was readily available for them to see each other as they were, might just let the outsiders see what their pain and the lack of a future had driven these innocent individuals to act so desperately for.

Jack knew full well that the nurtured relationships were so vital. Coaching them, as a father would coach his son, he told them, "Please, look in their eyes, get down to their level, and show them that our town was more than a rebellious, crazed group. Make them understand how in a different situation we could have been their neighbors, their friends, their soul mates. They need to know you can be the smallest kid on the block and bullied for only so long before something gives. You asked for help and you got kicked down again. There has to be a point in every person's life when they say 'Enough is enough!' I know what you do now is for all of us. Thank you, be honest, and hope that in time, we might be all we have left to offer." Turning away, he touched the cheeks of a few of the young as he headed back down the tunnel.

Asking that more warm food, drinks, and blankets be passed out, he wanted these folks to understand the compassion of the islanders as they made their way among the crowd of captives. Great excuses for introductions, as common needs were taken care of by the caring of the captors.

It never seemed to take long for all to mingle, and the questions and answers to flow. First there was strained chatter, but as the day went on, laughter and real conversation could be heard. No outside forces interfering with personalities; what you saw was what you got, as it was before the advent of TV, radio, and the internet.

The few hours passed quickly. Life had to continue as the groups had to be separated eventually until they were the captives and captors again. This time, though, it was a little different, as random individuals were shaking hands as many maybe new friends hugged their captor's goodbye. Maybe what Jack had been looking for had come true, as that imaginary bridge of trust had been started.

As the get-together was ending, Mitch scanned the departing crowd, trying to find Kate. Was she in there talking? He wasn't sure. The crowd exited the area and Kate was nowhere to be found. With more than a hunch, he left the safety of the mine and headed to the dimly lit town. Coming out of the darkness, he spotted a familiar figure. Rushing to his arms was Kate--all he could do was hold her, hoping she didn't bump his wound again. Did she really miss him, he wondered? In an instant he could tell that she had been crying as he gently wiped the tears from her face. The stress of a lifetime was weighing heavy on her shoulders.

She had her life wrapped up in her bed and breakfast. The business was hers as it was her parents' before, and their parents' before that--a family tradition of sorts. He hoped he could take some of the pressure off her, and ease her through what could come. That evening, the future felt even closer, sort of like a freight train rolling on with no brakes. There just seemed no rational way of ending this crisis without someone getting hurt.

In an awkward silence, they walked hand-in-hand as young lovers do, back to her dark home. It wasn't quite as romantic as it had been earlier. The salty smell of the ocean had been replaced by the diminishing smell of burnt wood. Much had changed quickly. Being human, you can prepare for only so much, and when the future you always planned for seems to be turning into a dead-end street, all you can do is hold on. The revolution had begun, and all they could do was grab the one they loved. In life, did anything else really matter?

Lighting some burnt candles in her dark room, Mitch held her close as she cried softly. Crying was made easier just knowing someone who cared was there, holding her tight. Feeling her warm tears on his chest, he could almost feel her pain. Then just insignificant individuals, together they were waiting for the dawn of a revolution. Two pieces of the big puzzle was all they were in this seemingly overwhelming tide of change, lying close to each other in a simple embrace as one wept and loved, as they knew the morning would surely come.

CHAPTER 18:

TIMES, THEY ARE A-CHANGING

The reality of the events unfolding finally hit Kate like a ton of bricks. Mitch didn't quite know what to say to her to ease her pain, since he had never been in the position to possibly lose everything he had. Losing her home was never considered when she bought into the rebellious plan. Walking through her rooms brought back good and bad many memories. It wasn't just a black and white situation then; it was more complicated than that. At that moment, there were no right answers as she tried to justify to herself that the end really justified the means, but it wasn't working.

Always having a comment to make, Mitch knew this was probably a good time to be quiet, while in a haze, dreams of a lifetime trickled by Kate. Her grief turned slowly into an unconditional acceptance, because what else could one person do in an event that was bigger than them all? With a little coaxing on his part, the two of them stepped out the front door into the morning sunlight. She turned her back on the past as she locked the front door maybe one last time.

She was wondering how a whole town could just walk away from everything they had known—a lifetime of preparation and plans turned upside- down for a principle. These people had an inner strength and resolve Mitch only wished he could summon. He knew full well that the islanders at this point were viewed by many as nothing more than traitors, regardless of the sacrifices they had demonstrated.

As to much had happened already, what could these folks possibly look forward to? Could these islanders see more in their future than the outsiders did? No matter how hard anyone rationalized their actions, Mitch couldn't see anything good coming out of their stand. Personal sacrifice was always hard, though these folks made it look like a walk in the park.

With Kate leaning on him for support, he walked silently through the town, both of them forced to witness what Mitch had too many times before reported on. To most Americans, this was just another all-too-familiar scene for some news report. The islanders were a displaced collection of people, some retreating with what few belongings they could gather as they sought refuge from what could harm them. The townsfolk really only had a two choices: retreat or surrender, and since they had come this far, what else could they really do?

Startled by the sound of children's laughter, the two looked in the direction of the sounds. Zipping down the road, Billy and Liam were cruising as they slid their bikes to a stop in front of the couple. Happy with just the right amount of dust flung in the air from the stop, they jumped off the bikes.

"Hey Mitchy!" Liam yelled while chewing a golf-ball-sized hunk of gum. "Where you been? We've been looking for you!"

"Howdy, Guys. I've been busy with a little of this and a lot of that, you know! Hey, shouldn't you guys be with your folks?"

Pretending they never heard his question, they asked

another one. "Hey come on, what's a matter with her? She's got all that black stuff under her eyes-- sort of scary, if you know what I mean."

"Come on, don't you know she's been crying, dork?" Billy interjected. "Haven't you ever seen your mom messed up before?"

"Don't call me names, jerk!" Trying to be cool, he shot his wad of gum out of his mouth like a bullet; it bounced off the ground like a super ball and in an instant was scooped up by a spying gull.

"Just eat it, Billy. You're just pissed off because a bird beat you to it," Liam said, laughing like kids do when they don't have a care in the world.

"Come on, Mitchy--you hit her?"

"No, of course I didn't hit her! You guys surely have some-where to be other than here, right now?"

Not satisfied with the answer, the little pests gathered their thoughts for the next verbal assault.

"Maybe you two love birds want to be alone?" Billy asked as he punched Liam in the shoulder. Not waiting for an answer, the two started chanting, "Mitchy's in love, Mitchy's in love!"

Screaming, Billy blurted out, "That's gross," as the two chorused in on some genuine laughter.

Having enough of the adolescent chatter, Mitch piped in, "You two undersized twerps get on back on your bikes and get moving, or you're going to meet the side of Mitchell you won't like!"

"Awww, come on, Mitchy--you're going to marry her, aren't you?" Liam screamed as Kate blushed for a quick mo-ment. Marriage had never really crossed Mitch's mind, but judging from Kate's reaction, it must have crossed hers.

Sensing Mitch's frustration, the boys mounted their bikes and pedaled away as one yelled out, "Later, lovers!" as they headed in the same direction as the folks returning to the mine. Mitch, relieved that the two had moved on, wondered to himself was the past so bad, that they had no other options? Times change everywhere, only this time, these people wouldn't budge.

Witnessing so much tragedy in his short career had caused tragedy itself to lose its realism. That day, almost seeing into the future caused those feeling to come crashing back to Mitch. What had happened on Macbeth would change innocent lives, and it had already changed his. To a God he seldom prayed to, he prayed hard that day, and that in the end all the sacrifice would be worth it.

Seeing Lynn in the crowd, the two went up to join her. Going past the marquee of the darkened theater, he read, "NOW PLAYING: Classic Film Revival, Orson Welles' *WAR OF THE WORLDS!*"

How much more fitting could that be, as they stepped over the crushed popcorn boxes and candy wrappers, once just everyday movie theater trash, but at that moment a harsh reminder of a better past.

The evening wore on and things remained peaceful. The militia had shown its hand, and that was enough to make the outsiders think twice about making another move. The governor they knew would not be quiet for long--it was a lot like playing doctor when you were a kid, the forbidden kid's game that was all about the future, and the consequences responsibility would bring. Mitch knew deep down that the islanders had pushed too many buttons to go back to square one. No matter what happened next, all were in this fine mess together.

Since cutting his writing future with the magazine, he felt a closer bond with these people. With his loss of a real job, his lifeline to the real world seemingly was wilting away. The islanders were, at that point, all Mitch had, and they had become his immediate future in such a short time.

Every man, woman, and child was involved in this planned crisis, Mitch, in his stupidity or nobility, would now be branded as one of them. With little regard for his common sense, which was in overdrive, he jumped feet first into the boiling pot. Was he a fool, or just plain crazy in love? That day's confused emotions had haunted more than a reporter's ego, as a feeling of some lost decency had managed to surface within. For whatever it was worth, he would march together with his town.

While Lynn and Kate talked, he sat daydreaming about the implications of not having a paycheck. Hell, why was he worrying? No paychecks are needed in prison. With a sharp crack to his backside, Peace snapped him back to reality.

"Whoa, big guy, that hurt--still sore and oozing back there!"

"Sorry, dude!" Peace said. "I forgot; just joking around. Everything sure is getting serious around here."

"I'm good, Peace. You know anyhow, my little sister smacks me harder than that. All kidding aside, we all could use a little laughter around here."

"I know the feeling. The whole island feels like one big funeral—and, I hate funerals. How are you lovely ladies doing?" Peace asked as he moved closer to them.

"We've had better days, Peace, but no use in complaining." Kate replied, a bit more subdued.

"Anything I can do?"

"Maybe another time, but thanks for asking. I'm just a little messed up--too much has happened, and I'm just trying to work it all out."

"How are you, Lynn?" Peace moved even closer to her, as he felt sympathy for all she had been through.

"I'm hanging in there. My mom isn't...she has been crying and scared about this whole thing. At night I hear her crying about my dad. You know, a lot of the mothers are really questioning why we are doing this now." Pausing, she reached for Peace's hand. "I really do miss the life I had only days ago."

Brushing her soft blonde hair out of her face, exposing a few tears, Peace replied, "Questioning the elders also--you're not alone!"

"It doesn't ever seem fair to anybody."

"Yeah, me either--I've rationalized it every way I could. We've all been sort of backed into a corner, the way I figure," Peace replied as he grabbed her other hand. "Hey, Lynn--as much as I want to stay, I have to go." Pulling her in for a hug, he felt the young warmth of her body against his, as she didn't want to let him go.

"Let's hang out later. It's been way too long, and I mean it." With a quick wink he gently pulled away.

"I'd really like that, Peace." Lynn had wished he would have held her a little longer, because in his arms the future didn't seem so bad.

"Mitch, I have to grab a few things, and I sure could use a hand--want to come along?" Peace asked hoping for a yes. "I'll even find you a warm one!"

"Miller time!" a willing Mitch replied. "I can't lift much, but who knows what tomorrow will bring. Let's do it, big guy--one for the road ahead!"

Thinking twice, Mitch looked back at Kate, almost looking for her permission, as she nodded yes. Times like this, maybe she was better off alone with Lynn.

He kissed her goodbye, as most lovers would. He wanted to. Wow, what had happened to him? Maybe a warm brew would help sort these feelings out.

Peace knew where to go. The shops were empty, and the only real noises were the gulls that really never seemed to shut up. The town didn't feel right, even to Mitch.

Being the kind of guy who never turns down a beer, he followed Peace as they pushed open the Daisy's door. With a passion for the suds, the two made themselves at home in the bar. Inside you could smell the years of stale beer that had seeped into the old wooden floors, a familiar stink that ranked up there with the smells of an old college frat house after too many weekend parties that only college boys could really throw.

"Baptism by beer," Mitch yelled, remembering his days in the trenches of an old Beta Ro TKE house. This bar, he was sure, had certainly had its share of baptisms. That day the darkened, well-worn tavern was just another cold building. With all its stories forgotten, its dedicated regular flock was forced to scatter. Only the creaking of sitting on an empty bar stools, pickled eggs, and the spilled bar nuts gave any testimony to the tavern's colorful past.

"You know beer is always good for the pain, Mitch."

"Kate said things heal faster on the island, something about the salt water in the air."

"Must be that live-in nurse of yours," Peace said as he slid Mitch a brew down the bar.

"She really is great. Why didn't she ever get married?"

"Who really knows? I remember at least two who really wanted her bad. In fact, if she had been younger, I would have jumped on that!" Peace said with a bigger grin.

"You know Peace, she really seems so right. Man, I've been with a lot of women in my day – some I'm proud of, more I'm not – but I've never gotten the feelings I get when I'm around her." Twisting open his beer, he flipped the lid toward the open can on the floor. Taking a long deep sip, he knew how good a warm beer could be.

"God, that's good!"

"You know it, Mitch--help yourself. Somebody's got to drink it; might as well be us."

"Peace, has she dated a lot recently?"

"No way, just a lot of one-night stands. Miss Quick and Easy most of the time, as the island boys called her!"

"Get out of here, really?" Mitch questioned.

"I'm just kidding. Kate's the kind of woman you take home to Mom, then take upstairs and spank her like there's no tomorrow. Ride 'em, cowboy." Peace was feeling good as he watched his beer buddy squirm a little.

"You really like her, don't you? And on the ferry over I really thought you wanted Lynn, from the way you were starring at her. I figured you for a cradle robber!"

"Thanks a lot, Peace. By the way--how old is your younger sister, if things don't work out with Kate?" Mitch joked as the two broke out into laughter, and for the moment, the Daisy sounded like a bar again.

Mitch wondered--did Peace really need his help with something, or was this the help he needed? You couldn't have shut him up if you had duck taped his mouth shut. Peace needed to talk to someone close to his age, even though he was sure Mitch was an old man. For the time being, the conversation flowed easily and both forgot about the real world outside the tavern.

Back in the city at his old job, Peace was so sure something was going to happen on the island that he couldn't keep his mind focused on his job. His island family meant so much to him, and if the whole town was going to blow, he had to be there. Deep in his heart, he knew right from wrong: but love and loyalty can sometimes blur that thin line between sanity and insanity.

He, as well as most of the working islanders, realized that the economic shackles the mainland had imposed were nothing more than bullshit. How do you take the surgical tools from a surgeon? Then, on top of taking away their livelihood, you hit them with more taxes. This action was a recipe for confrontation, nothing more. This state government was hellbent on intimidation, as their means to an end. Peace was told if you don't like it, change it. But how do you change it if the system is bad, and controlled by people who like things their way? That was Peace's predicament; he was on the island for the long haul; good or bad, it didn't matter...this was about family.

The two chatted for the longest while, like two lost buddies catching up and sharing the moment. Determined soldiers of beer, they did their duty as they killed the last of the amber glass soldiers.

Leaving the Daisy not as quiet as they had entered it hours before, the town drunks stumbled and burped their way down the street. Passing the machine gun nests, the guards laughed at the two stumbling, wishing they had been part of the party. Beer had been good, as Mitch's drunken mind raced on: no job, no worries. He was a free again, with no place to be on time to. Mitch's unintended evolution had taken place on that padded bar stool, as the real world just passed this island boy by.

CHAPTER 19:

THE RIGHT WORDS CAN SET YOU FREE

Mitch, being the true buddy he was, understood it was best to leave Peace by the side of the road as he puked up his earlier meal. Not quite the alcoholic he had surmised he was, he was better off his way, as Peace wanted nothing to do with Mitch's attempt at compassion, shooing him off. Alcoholic binges...just another badge Mitch wore well, earned from the many empty nights in the city, as he drifted along, hoping for some form of acceptance from the neon crowd.

A few short hours after the guys' brew fest, the island had been mobilized. The guard's arms gave the island's militia some real teeth. With four tanks, at least two dozen hand-held missiles, grenades, and more automatic rifles and ammo than anyone would need, the rebellion became an unpredictable force to the outside world.

Four sides of the island, thanks to the guard's gifts, were all armed and ready. They watched impatiently for an assault that most knew would have to come if the governor didn't give in. The islanders were not stupid; they were not fooling anyone. These disillusioned citizens knew they were no match for any modern army. Most secretly felt, when common sense wasn't lacking, that their only real option was a fair and peaceful settlement. Nobody wanted to die or even fight. All these folks needed was a chance to be heard, and to preserve their way of life!

What worried them the most was the governor and his track record: once a crook, always a crook. The way the governor saw it, he had two workable options: peaceful solution or a bloodbath. He should have known better and washed his hands of this situation and let someone more rational handle it, but politics are politics, and the governor felt he did no wrong. This was to be the mother of all fights, and he was going to win it.

Macbeth's anger hadn't been fictionalized and wasn't the islanders' fault; the seas had been over fished for years. Who could you blame and still be correct, when everybody was really part of the problem? Most of the islanders felt the politicians had a firm handle on the real villains, but the campaign contributions from the big players in the fishing industry sure came in handy in their time of need. It was apparent that the state government didn't lose any sleep over the islanders' demise, as many had their life savings tucked away in a fishing boat, docked in the harbor, collecting nothing but barnacles. In the real world, somebody had to pay a price so others would succeed, and it just happened to be Macbeth's turn.

Looking back, the island's story wasn't really that unbelievable: the administration's record on cover-ups and indiscretions set the record straight. Researching the story later, the media had a degree of sympathy for the simple islanders, while those on the edge figured they were just blowing bad smoke to protect an easy way of life.

It all depended on where you wanted to put your trust.

Regardless of who was right and who was wrong, that town had crossed the line between law and order. That morning as the 9-to-5 crowd was pouring their morning cup of coffee, the country was waking up to hints of a state of the union that maybe wasn't as strong as when they had climbed into bed the evening before.

After a sleepless rest, some warm clothes, and some welcomed food, the captured media pool was escorted to the boats. A quick trip to release their live offering of peace was the plan as the white flags on the boats fluttered in the breeze. In the salty air, two young men, Jimmy and Bobby, islanders for all of their short lives, now held the responsibility of delivering and freeing their live cargo. Out of the harbor they went, armed with only some emergency flares and a twelve-pack of Mountain Dew.

As they barely left the safety of the harbor, the two boats of peace were intercepted and surrounded by local law enforcement boats. With guns ready, the nervous law officers carefully watched as prisoners were released to their custody and safekeeping. The freed media, ever thankful for the island's hospitality, couldn't wait to be on solid ground close to a phone or computer so they could deliver their story.

What happened next should have been expected, but the islanders had made the same mistake before in trusting the administration. In a quick second, Jimmy's boat of truce was surrounded, cutting off any avenue for escape. His boat was quickly boarded with Jimmy thrown to the floor, beaten, and cuffed. He was seemingly an early trophy in this bizarre war, to be displayed and used as a pawn.

Bobby, knowing full well he was next, and full of youthful

invincibility, gunned his motors and made a desperate run for the safety of the harbor. With engines whining at full throttle, his boat skimmed across the water. All it took was one trigger-happy law officer and one all-too-lucky shot into the boat's gas tank, and the speed boat was transformed into an exploding hunk of twisted and burning fiberglass, wood and flesh. There was never a chance in that hell to rescue that kid, as his youthful spunk was extinguished in an instant.

What remained afloat after the explosion sank quickly beneath the consuming waves? There was no body, as it all tangled, sank, and settled together at the bottom of this unforgiving sea. This all happened under that ignored white flag of a simple violated truce. The governor had his first blood and felt totally justified, as he had blackened the islanders' eye, and unknowingly made their choice even more right.

If there was any, it would seem the justice that came out of this mess was the fact that this act of a coward had unfolded in full view of a shocked media. If this event wouldn't turn the public's passion up, what would? The law for once felt like the warriors they were trained to be, regardless of their unarmed victims and their simple act of murder.

Tonight under the spring moon, another mother would weep for her fallen son, while upon twilight-lit mainland the killer and his friends in arms, drunk and merry, would celebrate their deliberate and unchallenged victory.

Tom and Mitch stood stunned as a stiff ocean breeze blew the smell of the burning boat across the cliff. Together they had witnessed the sudden unjustified attack. Out of an uncontrollable rage, Tom's veins popped, as his face grew red in anger. Reacting to the moment, screaming like a madman, he ordered the tank to send a shot in the direction of the enemy. Then, almost hesitantly, he realized the media were still on board, and that they didn't need to become victims. With no options, he reversed his order to shoot. His common sense had prevailed, he knew that as bad as it was, this had to be the time to suck it up and find a way to turn this crisis down a notch, before someone else's blood was drawn.

"Damn them!" he shouted, as he flung his clenched fist in rage.

Knowing an eye for an eye would not work, he prayed that tomorrow's paper would strike the blow he couldn't.

"Our revenge must be sweeter," he cried, collapsing to his shaking knees as the pain of a child's loss dug the dagger of self-blame deep into Tom's tormented soul.

The poor boy, so full of youth, had given up his life for an ideal he probably didn't even fully understand. It was nothing more that the heat of a moment gone sour, as a boy trying so hard to be a man overreacted to a situation no one had seen coming.

Word of the loss spread quickly on the island. People who had questioned the cause now were outraged and full of fight as the imaginary drums of war beat louder. Any doubts about the cause were then replaced with even more danger-ous thoughts of a painful revenge. The devoted people were in a state of panicked frenzy, which in itself can be evil. Calm was urged by a few of the realists, as their voices seemed to be muffled out by the crowd.

In that tragic moment, for once Mitch was one of the few feeling rational; must have been the leftover beer flow-ing through his veins. Though he was never much of a public speaker, his gut feeling kept telling him that things were going to overheat if something didn't happen. Everything he had always tried to repress kept telling him he couldn't be quiet any longer. Not rationalizing, he pushed his way to the front of the growing crowd and, with a quiver to his voice, a public speaker was born.

"Can I have your attention?" he yelled as the crowd quieted down to see what this outsider they had seen around had to say.

"I know many of you don't know me, though you might have seen me around lately. I can't possibly feel all the emotions and pain you are dealing with. I know pain, I've seen it, I've reported on it. But please don't let pain destroy you. Channel it however you must into something positive. Your boys would have wanted that."

After pausing for a moment, he continued: "Sure, you all can work each other up into a frenzy and go out and shoot things up, but then someone else will get hurt. These are your friends, your neighbors, your family, and it's still about them. Life is way too short, as we all witnessed, so let's take our time and pick our battles and not make life any shorter. We will live to make Bobby's life worth his sacrifice. The world is listening. Don't let revenge destroy your chance at a future!"

Mitch figured by crowd's silence that he must have said the right things. Quickly he walked through the parting crowd, as he though maybe he had earned a little of their respect.

Pumped up from his speech, he figured maybe his words were flowing and that this could be the moment to write the declaration they so wanted him to begin. He knew these folks were counting on him. He wasn't sure what his words could do to help, other than giving these folks something to read.

"Four score and seven years ago," was all that kept racing through his mind. Sure it had already been used, but like a skipping record, it wouldn't stop.

In thought, he walked back toward his little part of the mine. Drifting out of the dimness, a whiff of cheap perfume greeted and enticed him as he was gently body slammed by his angel.

"I need you now!" Kate said, as Mitch looked around acting stupid.

"You were talking to me?" He knew of course she was, as he felt like that sex slave he always pictured himself as. With that seductive bedroom look in her big eyes, how could he tell that crazed woman no? He knew that when it came to cheap and easy sex, he was pudding.

In full control of the moment, Kate led him down to an isolated part of the tunnel, and made that poor Mitch do things he had previously only thought about doing to her. He was in love that night, as the island's declaration would have to take back seat to his lady in waiting and his overactive hormones.

Those minutes of passion in the labyrinth held a darkness few could imagine, combined with the feeling of rock salt on their naked buns equaled a rendezvous of lovemaking that neither would ever forget. The high flyers club had nothing on a dark tunnel--just another kinky story for Mitch to remember in his book of kink.

After his last distraction or attraction, he put off his project again, just for the time being, he told himself. As he located his scattered clothing, he thanked Kate for taking advantage of him and told her he really had to get started; he couldn't let the islanders down. Kate, sitting so naked and innocent in front of him, reminded him that she was not keeping him there, as she playfully crawled on all fours toward the man. His devils raced through his mind again. Fresh air or a cold shower had always worked wonders on cleaning up his problem. He knew with her distraction, he wasn't going to get started here. Reluctantly, he pulled away from her as he left the fatal grip of a renewed seduction from his queen.

With a firm intention of completing the job, he planned on heading back to Kate's house for some solitude--just what he needed, he thought. He knew it had to be fresh and catchy, something to move the islanders he hardly knew, and overwhelm a nation.

"Let it be," as the Beatles said--he was to be the author, no escaping it. He still couldn't see the whole picture and what was so important about this declaration, even with talking to so many about the issues on the island. Knowing how important it was to them, he couldn't connect the dots and the impact Tom had planned on it making. Before he left, Kate had assured him the connection was there, and only he could bring it out in words. Mitch, still not believing in himself on that task, could never argue with a naked woman, as she begged him to come back for a few more minutes!

On the mainland, local law enforcement figured the islanders needed to understand once and for all another reaction for their actions. With a few clicks on a mainline computer, electricity and phone connections were terminated. The island's link to the real world was over, as the crisis moved into another stage. It was hardly noticed, as much of the island had already gone dark; the only hint was the scattered sound of generators kicking in, and replacing what little the mainland actually provided.

The computers of the islanders went blank as the young internet was no longer their friend for the moment. Macbeth's keyboard junkies through the chat rooms had saturated the net with stories of the island plight. Sure, that day they lost their place online, but the story the children had told and sent was alive and well. Through the magic of the modern world, Macbeth's story had a chance to breathe, thanks to the people who felt their pain and pushed the message forward. Nothing more than a modern-day Paul Revere who rode on again through the electronic world, he traveled silently, issuing his powerful warning: they were coming!

Always one to let work wait, Mitch, walking away, became absorbed in watching a group of the island kids at play. The raw energy of a child combined with the utter absence of rational thought on the crisis above allowed the kids to run carefree through their little section of the mine. To a child, life in the tunnels was just another reason for a day with no school and a really cool place to hang out. Yet with a child's curiosity, Mitch could only wonder if some of the kids had any idea of the extreme sacrifices their parents above were dealing with to protect their future.

"Not a clue," he blurted out to himself, as their lives would continue, as the adults tried to carve some normalcy out of this absurd situation they had created.

Much older, of course, the adults' lives had been shaped by many triumphs and failures, and now they were forced to deal with the critical choices. As with all communities, some islanders were coming down the final stretches of their lives. What these folks would accomplish soon (or what they couldn't) would surely shape the futures of the innocents.

Walking out of the mine, Mitch couldn't blame the kids for enjoying the last free moments they could. Childhood was always just a flicker in the candle of life, some unfortunate times, snuffed out before it burned. With deep thoughts in his mind he made his way to Kate's house and settled in for a quick power nap. All that thinking and sex just made him tired. Mitch's homework would have to wait again; he had to sleep – it was an essential right he held ever so dear.

Out of a partial media blackout, some say orchestrated by the administration and the lack of credible information, the release of the media POWs then troops was welcomed by the public. Reporters with the scent of a big story on them wrote their versions of Bobby's murder. Many, to themselves, worried about possibly being detained again after the stiff warning from the governor as to how they had to be careful what they wrote, he didn't need their stories making it rougher than it could be for his men. The Massachusetts administration still governed like a small town from the '50s, and had many dark corners to hide people.

Tabloids and newspapers claimed that some of the governor's people had offered reporters cash for a positive story on the administration's actions. Most were also sure it was just calculated cash for stretching the truth. The governor would claim the real story was nothing more than fiction, as he was the fastest gun to deny or change the facts. It wasn't anything new with this administration; there had always been whispering about deep pockets and special interest groups sharing the same bed-- nothing new to many of the disillusioned voters.

Money, and a special favor, was always policy to this ruthless bunch.

With Elmer probably looking over the reporters' shoulders, most wrote a fair story and honesty had the edge. The media, of all people, knew the meaning of freedom of speech. They who lived by their words would be the last to mess with this most precious and important human right. Free speech had always preserved their freedom.

Giving the prisoners their own skiff, they motored out of the harbor. The news media were free along with the dozen troops as a peace gesture. No island escort, since they knew all to well what could happen. The news stories were published, and then waves of questioning swept through the state and ended up in the administration offices. Most boiled down to questions: why would anyone want to leave the protection of the state? What had caused them to take this drastic step? And of course no answers came--just more questions.

The governor's administration scrambled frantically as they tried to control the backlash from the news. The press spokesman, rarely speechless, was dumbfounded as he could be. All the minister of the words could do was deflect the damage as he was forced to retreat and collect his thoughts.

After a cabinet meeting where they all listened to the governor rant, they released a brief statement claiming the attack on the islanders' boats was an essential action in an unstable environment. Their law enforcement's actions, must not be condemned since they were involved in a very tense hostage situation, where innocent lives were still at stake. The situation was very fluid and negotiations were ongoing. Knowing full well this was not the truth, the spokesman had no choice;

he knew who he worked for, and his family lived paycheck to paycheck, so it was no big quandary for him when it came to his family.

The statement had worked for the time being. The governor knew all too well the islanders held a good hand with its collection of hostages. With Washington demanding some real answers, the crisis seemed to be getting stickier as federal advisors started showing up looking for the answers that never seemed to come. The situation on the island had to end soon, or it would be out of the governor's reach. He knew it, and his overwhelmed cabinet knew it too. He would not give in and negotiate with terrorists. He was tougher than they realized... or so he thought.

CHAPTER 20:
A TIGER WALKS AMONG US

A boy was dead, was it his fault? Tom wondered, as he watched the two kids running around the field outside of the mine playing football. He debated if what he got this town into was really worth the price. Wrestling with his resolve, he searched to find that inner peace and believe that what they had done would achieve results.

In a weaker moment, he needed to quell the inner voices that kept questioning his decisions. He knew full well with a short wave radio, he could make the call he never wanted to make. He moved slowly as he went down a level to the command room. It was empty--which was good, for he never wanted anyone to hear his doubts. Picking up the microphone, he reached the outside world and asked to be directed to someone from the administration.

With more than a few questions as to the authenticity of who he claimed to be, he got through. As the short wave hissed, a familiar voice answered; it was the man Tom had never wanted to talk to again. The governor, more than pleased with himself, was now the negotiator.

"I knew I would be hearing from you sooner or later."

"Well, I never wanted it to get this far," Tom said.

"It did, and the blood is on your hands, not ours. You asked for help and you took prisoners. The way we see it, you're all traitors, and have felonies awaiting you. If I had my way, you'd all be tried as war criminals!"

Tom was sensing this was going nowhere, but had to keep trying.

"We want to talk. I want no further bloodshed."

"The time to talk is over, buddy. The only talk I want to hear from you is 'We surrender!' You and your rebels are done. When you're relocated, your island will be the state's newest tourist attraction. Oh and while I'm at it, I should thank you for helping my re-election – I really needed this boost!"

Tom's mind was made up; there would be no use talking to this man. With a clear conscience, he now knew the direction he must take. The short wave line to the governor went dead as Tom calmly flipped the switch off.

Almost ashamed at his attempt, Tom felt better as the inner voices silenced this time. This was a call nobody needed to know he had made. He would sleep better, knowing that he had at least tried.

Next morning, with the loss of dead boy on their mind, sitting around the coffee pot, the men had their daily power chat with the elders. That day maybe they should have been drinking something stronger as well when they decided that the island needed to a show of force to prevent someone else's death. Tom was sure the governor thought he could just push his will around Macbeth; he needed to have a reason to think twice. A boy was dead and they were sure some in the world saw it as the island's fault.

Symbolic as their strike would be, there were ample

targets on the mainland. It would be an attack steered away from causing any injuries--more psychological, just aimed at causing some discomfort, confusion, and a reason to hopefully take the situation down a notch by a big distraction. With a governor, most were sure, who was hell-bent on the termination of the hold-outs on the island, something had to be done to prevent another fight.

Some of the elders focused on what could be done other than messing with the coastline. Negative as they were, Jack figured there could be a sense of truth to their thoughts. With trigger-happy troops, all this crisis needed was one gun-toting islander or guardsman to get wrapped up in a fight, and chaos would follow. They needed this diversion of violence to add restraint to an attack on the island they thought would have to come. No one on the island wanted any more bloodshed; one more life already wasted was more than anyone wanted to accept.

As each day passed, the governor knew his political life was dripping away with each moment the crisis wasn't resolved. More and more questions were being asked, while fewer and fewer were being answered. He and his cabinet hunkered down for the stand off. He knew he had the might to just walk over this distraction in his career, but what can you do that is politically correct in a time of crisis? This was new ground for this armchair governor; his greater-than-thou administration was stumbling.

Tom knew all too well that going by boat to the mainland was too risky in these blood-tempered waters. They had seen how a white flag of truce had only helped the officers aim better. The island surely didn't need any more martyrs for the cause. Young divers slipping beneath the waves had worked once and could work again. All knew a third time wouldn't stand a chance.

With a no hesitation and a few questions, the dive team walked into the dark surf. With the help of the back yard tinker of the island, a underwater tug of old plastic sleds, a few electric fishing motors, and a lot of fiberglass and epoxy was put to work as it propelled them silently and forward with their important cargo toward the unsuspecting Massachusetts shore.

Below the pre-dawn waves, the divers rehearsed their plan over and over again in their minds. Like fish from another planet, they were cutting silently through the deep water. The mainland for the most part was clueless about the passion of the islanders' resolve, but in hours would wonder what else they might have up their sleeves.

As fate would have it, two units were moving at the same time, one leaving the island, and one of the state's elite SWAT and tactical unit fast approaching. In their debriefing, the officer clearly made the case for arriving by way of the remote cliffs, surely their safest way in. Once safe atop the cliffs, they would be ready to deliver the administration's message by their supreme tactical advantage and surprise.

Sure, in theory the SWAT team's plan should have worked. The mainland didn't estimate the scale of Macbeth's rag-tag army's devotion to duty. This wasn't just a group of ten to fifteen groundhog-shooting good ole boys, but rather a group of disciplined, rehearsed men. Worse for the unit, these folks had a burning desire to protect what was theirs, and there is no treasure more valuable than loved ones.

Laying low on the cliff, Macbeth's militia enjoyed the benefits of the night vision goggles that the captured troops provided. Just like pirates from another era, nothing went to waste as their supplies were seized and then utilized. Grown boys, playing war for all the right reasons, guarded the cliff like this was their last stand.

With little talk and a whole lot of thought, the sentries watched as the small frigate quietly drifted in close. Closer it came, seemingly daring the rocky cliffs to try to snatch its metal heart.

In the awkward silence of darkness, the boat dropped off its live cargo, which was unaware that its every calculated move was being watched from atop the towering cliff.

The SWAT team rowed the rubber rafts in against the outgoing currents. Reaching the rocky beach below, one by one two ropes and grappling hooks were shot up the cliffs. Digging in the rocky surface, the hooks clawed their way into the cliff. The ropes drew tight as the weight of their climbers placed the burden of life and death on them. The team ascended the nylon with focused nerves in their race to rescue their brothers in uniform in their time of need.

With muscles burning, the men started reaching the top. It was a long climb, and their thoughts were more occupied on finishing this physical challenge than what awaited them. One by one, as the men rounded the top of the cliff, they were grabbed, silenced, secured and rushed away...just like hauling in a big tuna, even though they never seemed to wiggle as much as a caught fish.

Not much fight in those men. Together, with guns drawn, they were powerful, alone, and subdued; they were just ordinary men with everyday fears. Outnumbered and foggy in a new land, the dreaded tactical team became kittens for the cause. Chained together they were marched silently away.

With the catch of the day done, the men of the cliff tossed the empty ropes back into the welcoming surf, the only a reminder of a mission that went bad. An islander with a good eye shot a few bullets into the waiting rafts, deflating any chance of a possible escape from this side of the island. Alone in the field, a backpack came to life as a unit commander voice came across the radio as he tried to contact any of his men. Greeted only by silence and the few distant gunshots, he figured the mission was proceeding as planned.

Aboard the frigate, everything was normal as could be, as radio silence was expected. Who would have guessed or even noticed the magnetic cling of the little mines that were attached to the hull? The crew's mind was on recovering the team if they ran into trouble, and getting the hell away from this island.

With a power nap and a warm shower under his belt, Mitch walked out of the gray mine into the dawn, on a personal mission to smell some fresh air, as the recycled mine air wouldn't do any more. Too many smells, most of them bad, as he wondered to himself if these folks even knew about deodorant. Grabbing a strong cup of cowboy coffee, he filled his lungs with the freshness he had so quickly learned to love. City air was a thing of the past to this changed man.

The serene silence of a world awaking was broken at 6 a.m. by a few delayed explosions, which seemed to come from the back side of the island. Knowing this just wasn't a few kids lighting off M-80s, Mitch grabbed a bike and headed toward the direction of the blast. Pedaling on this kid's bike was made worse as his wounds only throbbed more.

Wondering what he had missed because of his nap, he got off the bike and rushed up beside the other men watching the scene below.

In gut-wrenching horror, he watched as the small frigate listed heavily to the starboard side. While flames poured out of a rear porthole, young men ran around the tilting decks just trying to launch their life rafts. Panicked as they seemed to be, all on the cliffs wanted to help, but only felt desperation, as the options to help were few. The boat was sinking much faster than any had planned, but then again the militia had never sunk a real boat. Things were going from bad to worse, as many knew they had just turned up the heat way too much.

In fear of the boat sinking too fast, Tom radioed back to the harbor and ordered a few armed speedboats out to assist in a rescue. In the next breath, Tom ordered a tank closer to the cliff, just hoping to give the speeding rescue boats some cover. They didn't need a repeat of other day's events.

With hardly a second to spare, a few loaded lifeboats slipped into the bucking sea. With more men waiting, a collapsible was being readied to be loaded when the ship burped a large belch and an explosion of air, and then flipped onto its starboard side.

In a violent mass of hissing and foaming water, the frigate slipped gracefully beneath the white surf. The only evidence of the ship's existence was the floating debris and some thrashing men in the frigid Atlantic water.

Observing the approaching rescue boats and doubting the island's motives for rescue, the two lifeboats started their engines and sped away trying to catch the retreating darkness. Gone without a second thought for retrieving any survivors, the sailors guessed it was the law of the sea: every man for himself.

The rescuers could find only a few oil-covered men in the surf. Pulling them aboard, the shocked boys stared at their captors like sailors from a war long ago, with their world shot out from under them by a U-boat, with big, wide eyes surrounded by wet soot and oil, dazed, they worried about the men still on board. It was too late: their fate was complete, though their deaths weren't planned. This event wouldn't help, as in time other families would be torn in grief as word of death reached their doors.

In the face of this mistake, the island's cause was still just, but many stopped for a moment to re-examine their reason for continuing the insanity. This had to stop; death had never been part of the grand plan. As bad as this was, it could only get worse as many wondered what the hell had they gotten themselves into.

CHAPTER 21:

SHE COULD HAVE BEEN MINE

With more uncertain feeling for what Mitch learned Macbeth's men had participated in, he quickly left the briefing. He didn't buy the "no pain, no gain" philosophy that some of the islanders did. Realizing that the loss of life on the frigate was an accident that was never meant to happen didn't help the bitter pill go down any easier.

That hour, the cause of the revolution couldn't have been any further from Mitch's heart. Almost to his breaking point, the man with no emotions realized then he had found one. Arriving at Kate's home, he collapsed in the recliner a desperate man. Having spent time in personal reflection as he trudged home through the abandoned town, he knew there was no turning the clock back on this unprovoked sinking. A price had to be paid.

It was a scary feeling seeing such a quaint town, void of its main ingredient: life. In an eerie kind of way, it reminded him a lot of the neighborhoods from many of the doomsday B-movies that he and his college buddies thrived on. What this abandoned town needed was some well-placed tumbleweeds and zombies, and a new movie set would be ready to shoot.

Too much wasted reflection on his part sure didn't help his

creative process. Mitch could imagine the haunted expressions on the frantic faces of the boys on the sinking boat. The face of death was never easy to deal with. Right or wrong, death was so final.

Kate's home wasn't much better than the isolation found in the mine. No electricity made it rough on the eyes; no Kate made it rough on Mitch. Too much had gone down in the last few hours, Mitch needed to talk to someone, anyone, but it wasn't going to happen. Grabbing a couple of candles, and matches, he pushed the darkness back. Then grabbing a warm beer from her putrid-smelling refrigerator, he settled his drained body down, hopefully to write by candlelight like the generations before had.

Sending his beer cap flying, Mitch tried to clear his mind, then his nose of the smell of spoiled food. Concentrating, he tried focusing on opening up his unused writer's path, like the Jedi he dreamt he was.

This was like homework all over again, even though Mitch never had done any more homework than he had to. Homework time was his private time, a time of the day to dream and doodle about places and things that existed only in his wandering mind: escapism, kid-style. To most, it really was more about early freedom, locked away in your private space while parents wanted to believe you were busy studying. If parents only knew what kids were really up to--thinking back, most probably did.

Jumping in and out of his dream state, he knew that in order to write well for these people, he needed passion and commitment. Precious lives, young and old, were depending on his yet-to-be-written words. Mitch knew he wouldn't bet the farm on himself if push came to shove.

How do you start, where do you start? He kept asking himself. "Four score and seven years ago" kept banging around the walls of his empty head, while the scared faces of the doomed sailors kept haunting his conscience. His mind, a scrambled collection of thoughts with serious reservations and doubts, unwillingly began the process.

In minutes, though, no matter how sincere his faked determination was, his mind drifted. With little to stimulate his thoughts, he stared around the dark voids of the huge Victorian room. Mitch could still imagine all the creatures from the worst nightmares of his youth. Those ungodly creatures always waited for him in the dark corners, even in his adulthood. Evil watched from the shadows, just waiting for that one misplaced step out of the security of the his tiny flickering light, and into their realm of darkness, the ultimate blackness, the type of darkness most nightmares thrived on. But tonight he was alone.

No matter what he tried, he couldn't think straight. Sitting, he listened harder as he thought he heard a creaky door open downstairs. All those imaginary creatures of darkness appeared, he was sure they wanted nothing more than to consume his inner soul.

Grabbing Kate's grandfather's cane, he prepared to face the unseen intruder. He was still a Jedi master with his light sword, shaking uncontrollably behind a closed door. Then, thanks to fear, he was just a child for the moment, more afraid of what the darkness could hold.

Not realizing if this was real or imagined, he heard the sound of light steps ascending the staircase. His mind raced into overdrive, ready to pounce and defeat this bold intruder. How dare this creature of the night invade his sacred domain and interrupt the good he was wishing he could accomplish?

The old door was all that separated him from his fears. With a turn of the knob and a slow creak, the door slowly pushed open. In what seemed like minutes the beast walked in wearing a sultry wisp of cheap dime store perfume.

With all that his shaking muscles could muster, he stood ready to whack the intruder into never-never land. Raising the heavy cane high above his perspiring head, he stood ready and willing to clobber whoever. Showing little fear, Lynn glided into the plain view of the twinkling candlelight. With a sigh of relief, Mitch stood down as his anxieties fled as quickly as they came. Thankful for the fact that he didn't have to demonstrate his mighty powers and embarrass himself, he was glad, and told Lynn how lucky she was that he didn't knock her into kingdom come.

Mitch, still shook up, was sure Lynn was more than over-whelmed by his generous decision. Without a motive, Lynn raced into his unsuspecting arms. Catching him off guard, all he could do was hold her tight as she cuddled gently in his grip. To feel that young, soft sensation again! Had it been so long that he had almost forgotten the sensuous softness of youth? Her schoolgirl innocence took what little breath he had left away.

Young and more than willing, she pulled away while her loose-fitting clothes started to drop quickly around her. A minute seemed like seconds before Mitch even thought he could stop her--but did he really want to? A goddess of his dreams was standing before him in the flickering of the golden candlelight…young, willing, and naked.

For the second time in such a short time he was speech-less. This beautiful woman of just eighteen wanted him to want her, and Lynn's body was all Mitch needed. In her nervous yet sensuous tone, Lynn begged him to take her. She had already unwillingly been taken by force, now it was her choice.

Not waiting for an invitation, she lurched forward even more, grabbing for him. Off guard to her second advances, he fell to the floor, trying to escape her next advances. Mighty Mitch was at a loss as to what to do with his hands. His hands went limp, while another part of his body grew hard. Trying to retreat further, Mitch's clothed body was covered and re-strained by this naked woman. This predicament was any sane man's unspoken desire. Without a rational thought he grabbed, felt, and finally, almost hesitantly, rolled away.

Lynn stayed there just wanting to be fulfilled and used, now just the object of his worthless rejection. She closed her long legs and wept, curled up alone on the soft bedroom rug.

Lynn was so young, and in her eyes, Mitch was her last hope. The only world she knew was possibly coming to an end, at least in her mind. For once, a woman wanted him to be the man he had always assumed he was.

Before he met Kate, he would have thrown Lynn or any other willing subject to the bed in a quick second, and ravished her as best a man could, but that day the preying animal in him was tamed. This was Kate's friend, young and vulnerable, and that lonely moment wasn't going to be her lucky day--or his, either.

Too young she was, and how would anyone ever adjust to a whacked-out situation like this? Mitch thought. He grabbed her in his arms, and she cried softly, as her visions of a husband and kids drifted away. Hanging on tight, all she could do was relish the warmth of his embrace, since her night of passion was only in Mitch's working mind.

In time, as always, he convinced her all was not lost. It wasn't her he didn't want; for once he was just in love with another woman. Yes, that was right; he was in love with another woman. What the hell had happened to him?

She almost trusted his judgment, since Mitch was from the real world. He didn't know what was more real: his world, or his desire for this innocent young girl. All he knew was that he kept getting new visions replacing his own little haunting gremlins that used to run naked through this demented man's mind.

It was kinky for him, and on this island life could be short. Got to get those thrills in when you can. Mitch assured her that this secret would be locked away in his mind for years to come. He was sure someday she would star again in one of his many untold fantasies…but not today, as he really felt compassion for this young girl.

As the dirty man he was, he couldn't help but watch her slowly dress. Trying to be the stud he thought he was, he walked her to the door. Kissing her softly on the cheek, he told her to wait, until the right man came along and he most definitely would. Amazed at what he said and did, that day the big bad wolf spared another willing lamb.

With gratitude to Lynn's interruption, his mind was distracted from the horrors earlier. With fresh visions dancing through his head, Mitch felt rejuvenated as his writer's paths seemed to be opened once again.

Within an hour or so and with the help of a few more warm brews, his hormones cooled down. A cold shower was what he really needed but with no electricity the shower was out of the question. Popping open another Bud, he pretended it was cold as he molded his slurred words on paper as he had hoped and prayed would help steer an island, and just maybe a nation.

Yet, his words still would not come. It was either the warm Buds or the thoughts of Lynn stripping in his mind. It's not often, if ever, that any guy gets a cheap thrill. It really wasn't cheap. In his earlier years, he probably would have paid for a show like that. Only that night the view of the dark deserted town brought his restless mind back to home plate.

Realizing the seriousness of the ever-pressing situation, he began to try to write in earnest. It was surely a burden no man ever really wanted, or a caring man could ever turn down.

Through the flickering candlelight, the words started to flow. Mitch had realized this was no longer just the people of Macbeth's burden, but his as well.

Reaching deep, he pulled out the best words a drunken fool with feelings could muster. He fought with fleeting rationality of the moment, just trying to capture in sentences Macbeth's years of frustration. Taking that frustration, he worked at molding the words down into a few moving, honest paragraphs that explained all and left confusion for none. The tabloids would need no more fodder from these struggling people. It was Mitch's time to add his wood to the fire of this smoldering revolution.

As the candles burned down, a weary Mitch stumbled down the steps into the rising sun. Morning, in all its fresh dew and bird songs, was upon him as the night that had held him earlier eased its tight grip on the home.

That morning light reminded him of how beautiful the town still looked. Mitch knew, as he watched an empty building with a door swinging open in the Atlantic morning breeze, that this crisis was far from over.

Document and aspirin in hand, Mitch walked away from what was. During another one of his drunken stupors, he created the best combination of words he could muster, fully knowing the real judge would be the outside world, and the people of Macbeth.

Walking carefully through town, now more accustomed to the cobblestones than before, he unfolded his document. Reading while walking, Mitch, a little more sober, read what he had just written. Reading out to himself, he listened to how his words flowed. He bounced his babble off the abandoned buildings, which gave silent witness to his written creation--sentences he hoped would be recited over and over again, as any author crossing his tired fingers could only hope and pray.

His words began.

WE, THE FRUSTRATED AND UNHEARD PEOPLE OF MACBETH, desiring a more perfect union for all, declare our independence from the grips of our mother state of Massachusetts.

Today is not just another day in the course of human events, but rather a unique day when one new state, a state comprised of one small and devoted community, was forced to act because of oppression and neglect. Stable and well-tried, this community is so conceived, and so dedicated to the right of freedom that all men and women are created equal, as a great leader once said.We are equally dedicated to its uncompromising democratic values, that a total act of devotion like this separation should ever be taken.

It is known that the actions declared here will surely test the morals and values we as a nation strive to protect. It has always been said that no man is an island. Someday it will be said that this lone island acted as a true nation: a great nation so dedicated to its way of life, guarding its God-given pledge to protect its citizens and their families with a loyalty to one another.

Furthermore, when another state government puts unnatural and heavy burdens upon a community of limited means, with the unnatural desire aimed at limiting its unique culture and way of life, for the benefits of others, a change must take place. Ignoring the need for honest compromise and negotiations makes visible the needs of our community and its people to take this extreme action, from which this secession was born.

Today, the fifth day of May, we declare our secession from the State of Massachusetts and its government.

We, the UNITED PEOPLE OF MACBETH, with heavy hearts, torn for our love of state and country and our simple but true love of our united community and its people, are compelled for a solution no matter what the consequences may be. We the oppressed feel the uncompromising burden placed upon us, have but no choice other than to drive us in this unnatural direction.

With open hearts and minds we pray and believe that this island we love and call Macbeth will not be reduced to a hallowed battle ground, concentrated with the blood of the young and old of your children and ours.

In undying respect for the Union, WE THE PEOPLE of MACBETH declare our independence, and forge ahead as a separate state governed by our own, and by God.

THE ISLAND OF MACBETH

*May God be with us and with you, in these coming days. God bless
the United States of America and God bless the state of Macbeth.
Signed, WE THE PEOPLE OF MACBETH.*

All was good in his universe, as Mitch walked down the familiar streets listening to the sounds of the sea. That day those
rotten fish smells for once felt like they belonged--or maybe
it was he who now belonged. His rebirth must be complete,
as the island for once felt like home...strange forgotten feeling of wanting and acceptance, which he had never really gotten to know. Now he was a weaker man, more worried about
whether this warm feeling would ever be taken from him--and
how would he replace it?

The document was done. He needed to get it to Tom so
his task was complete. No time to wait, as he moved quickly
for the anticipated delivery. Mitch wandered alone and wondered, peering in the empty storefronts as he tried to dream
of a more perfect union.

CHAPTER 22:

WE ALL HAVE TO DIE
SOMETIME

The next morning after searching all night, Macbeth's rescue craft slipped past the wreckage of the *Danny Boy*. Cautiously, they maneuvered it back into the relative safety of the harbor. Macbeth's crew, more concerned about the last survivor they found, docked the weathered boat at the swaying dock.

With the care reserved for a loved one, the town's quilting club waited on the dock to help the shocked victim. Visibly shaken, the young sailor gratefully accepted blankets and coffee, then shuffled up the dock following a few women and militia. In disbelief at what had happened, the sailor questioned the superiority he once so steadfastly believed in.

While a few of the rescue crew walked off the dock, a brilliant and blinding flash filled the early morning dawn. The screaming sound of guard choppers accompanied by a few missiles disturbed the moment. Macbeth's defenders were caught off guard and scattered for any cover they could find. Outgunned and scared, their earlier actions were now clearly to blame.

As the sound of explosions rocked the silence, the sky turned ablaze with flames and shooting rubble. The intensity only hell knew suddenly reduced a fishing shack and objects to burning piles. Modern weapons once again were ruthless, as they discriminated against no one in their calculated fury.

Those caught in the crossfire looked for any type of cover aside from the wooden boats they had just left, and, running for their lives, a few were gunned down. The new captive with no guards was running free, in a strange land filled with the sights and sounds of war.

The fishing skiff that was their rescue craft was burning like an October bonfire, as the old wood snapped, crackled, and popped. Streamers of flames shot skyward as the little bit of fuel that remained for the engine ignited and finished the boat off.

With the sky of the harbor aglow, a century of dried wood reacted to the allure of the spreading flames. With fear for one's own skin, the stunned men manning their guard post started shooting wildly into the morning sky. There were no real targets; only haunting visions of an enemy filled their overwhelmed minds. They had no doubt now that the sanctity of their island had truly been violated.

Hovering above the glow of many small fires, the chopper pilots had no choice but to return fire at the militia. With blast of small arms fire aimed their way, they were nothing more than big floating targets. More missiles were released in haste as the situation was unraveling for the invaders also.

Additional missiles then streaked widely through the town, the first burying its painted nose cone into poor Fanny's business. In one loud explosion, Fanny's was reduced to a burning pile of rubble, syrup, pancake batter, and memories.

It was too hard for anyone to grasp what was happening

so quickly. Mitch ran down Main Street, just trying to size up the unraveling scene of chaos, not really realizing the danger he was in. Stopping in the street, he saw a gun lying on the road where it must have been dropped in retreat. With not much thought about the pros and cons of his action, he picked it up, hoping to feel a bit safer with the cold steel barrel he commanded.

Feeling the intense heat of the fire from Fanny's, he ran faster. Keeping his head down tightly, gripping the silent gun, the rules of a rational society seemed abandoned. Choppers seemed to be flying every which way, following no rules of engagement, just dodging in and out of the safety of the darkness, randomly strafing the town and surrounding neighborhood.

Glass, wood, and debris were rocketed through the exploding air, as explosion after explosion rocked this part of the island. This was definitely a calculated show of excessive force, meant to get the islanders' attention. It clearly had their attention.

The islander's forts of sandbags provided no safety as one by one they were targeted and destroyed, sending clouds of sand and body parts rocketing through the sky. It didn't take long for Macbeth's defenders to realize their only hope for living was to run like hell. It was every man and woman for himself. Most scattered in many directions, while listening to the sick sound of bullets hitting metal and flesh in agonizing symphonies of pain and destruction.

A few of the militia, still brave in their retreat, shot back randomly, aiming their weapons at the churning night sky. Targets were many, but opportunities were few. It made no difference at which dark shadow they shot, it did little to slow them down. The bravest were no match for the wrath of attack choppers. The angels of death just kept coming back run after run, taking advantage of the panic they had masterfully created.

A chopper, intent on ignoring the random return fire, put down on the old wooden dock next to the burning rescue skiff. A contingent of SWAT guards jumped out of the chopper onto the creaky dock and secured a small rescue area with the help of a hot 50-caliber.

The island's militia, in blind confusion, was not ready for this heavy of a response. With overwhelming force, the guard quickly apprehended and shoved the dazed sailor into the side of the beating chopper, which vanished in a whisk of wind and salty spray; as fast as the rescuers had arrived, they became just a vanishing blur in the brisk night.

Mitch screamed for a wounded girl walking to get down. It was one of Lynn's friends in the wrong place at the wrong time. With not a minute to spare he pushed her down, forcing her face first into the hard ground.

"Mister!" she screamed, crying. "I'm shot!"

Without a moment to reply, Mitch shoved her pretty head back down as a blast of hot lead danced across the pavement inches from her head.

Spitting rock and dirt chips from her mouth, she looked at Mitch with watering eyes of shock. She couldn't find the words to thank him as she pulled him even closer. Pushing her back, he screamed, trying to shock her into action.

"You've got to get out of here--quick! Stay down and get into the damn woods and head toward the mine. Don't look back! I'm telling you, that's your only chance. Those other choppers will be back soon. They smells blood, young or old, I don't think it matters. You get the hell out of here while you have a chance. GO!"

He yanked her up and pointed her on her way. She didn't need to be told a second time as she ran scared, thankful for the new man in town.

Macbeth's scattered militia was in disarray, with the lines of communication nonexistent. It wasn't the all for one they imagined. A few with sense enough to do something about the slaughter brought out some of the captured handheld missiles. Busting open the wooden crates, the olive-green ordinances were quickly armed and readied. The men were more than willing, as the blood of battle was flowing hot within most, just hoping to have a chance to even up the score of the lop-sided battle and bring it to an end.

The mainland's next victims of this seemingly senseless show of force soon tasted the islander's wrath. With its engine exhausting heat, the missile was a blur as it streaked down the street. The chopper, more interested in strafing anything that moved, never saw it coming, even as its alarms sounded. One missile into the chopper's fuselage, and it was reduced to a flaming fireball.

Slamming sideways to earth in its final moments, into the drug store the chopper crashed. Years of memories from prescriptions to sodas were engulfed in the inferno. As if the searing flames weren't enough, the whole building exploded in a fuel- and ordinance-inspired explosion. In just seconds, Paxton's famous sundaes were just melted memories, and the old building joined the other raging infernos in town.

Overlooking the destruction from the pine-covered hill,

the captured tank started taking random pot shots. Lucking out in this wild skeet shoot, the tank crew hit a rear rotor of another chopper. Its rotor damaged, the screaming chopper started spinning wildly out of control. Spinning faster, then faster, its crew lost their bearings, as their reality became a dizzying blur. With no control of the chopper or themselves, all hope was lost as the doomed chopper slammed into the bridge of the sunken *Danny Boy*. In its final act, the glow of the burning chopper lit up the harbor. Unforgiving or maybe an act of penance, the *Danny Boy* cradled the smoldering fuselage in its steel grip.

The rest of the choppers, still all too sure of their mission, kept coming. This was much more than a rescue mission. Surely the term "rescue" was just a cover for the real reason behind the attack. Missiles screamed as they pierced the dawn, aiming at nothing in particular, just trying to cause random and unforgettable damage.

Mitch knew this shit didn't happen in America; everyone negotiates, everyone from the scum-sucking drug dealers to the crazed kidnappers get their chance. Why not here?

"What the hell is going on!" he screamed. Who could he blame for this insanity? This should never have happened, so why was it? Mitch was beginning to second-guess himself, as the flames and combat were just too close to his personal comfort zone.

On the edge, and almost out of control, he ran through the town. With survival on his mind he stumbled on some unseen debris. Falling like a hunk of dead meat, he thumped quickly to the ground. Then with the feeling of cold coagulated Jell-O on his face, he looked up to the horror of seeing some poor soul's limb lying next to him; a gold wedding band still held its place on the soot-covered finger of this piece of a man.

In horror, he pushed away as he stared in disbelief. The early-morning battle had lit up the red dawn sky. Black, billowing smoke and flames shot up and down the road. Mitch was sure the governor and his aides were happy in their revenge. Blood was so sweet, as this governor knew his name would never be forgotten.

From where Mitch had retreated he could see the old island homes, burning in the neighborhood behind Main Street. With nothing and nobody to stop the roaring flames, they engulfed home after home. A sickening, clammy feeling came over Mitch as he thought about Kate. "God, please watch over her," he prayed silently. Feeling more human, he felt the need for somebody more superior than mankind to help.

Not feeling safe in the open, Mitch ran up the hill to a well-protected fox hole.

Jumping in, he tried to catch his breath as he stared into the eyes of the defenders. Big-eyed scared stares greeted him, when he realized the soot-covered men were no more than boys with guns.

"What the hell are you doing up here?" Mitch demanded.

"Nothing, mister. We got caught here when all the shooting started." Rolling his body over, he exposed his AK-47, which he caressed in his young hands. "Me and my boys, we're ready to die for the cause, I think?"

"Bullshit, you're ready! That gun isn't going to help you against them, only slow you down when you should be running like hell. Put it down before you hurt yourself or us. Fuck the damn cause." Not believing this was really happening, he looked for the right words, but couldn't find them.

"You all know your parents must be going crazy worrying about you!"

"We just wanted to see what was going on, mister. We're sorry; we just got stuck out here when the fighting started. We're not fooling you--we're scared. Please help us get out of here?" the youngest of the three said.

"I don't know anymore." Pausing for a moment, Mitch said, "Maybe we're safest here."

Another boy, still curious, stuck his head up to look around. Pissed-off Mitch yelled, "That is, if we keep you out of sight. Get down--what is with you kids?" He didn't have the answers, and what he did have, he was afraid, wouldn't save these boys if they made a run for it.

In an unpredictable moment, their simple hideout became a target. A chopper must have smelled blood as it aimed its weapons toward the gunner's nest. Who knows how they were spotted: too late to blame anyone. Grabbing for their weapons, the boys shot back, shooting at anything, just hoping to make a good shot to scare the threat away.

In a flash, the boy next to Mitch who had been so curious the moment before took a burning shot to the chest. Mitch was helpless with all the bullets flying around them; all they could do was stay down while listening to the young voice gurgling for help. Mitch picked up his gun and shot back with a vengeance he had never felt before--unrelenting anger as this orgy of blood began while the angel of death waited.

Mitch had never felt the extreme need for someone else's death before. His skin became red and wet with sweat while all his energy centered on taking out the returning chopper.

His once-painful wounds were no longer an issue in his altered state of being, as he shot clip after clip into the dawn air. As far as his reality for the moment was concerned, there were no men in that chopper, just a killing machine going after a group of people, he had no choice but to protect.

Halting his fire for a moment, Mitch ripped open the wounded boy's shirt and saw the blood pulsing out of the gaping wound in his chest. With only a moment to spare, he ripped the blood-drenched shirt and stuffed a piece of it into the gut-filled hole. It was surely too late for this lad, as all they could do was watch as his life bled away.

The pilot wanted more. The job wasn't done until the nest of traitors went silent. With all the chopper's missiles spent, it still didn't matter. The chopper had its guns firing again and again for no other reason than to kill. With the rhythmic bam-bam-bam-bam, they filled their little area with bursting hunks of hot lead dancing through the dirt.

The boys with guns were beyond scared, crying harder as they pressed the triggers even more. Their moment of innocence had been lost, as they too would share the nightmares of war. With spent shells and warm blood covering the floor of the bunker, this foxhole was real.

Shrapnel blanketed the area; its hot metal burned its way into everyone's skin, as it burned through the soft cotton clothes they wore. No time to tend to the bloodied wounds, while they shot round after round toward the chopper. This was war and nothing less, as a child's fantasy erupted into hell's backyard.

As he swooped in lower, Mitch saw the pilot's emotionless face. He and the pilot made eye contact. With the look of nothing more than a scared killer, Mitch emptied his burning gun's last clip into the cockpit. He watched his bullets streaking on a mission of deliverance, as they danced towards the hardened cockpit. One shot was finally lucky when the glass of the cockpit cracked and shattered into a thousand glistening pieces of glass. Like a winter snow on a moonlit dawn, its pieces dropped to the raped earth.

For the defenders in the smoking foxhole, wrapped up in their frenzy for survival, a crack in the armor had appeared. Concentrating harder, they fired their burning guns at the vulnerable war machine. Piercing its aluminum-covered hull and cockpit with bullets, they watched the first sign of black puffs of smoke escaping from the skin.

Mitch, with nothing more than killing on his mind, aimed straight at the vulnerable cockpit and unloaded his clip into the dazed pilots. It was them or Mitch, and Mitch had a story to tell. The chopper with systems down veered quickly to the left as the pilot closest to Mitch collapsed in pain.

The shooting stopped as the chopper turned sharply away. Mitch and the boys watched the wounded chopper make one final banking turn up into the valley, then plunge almost in slow motion into the dew-covered field that spread out below the castle.

At the instant of impact, the chopper exploded into a giant glowing fireball, its flames slipping through the field casting an eerie glow on the ruins, depositing bits and pieces of metal and crew into the virgin field. The unlucky chopper burned away into a smoldering mess, as the forgiving earth had no choice but to absorb the insanity of the sins of the moment.

With victory at hand, the boys jumped in celebration

of their deliverance. Like a band of hungry primitive hunters finally killing the great menacing beast, they danced. Mitch never knew such joy as that of surviving, though it was eventually tempered by the reality of what had just taken place, and the wounded and struggling little friend.

The sun would rise slower than normal that morning, as the light of day revealed the carnage that had just taken place. His world had changed for the worse that early morning.

Mitch bent down to help the wounded youth by his side, the child pleaded no more. His once-bright eyes gazed at the heavens, but the life glow was gone. Touching his hand, Mitch could feel the warmth of life retreating as the cold of death invaded. He could only pray that this unfortunate youth was heading where his eyes stared. Death had never been easy for Mitch, only now it was many times harder with the death of child.

While morning light filtered in, the remaining choppers headed back out to the safety of the sea. The chopper crews were shaken up from the experience of a battle most had never anticipated. "Casualties" a word that had not been used by the guard in a long time, but because of arrogance, it was heard once again. Live and learn, the armchair generals would say, but no excuse they could create would ease or justify the loss of someone's life.

The romantic town Mitch had come to write about had been destroyed. What little was still standing, he was sure, would be burning in a short time. By most counts, four choppers had been shot out of the sky with no survivors. Macbeth suffered much for a small town: eight killed, close to twenty injured, some forever. There were casualties on both sides in a battle that should never have been fought. While both sides had showed their will to fight, carnage and destruction had won.

The once-peaceful people of the island were now warriors consecrated by blood of battle. There were dead, now instant martyrs for the cause, as loss and suffering had bred revenge and the potential for more pain on both sides.

Insurance agent John Dawson, with Pharmacist Little, lined up whole bodies, and pieces of corpses pulled from the wreckage of chopper. In a macabre ritual they lined the cold carcasses up like trophies from a great hunt. With their weapons of war in hand, they posed proudly for their grotesque pictures. They were the proud victors from today's hunt. Mitch almost caught the humor in it, if it hadn't been for the memory of the young corpse, lying alone and cold in an empty foxhole. These men had clearly crossed the line and now were killers for the cause: no turning back for these two.

The order that should have been given earlier was issued to whoever would listen:

"All non-essential personnel must go to the security of the mines," a voice said across the few still-working public address speakers. Most had no issue with this order; by then the feeling was unanimous, as all knew somehow they needed to turn this out-of-control situation off.

Tom and Jack, in disbelief, surveyed the damage, mystified that even this governor would turn up the heat this much. In stubborn denial, Tom wondered again if the cause was worth this. Tom had a strong feeling that both sides needed some kind of dialog before another slaughter resulted; maybe surrender wasn't such a bad option after all. Jack agreed for the most part, as long as it didn't involve surrender on Macbeth's part.

"Tom, I feel the same guilt you do. But you know if we give in, the blood we have already spilled will be in vain. If we give up at the first sight of blood and surrender, then we were never a real cause. I say we pray for those lost and injured, pick up the pieces, and stick to the plan. We can talk if they want, and we negotiate if they will, but we must stick to the plan!"

Tom agreed reluctantly and knew Jack was right, as much as it hurt. Distracted for the moment, he watched as Midge trudged up the hill to have a better look. Midge, always one of the strongest emotionally, wasn't herself that day as she cried for what had become of her town.

The governor had called the islanders' bluff. No matter how mighty they had appeared, in the heat of battle, the final score settled the bet. It was time to use the remaining hostages to the island's advantage. Human safety shields the POWs would be, positioned strategically around the island and highly visible. Tom had high hopes for this human ploy, hoping the aggressors would think twice about shooting their own, sparing both sides any further loss.

Mitch sat alone for a moment on the side of the hill watching the drifting smoke as the rain slowly began. Refreshing raindrops mixed with the bright rays of sun as she poked through the parting clouds. It seemed that nature was cleansing itself of all the sins mankind had just committed.

The sudden sound of gunfire had been replaced by the crackling and hissing of the rain, as it blanketed the smoldering debris. The rain had to be good, as its wetness put out the remaining hot spots of the town. The rain did not run clear, but black, as the rain tried in vain to cleanse the spoiled island.

That day Mitch and many others had crossed their personal lines in the sand. A journalist is paid to be unbiased and judge a story on only facts, and most importantly, never to choose sides. Journalists are to present the facts and let the reader decide for themselves. Mitch had broken the rule: he was emotionally involved with his story, and even more with the cause. Deep inside he knew he had intentionally picked up a weapon and fired it, and it felt good! In his furious revenge, he had also become murderer. He was now no better than the men from the choppers they had just destroyed. Does death make both sides equal? Does one bad cross out another bad? He had chosen his side; he was as guilty as all the rest, his neutrality a voided point. Baptism by blood--he knew it all too well. Mitch belonged again, just another of the family of Macbeth.

He remembered back to his forgotten family and they just didn't feel as close as before; he had found another place to call home. As sick as it sounded, his life was fulfilling again. Life and death walked hand-in-hand, and as he remembered from covering wars before, he knew sadly how close the two would work together.

Feeling lucky to be alive, Mitch felt unworthy to return to the foxhole, but knew he had to go. With no one else rushing to the task, he picked up the cold body of the boy. This young kid had deserved so much more...too late, though; his life was over. Death in a random act leaves little choice for the living, other than suffering.

Slowly walking with the added weight of the body, he eased on through the ruins of town. Fully knowing the pain he would deliver, he searched for the boy's parents, exchanging shocked and saddened stares along the way with whoever would look. Hopefully his lifeless body painted a picture of what these people could expect if an answer to this carnage wasn't negotiated soon.

Hearing a piercing scream, Mitch knew he had found the youth's mother. With little reason for his untimely death, other than the ignorance of youth, he handed his motionless body to his overcome father, who was now lost without his boy, forever regretting teaching him how to use a gun. A boy would always be a boy in his parent's eyes, but to Mitch earlier that day in the foxhole, the youth had been a comrade cradling his gun as they defended each other when the firing began.

That day was way too much for him. He needed one person who hopefully would listen. Searching the faces of the curious, he frantically searched for Kate, hoping to receive some needed forgiveness for his actions. Mitch knew the only forgiveness that could help would have to come from deep inside, and that wasn't coming any time soon. In his darkness, he still noticed the rainbow in the sky. What a contrast to what had just transpired…the beauty of nature, and the worst in mankind. Was God watching and smiling? Could it be?

In small gatherings, islanders questioned if there was ever to be a future for any of them. They were guilty, guilty of not wanting anything more than freedom. In their sorrow, repentance was only a heartbeat away, as the town's young and old remembered and prayed for all of their sins.

CHAPTER 23:

BIG BROTHER IS WATCHING

Issues and wrong decisions were spinning so quickly out of control on the mainland that the governor and his staff were on the roller coaster ride of their political career. The administration had made the big play and then it seemed was ready to blow up in their face. Sure, in their haste and ignorance they had rescued a sailor, but they had lost choppers and crewmen because of it.

Congress, with the feeling they were sitting on a powder keg, screamed at each other to do more than watch. The outspoken legislators wanted to know how any administration could have ordered his men into such an unstable situation. The governor and his cabinet were paid well to know what was going on. Who in their right mind would command the weekend warriors into the eternal pit without fully sizing up the explosive situation?

"As usual, too quick to thunder, that ignorant bastard!" the old house speaker said.

"Life to these political cowards has always been a show. For God's sake, human life has no worth to these crooks." The house speaker was old; he didn't give a damn if he shot from the hip and hurt someone's feelings. A point had to be made.

"Massachusetts is still in my union," he continued, "and unless all of you forget, we and the people are the union. If we had any balls – excuse me, ladies – we would draft a measure, condemning the actions of this runaway few of this out-of-control administration, and run the damn state ourselves while we sort out this mess. But--and this is a big but--most of you don't have the balls. Most of you are sitting there nervous, wondering if this old fart in front of you is going to make you do things your public won't like. Well, ladies and gentlemen, shit happens! I'll follow my conscience; I wish a few of you would follow yours. If you remember one thing, remember your conscience shouldn't be reflected by the polls you think you need to follow...get it? All of you, it is time to make a stand, and for once do the right thing."

His young congressional aide smiled ear to ear, knowing the uncomfortable spot this old geezer had just put his fellow lawmakers in. Shaking hands as he left the podium, a few really admired the gruff old man for his honesty, while the younger and newly elected in Congress, got nervous, as they could worry about saying the right words to preserve their political future.

The debate raged on, while the Speaker searched the aisles of the hall for allies. In his wisdom, he realized his views set him on a lonely road, although many a man and woman knew his way to be the right path yet chose a less prickly route. The session raged on until a tired Speaker, borrowing an antic from decades ago, took off one of his black wing tip shoes and banged it hard against his desk to get the attention of a worried Congress.

"Fools--and I say this loosely--I have neither the time nor

inclinations to listen to you argue any longer. We know in our hearts what the right answer is, so let's vote and save us all the rest of this humiliation."

A daring few in Congress wanted action, while most wanted more time to let the state settle their own problem. Many still hung on to the fact that any state has self-governing rights. The vote was taken, and as the political dust settled, Massachusetts was still in charge, with big brother watching more closely over their shoulder.

This was surely uncharted territory in a world of home-town militia, domestic terrorism, and a state administration getting too big for its own good. The federal government should have been involved, but the Constitution was specific about the federal government's role in a state's self-rule.

The Speaker and a few others demanded that martial law should be declared in at least that portion of the state. Outnumbered in a young Congress, all they could do was watch from the sidelines, while in her Oval Office a president, feeling the heat, worried about the many what-ifs and when the critical time was right for the commander-in-chief to step in.

Working the phone and calling in a lot of old favors, the governor was able to hide many of the blunders committed that day. Thanks to an effective partial media blackout, many atrocities were never witnessed by the media or the public searching for information. Limited coverage worked well for this lucky governor, while his overpaid administration con-tained the damage the best they could.

Like most events, in time the truth would sneak out, the truth every bit as damning then. Riding the wind of a free press, the scattered reports were snuck out by a few of the news crews that returned from around burning island. If just one of the reports was true and could be verified, it would shake the very pillars the governor had ruled from. Too many stories: who could you believe? It was still early as many tried to figure out what had really taken place on the smoldering island.

CNN seemed to have the most up-to-date information for the awakening public. Thanks to aerial surveillance and a keen sense for gathering the news, CNN was able to paint a clear picture. The governor figured he had clout, and he would use it to dissuade the news editor from blowing up this powder keg. The seasoned editor had been through this type of intimidation before, and at that time the fish had been much larger than this governor.

Getting his phone call through to the editor was no problem this time. With what she knew had happened, any editor would have wanted to talk to the governor.

"Hello, can I help you?" the editor answered.

"Honey, I am your governor. Can you put me in touch with the man in charge?"

"Now come on, who is really asking?" she replied.

"The big bad wolf," he said with a perverted little laugh. "Don't you worry that pretty little head of yours; he will want to talk to me."

"Well, sorry--there isn't a 'he,' and this 'she' is it. Can I help you?"

"Well, honey, congratulations. You're talking to Massachusetts' most honorable governor, but you can just call me Gene if you want."

"I guess I should be thrilled talking to you, right?" she sarcastically replied.

"I'm sure most editors would be."

"Yes, you're probably right, especially with all the trouble and embarrassment you've caused your state?"

"Honey, I didn't start any of these problems. These are little people with big unrealistic ideas and aspirations. I am the solution to their rebellion, and this back yard fight is going to be over soon, if you know what I mean."

"Oh and I'm sure you and your administration had nothing to do with pushing the island over the brink, right?"

Detecting a bit of sarcasm in her voice, the governor raised his voice into the phone. "You know, just because you're a woman and women have been held down in your world, you don't have to disagree with everything a man says to you, honey!"

Getting more than a bit agitated at the sexist clod, the editor shot back. "Don't you dare disrespect me and continue to call me 'honey!'"

"Well stop flooding the air waves with this sensationalized crap about Macbeth. My brave men are risking their lives trying to control this damn out of control situation." Pausing, he slowed down in order to catch his accelerated breath. "There is a time and a place for these colorful reports, but not now. You news people are all alike, just dying to sell a story, fill some space and sell more ads. You all are nothing more than legal whores! All of you!"

"Excuse me, what did you call me? And can I quote that?"

"You heard me. You have plenty of other bullshit to report on besides my state and administration."

"You're telling me I shouldn't be reporting on this?"

"Yes, I am. You're fanning the flames of discontent and sympathy for these backyard terrorists."

"Governor, we're just reporting the story you started."

"You ignorant bitch, I didn't start this mess, but I'm sure as hell going to end it."

"I'm quoting that!"

"This isn't a damn interview. Can't you see I'm looking for some help here?"

"Sir, the news has always been unbiased around here and will continue to be unbiased. This bitch, only reports what we see and what is fact."

"Bullshit, honey. You haven't seen shit. If your people don't ease up, we're going to make it rough."

"Oh, now you are threatening me?"

"Call it what you want, honey. Massachusetts is a big state with our share of bad people, some of whom would do about anything for some quick reward-- understand me?"

"I'm still not your honey, but I think I'll quote that threat, right after I call my lawyer. I still have a say around here."

"You know, really…who's going to believe you? It's your word against mine. What is it with you women when we give you a little power? Do you feel like you have to get back at all males for your years in the kitchen?"

"Governor, I have a show to run, and have less time to deal with a fool and his insults like you." With a smile of satisfaction on her face, she slammed the receiver down.

"You bitch!" the governor screamed to late into the phone. Knowing he had been beaten by a better woman, he slammed the phone down and kicked his trash can across the floor.

The justified CNN editor knew now that there was a lot more to the story than met the eye. With a feeling that something bigger was going on, she issued the order to start interrupting the news with the new headlines "THE BATTLE FOR MACBETH." Not wanting to waste any more time, she searched for information and reports from the many eyewitnesses, just hoping her reports could turn up the heat on an administration that had been untouchable for too long.

The college kids, as before, took interest in the increasing news reports on the uprising and retaliation of the island. Peaceful demonstrations were popping up at scattered campuses around the country. They gathered once again in Ohio around Kent State's peace rock, a hotbed of revolution in the '70s, and still a symbol of defiance. A few concerned individuals at first, then hundreds, chanted for answers, beating the old drums of revolution. The bell-bottoms and peace symbols were gone, but the mood of change and answers was still evident--a few remembered the pain, and laid flowers where the four students had fallen years earlier.

The news reports became more graphic as the day wore on. It was getting nearly impossible to hide the carnage that had occurred through the night. By the light of day, the total destruction became more evident.

Was it revolution, or was the governor's administration at fault? Regardless of who started this crisis, it had never been public policy to launch an assault on any group of American citizens. Negotiation had always come first – you just don't attack your own people. Something had gone so very wrong somewhere, and other people whose rights had been ignored for years wanted answers!

Scattered reports of social unrest started coming in. Senior citizens related to a few on the island, in a assisted living home became unmanageable, rolling wheelchairs, throwing dietetic Jell-O and bedpans at bewildered orderlies and nurses for turning off the breaking news reports. Some residents were temporarily stilled by being restrained in their wheelchairs, shocked at the thought of a government attacking its own people. Most, condemned to their final plight in the vestige of controlled retirements, were now re-energized by the plight of a people.

Many a forgotten veteran of past conflicts tucked neatly away in their homes were now ready to take up arms, grab their old uniforms if they could, and rally to Macbeth's defense, wondering if the government they had defended could really let this rogue state inflict this type of retaliation on its own people.

Elementary kids with relatives on the island locked their teachers out of their classroom, with their little protest attracting the local news while their concerned parents blamed each other's children for stealing their own child's guarded innocence. The children's crudely drawn pictures of protest were taped to the outside windows for all the media to see, expressing the compassion only a child could harbor for the plight of a fellow child in need.

In many churches, the righteous women with their religious purity and holy beads all prayed for themselves and for the eternal penance they didn't need; their little world was more frightening then, as their Monday through Sunday social structure seemed to be capable of unraveling. Would Sunday ever come so they once again could dress up for the community and show how religious they were? A few steps away, the homeless and abandoned on the street prayed from the heart for the lost, unknown souls on the island, forgotten and alone, a feeling and emotion they dealt with daily.

What had happened to a controlled solution, most wondered? A grocery store line became a line of confrontation as one point was argued against the other, while underpaid store managers became referees for a game that couldn't be won. When little cans of corn and beans became projectiles in a civil war erupting at a local Kroger, doors were locked for a cool down. These events started those little ripples that the islanders had hoped would surge into a great tidal wave of discontent. With a greater power's help, hidden feelings and emotions would surface and lead this country on a personal crusade for the good of all the Union, or so the islanders prayed.

Massachusetts was beginning to stretch at the seams; the police and units on the guard demanded to be informed. A people in the dark could be a dangerous thing in their quest for answers, and the governor knew that. In his world of partial truths, he also knew that if the public found out all the truths about what happened on Macbeth, his career would be over. In the administration's nervousness, the cover-ups continued, as one story was changed to another.

As far as the governor and his yes men were concerned, the deceit had to continue. The governor still felt safe in his concrete palace, surrounded by the body guards he kept. Some said the guards were there to protect him from his closest aides, all more loyal to his fat political wallet than to the soul of the man. With the governor's battle and bunker mentality consuming his every thought, the governor was hunkering down, waiting to wave his big stick one more time to solve this widening crisis. In his delusional mind, the presidency was still only a step away from his state's throne.

Anchored off the island, the guard still felt fully in control and knew they had the supreme firepower and the will to use it. To these men, the faceless people on the island were nothing more than modern-day barbarians, and the only good barbarian was a dead one. Their total destruction and eradication was best for them, to spare them the gallows--gallows that certainly awaited these contemporary traitors.

It was a pity that only a few weeks earlier these barbarians had been their friends and customers, many patronizing the coastal businesses. The island's money had always been good for the local economies. How quickly those in uniform with a cold gun had forgotten.

With beer smuggled on board one of the anchored gaurd frigates, a group of guards held a little party to relieve the boredom. Tempers flared as the group overindulged in the brews, when one remembered the date and the virtues of a beautiful girl from the island. She was no barbarian to this man, as she made this young guard's wildest dreams come true. Awash with visions of an erotic evening drifting through his drunken head, he was beaten to a crisp pulp, as he made a brave stand for a young island girl. This was just another example of an unplanned casualty of a situation and a people on the edge.

At the northern end of the island, volunteer firemen hunkered down in the abandoned weather station, a discarded government structure left over from the Cold War, adopted as a concrete bunker by the islanders. Thick concrete walls and sand bags made all the would-be defenders feel safe, protected from the elements and most unseen threats. The men would have been justified in their thoughts, if it had been just a war of hand guns. Modern warfare is never equal, as some would learn too late.

It was an early afternoon when the mainland's elite commandos tried the island's back door. Jebb Stuart and his son Nile were sitting out front watching the tall waving pine trees and listening to the methodical white surf pounding the rocky cliffs. Both were trying to be good lookouts--but still, a father and son, who never seemed to get to spend enough time together, had a moment. Today that all changed as Nile, for once, really talked to his dad, and for once, a father really listened.

It was a good day for both, as the other men inside the would-be bunker relaxed and talked like guys do when the women are away. The bullshit was flowing, as there wasn't much else to do while time slipped away. Visions of manhood and young women still flowed as freely as time. One man tried to outdo the other with stories of their manhood, all eager for an easy laugh.

Jebb heard the rustle of the birds in the woods, but didn't think much about it. Nature was still alive and well, seemingly handling the assault better than man. That all changed, as a single handheld rocket came screaming out of the dark cover of the spring woods, zeroing in on the open weather station door, an oversized target for any well-trained man.

He never even had a chance to grab his young son, as the complex vaporized, along with the precious lives. The simplicity of the attack was over before the men breathed their last dying breath. A tattered Macbeth flag fluttered on the flagpole atop the pile of mangled smoking concrete. As a spring day grew silent again, the commandos swept back into the cover of the artificial darkness of the woods, to high-five each other and rejoice in their absolute victory.

The island wasn't so big that Jack and the others didn't notice the loud explosion, followed by the rising smoke. When the weather station couldn't be reached by radio, Jack figured the worst. The assault had begun again. "Why won't they negotiate with us?" he yelled. Summoning his men, some kind of response had to be forthcoming, as Jack assembled a posse to investigate the obvious.

Nervous but more angered, some of Macbeth's militia applied their fresh war paint, and then planned their sweet revenge, all just waiting for the command that would set them on their way.

The media, as always, was fanning the fire of discontent across the country with the real story. Soap operas were interrupted with special reports on the growing crisis, while pissed off women lying on their couches in well-worn tent dresses threw fuzzy slippers at the TV screens for interrupting their precious world of soaps.

CNN slipped in the caption "THE BEGINNING OF A REVOLUTION" to all its news reports. Was it war or revolution? Paranoid coastal housewives started tying up the phone lines with questions and answers for whoever would listen to their growing panic.

Meanwhile, at some local neighborhood tavern, countless husbands fed up with their nagging and questioning wives drowned their sorrows in glasses of beer, reliving their tours of duty – mythical or real – to whatever barmaid or stool queen would listen. It never really mattered, though. Talk was good to these few, as it created the only tours of duty some of these men never knew.

Talk radio was buzzing, while none of the listeners wanted to talk about any of the over-talked school issues or crooked cops. Phone lines to an Ohio talk radio station were jammed with protesters calling for the removal of the morning jokester and his insensitivity toward the issue. For once, WNIR's Couch Burner was silenced. Most wanted a voice of reason through this time of uncertainty. All anyone wanted was to talk about Macbeth's struggle, good versus evil. Was it really a struggle just for them, or in the big picture of life was it really for all?

Most of the concerned portion of the public wondered and contemplated; maybe this really wasn't a crazy cult or terrorist group...or was it? The freed media made the country aware of that, and the enraged media screamed from editorials to front pages that these islanders were good and honest Americans. They were the Americans you never hear about, only it was their turn to get shafted. All of this was because nobody had the will or the inclination to listen to and possibly learn their problems. Through the smoke of island they listened then, it seemed to be too late.

In mid afternoon, the activity on the coastline was at a frantic pace. Truck after truck of military personnel and weapons arrived. The island had to be contained at any cost. With the secessionists blocked on the island, the state's administration thought the situation was containable.

Washington was getting nervous as its daily news conference was all about Macbeth. To Washington there were too many questions, and no new answers. The press secretary stuck to the administration's line. "We believe in the constitutional self-rule of the state government. Regardless of our personal views, we are a union of states. If we step over the boundaries this time, we will open up Pandora's Box. Until the time Massachusetts' administration feels it cannot handle the situation, we will stand by and be ready to respond with any reasonable request we receive."

The US Navy, gray and menacing, blocked the outer sea lanes. Since deep water wasn't infringing on the state's self-governing rights, technically Washington wasn't interfering.

The world was watching as the situation continued to sizzle and ferment.

Containment was a great idea, in theory, only the idea for containment was too late. The armchair generals and would-be politicians didn't have a clue as to Macbeth's next calculated move. The divers from Macbeth had arrived that previous evening, just looking toward the island and waiting for the sign that had to come for their turn to mix things up on the nervous coastline.

Jack and Tom never really thought the need would come to attack the mainland. The last thing those two wanted was to inconvenience the mainland's public. But with the attack on the weather shed, things were different now. A larger and final invasion had to come, and they were sure it would be deadly; a severe distraction was now their only option, and had to take place soon. The time for negotiation seemed to have run out, as Tom raised his hand, clasping the flare, and shot three distinct red rockets screaming into the air.

To the divers used to long boring days on an oil rig, these were turning out to be some of the hardest hours they ever had to wait. Sitting isolated under the cover of the boardwalk, running their bored fingers through the gritty sand, they listened to the clatter of the activity overhead. Unfortunately, they were witnesses to the scattered explosions and drifting smoke above the island, only guessing as to what the real score was.

The divers knew the island had survived by the increased military activity above them. What was the real damage? Who was wounded? Who was killed? There was no time for these haunting mind games, as they reminded each other to focus on their mission. All knew they had a job to do, if the survival of the island's people became their responsibility.

Jeff was watching the gulls dancing among the beach's trash when he noticed the first flare. He slapped Stu Babe on the side of his big head, and the two stared as the second and third flares flew. That was the sign: their real fears had come true, as they would wait until early evening to make their next move.

The hours passed as another evening quickly approached and the divers moved in. One by one, they blended into the swell of military activity on the main road, gathering again in groups of two, in their confiscated guard uniforms. The uniforms either ran too short, or too long, but for make-believe pirates in tight situations, they couldn't be choosy. All together again, they now marched in step with the beast. Into the henhouse these foxes went.

The sun was beginning to set and the safety of the approaching darkness promised some form of limited security, the mine shaft door swung open, and the determined island cavalry set out on fresh horses to right a serious wrong.

Galloping with the full retreating sun to their sweating backs, they rode two by two down the dirt-covered cobblestone road toward the ruins of the weather station.

Advancing like lightning to the open field, they spread out into one large, charging line of fear and snorting beasts. All as one, they came to a halt at the edge of the field, shocked at the sight of the smoldering rubble, now visibly shaken by the unnecessary deaths of their friends. There was but one purpose for their mission now, as the passion for revenge was ignited within each soldier.

The resting commandos heard the distant thunder coming down the only road. The thunder grew to a roar of a hundred hoofed feet, slapping every echoing stone with the beasts' mighty muscles. The unfamiliar noise caused the commandos out of raw curiosity to venture from their safety of the black forest to the edge of the clearing to watch.

The commandos knew for a short, almost reassuring second, that they outgunned whatever the militia threw at them. But it would be too late when the shooting started and the commandos realized that they couldn't see. Macbeth's sun blinded their limited view by shooting its evening rays straight down the valley at the confused commandos. Its distant rays scorched and burned into their panicking eyes as they strained to see and hoped for a small glimpse of something to shoot at. It was all in vain, as the sun's final evening rays evened the score. Macbeth's army with raw firepower took advantage of a large friend, when the order for an eye for an eye was acted upon.

With the screams of twenty-five wannabe Mongolian knights, Genghis Khan's lost clan was reborn, the crazed men and boys of Macbeth charged, then sliced and shot down the blinded commandos. Nerves shattered, the shocked and wounded commandos raced in fear, heading for the sudden deliverance of the cliffs. Military weapons and foolish men were fooled by such an old trick left over from a forgotten war, remembered by a child from a Sunday school lesson. God works in mysterious ways.

In utter confusion, a scared man was trampled under the feet of the horses as these beasts of burden did their masters' dirty work. This was the type of warfare that had long ago been forgotten, in a world that feared the bomb more than the beast.

Macbeth's revenge was measured in quick minutes. The three remaining commandos, scared and outnumbered, raced for the sanctuary of the steep cliffs. Chased through the dark woods by the skilled horsemen, they ran faster upon hearing the painful cries of their fallen comrades. Illogical in their reasoning, their minds were made up, as they tried to maintain their sprinting strides.

In a split-second decision, the delirious and exhausted men decided the deep water would have to be more merciful than these madmen on horses. Without a second look back, all for one and one for all, together they took a leap of faith down into the churning rocky depths. For that day, they would become heroes of the mainland and would feed the island's fish with their own fleshy offerings.

It wasn't the ending Ernie the plumber had wished, but it was final. The three commandos bobbed for a few minutes, then succumbed to the pounding surf. An eye for an eye sounded good earlier, but it sure didn't feel right then.

Death never really feels good, but even a reason like revenge still makes it no sweeter. Ernie looked toward his son, decorated with war paint and a few feathers sitting high in his saddle, an M-16 slung over his back. Confident and proud, he was enjoying his first victory, still too young and immature to realize the real pain it would cost the innocent victims who surely waited back home for their father or son to return.

Ernie was cold--not due to the weather, but because his emotions were strained. Sitting in his stiff saddle, he felt a warm tear roll down from his aged eyes. Turning away, not wanting his son to see, he looked into the eyes of Will the banker and saw tears streaming down his cheeks also. Inflicting pain was not a lesson either man wanted to learn, but learn it they must if they too were to live.

With their job done, the horsemen one by one turned their beasts away from the cliff and headed home. Ernie looked at his smiling son with a look of anger. Screaming loudly, Ernie swung his gun by its warm barrel and tossed it into the pounding surf. There had been a time when Ernie lived for his father and son activities, but this was a day he wished his son had never seen. He realized far too late that there was no valor in this shallow victory. It was just a job that had to be done, and some jobs sucked more than others. His son, then alone, questioned the pain in his father's face, realizing all at once that there was more to this man than he ever knew.

This crisis was hotter than Washington cared for. How long could they sit on the sidelines, and do nothing? A hard-headed people had seceded from the state; however, it might as well have been from the union. Washington was abuzz, as a nervous Congress screamed, starting to demand that their president to get involved. In an unnoticed instant, a cautious super power was about to blink.

President Beatrice Roosevelt, a distant descendant of a great president, humble and honest, yet cautious to act in the heat of the moment, was gravely concerned about the implication of secession. The union was only as strong as its leaders, and if this was any indication of their elected officials, shit was going to hit the national fan.

She and the Speaker of the House knew the conflict wasn't capable of engulfing the state. Many were still nervous, feeling this could be the beginning, maybe an excuse to trigger the domino effect in other towns. A lot of common folk who had a whole lot of gripes that just never seemed to get answered identified with Macbeth's revolution and thought that some good could come from this.

With investors worried and nervous over the potential of the crisis and secession spreading, the bull market reacted, as the Dow dropped 353 points. The stock market had always measured the pulse of America, and it was nervous.

Financial planners in Massachusetts and neighboring states who peddled mutual funds were afraid, as their potential client base dried up more quickly with every news flash that shot across the millions of household screens. Holding on to cash in times of uncertainty always seemed to be the frugal thing to do.

The gold and silver market crept up as precious metals became more precious, while more than a state watched and waited along with the forecasters of doom. Doomsday addicts for once were in their element, as all they had wished for could finally come true.

The crisis in reality simmered, while an alerted public panicked around the country. It seemed like a crisis of confidence. The mood grew ominous when each true or fabricated story came in. Who could they believe, when good neighbors said they heard the latest story…always from a reliable source? Who was this reliable source that always seemed to be one step ahead of everyone else? No problem finding something to talk about to your friend or enemy that day, as the vines of gossip sang loudly.

A few senior citizens and investors who had survived the Great Depression once again eyed stairwells to the roof, as their lifestyles of luxury hung in the teetering balance of desperation and despair. Too many there was but one way out, if fortunes vanished in the span of a day. How would the market react to the question of more secession or revolution?

Many fearing the worst eyed their stashed copper pennies in glass jars, as its metal content looked like it might be worth more than the respected dollar and the paper it was printed on.

Why would they all worry, for God's sake? The state guard could surely handle this small band of renegade people. Their minor revolt wasn't capable of threatening national security or any other state, the administration surmised. This was the governor's show as he preached to the federal government to stay out. If they wanted to help, the administration demanded they stop all these news reports that were fueling an already nervous people.

What could this president do? On one hand, she had firmly believed in the divine power of statehood and its independence. States didn't need big brother always jumping in. On the other hand, she had never trusted Governor Roe and his band of cronies.

In the end, she controlled the union and its destiny. History would judge and remember her decision, right or wrong. Whom do you try to please, and whose toes do you step on? She didn't have any better answer than Congress did. Something had to be done regardless. Life would go on with or without her, as her career was but a drip in the big bucket, and the fate of the union was worth the chance. The president couldn't hesitate much longer before she would have to make a decision and try to restore faith to a drifting state.

Hidden away in the recesses of her mind, the president wished she would have the opportunity to grab this slimy little man and drag him off his political throne. It was a messed-up thought for such a proper woman, but destroying him was but the tip of the problem. The state's political machine, full of greed and corruption, had a very long root.

The governor for years had built a network of political allies that lined his trenches, ready for the chance to pounce on the country's first female president. Many who fervently guarded the male bastion of society on its testosterone high secretly snickered over her untimely bad luck, in this still male-dominated world.

Even in this modern-day world, with the public more worried about the state lottery than government, there was room for corruption. Massachusetts in its greatness still had dirty secrets, while its governor and his friends hid a lot of needed cash, cold hard cash used exclusively for floating this governor's luxuries and sometimes illegal political agenda. It was a world with just enough dark spaces to hide these modern-day thieves who were not ready to let this ship of fools flounder.

In despair, and unable to get the situation out of her mind, the president flicked on the TV set and watched the screen in disbelief. On the coastline there were little old ladies and men with Depression mentalities standing in line to collect what little savings they had stashed away for a rainy day, while most of their real assets laid buried in jars or under mattresses back home. The sky was falling and Chicken Little just laughed.

The other bordering states were intently watching, wondering whether this crisis could spread, while most state administrations waited to see how the president was going to handle her first real domestic crisis. The dogs of war were perched as both houses picked sides down party lines. Today a woman was going to run for her political life, as she made the most important decisions of her political career. The country could only wait and worry, as the situation seemed ready to spin into chaos.

Mitch managed to repress the haunting vision of the dead youth as he went about what little business he had. It felt good to be in the fresh air, even if it did smell like a junkyard fire. It was hard to make any real conversation with anybody, after the battle they had just fought. Somehow reality didn't seem so real anymore after getting so close to death. Was war more real than reality ever could be?

Shuffling through a part of unspoiled Macbeth, he walked. Hearing a loud "meow," Mitch froze and slowly turned around to see a tattered, out-of-place Amadeus.

"Oh, that's great. Still alive, I see."

"Meow!" the battered beast screamed.

"You've looked better," he said with a chuckle as he knelt

down to examine the singed beast.

Pretending he almost cared, he petted the weathered feline, thinking if he were only half-monster, he could strangle this excuse for a pet and be done with it. He was still in a somber mood from earlier. Amadeus's death would have to wait its turn.

"Well, Lardo, guess this will teach you to run away from the hand that feeds you." Amadeus purred for once, probably because there wasn't anyone better around and Mitch would have to do. Scooping up the beast, he walked on just hoping this lazy blob of tangled fur would remain tame till he delivered it to the arms of a woman he truly loved.

Unbeknownst to Mitch, in both houses of the federal government a little- known document was presented. Macbeth's Declaration of Independence had been delivered quickly, thanks to an island diver and coastal sympathizer. With the lawmakers' curiosity boiling, they were assembled quickly for the presentation. Clearing his throat, the Speaker of the House addressed a joint session of Congress. With the voice of reason, the speaker read Mitch's words that resonated through the halls where history was made. Mitch's careful words became to some the sword of justice they were meant to be. Washington's movers and shakers intently listened with open minds, hopefully learning and maybe understanding Macbeth's plight.

In all of its pressed glory, Congress was truly scared and intrigued by such a simple idea--an idea that made some politician re-examine his or her own political agenda. Careers, for better or for worse, now hung even more in this precious teetering balance between law and order.

Massachusetts' once-powerful representatives were alone in the hot seats, as their thin-skinned colleagues in Congress abandoned them quickly for not having the power to see into their constituents future.

Politics was politics as usual in Washington. There were the majority of honest men and women, and a powerful minority of out-of-touch old codgers and hustlers. Term limits would certainly have helped; fresh blood is always stimulating in a stagnant situation. This day was every man and woman for themselves, as most had forgotten how tough the real world really could be, and how close they were to being flung right back into it.

As that document was slowly read, many in Congress squirmed at the words that seemed all too familiar. With morality and Main Street America seemingly at issue, the crooks (just politicians in disguise) that always seemed to wield the biggest campaign chests looked around to see if they had been noticed, all too used to providing lip service and catering to their pork barrel projects of the hidden contributors. There were so many unneeded projects that should have been dumped and scrapped, but somehow were always overlooked at budget time, while honest politicians with little say pushed on with well-intentioned programs. Good intensions don't buy a cut in a real-world budget…only in their dreams. It was a tightrope between honesty and bribes, the freshmen learned all too quickly. Honesty stood out like a scarlet letter to those who had forgotten the difference between right and wrong.

Runaway government in the states had gotten too big. To the common men and women, it seemed that lawmakers were just losing touch with everyday folk. Mitch had been seen the signs of this political ignorance through his years of reporting. It was possible for little towns and communities to be swept into the deep voids of a society. No voice and no vote. It was inevitable that some town would be ignored.

Back in the halls of law, a pissed-off Republican Congressman Cody Lehman from Brimfield, Ohio, not worried about making friends, lectured the crooks and elders of Congress on their ignorance.

"With the world shrinking as fast as it was, foreign aid should have been concentrated on our own shores. Screw the monsters overseas that you keep afloat, all in the name of pacification! Keep your nose clean and I'll send you American dollars. Kiss my big white hairy ass, all of you. You greedy excuses for politicians make me sick. If you could only see the whole picture, we wouldn't be here. Shit, what am I saying... you've seen the real picture, but you ignore the plain truth. Your tunnel vision sees nothing but greed, and who can help your agendas?

"Thames, you remember Massachusetts? You know where all that cold, hard cash comes from! The cash you keep hidden in that political war chest of yours. Have you forgotten who sent you here and why?" he yelled, getting even louder.

"No, tax dollars are not for your need-of-the-month club. Tax dollars are to help everyday Americans, not to help you. It was them, stupid! You ignorant bastards, you care nothing for these common folk. It's always been you!"

Lehman was hitting these men where it hurt, as they squirmed even harder. Clearing their throats, the guilty tried to disturb his rage. They banged shoes on their desks as the noise got louder. Lehman would not be silenced as he screamed into the microphones.

"We're all to blame, every last one of us! There is but one stand that we as elected officials must take. Help the people you represent first. Isolationism is dangerous! But so is the potential for rebellion within your own land. Keep the honest people that feed you happy, and the system has a chance to work. Screw with them and this happens. Fuck all of you self-righteous thieves--I'm ashamed of myself for ever crawling into bed with the likes of you."

Congressman Thames, unable to take it anymore, whipped his shoe in the direction of Lehman. Lehman, younger and more agile, dodged the projectile as he flipped the bird in the direction of the shaken old man.

"Silence this damn fool who makes a mockery of this Congress!" Thames yelled while chamber cameras filmed away at the medley in this usually solemn house. Congressmen and women turned on each other as good versus evil spilled out into aisles, while the Speaker pounded the gavel of law and order that seemed to make no difference. Bloodied noses and torn clothing added to the circus atmosphere that replaced so many years of grand tradition.

The security guards rushed in. Outnumbered, and with too little to go around, they could only try to restore some type of order. Congress needed a shake-up, and this day was as good as any other.

Thames, still feeling in control, stood up to speak surely to condemn Lehman for his banter. Once, all-powerful Thames could control the floor with a word. But as he spoke, many an honest politician, realizing the cost of freedom, stood up booing and banging, hoping to drown out the old man's words.

The louder Thames spoke, the more noise the silent majority made. Thames looked around at the hungry faces of the crowd and realized his time in control was over. Looking into the broad smile on Lehman's face, he and his old men's club knew their days were now numbered.

Without his shoe, Thames had a noticeable limp, and his brothers in deceit, shuffled out of the chambers, chased only by the thundering applause of the new Congress basking in the victory of such a simple revolt. Macbeth's words had scored their first victory.

The President, watching the closed circuit presentation of the congressional fiasco, saw the future. Too many signs gathering beyond the White House's front yard--as nation and her people were indeed concerned.

That night, all fifty-one states needed a true leader. Through the creeping darkness, a people concerned for the future and present slept a little less that evening, while the worst of nightmares kept drifting through their slumbering minds.

CHAPTER 24:

WELCOME TO OUR WORLD

The island's divers, too anxious to be nervous, needed only a few hours to finish their business. It wasn't a terribly complicated plan, if you had learned it and practiced it. All knew they had but one chance, and after the initial surprise from their bold plan, the window of opportunity would be slammed shut. The men knew their reality was another dimension away as their loved ones lay alone on an island under siege. Love and survival sure had a way of focusing their resolve.

In pairs, the divers easily found the targets. With little fanfare, they planted their plastic explosives and set the timers. Targets were chosen where their simple reaction to explosives would be felt the most. Many trips to the mainland and a lot of homework made setting the charges like child's play, as a well thought out plan came and went without even a flicker of detection.

The main electric plant relay station and wire towers were the main targets, followed by the pumping facility at the coastal water plant. Third was the fiber optics relay station, which controlled so much of what a modern seaside community counted on. These were all soft targets that many folks passed by every day and never really noticed, but which all played such a big role in their real world.

The consequences if the attacks were successful would be limited electricity, water, phone service, cable TV, and no working toilets. The bad joke, compliments of the islanders, would hit a portion of the population of the coastline where it would hurt. With a little luck, for a short period the affected area would be knocked back to a simpler time, and an unforgiving public was going to rise as they always do when times get uncomfortable. In days cabin fever would probably set in, as a forced isolationism would have no choice as it yanked at the coastal residents' every frayed nerve.

The guard could be in only so many places, as town after town would demand help. With limited resources and less communication, the lines of command would become tangled, as some would falter. Some guard units would start collapsing as men deserted out of necessity to make sure their families and loved ones were secure. Families would see visions in the night of the island's militia sneaking through their dark backyards, minds just playing tricks on the innocent. The next invasion for the time being, would be put on the back burner as Tom and Jack could only hope that this borrowed time would bring them the help they had so needed from Washington.

If all worked as planned, the state and local governments would be so busy trying to satisfy the demands of the constituents that the administration wouldn't have the time to be crooked. A few nights of empty promises, and the fear of the unforgiving public would wrestle with the nervous Governor and his administration. With no choice, they would be forced to scramble to restore modern necessities to a helpless coastline. Sooner than later the public would scream for a hot meal or maybe just a candle to burn at night to chase away the demons. In the dark many of the residents would have plenty of time to plan on getting even with the man that had made their nightmare come true.

Gathering in the hidden lair under a quiet boardwalk, the divers returned from the adventure. Slipping out of their guard uniforms, they suited up ready to return to their loved ones. Only one problem: one team had a different final agenda planned. A solid solution to everybody's problem, the missing divers thought: cut the head off the snake and its tormented body dies and everybody is happy.

That choice had been made, as there was no other guaranteed fix. The rationale they wrestled with was the ending of one life to save many. How right they felt as they planned their final solution--an act of courage, for the good of all.

The remaining divers couldn't afford to wait any longer for the other two, as the sun was starting to rise. With an uneasy fear of some kind of a loss, they slipped into the cover of the surf and disappeared into its embracing cool depths. Releasing the underwater tug anchored safely to the bottom, they started the electric motors and grabbed on for the ride home. Individually they prayed that the others had not been caught and the plan exposed. They prayed harder that their explosives hit the mark, as the mainlanders unknowingly went about their day.

With a final sick joke, the timers had been set for the 5 p.m. rush hour. Many overworked souls would be driving home, irritated and locked in traffic as the explosions along the small part of the coast began--not earth-shaking, but precise, as the focused damage they did would be acute and almost surgical in its precision.

When the clock struck five as planned, tiny explosions started emanating from little-known cavities in the ground. A few critical electric towers just toppled over in a tangled broken mess. Fiber optics and cables were shredded into a thousand different strands. Which line went with which line? It was just the island's idea of a needle in a haystack. Some surely noticed the small puffs of smoke, but most were just absorbed in the traffic jam from hell, which was only going to get worse as the traffic lights went dead.

As quickly as the explosions started, they ended; town after town came to a grinding halt. Residents went to phone lines only to find them silent. Water lines emptied as the main and backup pumps were turned into shrapnel. It was sure awkward at that, as all lives changed in such subtle ways. Alone in the bathroom with a simple final flush, the modern convenience normally taken for granted was gone. Most, not keenly aware of all that had happened, could only brace for the long days ahead.

That evening the coastline was truly in the dark, as the neon tubes and silver screens reflected only thousands of candle lights. The public screamed at each other for the TV shows they were missing, not fully realizing the change in lifestyle they were all about to receive.

The intial repairs would take weeks as the simplistic genius in the plan was realized. It was the rush hour from hell; no vehicles moved forward or backward. With road rage and chaos becoming apparent everywhere, local police stations had to lock their doors to keep out the throng of demanding residents. With no quick solution for this ensuing chaos, the frustrated officers combed through the emergency manuals trying to figure out what to do next.

Authorities just couldn't respond to situations and emergencies of the magnitude they were experiencing. Relief would set in only as the short wave radio went dead, to the relief of the stressed dispatchers. In hundreds of homes the unfortunate fumed, with veins surely popping as the blood pressure of the masses rose along with their tempers and fear, while all the traffic jam could do was snarl. The coast never had a chance to take a breath.

As the relay station smoldered, utility companies had nightmares they never could have imagined as they attempted to get power restored. So much was taken from this part of the coast, by so little. Everyday utilities now knew how vulnerable they were as the unthinkable was now believable--just another complication and a sacrifice for the virtue and rewards of a free society.

With the fiber-optic junctions in no better shape than the electric relay stations, no phone or cable was now the reality that most would be stuck with for weeks, thanks to this coordinated destruction. Members of that hidden society who hid away by day, living life through the TV, internet and phone, were lost, as the realization set in that they might have to actually face their worst fears, leave their homes, and face a live human being…or deciding what was worse: real isolation, or facing those outside they had tried so hard to avoid.

No back-up pumps or electricity at the pump stations meant no fresh water, no working sewers, no functional showers, and no working toilets. An unimaginable nightmare to a germ freak's controlled world. What would you do when your commode filled up and your room reeked? Sooner rather than later, the people would come to understand the simple luxury of an outdoor outhouse, or the usefulness of that big tree in the backyard. That unfortunate coastline of Massachusetts was simply thrust back in time.

The governor, unbelieving in his bad luck, had a manmade disaster on his administration's hands--an event that only a Hollywood screenwriter could have thought up. In haste, plenty of contingency plans were set in motion for all the wrong reasons, as the administration, local police, and the Red Cross scrambled to take care of the demanding refugees from the real world.

All the available troops the guard could muster became committed to the event. Reinforcements were out of the question, since it became evident it would be impossible to call them up. Along the coast, all the unit commanders could hope for was the men in the unit would feel the pull for their call of duty and come in. To many the decision would turn into a crisis of the heart and who would be more important, those little eyes of a child looking up at you while holding your hand for reassurance, or your part time job. It was an easy choice for most as the call of duty would go unanswered.

Many reservists loaded up their families in the cars, along with what little they could fit in, and drove off. The deserters of conscience, knowing what lay ahead for those who stayed in the affected area, headed toward the sanctuary of any relative or friend away from the dead zone. All the refugees, just hoping they had enough fuel to battle the clogged highways of evacuees leaving the coastline.

Vehicle after vehicle inched slowly along the main arteries and small roads out--going where, nobody really knew, all just trying to get away. In due time, lines of vehicles just ground to a halt as the engines running on vapors succumbed, abandoned as their passengers and drivers rediscovered the purpose of their legs.

All were faced with the shocking truth that they were out of touch with everyone in their immediate real world. A few of the new cell phones put out, but they too would eventually run out of juice; recharging was not an option.

The local coastal economies would have no choice but to shut down as the shelves emptied. Class lines so evident earlier were abandoned, as all were in the same boat; for once all residents regardless of wealth were equal in their discomfort.

One hundred years ago, most wouldn't have thought twice about hunkering down with a case of Spam and just waiting until things improved. That evening in the rushed cycle, modern life had its price, a cost modern Americans would probably have eagerly paid if they could just find the help they needed.

The day of nickel suckers and dime-store logic had vanished, along with the wisdom of its time. Grocery store pandemonium was apparent as a desperate culture realized for the time being that what was left in their cupboards was all they had, and waiting for no one, the refrigerator and freezers just thawed.

The weary divers eventually made it back to the island. Emerging from the surf, many questions would be asked, but with fewer answers, only one that could be no more evident as they looked back toward the dark and silent coast. In all its simplicity, the strike had gone smoothly and had worked as well as the calculated results had anticipated. Yet the waves on the beach still broke as Macbeth held its breath at the thought of what would come next.

In the Oval Office alone, the president was appalled at the severity of Macbeth's attack. She felt like she had been sucker-punched, knowing that she had not stepped in soon enough. How would history judge her? She was but a link in the chain of events that had already started years before her. She worried, as any mother would--was she too late to break up this playground fight?

Congress, who felt for the islanders now, thought twice after such a perverse act of domestic terrorism on the coast. The islanders were now threatening innocent lives. They had crossed the line of decency, giving a governor the reason he needed to justify his actions to his troops. The old men of Congress, feeling a bit defeated earlier at that, felt justified now in the coastal plight. They tried to work their back room deals, plotting their revenge on the silent majority of the House who waited for the next move, as once again right just didn't seem to be so right.

Through all this chaos, seaside towns that had geared up for the needed and anticipated tourist season turned into ghost towns, as time was measured in hours when it became apparent that life without utilities would be around for a while.

The guard, in a holding pattern, turned the heat down on Macbeth as some of its units slipped into its humanitarian role on the coast. With limited personnel, the mission around the island became one of containment. The resurrection of the seaside communities had become a priority, as one black eye had been enough.

As the islanders had been quickly labeled "domestic terror-ists," the governor was happy, as he could see the tide turning in his favor. He knew if he could pull this off and restore the coastline utilities, no office would be out of his reach. Without those coastal tourist dollars in the trickle-down theory, it would deny communities the needed funds that drove these entities through the long cold winters. Winters were always tough in Massachusetts, and if the governor came through, he would be the hero for saving the day.

Sitting on an unscathed front porch alone in his thoughts again, Mitch looked out over the remains of the town. Amadeus wouldn't leave his side, so he picked up and petted the furry friend he didn't need. Seeing that the smoke and smoldering had subsided, he waved at the few townies he saw. Most were just in a state of shock as they poked through what little remained. Most in denial thought that it never could have gone this far and destroyed so much. A wooden community was no match for real weapons, as all the dreamers had learned so quickly.

The sign that something was even worse was the familiar smell of burning flesh. The cat's ears perked up, maybe sensing it was meal time, Mitch, getting up, walked toward the smell and pushed through the brush till he came upon the edge of a small bomb crater. In horror, he saw the body of Judith McGuff surrounded by loosely scattered pictures of her dead family, and burned clothing from her opened suitcase. Her slender burnt legs were going in a direction God never intended. Only part of a limb remained on her half-naked upper torso, along with an almost sick satisfied smile on her soot-covered face. Her sad circle of life was complete, as a family was united again when her human world finally stood still. The former model had been discovered by a random shell. Weapons pick no sides, and their damage, as calculated as it was, still so random. Sometimes in a macabre way its damage is worthwhile to the victim. Judith wouldn't disagree. Mitch couldn't feel sorrow for her since he had come to learn that in the end this was what she had always waited for.

After a quick prayer for Judith, he grabbed a big armful of the feline and headed for the mine. The sooner he delivered the cat, the safer he would feel. Amadeus purred while he thought back to their moment at the bar only weeks earlier and wondered whom he could get to help bury her. He was sure he owed her at least that.

Walking along the road back to the mine, Mitch couldn't get the smell of burning flesh out of his mind. The smell of death is overwhelming; male or female, it's all the same. Rushing over to the side of the road, he grabbed a handful of spring flowers and crammed them up to his nose, just hoping for any scent to relive his mind of the smell.

With a brisk pace, he reached the entrance. The guards had lost the look of innocence and now looked like warriors as their mission guarding the mine had become life or death. Nobody knew what could be next, as no one had ever expected what had happened.

"Hi Mitch, got some pussy there?" a guard asked, half cracking a smile.

"Yeah there's enough here for both of us!" Mitch shot back, glad there was a moment for a little bit of comic relief.

"Hey I found the body of Judith about a half mile back along the road. She got hit pretty badly."

"That poor woman never seemed to have any luck. Maybe this time she was the lucky one? When we can spare some guys we'll take care of her. You might have to show us where she is," the guard replied as he let Mitch in.

"Yeah, just let me know when. I will gladly help; it just doesn't seem right, leaving her there," Mitch said, as he really hoped he would never have to go back and smell the body again.

CHAPTER 25:

THE WIDOW SHE WAITS

With a loud clank behind him, the metal door to the mine closed as Mitch's eyes adjusted to the dimness. An elderly soft voice drifted out of the darkness and caught his attention.

"Helloooooooh!" that voice of an aged angel said.

"Well, a hello to you also," he replied, not really knowing who he was talking to. As his eyes made the adjustment to the lack of light, he recognized the widow Piddle, as he then handed her the flowers he had grabbed by the side of the road, hoping to help her day.

"Hey just ignore her--she's been sitting there for hours. I think she finally lost it," a frustrated guard said. "I can't seem to reason with her anymore. She just keeps repeating the same things over and over again!"

Mitch could see that the widow looked much older than he remembered from a few days ago. Just rocking back and forth, she repeated over again that her husband was coming back for her, even though her home was clearly gone, as was her husband. It was sad--she must have suffered from some form of dementia; life was even stranger, as she lived in some dimension of her own reality. Just calling out to whoever would listen, she suffered, locked away in her mind, waiting for her knight who would never come.

Never being one to care, Mitch felt the unusual need to help as he tried to move her away from the cold entrance to somewhere more comfortable.

"I don't want to go, honey! Please just let me sit here. Elmer's coming soon, real soon. Where is he? Dinner's been ready and the kids have soccer practice tonight!" she said with that confused, scared look on her aged face. Widow Piddle was fighting her own war in her head, and she didn't even know it, and Mitch knew no matter what he said, he could not win. He left her there as confused as when he found her, with the flowers scattered at her feet.

Leaving her be, he felt the sorrow he knew so well. He had seen that look before in a parent, as he learned the hard way about Alzheimer's. The curse had robbed his father of what dignity he had. Locking his dad away in a world full of confused voids, he struggled to make reason out of the reflection in the mirror that was him. No matter how many family members were around, he was always alone as he struggled to find his parents who had died so many years before, but lived on in his tortured memory and only contributed to his nightmares. His pain lived on daily as his loving caregivers wondered when death would come and end his living hell.

For a man who thought only of himself, Mitch had learned sympathy from his short stay. Ignoring the widow Piddle's plea, he walked back over, picked up her packed suitcase, and reached for her soft hand. Without a second thought, he became whoever she needed as he led her away to a better spot.

The mine, for the time, seemed much quieter with the kids not seemingly around. With all the destruction, moving them lower in the mine seemed to be the right thing to do. *Were Tom and Jack worrying more than before?* he wondered. Mitch had seen the absolute carnage outside and was worried himself.

With the seaside fishing town nothing more than a smoldering memory, Mitch started to entertain haunting images of what could come. What was the real objective? Did the end really justify the means? With an island population displaced, what was left for them? They could rebuild, but would a population away from the island be hell-bent on revenge and not stand for any of them living in their backyards? Too many nagging questions, as he wandered with the widow, looking for someone to give her a hand.

Entering the mess hall with widow trailing him, he sat her down and poured her some tea--*All old women like tea*, he thought. Across the table, one of the boys from the battle, still covered with some of yesterday's blood, stuffed a Twinkie down.

"Hello, mister!" he said as he licked his soot-covered fingers, making darn sure he got every little bit of that creamy white filling. Was Mitch so old that he was now called mister? Wow, what was the island doing to him?

With Mitch not responding yet, the boy asked, "You want a piece?" He wanted to respond, but that "mister" thing had him agitated as he helped the widow drink her tea.

"Sorry, I was occupied in thought, but no thanks."

"Mister, something's been bothering me real bad." *There goes that mister thing again.* Mitch went to another level of frustration.

"What's going to happen to us when this is all done? I mean, we really shot at them...we even killed some of them...and I know it was us or them, but who is going decide who was right?"

With a sigh, he looked scared and nervous: "I'm no dummy, I know we can't hold out forever; it's just a matter of time." He was agitated, and had every right to be, as he couldn't have been much more than fifteen or sixteen. Mitch deep down knew his life was probably over, because if he wasn't killed, he could surely look forward to a life behind bars branded as a traitor--probably in some military prison, hidden away and lost. No matter how hard he looked, he could see no light at the end of this poor kid's tunnel. For the kid's sake, he hoped God was more merciful than the governor.

Finishing another Twinkie, he continued, licking the wrapper as he talked.

"You know what we had to do in that foxhole was nothing more than life or death. If I hadn't aimed at them, they would have taken us out – there really was no other option! Those other boys and I did what we had to do; that's all that matters, no matter what they do to us later, and I am starting to wonder if there really is going to be a later. Mister, I'm not a murderer, am I?"

"No, you're not a murderer; you did what any other person would have done if they were in your spot. In your heart, you know it, so just get on with it and don't worry, keep your head down," Mitch responded. "It's not over by any means!"

He must have said something right, since the kid shook off his uncertainty and dove into another pack of Twinkies. Widow Piddle must have seen her chance as she escaped out of the room and headed on her way to nowhere in particular, smiling as her unseen angel led her on her way.

Meeting later that day with Kate, Mitch couldn't have dreamed how beautiful she still was from being stuck below the surface, but he wished he could say the same for himself. No shower in days, as hygiene had no real meaning anymore. He knew he had to be ripe, and wished he could find a bottle of Old Spice to tame his smell. Not that any of this made any difference. He knew from being close to a lot of these folks down there that he wasn't alone in stink. Thinking about the coastline, he knew they had to be experiencing the same unfortunate hygienic fate they all shared.

"Mitch, I just heard how you took care of Mrs. Piddle. I knew there was a grain of caring locked away in you somewhere," she said as she came in closer to him for that kiss she wanted.

Backing off a bit, he said, "Just the Boy Scout coming out in me." Knowing he needed a shower, he pulled back more. "I need a shower bad, Kate."

"What, you want me to suds you up?" she said with a giggle.

"Yeah, I wish we could!" he exclaimed, just wishing sex would cleanse his feelings of guilt.

"Have you seen Amadeus?"

Shit, he said to himself realizing he had let the ball of blubber down to help widow Piddle out. Pretending he hadn't heard a word, he searched for excuses so he could sneak off and find the ball of lard.

While visions of a permanently lost feline danced through his head, Lynn and her friend Heather came out of nowhere carrying the cat. Mitch breathed a sigh of relief.

"Look what I found wandering around, Kate--looking for some food, of course!"

Running as if she had found her long-lost friend, she screamed, "Amadeus, you're alive!" as she grabbed her beast.

"Jeez, you smell! What have you been into?" All the cat could do was purr, and look at Mitch out of the corner of its eye. "You and Mitch stink, you both need a shower!" *Only if you and Lynn come and help*, Mitch thought to himself. All he could imagine were vivid flashes of Lynn lying naked in front of him. She no longer was that girl he met on the boat. In his mind she was a seductress, just wishing she could please him. Even in a war his hormones raged, as he felt like the perverted man from before the person he had despised so much.

The four of them tried to make small talk, but Mitch was useless. He really wanted to make conversation, but his over-active mind kept undressing Lynn. Kate looked at him funny, wondering what his problem was. He wanted to be good, but his thoughts needed the distraction. It had been a long day, and Kate had her feline family back. Someone was getting cleaned that day, and Amadeus seemed like the best bet. Kate sensed he'd had enough of their chit-chat as she told the girls goodbye and turned to him to leave.

"You ready for that shower?" she asked, thinking for a moment that Mitch's mind had to be somewhere else.

"Kate, give me a few minutes. I got to do a couple things."

She blew him a kiss as she walked away toward the shower room, holding the cat. "Don't be long!"

Lynn, seeing her chance in her playful innocence, knew what she was doing to him. As Kate walked out of the picture, Lynn lifted her shirt as she flashed him a quick peek. With her temptation just staring at him, he turned away in embarrassment as his hormones hit warp speed. He could tell the pain from his initial rejection of Lynn had worn off. She had been raped savagely, but he never could understand her latest actions. He thought maybe this was the best way Lynn could deal with the trauma of the attack.

With a quick turn, he looked back hoping for another quick peek. He wondered, with the potential for his life to be cut short, if he should try and go for it? Seeing his male interest piqued, Lynn licked her soft lips as she teased him once more. Mitch was only a man and could take no more. More than afraid to say goodbye and have to look into her eyes again, he ran after Kate, getting as much distance as he could between his thoughts and Lynn's body. He knew he was safer from his temptress if he left. Lynn, with a little satisfied smile and a tear in her eye, was sure she had caught his attention, as she had used her powers on a very susceptible man who had passed her test, even though Kate really was like family to her.

Kate should be the only thing that filled up the darkness in his mind, he kept telling himself as he fought off the recurring visions of Lynn. Questioning himself, he sensed she hadn't been nearly as easygoing as when he first met her

He walked up to Kate as she began to scrub the ball of fur. She turned to him and asked, "Glad you changed your mind! Have you ever thought what are you going to do when this is over Mitch?"

Looking for some personal redemption from his thoughts, he replied, "Wrong! What are *we* going to do when this is over?" Getting that clammy feeling that he wasn't going to squeak out of this, he fidgeted. He was no fool, and he knew it was going to be nearly impossible for any on the island other than the kids to get a second look. He wished someone would jump in and help the islanders, but with few options for negotiation anymore, their fate was all but sealed. Looking at Kate softly washing the cat's fur, he had a feeling that luck would be on her side. Looking into her eyes, he tried to wipe the naked vision out of his looped thoughts. Lynn was beautiful, but Kate was who he needed then.

Driving slowly along the edge of a congested highway going into the capital, the two from Macbeth, still dressed as guardsmen, maneuvered through the abandoned vehicles. Driving the stolen jeep, they ignored the obscenities hurled in their direction. It was bad for any in the guard, as the heat had been leveled on them for the worsening situation on the coastline. Innocent scapegoats, but someone had to take the blame. Those stuck in the grid lock questioned what was so important to these two soldiers as they weaved in and out, just trying to get to where everyone was leaving from?

It mattered: time wasn't on the islanders' side. The governor too knew time wasn't his friend as his window for closure on the conflict was closing. Hunkered down in his office, he knew he had escalated his blunder. With the help of Macbeth's divers, it was now his move. Not a moment went by that he didn't plan his sweet revenge. Never knowing what was next, in due time he would meet the two islanders who had planned their surprise for too long over some ice cold brews at the local pub. The governor was to be the guest to their party--he just didn't know it. Surprise was always good, if it was on your side.

CHAPTER 26:

THE FOUNTAIN OF YOUTH

The news trickling back to the islanders about the success of the attacks on the coast gave all a remote glimmer of hope. It was a desperate hope of achieving a workable solution and keeping this insanity from getting any worse--hope from others' suffering. Dangerously sick, in a demented kind of way, as Mitch saw it. In any war, most clear minds never think straight in the heat of battle.

It had to be the pressure in a life-and-death struggle that overtakes common sense. He didn't know or care what the answer was to the real virtues of war. For a time in his heart he knew the good guys had won the battle. Were the islanders really the good guys or just more misguided players in the political and business evolution as a society redefined their values?

Trying to justify the struggle, Mitch figured all those innocent victims on the coastline were just the unfortunate victims in a growing social struggle. They, like the islanders, were now forced to flee their homes. All were, much more than they knew, dependent on the luxuries they took for granted, and then with them gone had a driving need to search for their lost life, temporary as it was.

With the completion of the island's bold assault, every

news show, paper, magazine, and website put their own spin on Macbeth. It was a struggle in futility for the media to try to get any story out of the island. The president, with an executive order, had imposed a blockade around the hostile area. The government's lesson had been learned the hard way. With a focused objective, she knew no more mistakes could be tolerated on her watch, no matter what the governor said.

With their real world turned upside down, paranoia and a seething revenge took root on the coastline. Helpless friends and family with loved ones on the island became intentional targets of a rabid media feeding frenzy. These uninvolved people had become innocent victims of Macbeth's backlash. Victims by association were now condemned to spend the duration of the immediate crisis and beyond, cowering behind locked doors and blackened windows. Most hoped to remain anonymous as the press sought them out, searching for pools of gossip to come up with any story pertaining to the island and its people.

In an unintended benefit of the media, their numbers provided a degree of safety to these victims. The media vehicles provided a rolling barrier between the victims and the other members of an enraged society, hell-bent on an eye for a eye, just looking for someone to blame and hang. It was bad that help didn't come sooner to some.

One evening a out-of-control mob, not willing to take no as an answer to their appetite for revenge, surrounded Tom's brother's home on a quiet dead end street. A good brother he had always been, raising his seven children, just trying to make a difference in their middle-class lives. Without warning, Tom's brother was dragged from his warm bed, half-awake.

With his children and wife watching and screaming in horror, he was strung upside down like a side of beef, and with a single slit his thick neck was cut open. His life bleeding out of him, his family in shock could only cry and pray that they were not the next sacrifice to the unrestrained whims of a mob gone over the line.

An old-fashioned lynching, with only one difference: the mob was united, black and white, with genuine anger not directed at the color of the skin, but at an untouchable brother hidden away on an island. Many watched with a smile, as nobody tried to stop the mob. All participants seemed satisfied and content, doing their part to solve the crisis. A family, destroyed and shattered, knelt below the dripping body as it cooled off in the refreshing night air.

The mob moved on while a few remained, realizing too late the damage that had been done. Common sense had fled as fast as the electricity was depleted. Would life for any in the mob ever be the same, as they washed the fresh blood off their hands? When rational thought returned, the useless waste of a good life would haunt many for years to come, as they too would be like the Germans who looked the other way as the Jewish neighbors took punishment for their innocence. A few knew all too well that there was no turning back on this crime, and all they could do was cut him down and end the vision of the nightmare.

Patrolling the skies above the island became the U S Air Forces mission. Indirectly, the president had ordered flyovers so that the situation could be monitored and real-time intelligence could be obtained. The islanders tolerated the intrusions, as there was nothing left to hide and they were not in any position to pick a fight with Washington. Tom made sure the hostages were positioned where they would be seen, with the hopes that just their presence would deter any additional bloodshed. Never one to guess anyone's moves or motives, he just prayed that the US military didn't consider them expendable.

Off in the distance, anchored, ready, and clearly visible from the shores of Macbeth, were the Navy and her big guns. As hours ticked by, an armada of frigates, destroyers, and even an aircraft carrier off in the distance surrounded the small island. Most were aware of this buildup as they clearly overshadowed the few guard ships. The president was firm that this mighty presence was to prevent the coastline from suffering any more from this unnecessary conflict.

Even the extreme show of force did little to reassure those on the coast. Emotions and fear were running wild from home to home. The crazy rumors circulated faster than the sound of a free cash giveaway. In a distorted reality to most of the uniformed, they expected that behind every garage or shed was another blood-sucking terrorist. Modern-day kamikazes were being smuggled in from the island, all with a mission aimed at the innocent residents left behind. To them in this delusional state, no one was safe while the island still controlled their future.

As all of this spun out of realism, neighbors who had been good friends for years stopped trusting each other in a moment. All too often, they nervously peeked out from behind their curtains, standing poised and ready, holding their loaded broomsticks and their dustpan shields, waiting for the attack that surely had to come.

To many it was safer for the time being to let lawn work go. Each other's prized yards and gardens were not as important as they had been in days before. This war had hit home, and that lawn could be the next front line as the mind games took over.

All those guns hidden and locked away became visible on the streets, in the neighborhoods, and in many a back window of pickup trucks of all the new proud and armed rednecks. Everyone seemed to have a gun: from the hip-toting macho men living out their cowboy fantasies to the little kids carrying around their favorite Daisy BB guns. Men, women, and boys were just living out their favorite armed dreams, as a piece of metal by your side put a little jingle back into their strut, and many in their favorite polished cowboy boots delivered the pain as the corns on the toes protested. It didn't matter; they now felt in control with that loaded piece in their possession. Chewing mouthfuls of tobacco, they let all the people know there was a new sheriff in this town.

The situation had risen to more of an event than anyone had ever anticipated, as the coastline was quickly slipping into a war of paranoia as its people panicked. Scattered reports started filtering in as common folks started shooting each other by accident; the wounded had been in the wrong shadow at the wrong time. It was time to think twice about going next door and borrowing that egg from Bessie Mae. With so much uncertainty, neighborhoods and businesses became a little more deserted, and most folks just hunkered down and guarded that little piece of turf they called home.

To the forgotten couch people, accustomed to living their reality glued to a TV, any report they were lucky enough to receive seemed believable. With dark screens, they still assumed their daily position and waited for the idiot tube to come alive again as their reality was put on hold. Nervously fidgeting, they absorbed any information that was churned out from the local gossip chain, as all knew the story only got larger. The ladies that lived their lives in an oversized housecoat did their best to cope as their junk food stockpiles dwindled, and they started believing the end was at hand.

Owning a business was rough; as shelves emptied and restocking was no longer an option, many a business just locked up. The black market experienced an unprecedented rebirth at the expense of the honest. The thieves with the toilet paper, cigs, brews, spirits, and munchies knew they were holding a king's ransom as they set the prices at their whim.

As the days drew on, it seemed the state guard kept getting smaller. Desertion seemed to be the word of the moment. The stress of loved one alone during this crisis seemed to be doing more damage than the actual enemy. The reports that did surface confirmed that groups of guardsmen, stronger as a group, just walked away to rejoin their families, while other guardsmen flatly refused to participate in any other acts of violence against fellow countrymen. It was apparent that weekend warriors were better suited to someone else's soil. It was a tough choice, as they too heard the rumors, combined with loss of communication with those they cared about; all equaled an unsettling predicament for the soldiers. Any loving heart can really pull in only one true direction, and men of the guard were no different from anyone else.

Sitting back in the musty mine communication bunker, wishing the day would go quicker, Mitch grew tired and annoyed while listening to the constant garble from the short waves. It was important to know what was going on outside of their world. It was getting harder to realize what was true and what wasn't, as many an armchair quarterback would give their spin to an already out-of-control story. The busy airwaves held nothing more than talk radio on a short wave channel, and any individuals who liked to hear themselves talk added their thoughts to the growing uncensored story.

It seemed like after almost three weeks in the mine, life was settling into a dull routine. The children of the light now became the children of the darkness. The parents and trustees tried to keep life as routine as they could. For the sake of the children, school had resumed, just in an unconventional classroom. Their playground, still fun and noisy, was but an empty section of a tunnel. The location didn't matter; the boys still chased the girls, and recess was still a free for all.

An old tool room that had been carved into a side of the shaft became the chapel and a well-used refuge for the faithful, all praying hard for their deliverance, while in the back of the room, leaned up against the wall, waited their loaded guns. No particular religion dominated the space, just whoever their almighty might be, as at that point any greater being was welcomed by the devoted.

"War was hell, and not like in the movies!" Mitch's dad would always say. Yet that recent war of few battles seemed harder for some reason, harder when you're staring into the bright eyes of a two-year-old, too young to understand the utter stupidity of an adult world. Youth in its purity was shaped daily by reality, which at times was like a cancer that would, given the opportunity, kill the pure thoughts.

One thing was for sure: the children adapted better than the adults. All day long you would hear the innocent laughter of kids just being kids, laughter that Mitch was sure still brought joy to some and tears to others. The older and wiser couldn't hide their feelings while their worry would show, as they could almost envision what lay before them all. With the wisdom of age, the adults would watch the little kids shine, as they would run or skip by, seemingly oblivious to the events above. It was better that way!

The routine did just drag on, thank God, with no new action above. Negotiations seemed to go nowhere as no guarantees ever came forward. The administration still held its ground, as they were determined not to negotiate with terrorists. Time, they felt, was still on their side, as the violence had taken a rest.

Bored and curious, Mitch felt the need to talk with Peace who had told Mitch he was working below. Jumping on the first elevator he could find, he flipped the switch down and slipped deeper into the security only the earth's cold depth could embrace.

Creaking down the shaft, he thought about the retired islanders and how their golden years were now so far from what they had dreamed about. It was the art of sacrifice, which so many of the older folks had already experienced a world war before, but were forced to be played out again for the cause-- they were a greater generation.

Mitch was getting goofy as the lack of sunlight and fresh air started messing with his senses. Losing the two parts of nature so many took for granted was unsettling in an unseen way. Cabin fever was setting in as many became restless. Little

THE ISLAND OF MACBETH

insignificant things blew up into full-blown confrontations, as people's logic seemed to be getting pushed to the brink.

In the tunnels, days became constant nights, as one unknowingly lost track of the time. All could sense things getting tenser as the days passed. Randomly noticing the dazed look of adults easily spelled out their frame of mind. There was little anyone could do or say as a cloud of mass depression seemed to settle on the mine as some just tried to make the best of a bad situation.

On down the seemingly endless shaft he rode. Being no more than an oversized chicken in the darkness, he contemplated his possible end. Mitch realized that maybe he did feel safer up above, down here if he got injured, no one would ever hear him scream.

With a neck-jolting jerk, he felt the metal cables tighten as they pulled the elevator to a stop. Needing no other reminder to get off he bolted for the elevator door, as he moved into the dimly lit tunnel.

Wondering why he needed to always be so curious, he peered into the overwhelming darkness of the tunnel. He smelled the unmistakable smell of seawater as he felt a slight breeze upon his face.

With all the talk he had gathered, he sure figured there would be more down here than this blackness. Had he gone too far? Where were all the people and supplies he sought? More confused than ever, he crept along as his curiosity drove the man.

Taking a big step forward, he hit the dirt hard, tripping on some unseen rail. Realizing he had the flashlight for a reason, he switched it on and pointed it in the direction of the extreme blackness. Scaring him for an instant, a reflection from an old headlight greeted Mitch. It was a childhood fantasy for him when he saw the ancient mine train; at a quick glance it became evident that it was all rigged up for electric operation. Someone had spent a lot of time on this project. The rails all glistened with the shine of use, he noticed quickly.

With a quick step up, he was seated in the engine. Should he or shouldn't he, he wondered as he looked curiously at the on/off switch. *Well, why the hell not?* he thought, as he flipped the switch to on. With the familiar noise of his childhood fantasy the clickity-clack reverberated through the tunnel as he edged the throttle up a little more. The beam of light from the engine quickly crumbled the darkness before the train, while he made whistle noises that echoed. Where he was going didn't seem to matter at that moment; he was secured in the metal frame of the engine as it pulled the two cars that, for an unanswerable reason, seemed to be set up for passengers rather than salt. That moment, regardless of the reason, he was the engineer and a fantasy on his bucket list had finally come true.

Enjoying the moment, he stared ahead, not knowing when he was going to have to slow down, thinking to when he finally would meet Peace, about the answers he would demand. The bright beam reflected off the shaft walls that were straighter than the tunnels above--these tunnels were different and just didn't seem like they could have been part of the old mine, he surmised.

Time went by fast; he whirled along with the wind in his hair, almost oblivious to the possible danger ahead. Whisking along the narrow shaft, the smell of salt water and diesel fumes only got stronger.

Breaking out of the darkness, a single strong beam of light appeared ahead, seemingly guiding him to the end of the line. The light soon filled the huge cavern, as he flipped the train throttle off and coasted to a gentle stop.

Unfolding before him, a magnificent cave appeared. One bright light strained to illuminate the big dome of rock. Mitch was sure this was no man-made creation, as it was too divine in its simplicity for man's clumsy hands. It was a cave with a natural beauty, with pillars and stalactites of salt too numerous to count. What a tourist trap this could have been! Why hadn't anybody exploited it before? He was confused by the neglected economy of the apparent ace that had never been dealt. Leaving the train, he stood in awe, as he could only stare for the moment.

Eager to see more, he followed the path he could recognize easily, as he could follow the many footprints cut into the rough sand. Like breadcrumbs he followed them until they abruptly stopped at the end of the chamber. Shining his little light ahead into the vast underground pool, he saw that not a ripple disturbed its glass-like appearance. While his light danced across the surface it picked up the many colors of small pools of oil, maybe just a sign of pollution in the purest of nature's cathedrals.

His curiosity now running rampant with theories, he turned away from the water and was scared stiff by the single rocking figure of the widow Piddle as she sat in a small pocket in the rock. Oblivious to his presence, she hummed a soft Irish tune, almost too quietly to hear. She was totally at peace with herself as she sat next to Elmer's cold coffin, the coffin that Mitch was sure they had buried days before. She guarded her husband's coffin in the darkness, as she had stood by her husband in life. Maybe she just waited for the time when the two young lovers would once again walk hand-in-hand.

"What are you doing down here?" Mitch yelled out of shock rather than compassion.

She looked at him as if he hadn't even spoken. He stared back, not knowing what to say next. With the voice of a nana she came to life. "Elmer and I have lived here our whole life. We're too old to leave now. They're young, so I told them to go without us. They're all gone now, but don't you worry. Someone will be back for you soon."

There was so much care and love in her voice, yet so sick, Mitch thought. Someone had to be looking for her, or maybe not. That day must have been her lucky day; she could have died down there alone. Would that have been so bad?

He tried in vain to get the widow to go with him, but she wouldn't have any part of it. He was cold--and the big empty space had yielded up all its secrets, he thought. Many other thoughts were on his mind and he knew the widow would get in no trouble as she sat guarding the coffin. He couldn't help it; he continued to worry that she might fall in the water, confused and alone. But he knew she was content just being by Elmer, and even in death he guarded her. It was best to leave her in peace and find someone else who could maybe convince her to come back up.

Leaving the widow, he noticed the bouquet of flowers he had given her lying on top of the casket. With a quick wave goodbye and a smile he left. Turning back one more time, he reminded her that someone would come back to get her, but she didn't seem to care, as she didn't even acknowledge him leaving. Everything she ever needed was there; everything else was just frosting on the cake.

No sign of Peace or anyone else…and still no answers. It seemed all he had accomplished was to create more questions, as he climbed back into the train. With all fingers crossed, he really hoped this train had a working reverse.

Flipping the switch in the opposite direction, he eased the throttle back; she sprang to life and chugged back to the elevator. With no lights guiding him back, Mitch could only trust the rails as the train entered the eerie darkness. In pitch darkness there were no shadows, as he thought to himself to ease his mind. What were the widow and the casket doing down there? He had time to draw conclusions, but none really added up.

Back within the marble walls of the capital, the governor and his administration were witnessing the inevitable. Pacing back and forth, the governor still felt safe, yet a little uneasy in his guarded office. At that point there wasn't much a figurehead could do, as it seemed he had less control as the hours moved on. He and his chosen few had the gut feeling that it was well past the time of damage control, as the situation had surely gotten the best of them.

It seemed to those noticing that the governor's political backers and allies knew the time had come to gather anything of worth and "get the hell out of Dodge." They had sternly warned the governor about Washington; he just hadn't been ready to abandon his ship. Politics was still in the old crook's blood--and for a reason lost to most, he felt in his delusional mind that he still held the answers to the final victory.

He knew he couldn't let on to what really had happened.

Most thought it must have been out of fear for his future and safety. Instead, in his mind, it was time for him to go to the front line and calm his troops. His staff could almost sense his fear. Little did he realize that desertion hadn't happened only to the guard, but also his staff had dimished. Like the rats they were, they had loved ones also, and the defeated governor just wasn't worth their loyalty any more.

He hadn't always been that way, and had gotten into politics to save the world. Little did he know how badly the party machine needed to control him. It was subtle at first until the dollars rolled in…he was no longer just a boy from the country; he worked for them. That was the real world, with big-time politics: play the game, or get out…but he stayed!

The old man felt he had one decision left to make. Would he continue trying to negotiate, or just storm the island and be done with it? What could negotiations accomplish other than another dead end? What would an invasion of the island do besides create many more unwanted heroes or martyrs to the island's cause? In his fleeting reality, the governor knew he had little time to make his choice as he looked around the room for his missing aides.

It was only a matter of time, he knew Washington was taking over. It was the bottom of the 9th, bases loaded, "Make it count, old man!" he said to himself softly. These islanders had ruined his future. Someone had to pay for his sins.

CHAPTER 27:

A BEAST IS AWAKENED

He never truly had been in love before. In high school, Mitch's overactive hormones were constantly lusting after someone. It was a time in his life when he thought infatuation lasted forever. At sixteen, love was just another four-letter word that had more to do about getting into some sweet young thing's pants, rather than unlocking the beauty in a relationship.

Mitch knew better then. Age along with a learned wisdom had a way of hardening your visions. It was either infatuation or love with Kate. He was under a month into the relationship, and he could have proposed and said "I do." The only thing standing in his way was the possibility of life behind bars.

He just couldn't help but wonder, "How could you be so crazy in love and still feel so alone?" He worried more about her than himself, and he was the one that had been wounded—and who was, by his own inner account, a murderer. It had to be love; Jake the Snake had called it in a song of his years ago. Those damn warm fuzzy feelings kept messing with Mitch. He couldn't shake them--he had been infected and there wasn't any prescription for his love-itis!

All things considered, the situation had really quieted down on the island, with the exception of Kate, who worried. The mine, with its regimented activities and chores was still a flurry of activity. Islanders were still being organized and settled into their jobs. You seldom saw the children anymore; Mitch had heard they had been moved to a safer portion of the mine. He wanted to know where that safer portion was for his own neck when the time came, but as before, his questions went unanswered.

Reaching the end of his journey back up the shaft, he sent help back for the widow Piddle. The guys agreed she wasn't herself anymore since her husband passed. Mitch had never been with anyone long enough to know what a true loss was, other than his parents. He did feel a genuine sympathy for the widow. At least she really had found her true love, and had loved enough to earn her sorrow.

A couple of the men felt the need to question him about his motives for going down the shaft. He had played dumb before – a trait a reporter picks up quickly if he or she wants to survive – and it was time to play dumb again. With a few crazy answers, Mitch left them scratching their heads, and they walked away, satisfied with his stupidity.

Keeping an eye out for the widow to no avail, he hoped they had found her before it was too late. One of the boys said she had been found and was safe, though just a little more guarded, for her own safety--a good thing, he was sure.

Jack and the men held to their coffee routine; some things would always be important. Mitch joined them and learned that the many seemed to be in a constant emotional struggle, and were consumed with worry. Tom had confided to a few in the militia of what was happening to friends and relatives back on the coastline. Mitch knew, and agreed it probably wasn't the best thing to be spread around the mine, and if it got out, it sure wouldn't change the resolve of many. If Kate had family over there, he hoped they got as far away from this state as possible.

The confinement and inescapable darkness were starting to affect everyone, and Tom and Jack were no different as both seemed to look a little more ragged and thin as the situation drew on. The islanders' lives and futures were a terrible burden for anyone to carry. Negotiations had hit a snag, as lately all the men seemed to get over the airwaves was a disturbing static.

Macbeth's militia all seemed to sense that the big battle had to be just around the corner--and most folks unfortunately agreed. They still wondered why both sides still couldn't sit down and work it out. Most knew that the coastline was still dark, which meant mainlanders were still dealing and angry with a lack of utilities. Talk was really going nowhere, as neither side wanted to take a step back--or if they did, you couldn't tell.

The coffee club, in their caffeinated wisdom, knew the administration could not let the situation drag on. The governor, with his neck on the line, was seemingly being pushed in a corner. Tom knew all to well you couldn't corner a wounded animal without it lashing out, common sense for an uncommon situation. "Pass the cream and sugar, please!" was heard, as the talk continued.

One thing that seemed to get under folks' skin was the lack of instant or even old news. Many wondered what was going on in the real world. What were the common folk of society feeling about the crisis? Could it be anger, frustration, or maybe just disbelief? Any tidbit of information would have helped the islanders' frayed nerves. Mitch knew all too well that not knowing the whole story in a crisis will drive anyone crazy. The future rolls on by while you're seemingly stuck repeating the present over and over again. It was unfair, and an uncalculated twist of fate as this unknown played against the islanders and silently took its toll.

Mitch had it figured out, but did anyone at the time understand the islanders' plight? He knew it was a damn pilgrimage for passion--passion for what was right and what was wrong in their little piece of the world. At that point it was just more water over the dam, as the governor had moved on.

With boredom setting in, Mitch resorted to moving about the tunnels, looking for anyone, or anything to do to occupy his time. As he approached the entrance to the mine he ran into Billy and Liam trying to get a look at outside.

"How you twerps doing?" he yelled.

"Hey there, Mitchy!" Liam responded, happy to see him. "We're doing pretty good; just getting a little bored around here with everyone gone."

"Gone?" Mitch asked.

"Come on, you know! The kids and moms are being snuck out of here one by one!" Billy injected. "They got that secret passage that they sneak out," he continued as he kicked his foot in the dirt, digging at a rock, still with too much youthful energy left to burn.

Good plan, Mitch thought, a*nd with that cave below, very plausible...maybe that was it.* But using common sense, how could they get past that blockade? He knew the navy was even more paranoid than the islanders; the mainland had been burned once, and he was sure they were not going to let it happen again.

The guard at the entrance told the boys to shut up and stop spreading rumors. The boys were sure as they yelled back at the guard.

"Make me shut up, old man!" Billy yelled back as they moved away.

"Come on, guys--ease up," Mitch said as he thought more about the clues he might not have been looking for.

The boys said they had to go and saluted Mitch goodbye. Liam turned back and said, "Hey, there really is a double secret passage out of here!"

Mitch wished it were that simple, as he wished again that he was still young enough to have that imagination that all kids possess.

Nobody really felt much like joking anymore. Kids still were kids, just a little more scared, and afraid to admit it in front of their buddies. If dreaming is what got them through the day, let them dream, he figured. There was no point in arguing with them about magical passages or escape, since reasoning with a child usually goes nowhere. Again his mind wandered to the lower tunnel: could it really be possible? Mind games followed him everywhere.

Tom had been trying to negotiate with everyone from the despised administration to the head of the local Little League. Some sympathized; others didn't give a rat's ass to what happened to the damn traitors. The governor had nothing to say other than lay your weapons down and march into the streets with your hands high. Most knew this would have been over weeks ago if it wasn't for the POWs, and the way they had been used as human shields. Historically, excessive force has always been the easy way to answer and an out-of-control stalemate.

Claudine and her husband Dewey had been living around their short-wave radio, sort of an unofficial Free Macbeth radio. It seemed to be the way to get any information out to whoever would listen. The islanders knew this, as hundreds of messages were left for the couple just hoping that they could get them out to their loved ones they missed so dearly.

Through the short wave, the islanders had learned of the protesting that was popping up on some of the nation's college campuses, and they thanked God for the open minds of the students. It seemed that older folks just got stuck in their groove of life and couldn't seem to look left or right as most of their minds had already been made up when dealing with the islanders. Old lives, filled full of their own personal tragedies; one could hardly blame some of them for not wanting to abandon the security of familiarity with right and wrong.

As bits of information trickled out of the communication room, they had learned that many of the guard had been busy trying to restore some semblance of law and order to a coastline without utilities. It was still a free-fall, as nobody seemed to know what anyone else was doing. Soldiers were only human, and the demands could only be taken for so long, especially when nerves were on a short fuse.

Word came over the short wave that President Roosevelt wanted to talk to the islanders--that was, if the source could be trusted, which was doubtful. The elders wouldn't believe that she would get involved, but the president appeared to be the last hope for Macbeth. Tom secretly held out hope that she would help lead the search for a peace to spare any more unnecessary tragedy. The problem was the unreliable and unverifiable communications, other than the short wave--smoke signals would have been the next best thing.

With his aides scattering fast as the crisis drew on, the governor sat in his office almost alone. Deep inside, he knew he was about to make his last command; as he could feel his grip on the situation loosening, he yelled for one of his last loyal advisor. "Damn them! This catastrophe is all about an insignificant little town that should have sold out when we asked them to. In their ignorance, they had to be different and ignore the greater good as the real world passed them by. Little ignorant tramps, pustules of pestilence forced to be doomed to the dark abysses of a new world order. Forgotten and alone as they rot in their dark squalor they so blindly defend with their lives. So be it, damn them to eternity!" The final solution had been made, with nothing else left to say, the governor was ready to order the final assault.

When the solution was put in motion, Washington should have been brought into the debate, but the last of the governor's inner circle had been itching for a suitable revenge and wholeheartedly agreed with the covert action. Was it ever really the guard's place to question their administration on state policy? There was still a situation with the possibility of spiraling out of control, with an island full of terrorists. The guard's sworn duty was to defend the state--and defend they would.

By the time the troops and choppers were reading for deployment, the security guards at the state capital didn't give it a second thought as the two uniformed men slipped by the bronze door into the empty capital rotunda.

The two men headed unnoticed up the back stairs, all too familiar with their route as they went toward the governor's private floor. These strangers from Macbeth were all too eager to complete their most solemn mission of a devoted destiny for those still under siege miles away. In their minds their solution would be the sacrificial gift of themselves for their just cause.

With her calls not being taken by the governor, the president had enough. By God she was the president – everybody answered her calls! Her administration had to know what was going on, as a troubled congress was stewing.

Like the sly fox he thought he was, even in his inevitable political defeat for his inability to restore utilities, the governor ignored the president's messages. For a brief delusional moment, the governor felt he was more powerful than the president. Regardless of the chaos his administration had created, his world was complete, even in his vision of an insane reality, nothing more than the bunker mentality he then possessed.

The most powerful world leader snapped; she was not used to being ignored in a time of crisis. She was the president, ignored in private by her husband, but not that day by a lonely governor. All it took was one call for the commander-in-chief and the army was rolling. She and others had seen the CNN pictures of rioting and looting in a few of the coastal towns. She had been affected by the irrational insanity of the moments, and as a mother and leader could not stay out of this crisis a minute longer.

Questioning herself, she wondered how long this state had been on the brink of turmoil. How could she as president never realize the potential for this act of despair? Were other states or communities on the verge of a similar crisis of conscience, cast adrift in the world? The world had gotten smaller with technology, with too much time on foreign policy; her domestic policy took a back seat.

The president had more questions than answers, and she was no more informed that the general public. That was her issue with herself, but she would have plenty of time to reflect on her lack of knowing later. It seemed in her mind that maybe the people of Macbeth had gained some credibility--as she witnessed those demonstrating for the islanders, they couldn't all be wrong. When and if this nation was on the verge of another civil war, would she know it? Adrenaline was flowing, as she knew the critical moves she would make would surely be her defining moment in history.

The moment had come for the Massachusetts coastline to be brought back into the control of the Union. With a determined stroke of the pen, she enacted martial law! Next she wanted a copy of Macbeth's declaration, the one that all the newspapers and tabloids had gotten their hands on first. She wanted it now; a frantic aide sprinted to quickly grab a tabloid with the document out of his office.

All across the nation, many were experiencing the unfamiliar terror of being out of touch with friends and family stuck behind in the affected area. With multiple lines down, few phone calls went through--occasionally a few would be answered by an annoyed operator miles away.

A part of the nation once so solid realized how vulnerable they really were as Massachusetts' government office shut down while the mess was sorted out. The rest of the nation--a bit more jittery, not ready for any kind of mass hysteria--went through their daily routine just looking over their shoulders a little more often. Housewives out on their weekly shopping chore fill their carts up extra heavy, and the once full grocery aisles seemed a lot emptier. Nobody was going to panic, but something seemed to be going on. Who really noticed the silent concern setting in, other than the gas station owners who had to deal with the long lines that just popped up? Did other folks have questions with their elected officials also, or were they just stocking up? It was a *War of the Worlds* scenario, as nobody knew which rumor to believe.

It was funny in a weird kind of way, as the employees of convenience stores emptied of their stock of beer and chips saw the potential for a national crisis; out of Bud and Miller Lite, the gravity of the situation hit home hard. Scattered and crazy reports came into the newsrooms as one reported a hijacked Coors Light distributor's truck full of product stolen at gunpoint. To the victor, a truck full of golden brews…which in the coming days would be worth its weight in gold, as many really needed their mind juice to help them weather the impending crisis.

Unconfirmed reports were radioed to the islanders about another small town further down the coast barricading their local government officials out. The sheriff was called this time; blocking their way stood men, women, and children standing arm to arm with shotguns, 22s, Red Rider BB guns, and baseball bats. The officers with their riot gear stood down, as they were sure they were not going to make the same mistake the guard had.

As parts of the country seemed to be drawn into the paranoia, the president couldn't ignore the pleas anymore. Massachusetts' own House of Representatives had a backroom meeting and made a secret call requesting federal help. Some of the governor's men in the House thought it was political suicide for those who did it, but only if the governor survived the mess. Fortunately that day some thought with a clear conscience and did what the heart knew was right, instead of their pocket.

At about the same time when the first wave of guard choppers was getting ready to leave, the distracted governor alone sat sipping a scotch as he thought he heard the oak door to his office open. Turning to see what problem he needed to handle next, he was greeted by two quick blasts from the cold steel barrels.

He was dead before he could say "shit." He fell quickly to the floor in a crumpled mess as he stared into the eyes of the two satisfied assailants. His term was over. The two quickly ignited a special cocktail and threw it against the wall. Closing the door before the explosion they vanished down the dark silent hall. A pool of warm blood pooled around his chest as the corpse twitched no more.

After the order from the president, the army was on its way to the state's capital; it would have been easier to invade Cuba rather than get into this city. With the uncontrollable panic and abandoned vehicles, the way into the city was blocked. An army that had come to restore order was condemned to ride the middle of the road, as the people they swore to protect escaped in the opposite direction. What was going on? Had these people lost their minds and their common sense?

It seemed the advancing troops were nothing more than an obstacle to many of the panicked citizens looking for safer ground. The army, in its role, didn't feel like the saviors a lot of them had pictured themselves to be, as they finally marched on foot into the capital. All that name-calling directed toward them drove home the point that this state was on the edge of reason. To a few of the older press corps watching the scene, it reminded them of veterans returning from another unpopular conflict in the jungles of Asia, just doing their duty. God and country would still be proud.

"Proceed with caution" were the words passed down from man to man. No officer had to repeat that order twice, as many of the troops felt a bit safer in their bulletproof vest. The capital was still a bit away and soldiers had plenty of time to think as they moved in.

Away from the insanity of the coastline, concerned family and friends of the islanders were not going to take this sitting down, as the stand off proceeded. With visions of using themselves as human shields on the island, the reinforcements in the makeshift armada of pleasure boats sped on toward Macbeth with a renewed vision of a workable peace. Fast approaching the ships of the blockade at full throttle, the officers of the blockade hadn't a real clue what to do with the multitude of unarmed boats approaching.

The flotilla of the concerned advanced, speeding ever faster toward the island. It was then their turn to become part of the revolution as they in their actions had dumped their earlier convictions of right and wrong, while they aimed to do nothing more than break through the blockade and get onto the island and help.

Alone in the Oval Office, the president, a bit wiser from understanding the island's declaration from the crumpled tabloid, was moved by its clear simplicity. Wiping a tear away from her aged face, she understood to a degree the islanders' fears and faults. In a cold panic she ordered her staff to move faster--there had to be more she could do, as Macbeth's doomsday clock ticked down.

CHAPTER 28:

BLOCKADE

The armada closed in on the waters around the island. The comical flotilla of all sizes of cigar boats, speed boats, fishing boats, and large live-in pleasure boats charged in one direction through the waves. All were filled to capacity with families, friends, and sympathizers of the islanders, all consumed about the uncertain future of the survivors.

Like the islanders, the folks of the armada had little real information. What news did trickle out of Macbeth was nothing more than rumor fueled speculation, which could be a nightmare if true, which did little to help the caring souls whose emotions were already on a roller coaster ride from hell. Supporters tried their best to focus their energy on the islanders and their immediate fate, as their unchecked minds sawed away at the little bit of reality they held close. Just maybe if some real information had come out, they wouldn't have felt the urgent need to jump into the conflict, but then maybe if more info had come out more would have joined in. Regardless--family, love, and blood ran deeper than respect for the law.

Jack's uncle, a mainlander by trade, but still an islander by heart, had organized and led the pack. Cutting a deep wake into the dark-blue channel, the armada cruised. A non-violent group of US citizens, an extraordinary day, together for one reason: a mission of mercy. Their quest wasn't an act of aggression, but rather, an act of defiance against what they saw as wrong. Gaining momentum, the boats aimed straight at the naval blockade.

The navy saw the boats coming--too many craft coming too fast in too many directions. Confusion was rampant on many of the naval bridges. All the officers waited for was someone to give them direction for a scenario they had never prepared for, as no one wanted to be the first to fire on the innocent.

The naval forces had been notified not to let anybody or anything off the island. The question and confusion about the orders continued, as directions were unclear about folks trying to get on to the island. Shoot them? Apprehend them? What do you do? Public attitudes seemed to be changing, as many listened to the radio and heard about the growing protest and cover-ups. Massachusetts administration clearly was becoming the bad guy.

Word came down from the commander to stop the boats. Who knew what those determined boaters could be smuggling in? A few of the captains preached that in order to have a confinable situation upon the island, the population had to be controlled on and off the island. But from their by-the-book logic, they still knew it was a lot easier said than done: just like a skeet shoot, with too many targets going in too many directions. Large naval boats were always better in battle against something their own size. These little pleasure boats were like flies on a cow's backs...swat all you want, but more just come back.

This maritime dilemma was turning into a moral crisis for the crews of the navy, targeting their own fellow countrymen.

These would-be targets were the people who put their hard-earned tax dollars into the weapons they aimed. It was more than just pulling a trigger, as all learned and questioned the order they hoped never would come.

The flagship made the first attempt to follow orders, shooting a thundering warning shot. The deadly projectile swooshed over the heads of the boaters, exploding harmlessly in the distance. The new recruits from the coastline were too determined to let the latest threat stop them. Spitting fresh wake in their faces, they cruised on even more dangerously close to the large ships, seeking bitter safety in the closeness that the large gray hulls provided.

By then it was fruitless to attempt to hit any particular craft with the navy's vast arsenal. Someone was going to get hurt as the small boats started weaving in and out of the navy ships' hulls. With limited maneuverability and visibility, the large ships could turn only so fast, as one and then another tried to avoid the almost-certain catastrophe.

All knew it was bound to happen: too many boats going in too many different directions. The cabin cruiser "PARTY CENTRAL" happened to be in the wrong place at the wrong time. Someone on the bridge of the wooden boat became confused in all the commotion and zigged when he should have zagged as they inadvertently turned into the path of the large destroyer...just too many tons to turn or stop that quickly.

The aging destroyer's bridge tried to avoid a certain collision, but her abusive size would have nothing to do with it. Good intentions count only in church, as the destroyer bearing down on the small craft cut the boat in half. Crushing and crunching the expensive boat like a hunk of brittle balsa, the destroyer never flinched in her appetite for destruction.

The screams for help didn't last long; most were just holding their last breath as the destroyed boat slid beneath the waves. The helpless pleasure boat, doomed by one bad mistake, was gone in minutes: no lifeboats, no bodies. This grave mistake was just another unintentional accident, caused when reason takes a back seat to common sense.

The aquatic rodeo continued, as an overpowered cigar boat lost control shooting over a wave from the wake of a large vessel. Rooster tails shot high and its twin engines whined as it slammed into the side of an unforgiving missile frigate. To the sorry occupants, for a brief second they knew what slamming into a rock wall felt like, until their world went black. The boat in its lightweight construction only dinged the metal hull. Its powerful engines drove the cigar boat forward, destroying itself completely in a flurry of pieces and parts.

The destroyed cigar boat's countless remains crashed back to the surface in a smashed heap of bobbing parts, while the frigate's horrified crew could only watch. The biggest part left of the overpowered boat bobbed for a few minutes with its crew still strapped in, then slid silently away. They waited for the survivors to surface, but that moment never would come.

The president was glued to CNN, as was a good part of the nation, and watched the chaos unfolding in real color. Fearing more useless causalities, she ordered the naval boats to hold their positions, cease fire and drop anchor. Screaming to her top military aide in her oval office, she yelled, "For God's sake, you can't stop them--let them go. We're not going to create any more martyrs than the island already has." The president, focused on saving lives, caused a sigh of relief for the captains of the blockade. The burden of making the ultimate choice had been lifted. Lowering a few rescue skiffs, the captains hoped there would be survivors.

In all the confusion, the navy had managed to stop a few of the boats and detained their crew for their own safety. A majority of the boats broke through the blockade and made it to the island harbor. Throttling their engines down, the blockade runners were greeted by the eerie remains of the sunken *Danny Boy* and the charred wreckage of the chopper upon her deck. Squeezing past her hull, the armada headed to the docks and the cold grasp of the silent empty harbor. Shocked at the charred remains of what used to be the town, they were greeted by the cold loaded guns of the guards who had silently secured the harbor. The guards meant business, as boats were secured and crews quickly apprehended.

The would-be reinforcements were led away for their own safety, as the harbor had the potential to be another killing zone. It was better that those new recruits for the cause not be seen by their loved ones, as the uprising needed no more fuel than it already had. Refueling a spent cause in that rebellion would have been a waste of good blood.

Jack's uncle, aboard the *It's Miller Time*, hit the deck as he saw what was happening to the other crews--telling his crew to hit the deck, he made an about- face with the boat. With hot lead from a machine gun at his back, he exited the harbor. Fully aware of the impending situation, he sped through the naval blockade. With guns aimed at his spraying wake, he was given ample breathing room and a second chance at freedom. Only he didn't know that his guardian angel at the moment was the president, who was calling the shots.

On the cliff, the lookouts witnessed what was happening in the harbor below. Helpless and more outgunned as the minutes ticked by, all they could do was bear silent testimony to what had happened, thankful that no one else was hurt, and that the show of support made all realize that maybe their cause was beginning to gain some steam. Dedication from others recharged their tested emotions, as a glimmer of hope would be spread by word from one to another. That cliff that day became their altar as they knelt in a prayers of thanks that they had finally been heard.

Mitch, being one of the few observing this, had a thought that maybe the intensity of the conflict had been turned down. He was wrong as he then saw all the fresh weapons and troops being brought in, and knew then it was overkill. Watching Johnny, not more than seventeen, hugging his Uzi, he realized his youth was gone. With random growth of a beard on his smudged face, he realized he was looking into the eyes of a warrior, not the same face he had first seen weeks earlier checking out the girls coming off the ferry.

"Hey, Mitch," he asked. "Are we getting out of this alive?"

"Alive? Hell yes, Johnny; too many folks are watching us now," he replied as he tried to come up with his best lie. "The governor couldn't be that stupid, to do something big now. We all just have to be careful that no one is too trigger-happy; that's all I'm worried about."

"Yeah, that's what I thought. Just sitting up here thinking... I know I'm screwed. I'm probably not even going to finish my senior year." He paused for a moment. "Well yeah--maybe I'll finish it in some fenced-in detention center."

"Oh, come on, you'll be okay. Just get rid of that gun as quickly as you can when this all ends--just go back to being a dumb kid, and claim innocence."

"Sure, Mitch; I can do that simple enough. But yeah, I haven't even gotten laid yet. Man, I am really screwed," he said as he shook his head.

He truly felt bad. Johnny was right--and he probably wasn't going to get laid until he walked out of those prison doors many years later. Mitch hoped when this was all said and done he would be lucky enough to walk out at all.

The conflict sure had the feeling that it was entering a final stage, as more troops seemed to be arriving in the harbor below--eager to prove their point, do their job, and return home to their families. By then with the islanders' retreat, over a half of the island had been secured and in the guards' control. The big push to the mine and the final battle had not begun, while a majority knew the decision to attack had probably already been made.

In her seat secured in her chopper, the president, scared, pondered her next move. Going to the coastline and the action, she was going to make a firm show of support--and for all those antagonizing generals, she would demonstrate her resolve.

Some of the diehards for the cause had planned for the final siege as they had been busy booby-trapping the road leading to the mine. The bunker mentality had set in. The ultimate redemption in the islanders' vision of a workable peace seemed to be vanishing as the fresh troops rolled in. The militia's options became fewer and fewer as this new saga of an American reality played out, as a glued to the TV audience watched with anticipation wondering when the end would come.

Nobody in the mine would admit what was on their minds, but alone with their thoughts and family, they all wanted it over. All of them--dirty, damp, cut off from the real world--knew there never really had a chance for any other outcome; too much had happened to go back. At this junction in time, a warm, safe jail cell with clean clothes sounded good...things really had changed. Tom and Jack, with their travel mugs of steaming coffee, overlooking the carnage of the town, out-gunned and outmanned, both understood there never could have been any other winner.

With all this soul-searching, all Mitch could think about was a bowl of Iona's Beef Goulash over a steaming plate of sprats. At that point, real cooking was a thing of the past; he was almost getting used to all the gruel and mystery stew Midge made in the communal pots. The hungry couldn't be choosy, but he knew at least their bellies were full.

CHAPTER 29:

THE FINAL ASSUALT

While the governor was still bleeding out, the final solution had started, with a wave of guard choppers coming in low over the muck fields, with Def Leppard's "Pyromania" blaring from one of the chopper's loudspeakers. Mitch heard in the distance the stuck tank firing wildly into the churning air. For the green tank crew, it was like target shooting with terrible aim; too many targets, and no hits. Shooting a tank's guns and a shotgun are two different things: a critical point the two individuals in the tank learned all too well.

Nerves of steel sealed the fate of the crew. They must have felt like defenders of King's Arthur's modern court going to battle in their suits of armor, overconfident, yet firmly unaware of the odds they were up against, when dealing with military grade weapons and trained crews.

No one will ever know if the tank crew saw the missile coming. Sharper than a knife and deadlier, it pierced into the thick metal of the tank and exploded. The burning end for the two was quick, as the sounds of their sizzling flesh and screams were silenced by the sound of chopper blades passing overhead of the burning wreck.

The choppers, waltzed in through the smoke billowing from the burning tank in the valley below. The rising smoke reminded the chopper crews of the mesquite-like smell of a down-home southern BBQ, with just the right dash of diesel fuel. Two souls joined the list of the dead from the cause, as their angels led them safely away.

The airborne cavalry, enjoying the supremacy of the day, flew down Main Street into what little reminded of the little town. The crews searched for safe ground to land, only to find it, and then be welcomed by the well-aimed sniping of some of the militia's hidden men.

By sea, the second leg of the unchallenged invasion, the armored division, landed with little resistance from the island. This town was the guards', as Macbeth's dwindling militia hid away and continued their doomed hit and run assault they never wanted to have.

The guard should have been stopped, but going by the presidents orders early they went in. This president wasn't getting the break she deserved.

The cautious guards, all too familiar now with the militia's record, were for the most part unaware that they were being fired upon. The noise and confusion of choppers landing and taking off added to the circus feel of the event. The random sight of soldiers wounded and falling finally drove the seriousness of the point home. With radios squawking orders, the guard for the humanity of the event ran for cover.

A unit commander, enjoying his first real inklings of a battlefield command, had enough of the lack of respect his guards were receiving, ordering Macbeth's sniper hideouts destroyed. The commander smirked with satisfaction about the thrashing they were about to receive. A gift basket of hand-held missiles was just what the doctor ordered, as he adjusted his seat to observe the show.

Real ammunition transformed pools of revolution into easy prey, as overkill was the word of the day. In reckless blazes of glory, the surrounding landscape transformed itself into multiple fire storms, as all living within ceased to exist. From that quick firefight, these burnt offerings in their sniper's dens were overdue payback for the guard's earlier failures.

Vietnam-era choppers kept circling the edge of the muck fields, while chopper after chopper set down and released its live cargo. A second backup unit, not really eager to push forward and join the battling force already assembled in the ruined town, sat down and reluctantly waited for a command.

Those manning the communication station in the mine hearing the guard's confusion on the radio, knew the final battle was here. It didn't take long to spread the word as their worst nightmares were finally happening.

Billy's mom came running thru the tunnel, screaming, looking for her son. Mitch told her to calm down even though he hadn't seen Billy and his friend recently. "Mitch, you don't understand--you have to help me; they are not in the mine. I have looked everywhere!" the hysterical mother yelled.

"Screaming at me won't do you any good. When and where was the last time you saw them?" Mitch shot back.

"I can't remember. Those two are always just around getting into something."

"You've got to think hard; things are nuts outside, now sure as hell isn't the time to be second-guessing," he responded, knowing she wanted him to do what he didn't want to do.

"Billy and Liam were together, just playing soldiers or something--'all for one,' they were saying. I don't know much more. I just don't know. They're just boys; please, you've got to help me--they would listen to you!"

He stared into her tearing eyes, knowing his better judgment said to stay where it was safe, he realized he was probably
the only one who knew where his young friends were. Hoping
they would come cruising down one of the tunnels, he stalled
for time. The moment never came. Mitch gave in and said reluctantly he'd find them. He had no choice--he had to go. The
lost boys were his friends, and the group's earlier words haunted him, "All for one, and one for all; friends for life."

He had a really good idea where he would find them.
Knowing Kate would worry, he told her he would be careful,
but had no choice but to go. She, stunned at the thought of
him going out into a battle zone, pleaded with all she had for
him to let someone else go. All that remained of her simple
world was slipping through her fingers.

Two women, both with tears: one worrying for him and
one for the children. Maybe being outside of these tunnels
wasn't as bad as Mitch had imagined. Women's emotions...
Mitch never had learned how to handle the human side of a
lady.

Time was a blur. He couldn't remember the last time when
he had full night's sleep with all of Kate's nervous fidgeting.
Mitch was dragging and needed a quick power nap, but nap-
ping now just didn't feel right. With a purpose, and his biggest
wound bleeding again, he leaned forward and grabbed a waiting AR-15. The boys needed him. In the distance the sound of
the battle in town made him forget all about his lack of sleep,
while the thought of death consumed his immediate reality.

Kate insisted that if Mitch was going, she was going also.
Kate was so sure she had lost everything else; she would be

damned if she was going to lose him. Mitch knew he should have been thrilled, but this was one of those times when he would have felt safer alone.

Arguing with a woman who had her mind made up was going to get him nowhere. Mitch talked the gatekeeper into opening the concrete door of the mine. With a strict warning from the gatekeeper about coming back in, they then slipped out into the cool air on their quest. If Mitch knew those boys, he was sure they were somewhere deep within the walls of castle Macbeth. Alone and scared, he pictured them just doing what boys who grow up too fast do in times of war. With a grand vision of invincibility, the two energized kids were caught up in the frenzy of the moment, protecting what they felt was rightfully theirs.

Climbing up the hill while staying hidden on the path to the castle's ruins, Mitch glanced over at the harbor. The once-quaint town of his story was no longer. It looked like a battle zone, with tortured, ruined buildings, wrapped by a hillside of smoldering stumps. The picture in his memory, of the seaside town, sacrificed itself to the new era, as all he could picture was the unrestrained destruction he had just seen.

The Flying Daisy was still moored, but looked as if she had taken a direct hit as she sat low and leaning dangerously. The valiant sub's colors, her cross and bones still flapping defiantly above her ruined deck. It was hard to see it all with all the smoke. What if the young boy's story only could have been true? Mitch could only hope, as he pulled Kate to move quicker and stay hidden, pushed on by the hint of the intense heat from the burned-out hilltop as it grabbed for their fleshy backs.

Mitch, fearing the end, knew the guard had a solid foot-hold on the island. In the ashes of the burned-out town square, some choppers rested after delivering fresh reinforcements for the governor's final solution. What happened to the mi-litia's calculated response? Had they given up, and left to be with their loved ones?

He had pictured Tom and Jack valiantly leading the final charge. Now with the imminent threat looming, the leaders of the rebellion were probably smart, hiding away in the security of the mine where he and Kate should have been.

Mitch thought too soon, as a half dozen hand-held missiles burst into the air, originating from the ruins of the burning buildings themselves. The streaking missiles, pretty in their own kind of deadly way, sent the guard diving for cover. It was nothing more than an old-fashioned trap, set especially for the unsuspecting.

Dozens of hidden rifles started piercing the chilled air, sharing the stage with the two long-forgotten VFW howit-zers as they sprung back to life. With artillery blasts from a war long forgotten, the surrounding hill came alive with the thunder of a more honorable age. The mighty howitzers hid beneath a lush tent of pines, while the smoke of their mighty blast gave away the forest's hidden secrets.

Unsuspecting choppers, one then another, started explod-ing wildly as their thin fuselages were violated by some lucky shots. The battle-shy weekend warriors scurried for what little cover they could find, as their grip on the town seemed in doubt once again.

The undamaged choppers quickly returned fire as best they could from where they sat. Two choppers now lay burning in crumpled piles of wire, metal, and flesh.

The guard had no time to lick their wounds—it was move or be annihilated, as they took to the offensive, pushing into the cover of the destroyed town. Shooting while they moved, cutting down whoever they could target, with the militia's surprise the town fell for a second time.

Whatever injustice the islanders had complained about became wiped away in the carnage they laid upon the guard. Sympathy can turn to anger, then revenge, in the blink of an eye. When guardsmen lost guardsmen, the simple peaceful balance in this unspoken, limited truce became null and void—it was a violation that changed all the rules, and caused the gates of destruction swing open this day.

Young bodies lay still; others, still clinging to life withered in sweet pain upon the bloodied ground.

In despair the old howitzers targeted what they had always symbolically protected. The buildings in town were now only hiding places for the advancing guard, destroyed shells of their former selves as the ghosts of the inhabitants of the years before vanished with the drifting smoke.

The beating lifeblood of the town, its people, now tucked away in the safety of the mines. Its depth, seemingly unaffected in the moment, willingly absorbed every impact and explosion from the land above. Muffled, the sound of the explosions dissipated as the waves moved further below, while mother earth could do nothing more than continue to absorb humanity's faults.

The media sensed the carnage on the island. With little more to report than the smoke and sounds of battle, their creative stories would make the front pages and the headlines of the evening news.

On the mainland, just looking for a reason, copycat fanatics were taking up Macbeth's cause--not because all believed in it; some just had a previous score to settle, and the time couldn't have been better. Looking toward the coastline you could see streams of smoke filling the some of the voids of the coastal sky. Disillusioned voters, voted their vengeful conscience as the law became preoccupied with a solution as their votes turned to violent action.

About the only thing left that Macbeth supporters could do was protest-- and protest they did, as the peaceful marches became battles of words, with many escalating beyond that. The views were too well-defined, and for many there was but one right and one wrong.

Macbeth's cause and action gave reasons to many to vent their pent-up anger, released through arson, looting, and rioting. A few smaller government buildings, one housing the welfare offices were the targets of some pyromaniac's get even with the bureaucracy wrath. A coastline, with its limited resources to respond, was tied up with one too many scenes of crime, causing many businesses to finally shut their doors and wait for the vengeance of the crowd to ease and pray they didn't destroy their business.

In the capital, flames poured from the office of where the dead governor lay, burned for eternity, a fitting end, as his body sizzled. Damn the man, surely he was. Forgotten this man would be, buried alone, condemned for his crimes.

All at once it became even clearer to the president, in three defining words: "WE THE PEOPLE!" This was turning into a small revolution, by the people. With dissent apparent it would seem only the president had any chance of stopping it. An anxious world watched, while many small communities were waiting and wondering how this event would ultimately change them.

Approaching the castle, they witnessed the remnants of the militia's tired army. He knew reinforcements were never coming; the candle of hope seemed to dim. The time to change their minds for these men had clearly past. This dedicated militia clearly involved with their defense had their spirit wearing thin.

The human shields and Macbeth regulars were no longer the captors and their prisoners, but friends. The two groups learned to understand the others as understanding replaced fear. Macbeth's militia knew that the POWs could never have been used as human shields. The captors had taken great measures to assure their safety. Human life still harbored dignity, as the rights of mankind were still evident on portions of this island. Fearing the end, Macbeth's last wild cards, the POWs were turned loose and allowed to seek the safety of shelter.

Macbeth's militia, were more alone than ever before, could only watch and wonder how their end would come. Looking over the lush green valley, most probably dreamed of a happier time, when families and children would play in the green fields below, gazing at the ruins above.

In the soft breeze, one could almost still hear the sound of an impromptu Thanksgiving Day touch football game, when the biggest battle consisted of making it to the other side of the field with a worn football in your hand. Listening, one could almost imagine the silent sound of two lovers absorbing each other with the night sounds of the crickets and smashing waves, lulling them into a lover's trance. Thank God for the fond memories; for some, memories would be all they had left in the short time before death would greet them.

In a moment, Mitch and Kate had walked up the grass-covered slope toward the ruins. Both were eager to find the boys and go back to anywhere safer. Breaking the uneasy silence between them, Kate asked, "Mitch, how scared are you?"

"Scared of what?" he said as he kept glancing over his shoulder, looking for the guard's advancing column.

"Dying...you know, that's all that seems to keep running through my mind," Kate said pausing as she tried to keep up with Mitch. "I really have nothing left, other than you. Really pitiful if you think about it."

Mitch thought to himself, wasn't he enough? Pausing on the hillside for a second, he spoke. "Pitiful--what? Kate, pitiful is those mothers grieving about their dead sons. It might appear pitiful, but we know where we stand. We have two young kids up here that need someone, and that someone is us. We've got a blood-hungry army behind us wanting our hides, and I'm going to be real scared if we don't get our asses up this mountain soon, and into that damn castle. Sorry to be blunt!"

With the tone of his voice rising, Kate broke into a trot, with him now huffing behind her. Getting closer to the castle, the two were greeted by a few quick shots placed well ahead of their advancing path. Judging by their shooting, the militia couldn't see who they were shooting at. Not happy with the thought of being the crisis' next victim, Kate screamed insults in their direction, causing one of them to fire again.

Using what little energy he had left from the climb, Mitch worried they might figure out how to aim. Without a second thought, he leaped forward onto Kate's petite frame, with the weight of his body slamming her face-first into the ground.

"Are you nuts? Get off of me!" Wiping grass from her face she screamed at Mitch, "We could have been safe in that mine...instead they're chasing us from the rear, and shooting at us from the front. Has the whole world gone mad?" Kate yelled as she spit dirt and turf divots from her mouth. She was not quite the lady Mitch had dreamed about, but all woman now.

Realizing he was probably crushing her with the weight of his body, Mitch relented and slipped off her. Out of breath, he turned to talk to her. With sweat dripping from his body, he told her to take off her bra. She looked at him like he was some madman who had lost what few marbles he had left. Turning away, without answering his seemingly perverted questions, she leaned up.

"Kate! I'm dead serious," he screamed. "It's no time to be a prude. It's either your white bra or our hides, and this has nothing to do with sex." More hot lead in his body was not Mitch's idea of a good time. Looking over his shoulder, he saw the advancing military column closing in behind them.

Mitch, not as perverted as some of his ex-girlfriends would testify, at least no more than the next guy, had an idea. With limited resources for a flag of truce to spare their souls, Kate's bra was their only hope--not the triple D cups he wished for, but at least white.

With the help of his male persuasion, Kate felt compelled to volunteer her brassiere for the sacrifice of life. With the lively words "Prude this!" she threw her guarded undergarment at him. Even on a field of war, a turn-on is a turn-on. He had watched intently, as Kate weaved her padded bra out of her loose shirtsleeve. He would have loved to peek, but one too many gun barrels had his attention.

Caressing unknowingly the warm soft garments in his hand, Mitch tied the bra to gun barrel and waved it furiously in the air. Standing up with Kate tugging on his leg, realizing the chance he was taking, she tried to pull this fool down. Lacking better sense or options, he walked forward dragging the newly liberated Kate.

Approaching the sandbagged entrance without another gunshot, the two heard the growing sound of a chorus of male laughter. The threatened men echoed as their flag of truce came into plain view. In her embarrassed state, what could Kate do but smile, even if it was for such a simple pleasure.

There was relief on the faces of many when they recognized Kate. Beauty and war have always mixed. She, the town's hidden rose, now secured her worldly vision among the noblest of Macbeth men, all then absorbing Kate the braless wonder. In her embarrassment, Mitch realized the true woman she was. Grabbing her muddy chin gently, which she hung low, he told her thanks, then sorry for her having to endure the embarrassment, as she reached for her bra, with a background of hooting men.

Echoing from somewhere in the halls of these ruins, a bagpiper piped his tune in every direction. They were soothing melodies; Scottish tunes that at one time had been a call to arms for the legions of true believers of a forgotten time. With the melodies echoing to all the worried souls, an eerie calm prevailed.

In the distance, a moist fog rolled into the valley below, soft and billowing, yet suspicious of the terror that often is associated with nature's white cloak. The guard column marched on, unsure of their desire for another battle, moving a little slower as the intended target came into view.

CHAPTER 30:

WHEN DO WE WAKE UP?

Jay, the obnoxious grocer, guarded the gate to the castle as if it were his prized cash register. Jay wasn't very threatening, with his round bald head and a belly that would jiggle when he occasionally laughed. Not to go unnoticed, he spoke out, "Are you two fools out of your minds walking up here? For God's sake, this isn't any place for a lady."

A crude voice from behind some sandbags joined in, "Hell! She can be my fool any day! Come on in, honey; I'll show you my big weapon."

"Shut up, Bernie. I'd know that crude little squeaky voice anywhere," Kate replied sounding a bit relieved, thrilled with the attention, and glad to see humor still prevailed.

In a moment of desperation to return to his old life, all Mitch could think about was Kate. She was so strong, yet so gentle. She really was more than beautiful. That day, for another time in his once-routine life, the wanderer realized he was in love. Kate was one of his reasons for abandoning everything he had grown to know. Without a thought of her own safety, she stood by the side of a man she barely knew. Without hesitation, she trusted his every decision, yet questioned their cause, which Mitch the visitor had become so absorbed in.

Mitch's life, job, meant nothing to him, as the thought of death consumed his every thought. Life was still so simple, like the passing of night and day. In an instant, though, everyday reality became complicated passion, when one worried about loves and lives that could be lost.

Resting on a sandbag, Mitch tried to talk to Jay as he shoved an apple turnover down his throat. "I'm looking for Liam and Billy. Have you seen them?"

Jay, with an overpowering smell of Old Spice drifting away from him, seemed a bit perturbed at Mitch's invasion of his space. "City boy, all I've seen in awhile are those of us here, and now a beautiful woman who doesn't belong here. This isn't any place for a woman, especially her. Shit, no real man would bring her up here in the first place. You city folk just don't get it; if you did, you surely wouldn't be here listening to me yell." Kate walked past the two men and slipped behind the crumbling wall for the privacy she deserved.

Feeling a bit unappreciated, Mitch bit his tongue. A thousand comebacks to Jay's ignorance invaded his head. Opening his mouth, he realized this overweight excuse for a guard had him speechless. Sparing the comeback of Mitch's spiny wrath, a sweet voice drifted out from behind the wall.

"Jay, Mitch didn't bring me here. I came with him." Pausing as she gathered her thoughts, she continued, "I'm sure somewhere in that head of yours, you probably remember love. That is--if you can think past your temporary ignorance, you might just understand how I feel. It doesn't matter, though; I know you really don't have a problem with me being here... do you, big guy?" Kate spoke out. Jay, with his male feathers ruffled, turned and walked away. Kate had put Jay in his place.

"Mitch! What did you do to my bra? It won't hook." Mitch's little demons were happy, as a little grin crossed his face. *Chalk one up for the good guys*, he thought as he pretended he never heard a word Kate said.

Kate, abandoning her attempt at fixing the bra, tossed it into the rubble and walked on through the ruins. Stone walls and sandbags were no defense against guided missiles, he guessed, but at least the heavy bulk of the fortification granted some form of limited security. What good is a false sense of security anyhow, if your security still could easily be breached? In the heat of battle, hidden away from your family, you still could die alone. Dying in battle was nowhere near the glorious end most pretend warriors dreamt about, even if it was a martyr in murder.

Walking on through the moss-covered halls, the two overheard some older teenage boys guarding their space on the wall, young boys who wanted nothing more than to prove they were men. In their immature ignorance, their youthful spirit showed, while most of their banter trivialized the importance of the potential of the upcoming conflict.

Down the hall, Kate greeted most of the young men by name. In her gentleness, she had a kind word for all, while Mitch scanned the ruins seemingly in vain for the two lost boys.

Seeing Joey Miller, one of the many Miller boys, she called out, "Joey, why aren't you with your mother?"

"Ah, don't you start on me, too. My mom's had a fit already," Joey replied while he tried to escape another female's wrath.

"You just turned sixteen and these men coming have real guns. This isn't your battle--and since when did you stop listening to your mom?" All of a sudden Kate realized the stupidity of all of this chaos, as it all was becoming more evident that she was losing her grip.

"Joey!" Kate screamed, "since your dad died, you became the man of the house. If your father were here, I guarantee you wouldn't be." Shaking her head in denial, Kate, in futility, reached over and grabbed Joey to hug him. Sensing an uncomfortable position, the boy, a bit embarrassed, pulled back, not wanting to be reminded of a caring touch, at least not in front of his armed buddies.

"Katie, not here, "Joey whispered quickly in her ear. "I got a job to do." With his buddies watching him closely, he cleared his throat of the warm fuzzy he was feeling and walked away. Still a boy, carrying a gun much smaller than his pride, he climbed up the wall to man his position. Kate wondered where all the years had gone, then remembered years ago when she babysat that beautiful blue- eyed little boy who was now a soldier.

Yelling the lost boys' names, deeper into the ruins the two searched, stopping abruptly when they heard the tower's bell start ringing. A boy of no more than fifteen hammered away on the old school bell as if there were no tomorrow. "The guard is coming!" he yelled, as he beat the bell even harder. The laughter died down, as all the militia ran to their posts.

The president, trying to ignore her motherly instinct, thought hard. With her keen intuition for trouble, she listened to CNN trying to keep pace with the rapidly changing situation. Her young grandchildren wrestled unconcerned in the hall just outside of her reach. Sensing frustration in her actions, she glanced at their innocent purity, and realized the importance of the job she had left to do.

Her advisors, in all their political might, were at a loss for action. Events were happening on too many fronts, and no one could fathom which front to tackle first. At a loss for what needed to be done first, her aides decided to wait for the president since the ultimate decision was hers.

The president, surfing the cable channels, saw the multiplying newsbreaks, before her aide could bring her up to speed with the changing situation. A battle appeared to be raging on the island, and she knew nothing about it. "How could this happen?" She demanded answers. This president, even though a woman, was still the commander-in-chief of the most powerful army in the world. Yet this lady was the last to know of a battle taking place on American soil. Things just didn't add up, as the lady of grace searched in vain for the answers.

Law and order had broken down in Massachusetts. For the first time in the modern era, this was a state on its own. While lines of communication with Washington went dead, a political system was cast adrift in a sea of chaos, with nobody steering the floundering boat. A sleepy corner of the world now became ground zero, and an out-of-touch world could only guess what would happen next.

Tuning in to talk radio, alarmed citizens could feel the tension in the air. Talk show hosts were having a hard time controlling their shows. Never had talk radio lit up the minds of so many. Phone lines were tied up for hours, with everyday voices waiting and wanting to be heard.

The referees of the airwaves scrambled for the high ground as frustrated listeners vocalized their fears. Airwaves were taken over by a public who would not shut up, with the talk show hosts trying in vain to control the direction of their shows. In disbelief of the power of the people, many a challenged host pulled the plug on their shows, frustrated and in utter despair at a fan base that seemed to have crossed the line between reason and insanity. Alone in their isolation booths, the hosts scratched their heads and wondered if the dark side had prevailed.

Meanwhile, the internet had worked its wonders. That day, for once, in a society on information overdrive, the islanders' views were online to whoever cared enough to read and understand the issues. Macbeth's website was experiencing so many hits, it was smoking. People related enough to the island's concerns and issues that they spread the word.

All citizens deserve a real future, the president thought as she watched the playful exuberance of her grandchildren. No more beating around the bush; Macbeth wasn't going to come to her. This president was going to Macbeth, come hell or high water. Determined, she screamed for her chief of staff to get her helicopter ready!

Getting his cue, the president's chief of staff, Lowell Finnegan, immediately responded. "No president ever goes knowingly into a war zone; it's absurd; it's unheard-of! Madam, have you lost your mind?" Raising his voice even more, he rambled on to himself, visibly upset at the president's notion.

Replying to his concern, she yelled, "Damn it, Lowell! Only one other president ever had to deal with a civil war, and he was not one to stand back either. Things are unraveling faster than I can control them. I know as well as you that parts of this country were on the edge, and we should have started way before. Macbeth was just the excuse that got the issues exposed. Get me a damn helicopter! For once, in this town of phonies, we really have no time to spare." As her aide digested her words, he raced down the hall, shaking his head.

It was so true. Somebody had to stop this battle, but nobody seemed to be listening. The guards were tasting blood, and the armchair officers loved it. Adding more fuel to the fire, they had sent more questioning troops to battle. The thrill of war, no matter how small it might be, had engulfed their common sense, and what had been so wrong yesterday was now so right.

Desperately looking among the ruins of the castle for the boys, Mitch and Kate had a chance to talk with many of the dug-in defenders. The two realized how out of touch many were, alone with visions of their loved ones, stuck with that last parting glance as they went off to war, a haunting vision of love that only helped focus the men on their mission.

Jack and Tom were manning a position just like the rest, both probably dealing with their inner demons for starting this conflict in the first place.

"Mitch!" Jack yelled as Mitch walk by. "Got one hell of a story, didn't you!"

"More than I ever wanted!" Taking a deep breath, Mitch spoke out. "It's not too late!"

"Too late to do what, end this conflict, Mitch? Do you want us to drop our weapons and walk? Mitch, we're all damn traitors--you know that. They can't let us go. We're going to be their examples. You know, like I do, society was built by simple examples like us. Law and order always works best with fear. Too many folks with too many agendas, just waiting to see what happens, take our place, and help pick our bones. There really could never have been any other way, just no way out!

Sorry, Mitch; heroes aren't heroes until they're dead." Turning his head to look out over the valley below, Mitch knew Jack was right; he patted his trembling shoulder and walked respectfully away.

"Good luck, Jack," Mitch said as he grabbed hold of Kate. For once Jack and Tom felt the isolation they had imposed, as they felt Macbeth's future resting on the outcome of what happened next. If the islanders had only known their dime store revolution had already changed the stride of society, the end might have been avoided.

Mitch thought hard, with the sounds of the battle thumping away in your head, one wonders if it is a dream, or if this is now reality. Sacred dreams and visions of your loved ones danced in an orgy in your twisted mind, as you dealt with your day-to-day routine. It is a devastating thought to any loving person, the possibility of never seeing a loved one again, no matter how important the cause might be. Blood is thick, and only gets thicker in the heat of battle. While loyalty may wane, family ties move on, hand in hand.

The ensuing battle had been turned up a notch as screaming guard jet streaked across the horizon and started pounding the hills on their way to the castle. The old howitzers overlooking the town were no match as the precision bombs took them and half the surrounding hillsides out, causing small avalanches of dirt to cascade down the hills, grotesquely engulfing the small neighborhoods in nature's overpowering wrath.

The thundering sound of the reverberating bombs made Kate a target of a few young boys who now realized they were not ready to be men. With tears of fear, the boys realized war was hell and not what their childhood dreams made it out to be. It was too late for them, as they had made their ultimate decision, as the piper called them to join his march of death.

The sound and shock waves loosened Mitch's resolve, while he tried to grab Kate and hold her tight. She was the closest thing to a mom for many boys, as she tried to comfort them the best she could. Grabbing her slender figure, he ripped her from the clutches of one too many pairs of young hands. Kate would do none of them any good dead, as Mitch pushed her to the safety of cover.

"Mitch! What are you doing? Let me go!" Kate screamed. Mitch had no time for answers, as he pushed her to get down to the ground. Not taking his silence for what it was worth, she hit him.

"God damn it, Kate!" he screamed, realizing the Lord was not whom he should be damning, but whom he should be praying to, as the outside walls of the castle shuddered, when an explosion ripped into the old stone wall.

Scared and irritated at Kate's boldness, Mitch, like the lunatic he was, screamed again at Kate. "Kate just follow me! It's your hide I'm trying to save, not just mine." Kate looked at him realizing he was scared.

Somewhere on the outskirts of the town, the few snipers remaining were harder to hit. Their slyness resulted in the use of more bombs, bombs that burned. Once exploded through the flames, a manmade darkness rolled across a portion of the island. In the confusion of war, one could not tell whether it was day or night. The smoke from the few bombs filtered out what little light there was. All at once this little part of the island was plunged head first into this nauseating darkness, while everyone's senses screamed at them to run.

Unseen through this blanket of soot, a few more hand-held missiles streaked from their unyielding cover. Their aim, working like there was no tomorrow, led the warheads on the mission of revenge.

An unsuspecting phantom jet, with its engines glaring red hot, was hit violently, crashing and burning uncontrollably into the ashes of the church and its cemetery. Within this fireball from hell, its force and fury destroyed in a blinding flash any reference to the many forgotten generations buried below. Everywhere you looked in the crater of the impact, broken and burning caskets, pieces of jet, and smashed gravestones scattered among the bones and tattered clothing of the elders.

The heat below in the valley was intense as you could feel its warmth in the flame-induced winds that swept up. There was no battle front anymore, just smaller battles around the tiny island. Small pockets of Macbeth's once-grand militia held out hope, now just trying to make heads or tails of a situation gone berserk.

Unnoticed stories of heroism and acts of courage unfolded from the battlefields, while many of the witnesses died before their stories could ever be told. The real battle was now more about survival, as the big picture became small again. Most combatants were worried about seeing tomorrow, since another battle raged in their troubled minds as surrender took on a whole new meaning.

With the battles on the island, the mine's thick door was shut. In an instant, the locks made it impenetrable. The islander controlling the gate knew it would take a well-placed nuke to take it out, and hopefully no rational lunatic would take that chance. The advancing guard could only climb around the door looking for a way in, which there wasn't, with the tools and weapons they had.

Dodging the few scattered bullets of the remaining militia, the guard kept searching for a way to penetrate the door, as they too finally realized their fruitless pursuit and scattered for cover.

What ashes and rubble remained of the town was now firmly in the guard's hands. The officers kept pushing, knowing they had gone way over their line in the sand with this president. Their only possible redemption would be to wrap this up quickly and give it back to the union, coming home maybe, as heroes for saving the tragedy they started.

In the castle under Macbeth's flag, all knew the final assault was here as the sound of the battle only drew closer. The two still had found no sign of the boys, as precious time ticked away. Mitch cold only hope, for the children's sake, that they were safe and ready for whatever came next.

Kate, more afraid than ever, stood by Mitch, wondering what this man she thought she knew would do next.

He did not want to lose it. If he succumbed to his emotions, Kate would certainly be lost. He was still a man as he gently pushed Kate on into the cold cellar, where he first entered the castle weeks before. Torn between helping the men above and the woman he loved, Mitch sat by her side, while the fresh smell of an exploded ordinance danced in their nostrils.

"Hey, I'm sorry for hitting you back there," Kate, blurted out. He could be cruel, but that moment was not the time. Gathering her shaking frame in his yielding arms, he softly kissed her soot-covered head. With words he reserved only for his parents, Mitch said he loved her, as his little world was now complete. If death came now, at least he knew he had truly loved.

The president, and a nervous aide by her side, commanded from Marine One. Escorted by military choppers and a few air force fighters, she meant business. Her military entourage, all engines roaring, evoked the mixed emotions and respect of the state's guard ships below, as one by one they were boarded by the waiting marines.

Approaching the war zone, the president could see the smoke of the battles. At a loss to control her overworked feelings, she cried out, "This is too much, it has to stop." Who was left to listen? she wondered. With tears welling up in the wrinkles of her eyes, she felt powerless, while the carnage continued in man's own hell below.

Caressing Kate gently, Mitch felt for her, as her short life was now in imminent danger. He, the great provider, had nothing to offer her, other than the warmth of his arms. How he wished she were back in the security of the mine, rather than by his side.

Within the castle walls, all had no choice but to hear the increasing sound of guns from within starting to shoot at the advancing threat. Soon it was a chorus of gunfire, as the ruins came alive in battle. Mitch and Kate's little hideout became a random target, when the lead and shrapnel started bouncing around their crumbling room.

Screaming in panic along with the wounded screams above, Mitch told Kate, "Go for that hole in the wall." She looked at him as if he was crazy, but she witnessed the horrified look on his face. That look convinced Kate, as she crawled quickly into the dark hole. He followed as the close thump-thump-thump of something hit the building above. Screaming, "Crawl faster!" through the trembling hole, they went. In a split second the floor gave out below them, dropping the two deep into another room.

With the wind knocked out of Mitch and Kate next to him, he cleared the dirt out of his eyes and looked up and saw two boys who had grown up too fast. "Damn, Mitchy, are we sure glad to see you," Liam yelled out. "We're scared real bad, he pleaded as he started to cry.

Mitch, coughing and gasping himself, told the three to get down, as the battle intensified above. Together they huddled and covered their heads, praying to whoever they needed. If there were angels, they were with them as their world above seemed to disintegrate around them. With every falling stone, it seemed one step closer to their divine they came.

It was a sick cowardly feeling that overcame Mitch being trapped below. With the heart-throbbing screams from the men defending above, he questioned his resolve. With each blast or gunshot, Mitch knew that could have been them. Only one lucky shot, and the final chapter of his book of life would have been finished, and Mitch would be up above with the rest of the martyrs of the cause. Dying with dignity for the brave of the island was irrelevant. In any war, could death with dignity really ever be achieved?

CHAPTER 31:

WAS THE GAIN EVER WORTH THE PAIN?

Political careers were toast, as the president was one pissed-off politician...more so since things got out of hand. She was irritated at her shortcomings and the unmistakable fact that this could happen during her watch and under the noses of her administration.

In a quick and unprecedented move in the history of this nation, the president chose to speak to the nation using the best means available, the Emergency Broadcast System. For another time in our nation's history, every airwave available to the population of the United States would carry the president's live voice. Her move had one goal, to save a nation--nothing less, as a portion of her country was clearly in turmoil.

The president's time was precious as she chose to speak from a moving helicopter entering a live battle zone. Her advisors were beside themselves at the thought of the commander-in-chief in that big chopper. What a great target, they figured.

The president never was a comfortable speaker, but today she would speak from the heart, filled with an unbridled conviction and an unstoppable determination for justice. This cause could never get any closer to her emotions. Being a mother and grandmother, this lady would speak for the generations that could not speak for themselves.

On the island, those listening in the mine and the battle-field to the short wave radios realized that day in radio land this interruption was for once not a test. All stations went silent as the emergency broadcast signal came blaring across the air. Then as the emergency signal went dead, the president's determined voice came across the waves, a confident calculating voice, reassuring, determined in its quest for quick justice.

In a scolding grandmotherly tone, the president spoke. "To you that are listening, the American people and the people of Macbeth, make no mistake. The union is only as strong as its people and its laws. Today you the people have spoken with your actions, some demonstrating their lack of resolve by rioting in the streets and their total disrespect for law and order.

"I have watched the news reports like you, and I have witnessed what has taken place in Massachusetts. Our law does not work with the present state administration in place.

"As of noon today I have ordered the army and navy to blockade the capital and parts of the coastline and treat it as a foreign territory. I have sent troops into its capital to take into custody what is left of its corrupt administration. In due time, our courts can sort through who is innocent and who is guilty.

"I have mobilized neighboring states reserve units still loyal to the union to patrol their states and control and suppress and developing situations. This crisis will not be allowed to continue.

"Martial law will be in place for the affected area until we feel the situation is safe enough for it to be rescinded. I have also put our entire military on the highest state of alert since the Cuban missile crisis. I do not want any other foreign nation getting any ideas about joining in on our party.

"Massachusetts's day-to-day running shall be controlled by the federal government until a time when Massachusetts can satisfactorily and fairly govern itself.

"To the innocent and law-abiding in Massachusetts, be firm and fair. Bide your time and bite your lip until order returns. Remember, the safety of yourself and family comes first. It is unstable times within, and the situation merits extreme attention and caution.

"At this time I have instructed our United States Armed Forces to take control and end the battles on the island of Macbeth. It is not evident at this time who exactly is in control of the guard on the island. Until it is determined, they will be treated as hostiles and subjected to the same treatment as any invading nation would be treated to. A fair and unmistakable warning is being issued as I speak to all forces on the island.

"To the people of Macbeth, I cannot feel your pain, but what you did was wrong. I wish we could have intervened and solved this before you chose the path that led to these drastic actions. Hopefully our courts of law will understand what drove you to this. I for one will observe, demand, and pray for a fair and unbiased trial for all on both sides.

"To the guard and militia of Macbeth, lay down your weapons now, and the guard is to move back to the what is left of the town or be treated as traitors and subjected to the laws and might of the land. I am still your Commander-in-Chief. What you are engaged in now has not been ordered. Cease hostilities!

"To Macbeth, I am demanding an immediate cease-fire and a suspension of all hostile actions. I would like to meet with your leaders soon and set up the framework for a permanent disarmament and a clear cease-fire with terms fair to both sides. To demonstrate my faith and resolve on my demands, I would like to meet upon your island as soon as a time can be set and an area secured.

"To America, it is time you receive this wake-up call. Democracy is by the people for the people. When you don't vote and get involved in the system, remember the people of Macbeth, who have voted with their lives. A government is only as good as the people voting it in. God Bless America, and let us pray for all of those fighting and dying upon Macbeth."

With that, the president had finished the most important speech of her life. A leader among men and women had emerged from the shadows of gloom to lead this questioning and stunned nation forward.

Deep in their dusty hole under the ruins the four of them could only imagine the intensity of the raging battle. With each passing minute, the fighting seemed to intensify. Projectile after projectile struck within and around the castle. With each explosion the walls seemed to shudder in agony.

The smell of spent gunpowder was nauseating, fooling everyone's limited senses. The four of them in a confused state gulped feverishly for any bit of fresh air they could smuggle into their starved lungs. Then, as quickly as the battle seemed to accelerate, it died. The killing had ended and the earth was still. An eerie quiet was broken only by the crying of the dying and wounded above.

Kate, the first to move, worried about those groans above. "Mitch! Get up! We have to help!" she cried. The agonizing cries evoked sympathy any caring soul could muster. Mitch would be of no use to her, and she knew it. The brave man he thought he was would not lend itself to the blood above.

"Kate, I'm hanging back here with the boys. We'll be right behind you," he said, fully knowing the sight of wounded always made him question his true manhood.

Emerging from the security of the earth's cocoon they found no warmth, but instead the realm of death and intense destruction. It was a smoking painful world where mankind had shown its worst as the living now suffered.

How could man one day go from being good neighbors, to friend and bitter foe? It only took one man's greed for power, with his flock all too eager to follow. War must somehow be bred into man and restrained in most.

Each community is its own, yet it shouldn't be measured and judged by its unique social fabric. Macbeth's ideals were set. The system worked, yet it wasn't flexible. These points, Mitch was sure, would be discussed and argued for years to come. One thing for certain: change had come. There was no stopping it now. Tragedy creates stories, heroes, and legends, and Macbeth and its people would not be the exception.

Mitch pondered as he stepped among the dead and wounded. Lord knows he wanted to help, but not having the knowledge or stomach could only prevent him as he led the boys. Kate, without a second thought about her vanity, was busy ripping her blouse into bandages. Soon she knelt there so beautiful, almost topless, sparing just enough blouse to cover her. She gave no second thought to her modesty. This wasn't something sexual now. This was life and death. Not sure of his own feelings, Mitch tossed her his shirt to wear.

Passing a toppled stone wall, Mitch heard a barely audible

voice coming from underneath. "Where are you?" he yelled back.

The soft voice of a child came back: "Help me, it's so heavy..." as his voice seemed to give out.

Mitch, like the dog he once had been, started digging through the rubble, looking for the voice. He screamed for help, as the stones only got heavier. Liam and Billy were the only ones who answered his call. All for one, they dug down till they hit soft flesh. Thinking it better that the two youths not see what Mitch thought he would find, he had them stand back. Reaching down, he felt the lukewarm flesh as he pulled one of Kate's former admirers from his temporary grave. Fighting back his emotions, he cleared rubble off the dust-covered youth. *Could any revolution be worth this?* silently he thought to himself. Mitch carefully pulled the boy out.

"I'm cold," another voice said from the same hole; with his blanket of rubble gone, some other dusty flesh moved. Frantically Mitch and the boys reached in and pulled another youth from the ground. Joey Miller had learned his lesson well. Too weak to walk, but still strong enough to hold his gun, revenge instead of fear occupied his mind. Joey lost more than blood that day, as battle had robbed him of his youth. Through his tears of anger, the next avenger of this massacre had arisen.

The three of them dragged the two to a flat area in the rubble, joining the wounded that were drifting about. It seemed more were wounded than standing, as the foul smells of blood, burnt flesh, human excrement, and gunpowder mixed.

Kate and some of the men bandaged as much as they could, all just praying for some form of real help. Aspirin, duck tape, and blouses didn't go far in a life and death scenario.

Kate was truly the rose and Mitch the thorn, in this true hour of need. There were men and boys who only a short while ago were alive with yet unfulfilled dreams that ended, as did their breath. The floor was becoming slippery with blood when Mitch had to go--this man of steel was about to get sick.

When his stomach emptied, Mitch climbed the battered wall to get a clear view of the destruction. Looking around, he realized the guard had not been spared the agony the militia were all sharing. Bodies and smoking vehicles lay scattered and destroyed, turning the lush green fields into a killing field. The dead were left among the dandelions of spring, just maybe symbolizing the rebirth of the true believers.

Off in the distance they could hear the ever-increasing beat of the choppers, coming in for the final kill. "God, have you no mercy?" Kate screamed from below as Mitch yelled back for Kate and the boys to take cover.

There was no fight left on either side. It was time to surrender, as Mitch scurried around looking for something white to wave in the smoldering air. He just hoped he was in time to save those of them that were left. Too many would be mourning tonight. The death and destruction had to stop, as he prayed like he never prayed before.

The heavy thumping of the blades intensified as Mitch in desperation pried a dead man's gun from his crisp fingers. He grabbed a bloody t-shirt off a corpse, tied it to the rifle, and thrust it high into the air, hoping it would be seen before another round was fired.

He ran for the entrance of the castle like a Texan ready to make his last stand as a mighty chopper slipped up in the valley, then hovered in place less than fifty feet in front of Mitch.

Like the angel in his dreams, Mitch saw the Red Cross on the chopper sides and realized his most important prayer had just been answered. Falling to his knees, he dropped his gun and broke down into the tears no grown man ever wants to shed. A weak cheer of relief echoed through the ruins of the castle as the wounded and living took a big breath again. An army of fresh medics had arrived to take care of man's act of carnage.

In the confusion, a messenger from the mine arrived, looking for Tom or Jack. Tom was busy helping the wounded and dying, and Jack couldn't be found. "The president is coming. She's really coming!" the young boy shrieked.

"She's coming here?" Tom yelled over the beating blades of the chopper. The boy, out of breath, stared at the carnage his young mind couldn't accept and nodded his head yes.

A guard ran up to the gate of the ruins, carrying his own flag of surrender; he explained what the boy no longer could say. "The president has ordered a cease- fire. All the guard troops are to pull back into town and lay their weapons down. It's over, man! It's over!" he yelled. The guard's words traveled like lightning through the ruins, as the militia gave thanks for the gift of life they all now shared.

With a slow motion, Tom laid his head in his hand and prayed. Whether he prayed because it was over, or for the dead, it didn't matter.

The president never stopped believing in the nation and the union. This grand lady had demonstrated that she was willing to die for it. This simple act of courage meant more to the men and women of Macbeth than she could have ever imagined. At that moment in time, any man of Macbeth would have gladly defended her, as the healing had already begun.

No longer needed, Mitch gathered Kate and the boys and headed for the gate. The slight stink of Old Spice was drifting in the ruins. Turning a corner Mitch saw Jay's cold torso, or what was left of it, slumped over a half-eaten box of Twinkies. His cold stare of death covered his swollen face. In his mouth the remains of his last Twinkie were covered in his gravy of blood. He probably never knew what hit him, since guarding his post had become his passion. In death all his imperfections were erased, as he chased the great Twinkie in the sky.

The four of them joined what was left of the tattered and bandaged island militia and headed home. In tattered step, the lone bagpiper still piped a tune as they abandoned their last stand. Lending a humble spring to their tired step, they marched through the blood-splattered field helping those they could, praying for those they couldn't. Death surely had visited his share of lost souls this day.

Mitch pondered how man's extreme anger toward each other could vanish in the blink of an eye. Was it truly the baptism by blood? He had no answer, only compassion for the price both sides had paid. The retreating columns of both armies mixed and marched in the ever-increasing procession of pain.

He, still a journalist, could only wonder if this flowering field of destruction had become the Gettysburg for tomorrow's generation. He hoped that this newly consecrated field would someday honor the memory of these two groups of patriots both fighting for reasons they had so strongly believed in yet few really understood.

Time would sort the whole mess out, as all moved on without their sets of convictions, alone in thought to the unnecessary loss all had experienced. The two sides left their dead to guard the fields, now watered with the fresh blood of this generation's sacrifices.

CHAPTER 32:

IS THERE EVER A REAL PEACE?

The guard, with respect to the will of the president and the backing muscle of the marines, ceased all hostilities, and more than willingly laid down their arms. Peace came easy to the warriors, all eager to resume their real-world roles. Following the president's orders, the weary troops assembled in the ruined remains of the town, eager and ready for deployment back to the mainland.

Eagerly the president's backbone, her marines, had landed in full gear more than ready to guard that thin line that separated war and peace. Both sets of leaders felt that the need for violence had certainly been turned off as quickly as the waves washed in and out of the harbor.

In the days since the hostilities ceased, the mine had been opened again as those below breathed fresh air again. Because of the fear of the what-ifs, the entrance was still heavily guarded while negotiations took place. Trust would take time to be earned, as the state's administration had turned the clock back on trust.

As the president managed the crisis, the marines with strict orders stayed away from the islanders' half of Macbeth. Tom eagerly suspended any type of hostilities to the welcomed marines.

The president, more aware of the situation than her aides, agreed to their strong objections to personally meet with a contingent from the mine.

Amazed that this president would meet with them, Tom knew no matter what, when peace was worked out between them, he and the fighters of Macbeth would always be marked men. Too many guards had been killed for all of this to be just swept under the table. Outside the security of the island there would always be someone hell-bent on seeking revenge for their loss. It was a given.

Jack was never found. Most figured he was buried under some collapsed wall. For him it was probably better that way, since the courts would not admire the man the way the islanders did. Men come and go, but heroes for the cause would ride the clouds.

The coastline had sections still in a primitive state, as utility repair crews scrambled to get communities up and running again. The coastal residents blamed everyone but themselves for their bad luck as they directed their anger to whoever was close enough to blame. It didn't matter, the sooner power and water was restored the quicker people moved on with their lives. Forgiveness could never come soon enough!

Regardless of the final consequences toward Tom and his militia, peace had no option other than to be reached. Some towns were still occupied and under martial law as the need for progress toward reconciliation had to be achieved. There were still fringes of common folks who still were on the verge of rioting, but had pulled back as the island and situation had quieted down with the president's strong handed intervention.

In his guilt, Tom realized how much the US meant to

him. It was truly pointless to draw anymore into this boiling pot; the point had been made, and Tom was more than willing to broadcast that appeal to all the supporters of the cause he had never met. Change had come, as many political thieves were swept out of office; the guilty knew who they were, and reacted quickly to save their own skins. Change had come!

Not the quite oval office, but in the privacy of her chopper, the president and Tom had met. He was moved that she would meet with this secessionist. She quickly realized how sincere he was, and how this never should have happened, but it had. Together the two worked out an understanding and framework for peace, both only wanting what was best for all, thinking more about the future regardless of theirs.

The Treaty of Macbeth, as it would be remembered, was really more than a document of peace, but rather a blueprint for the future. It was agreed the country needed to refocus on what made it great, and this president had proved she would deliver. Tom had seen the caring in her eyes as he hugged her tight, and then left satisfied that the dead on both sides had not all died in vain.

The handwritten document would be presented to both sides; both knew it contained the truth and had to be accepted to stop future bloodshed. The limited war was over; the damage had been done. Life could never be the same, as Tom and his tired few re-entered the mine for the security, as most were still too gun- shy to be seen in the open.

Mitch should have followed them back in, but Kate was on his mind. She still thought she could help somewhere, and he would stay by her side. Heart beating with anticipation for their future, the world seemed to open up ever so slightly to them once again.

In the mine, the patriots--as they saw themselves--discussed and prepared for their ultimate fate, knowing many would be locked up and others on the run. It was a hard thought, being separated from each other, knowing all they had gone through together. Some thought maybe they could move somewhere and rebuild their lives, while those more rational knew it could never happen. Most would be destined to try to blend in somewhere and become another nameless face and forget they were ever a part of the rebellion--if not for them, then for their children, who needed a clean slate. In death the governor had his last revenge on this dead island, soon to be uninhabited, as only nature and time could heal and cleanse this graveyard of humanity's ignorance.

A part of the peace accord was the release of all remaining prisoners. The islanders, being men of their word, released the remainder of the captives, who thanked them for their caring treatment. The line between captivity had been broken as more were close friends after the many hours spent with each other.

There were those few die-hard prisoners who would not harbor the same gratitude that most did and would sooner turn on their captors with a loaded weapon. Without a country, and as bad as that sounded, it was just a preview of life to come for the islanders, branded by some as traitors and cast adrift in many anonymous communities wearing an invisible scarlet letter.

It was a sad fact that to rebuild Macbeth would never be financially possible, as most insurance policies had clauses in reference to wartime. Loans or grants from any institution or government would be ridiculed by the public. If the mainland felt it was their responsibility to rebuild, the cost could strap the state for years.

Their lives were destined to be lonely ones. Some would say life is still better than no life at all. The price for peace was steep. The islanders prayed the next generation would forget their sins.

Mitch surely felt for the children who unfortunately would be haunted by the ghost of the crisis for years to come. Children could be so cruel to each other, as he knew so well. The endless taunting and associations with the traitors would bear heavily on their futures. He was sure again that from colleges to the job market, the kids would be branded as troublemakers, regardless of their innocence. He hoped that just maybe some would find peace in some little forgotten corner, and have a place to eventually call home.

Kate, being more optimistic than Mitch, thought time would heal. With education and discussion, the US would be better off because of Macbeth. In years to come, hopefully they would see the situation for what it was, and not what the tabloids reported.

It was lonely in the mine anymore as the days passed by. The dark voids seemed to hold fewer people as many must have moved to their own space. All most wanted to do was to be outside and escape the smells and dampness of the tunnels.

Needing a break from the mine, the two walked slowly through the carnage of the town. They were two lovers holding hands just staring at the ruins, sometimes too shocked to talk. He could almost picture his old editor drooling, just wishing she had his story. *Serves her right*, he thought. *This would*

have been the story of her career. He knew with satisfaction that
the thought of her having a rogue reporter on the island during
defining battle would haunt her for years to come.

In a selfish way he knew his life would be better because
of the island. It was only common sense that any tabloid or
filmmaker would pay him a king's ransom for his story. Hell,
at that point even his autobiography would probably sell. To
Mitch then it was more than the money. Bloodshed had a way
of sharpening your distant perspectives. He was a new man,
who deeply questioned his future.

He knew all too well he wasn't innocent, by any means; he
knew he had participated in the crime. No matter how hard
he tried to wipe the shooting and killing out of his mind, the
crime was dug in. He would be told by many later in life, "It
was you or them, Mitch." Sure, that sounds fine, but how does
that stop the images of the young face alone in that cockpit
gasping in horror knowing that he is going to die because of
your luck? Mitch had always wrestled demons of one kind or
another. But this demon had a super glue of a grip, and he and
Mitch would grow old together. Sadly, he knew that was the
price he would pay for his once-in-a-lifetime story.

The more he thought about his options, the less he realized he could write. How could he ever write about the lost
lives for cash, when he could still feel the lukewarm skin of a
young corpse as its life-giving warmth retreated? They died, he
lived--all random acts of good or bad luck, nothing more; how
would he ever deal with it? He grabbed Kate closer, and wiped
a tear from the corner of his eye. His personal battle had only
just begun, as he would search for that inner peace he would
need for a long time to come.

CHAPTER 33:

BEFORE THE END

The final insult in itself was almost surreal: one naval officer, anal in his respect for law and order, torn by his sworn duty to his commander in chief and by the loss of his son, killed in the battle during the final assault. The officer with his sorrow overruling his common sense caved into his need for revenge.

It was too easy, as many of the sailors relaxed as the tension had eased, then alone at the weapons console it was only a code and a simple push of a button when his decision had been made. He had decided his missile frigate would be the sword of justice, since he knew the punishment these traitors would get would never be good enough for his loss. His officers stood in horror as they peered through the locked door of the weapon room and could only watch.

In a flash of brilliant white light and smoke, a cruise missile launched. The commander was in full control of his actions. He knew the deed he had just initiated was uncalled for, with a peace being achieved, but to him this action was clearly justified. Then placing his pearl-handled revolver to his head, he committed one final insult to humanity. In a single blast he delivered his verdict in his own personal trial: guilty! At that moment, maybe a son and father were reunited.

Out of the brilliant blast the beauty rose, slowly at first, then engine kicking in as it thundered and arched its way gracefully, streaking away on the short mission and rendezvous with Macbeth's future.

The mine's thick cement door had been open, letting the fresh air seep into its shafts while expelling the smells that had gathered. There wasn't much activity around the entrance other than a few guards going through the motions.

Mitch felt detached as he was seemingly unnoticed by the others going about their business--was he an outsider again? In the last few days he had seen less of the people he had grown so accustomed to being around, but knew most were probably getting what was left of their lives back together. It was pointless anymore to ask any questions, as most seemed set in the fact that their way of life was coming to an end.

Why wouldn't anyone at least want to be outside enjoying that big blue sky? he and Kate wondered. The warm sun on their pale faces only helped hide the tear streaks and look of confusion they were experiencing. He figured it was still a matter of trust, and too many loaded guns keeping the peace on the island, which he knew scared many into thinking twice about leaving the safety of the mine.

Billy and his buddy had vanished, along with their family. At least Mitch was a saint to someone. He knew the two boys were still pretty shook up after the battle. Children seldom see death as close up as they did. No one would ever blame their mothers for sheltering them a little more carefully after that. Mitch and Kate were much older and they were still trying to digest all that had happened--it would take time, if ever.

He knew better than to try and talk to Kate anymore about the rebellion. He knew if he brought up what had happened he had to be ready to deal with her depression again. In time, he knew things would click. Trying to get through the day he searched for any humor he could muster, just trying to get her to crack even a faint smile.

He learned after assignments in the war-torn countries that life went on. It might never be what you remembered and trusted--it couldn't be, but it was life. If you could only shake those dark clouds that hung on in the recesses of your troubled mind, just waiting for the moment to lash out and tear at you again...to Mitch it was almost like that bad date that never ended, and any door you opened was another dead end.

As she grabbed his hand and looked into his eyes, he knew Kate wanted something.

"Mitch, I want to go see my home; will you walk with me?" How could he tell her that he knew what this would all lead to? He knew when she saw her burned out home that he would not have the right words to comfort her. Mitch knew either way he was going to regret this.

"Sure, Kate, whatever you want--but are you sure? He caved in; he was no fool, and he knew she already knew his answer and nothing he said would change her mind. He held her hand tighter as the two headed home.

"I've been thinking more, Mitch--what's next? You going back home to write that big story you always dreamed about?"

"Hmmm, well...you know I got all those women just waiting to get a piece of me. Just kidding--you laughed, didn't you?" She wasn't amused.

"I don't know, Kate; do you think they are going to want me to be a journalist again? I figure they want me for the story I can tell and then dump me. I'm a killer now, or maybe any mother's worst nightmare." He laughed, realizing he finally had a badass reputation." Are you trying to get rid of me?"

"Mitch, please be serious!" she said as she pulled away.

"Serious! I stuck around, didn't I?" He knew he better ease off; she wasn't ready to deal with his remarks just yet.

Approaching a few burnt-out buildings; Kate grabbed him again and pulled him toward the remains of Fanny's. Both just stared, looking for any reminder of the past. Kicking in the rubble, he found an old breakfast platter and some twisted forks.

"Makes you sick, doesn't it, Mitch?"

"So many pancakes, so little time," he said as he licked his lips thinking back to the last full stack he had there.

"Mitch, for God's sake, this was all Fanny had. What's she going do now, smartass?"

He was wrong. He needed to just shut up, but he couldn't.

"Kate what are any of us going to do? All we can do is watch the pieces fall into place and remember we have no control where they go. Let's enjoy the peace we have now. You know as well as I that once we get off this island, the real circus will begin." Turning his back on the ruins, it was her turn to follow him. "Let's get going. I want to make sure we have enough time to get back to the mine before dark." What more could he say? He wanted nothing to do with the serious side of life, while the nightmares kept chewing away at Kate's reality, the woman he loved.

Mitch hadn't felt this lost in a long time. The sense of frustration reminded him of his own shattered feelings. It was hard to deal alone with the tragedy, once more he was thankful Kate was near.

The island was hallowed ground for both sides, dedicated by the men and women who perished. Where could you go from here? What story do you write? What could equal what unfolded here--as an afterthought, nothing seemed to amount to anything greater than this unfortunate story.

Mitch knew then there was no way he was going back to work anytime soon. His old life seemed so insignificant anymore. He figured all the guilty would have to do some penance to make them equal to the dead. What some of these folks had lost was more than he would ever have had. As insignificant these battles would seem in the years to come, they had managed to rip open some national wounds. Sure, everything heals--all most could do was hope the wounds healed much stronger this time.

Sure, he could make some easy cash for all of this if he wrote, but he still had to come to terms with it himself first. "Don't let this get to you," he said. "Any war is hell. Mitch knew it all too well now.

Looking over at Kate, she was so beautiful, but in an instant his thoughts were shattered as the missile came cruising down Main Street, sweeping past them in almost a slow-motion blur. Was this really happening? He wondered as if he was only dreaming. He knew he wasn't: a missile no question, no conscience, built for two reasons...death and total destruction.

Standing there in stunned silence, they could do nothing. No time to warn anyone as that helpless feeling hits you. You know someone's world is about to explode as that sick numb feeling takes over your being.

Kate screamed, "No!" Too shocked to realize what was truly happening, she fell to her knees praying to God, asking why

He needed any more blood.

Turning around quickly, realizing the force of the explosions would be extreme, he reached down for Kate. How could she cry any more? She had to be numb from all the tragedy. He held her tight; as he looked for a spot to escape the explosions.

The missile would have no problem finding the target--the door to the mine was wide open, almost welcoming. With nothing to stop it, into the shaft it went. What seemed like a few minutes were only seconds, when a growing echo of a large explosion seemed to grow from the bowels of the tunnels. The wounded mine spit fire and smoke as if gulping for fresh air as it imploded from within.

The force of the contained explosion shot out like an explosion from a gun barrel, knocking Kate and Mitch to the ground. The heat was searing as the titanic roar threatened what little hearing was left. Quickly the two were surrounded in a filthy cloud of nauseating gas as the clean air was scattered. Anything left alive--including Mitch and Kate--struggled to catch their breath as they gasped for anything safe to breathe.

He gasped for his next breath, too concerned with living to just worry about Kate. She was his everything, wasn't she? Rationalizing that he was no good to her dead, he placed his sweaty shirt over his mouth and nose and searched through the cloud for her body.

Her coughing while struggling to catch her breath made it easier in the temporary darkness to find her. He lay on top of her, hoping to protect her, even as the wet shirt was no match for the grit from the explosion as it easily found its way into his throat. *Find cover or die*, his brain kept screaming as he struggled harder trying to make sense of the blindness. He grabbed Kate's body, and the two clawed their way to any salvation they could find.

Getting nowhere fast and on the verge of passing out, they stumbled into the wreckage of one of the doomed choppers. With an ounce of strength left, he opened the battered door and threw Kate and then himself in.

Slamming the door behind him, he cleared his eyes, revealing the carnage and the deteriorating guts of the two dead pilots. Kate didn't blink an eye as she had finally come to accept the consequences of death. Death was never easy, but easier that moment, knowing full well that because of the pilots untimely demise, Kate and Mitch would live.

In a moment the destruction was complete. All that remained was the shifting and settling of the loosened material as the entrance was sealed tighter than a tomb. Nobody could have survived the blast--and if they did, the explosion had easily sucked all the breathable air out of the shafts.

With the ultimate act of this coward--or to some, a hero--the struggle for Macbeth was over. Those in the mine had their freedom, as they had to be in a better place that day.

Sitting in the chopper, they sat motionless after having witnessed this act of revenge. Kate knew the life she had grown up with was truly gone, as a good part of the island's people that were spared, were vaporized and buried.

Looking over at her, Mitch noticed she was smiling. He thought he had finally started figuring out women...and then this. Had she finally lost her mind and become immune to pain? He didn't know, but he just grabbed her and hugged her tight as they waited.

The sound of chopper blades could be heard as Mitch

opened the door. Having had enough time sharing space with the overwhelming smell and flies, the two stepped out. The two survivors, one in denial, the other in a daze were surrounded by marines and medics. It was their time to be rescued. Macbeth was done; it was time for someone else to start picking up the pieces.

Starting to scream, Kate was crying as the medic tried to help her. Mitch jumped in and held her as she buried her head in his chest. Holding her tight, he felt her bare and burned skin on her back. She was hurt from the blast and didn't know it as he motioned for the medic to come back over. Feeling the burning sensation himself, he knew he could wait.

As the chopper rose, in the distance Mitch spotted some men walking down the side of the hill. It looked like they had come from the castle as they hobbled down the hill carrying Macbeth's flag. The ruins were now more deserted than ever as it halls were empty again, left for nature to clean up.

While the chopper gained altitude, he looked out the window one last time at the island. Through the dissipating smoke, he could see the *Daisy*. Trying to make reality out of confusion, he noticed the sub lying on her side. It seemed that the sub just didn't look as real as it had before. One thing for sure; it was destroyed and wasn't prowling the sea again. Nothing down below looked real anymore, just a mass of destruction ready to be bulldozed over. The chopper moved quickly as Mitch tried to figure out if he still had all his marbles. Approaching the crest of the hill, the castle became visible as once again the stars and stripes flew upon the flagpole guarding the top. Strapped in tight, he couldn't help but feel what could be next as the protection they had on the island was definitely ending.

In a quick thought, Mitch guessed in the long run it was better that the whole thing ended the way it did. Modern society never really would have had a place for these people. There were just too many casualties on both sides, with too many hard feelings and destroyed relationships. Trust would always have been elusive, as most would always have had to look over their shoulders. Calculated death had a way of turning people against each other for generations to come.

Kate felt like they should have been given the chance to stick around as the rescue effort got underway, but judging from the force of the explosions, it would only be a recovery effort for the bodies. It was better to remember the islanders in life.

Both knew that for the three dozen or so who had managed to survive, their future would be a hard road. It was going to take a long while to get on with it, as the impact of the mass death started to sink in. The haunting images of Billy and Liam or of Midge and her pancakes, Peace and his love for the island, and the strength and leadership of Jack and Tom would follow both through life, as well as the other faces that had started feeling like family to Mitch. Feeling more tears beginning down his face, his emotions had won as he grieved for his loss--looking out the window hard, he didn't want Kate to see his pain.

Mitch knew he was the story he had always sought; he just couldn't write it. Feeling a bit alone as he kept holding her hand, softly he prayed to God the one he never had any use for, to please let his healing begin and end his suffering. Maybe he and Kate would have been better off in the shafts below with their world. As the coastline passed below, into the heartland they went, hopefully to a lonely spot where nobody would know their names.

CHAPTER 34:

THE END

The fog had dissipated enough, allowing the two to see the quaint seaside town. In a moment the tranquility of the day was spoiled when a single shot rang out from a dark corner of a building. Looking at Mitch, Kate's eyes rolled back into her head as her body went limp, falling to the ground. A pool of velvety red blood gathered around her head, only intensifying the pain Mitch was feeling.

Awakening with a jerk in a cold sweat from another of his seemingly never- ending nightmares, he sat up and tried to focus on the walls of the hospital room that were becoming all too familiar. "Macbeth," his great American tragedy, kept racing though his mind, as the beads of sweat ran down his face. Kate was fine, he knew, just a few halls away as she too dealt with her inner demons, just praying her days would go faster, to ease her pain.

The rays of the morning sun shone through his locked window. Mitch wasn't sure if he'd ever be able to look at sunshine like he used to. He was truly more vulnerable, and had learned to understand the extreme value of life, and the responsibility to preserve it at any cost. A lot of good it did for the dead.

In one of his Walsh theology classes, it was said "there is no greater difference than heaven and hell, right and wrong," It still made no sense to him. Those survivors from the island had witnessed the best and worst in humanity and lived through it. It was probably best then to not judge a whole group of people by one event, but judge them on how they lived, loved, hated, provided, fought…and ultimately failed.

Mitch's story would have to be that. A story centered on how a dedicated people had lived, and how a braver people had died to make the union and smaller communities like Macbeth more perfect.

Almost a year later, as time had trickled by, Kate and Mitch had learned enough to deal with their nightmares. Each day, it got a little easier to crawl out of bed for Mitch, though both still had occasional haunting reminders of those who had perished. Life to both almost seemed surreal. Everybody's little problems didn't seem as big as they used to be. They walked the same streets, but deep inside they felt different. They felt tainted by the blood on their hands and the tragedy they had witnessed.

Mitch had tried to snap Kate out of her daily gloom, but she just shuffled along in a daze at times. She seemed to carry the weight of Macbeth on her frail shoulders. He was getting worried about her, as she ate less, and was always afraid to sleep for all the unwanted visitors who kept invading her guilt-filled head…a guilt created by her living, while the world she loved had died back on that island. Mitch knew if he hadn't been with her through the last year, she probably wouldn't have been here either. Depression was taking over her reality and no matter what he did, it didn't help.

Being in a one-sided relationship, at times he realized that when you truly love someone, there is no pain worse than watching the one you love self-destruct. He knew she loved him, but he just wasn't enough. He understood that, but he still couldn't accept it. Help was needed, but where do you find real help that could help you deal with what she went through?

Later, after getting released from the hospital, the two had tried to live anonymously. That was nearly impossible when their pictures had been splashed across every type of media across the nation. Word would eventually get out about their new hideout, and the paparazzi would soon follow as they raced to get the shots of their thin worried faces as they scattered, searching for any type of security that silence and darkness could provide.

"Why can't you leave us alone?" Kate would cry. "Damn you!" this once-compassionate woman screamed, as she would run flipping off the scavenging media. She was turned into an animal as she fought for her sanity and privacy.

The paparazzi loved her aggression, as her picture would be taken as she snapped in her moment of desperation. What more could Mitch do, as he would try to protect both of them from the hungry pack? He was better off, because his focus was on helping Kate, and he had grown to care more about her than about himself. Knowing the depths of her pain every night as she wept, he was scared, as he never knew which direction to turn to protect his delicate little flower.

There were other survivors, who were reduced to victims of the light as they were forced to hide away until dark, just praying that they would not be seen. Most had learned that they were unsure whether the public would congratulate them--or on more than one occasion, spit in their face. Most had no real friends anymore, other than each other. Sure, they had interested parties come into their lives, but most saw only dollar signs as they maneuvered in to capitalize on Macbeth's remaining disciples. In essence, the remaining islanders were the New Age lepers, as they had no other choice than to hide away from the peering stare of a frequently thankless society. Alone, they prayed for any kind of redemption that would save them for the unforgiving spotlight they were under. Sad to say, too many prescription pills and booze had become their best friends.

Other than the bags of hate mail and the few letters of support, the mail wasn't worth reading. Mitch got his jollies reading the letters from all the lunatics just waiting to put a bullet in his head. Too many broken and hurt families created a new group hell-bent on vendettas stacked against them, which kept all the survivors moving so it would never be easy to track them down.

Once in a while Kate would have a good day when she would talk softly, with an almost childlike sound, no longer the vibrant, self-assured woman she had been. Life, it seemed, was almost a burden to her; as Mitch prepared himself for her end he was sure was coming, if she couldn't snap out of her dream.

Mitch, with dwindling funds, had to cave in and take the cash advance for the movie rights to Macbeth's story. He felt as if he was robbing the souls of the dead, but he was flat broke and they moved too much to secure even a minimum-wage job where he couldn't be spotted. With the funds he did help the survivors he could; other than family and friends, financial support was thin.

Often on any dark night Mitch would lie next to Kate as

she thrashed about the bed with her unending nightmares, and he wondered how it would have been if he had never taken that assignment on Macbeth. He probably would still be sleeping around, enjoying his so-called friends, still searching for that perfect woman. Looking back…that was fun, wasn't it? he wondered. So many women, so little time…say goodbye in the morning and on with his life. Wow, how could he think of that with the woman he loved lying next to him teetering on the edge of insanity? Life just sucked anymore; he had gotten what he wanted and was stuck. He knew it did no good to dwell on the past. He and Kate needed a real income; maybe then he could buy the security and privacy they needed to survive.

The survivors all formed a tight network where they could all keep tabs on each other without the invading eyes of the media and curious neighbors. It was this strong support group that seemed to help chase the demons away.

One evening, word came through a friend that another island community off the coast of Washington state had supported their movement, and welcomed the group with open arms to visit and maybe join them. Most of the group felt reluctant, not wanting to believe there really were people on their side, and at that point Mitch was grasping at anything that might help Kate snap out of it.

"There has to be a point when we trust some people again!" Mitch said to the small group of survivors. "I need all of us to think about it!" he continued.

The invitations stood, but most still were too afraid to commit. Mitch never was one to give up easily, as he worked on Kate and some of the others for a few months to reconsider the offer. Did they just get tired of hearing him ask, or were they maybe ready? A few months later, the trip was on.

It took some pressure from Mitch, as he agreed the group would travel by night and sleep by day. They would stick to the highways, where they would blend in and just be like any other traveling group. Sneaking in through the doors of the rest areas, they would be in and out like a thief. For Mitch, the smell of Old Spice in those restrooms seemed to greet him and always jolt him back to the blood and stench of death, but he was stronger now.

The travelers were all too aware of the scarlet letter they all seemed to carry as they hid their faces, just praying no one would recognize them. It was a long journey and the sound of the road echoing in their big vans seemed to relax the group, as they knew they were safe as long as they were moving. In and out of thought, they pondered the next chapter in their lives, just hoping maybe the next stop at the end of the coastal road might be the one they prayed for.

Coming to the end of the road, he heard the gravel skid out under the weight and braking of the van. Grabbing their suitcases, the group shuffled down the dock to the waiting ferry. Déjà vu to Mitch...another time, another place...but he was sure he had done this before.

The cold salty spray irritated his three-day stubble as he stood peering over the front railing of the lunging boat. The Atlantic was not match for the Pacific's fury as the waves pounded the boat. Raising his hands, he felt the cold spray on his face as the pain from the salt let him know it wasn't a dream. Kate looked at him and smiled. He wondered to himself, had her healing begun?

"Mitch?"

"Yes, Kate?"

"You worried?"

"No, I'm not really anymore, just more curious. Nowhere near as worried as I was when I thought I might lose you!"

Clearing her throat, she continued, "What if it's a trap? What if the invitation was just a ruse? You know we are trusting people we don't even know."

"Yes, we are, Kate, but does it really matter? We weren't getting anywhere back there. How many more empty dark rooms do we have to live in before we realize we deserve to live?" Mitch knew this had to happen. "I'm tired, Kate, and I'm damn tired of hiding--we have to find a place to call home."

"Home? Home is gone, Mitch. When I lost those people, I lost my chance at ever having a home ever again."

"What are we? The rest of us, we don't count?" he replied.

"You know what I mean. I love you all, and it's just so damn hard." Kate was upset, but Mitch knew what she meant. It was silent again, other than the sounds of nature as the ferry finally rounded the island and headed into the harbor.

Squawking seagulls always seemed to be the greeters; only the bellowing seals made it any different. The ferry blew its horns as the pilot threw the engines into reverse to slow down the forward momentum of the boat. The gears clanged, and then stopped as the ship edged in to its waiting berth.

Smelling the all too familiar smell of fish parts, Mitch felt at home in a strange kind of way. No demonstrators or photographers waited to snap pictures-- only two boys waiting for the ferry's ropes to tie her to the dock.

More than a little leery of abandoning the serenity of the

rusting ferry, Kate followed her man off. With his face still stinging from the salty spray, Mitch glanced as the two boys raced away on their bikes. For a minute he thought about Billy and Liam, but he knew better than to go there again--after all, they were safely locked away in their innocence--in his mind, forever young.

The group stood on the dock; with no one stepping forward to decide what to do next, Mitch volunteered as he asked a deck hand where they should go.

"Well, I know there is a group waiting for you all, just got to find them." Sucking a well-worn straw, he smiled with a quick wink. "Friendly bunch...don't get many visitors, though. They will be glad to see you all. Well, I'd love to chat, but we got a lot of supplies to unload, and we still have to go back--good luck!" With that, he jumped back on the boat and went about his business.

Approaching the town, the group followed Mitch. In their uneasiness they almost resembled early immigrants carrying all their worldly possessions as they shuffled on through an unfamiliar town.

Seeing three little girls no more than ten or eleven, playing with their dolls while peddling some lemonade, Kate brushed Mitch aside and asked for their help.

"Hello, my name is Kate, and we are looking for some people who are expecting us. Are your parents or anyone around who might be able to help?"

The girls looked at each other and giggled.

"Well I'm Holly and these are my friends Shira and Kendal, and we're not supposed to talk to strangers, but everyone knows you're coming, so I guess you're not strangers!"

"Hi, Holly--those sure are beautiful dolls!"

"My brother doesn't think so...right?" Shira nodded, being the quieter and more timid of the bunch, while Kendal poured lemonade.

Holly, not wanting to miss a sale, spoke up again.

"You guys look real thirsty and we have some homemade lemonade for sale and it's only ten cents a glass. We're saving to buy a real baby, you know!"

"A real baby?" a surprised Kate replied.

"Yep--these dolls are fake, and we're almost eleven and ready for a live baby!" Holly exclaimed, very sure of herself. "We are Brownies, you know, and we even took a babysitting class, but not Kendal--she learned to shoot arrows instead!"

"Wow--that's definitely a goal, girls," Kate answered as she looked around for any adult to step in.

"You know, girls--sell me enough lemonade for all of us. We're all thirsty, and here's 5 bucks!" Mitch injected. "And can you give us directions for another 5 bucks?

The girls looked at each other, screamed, and danced at their newfound wealth.

"Oh yeah, ten bucks! Oh yeah, ten bucks!" they chanted.

Giving him the motherly scolding look, Kate put her hands on her hips as she said, "I can't believe you're bribing a child-- now that's a new low!"

"Oh, come on, Kate--it's for a real baby!" he said with a smirk as he enjoyed the Kate he had missed for so long.

The girls, thinking they had made the big time, poured lemonade like the pros they were. Tapping Mitch on the back, Shira then pointed her finger at a big two-story building down at the end of the street.

He gave the girls the cold hard cash, and they thanked Mitch over again as the group puckered up and slurped down the homemade swill.

Scanning the whitewashed building, he looked at his target. Approaching the building, he looked twice in disbelief as he noticed an almost familiar sign, "Flap Jack Heaven." *What a great tribute...or coincidence*, he thought. It really would be great if it were a tribute to a fine lady and a mouth-watering institution; salt, sugar, and grease always brought it back home.

The rest of the survivors followed as Mitch turned the handle and walked into the eatery. With the brass door bell ringing overhead he stopped in his tracks and stared ahead in disbelief as the packed room erupted into jubilant screaming! Kate and the rest of the group hesitated as the group was sucked in.

"Get in here--and what took you all so long?" Midge screamed, racing to hug anybody she could. Tom, Jack, Peace, and all those familiar faces jumped into the celebration, as the tears of separation and reunion flowed.

In shock, some of the group could only stare as they absorbed what was really going on. Questioning their sanity, they thought twice, as if this couldn't be happening.

"Come on in and sit a lick--we got a whole lot of explaining to do!" Jack yelled.

In disbelief they all stood stunned and shaken. Months of bottled- up anxiety in Kate came flushing out in her in streams of tears as Lynn ran up and grabbed her, holding her tight. Mitch could only stare at all the faces he thought were long dead. Feeling a blob of fur rubbing against his leg, he snapped out of it as he saw his friend, a much thinner Amadeus, uttering an almost genuine purr.

Still holding on to Lynn, Kate reached for her cat as she buried her head in the soft fur. She was weeping uncontrollably; her world felt almost whole again as she erupted.

"But why?" she screamed.

Jack a bit caught up in the moment cleared his throat, while he tried to hide his emotions. "You all know sometimes a kid's story does come true--big caves and a magical sub. We all really need to sit back and talk about it; we really had no choice, Kate."

Afraid to talk and expose his building emotions that he had learned to hide so well, Mitch glanced away, hiding his tears. Looking for the perfect spot to stare at and not be seen tearing up, out the window he looked toward the harbor. In confusion he saw the skull and cross bones flapping atop the mast of the *Flying Daisy*. In a micro second all his questions were answered as his mind became clear. He had a family again!

Putting his big arm around Mitch's shoulder like any caring father would do to his son, Tom spoke, "Great little community here, all because of a little town called Macbeth. You all know some towns never really die, they just move on. Kate there's this little old bed and breakfast up the street all paid for, just looking for someone like you and Mitch to move in... interested?"

Kate, still overwhelmed, stroked her cat; her eyes got a little of that youthful tingle back as she looked up at Mitch.

"What do you think?" she said softly. What could he say as her brighter blue eyes melted him away...he knew that he was in love with her forever.

"As long as I'm with you!" he said, as he turned toward

Tom. "I've got to know, Tom--why?" he asked.

Replying, "Somebody had to survive!" Tom walked over to the mixed group of survivors, reaching out for them. "You all helped make the illusion all the more believable. Thank you for the sacrifice you endured for us."

"I just don't get it? How did you pay for all this? The journalist in Mitch inquired.

"The *Danny Boy* was real good to us, as was the president. The ship carried a lot more than drugs. We figured the cash she held had to be heaven-sent. We all just bought this little bit of heaven out here. A dying town, with a group of welcoming residents who understood our plight...things always seems to work out, don't they!"

Jack, speaking up in his bold voice and showing that big Grandpa Walton smile of his, said "Welcome Home!"

With a twinkle and a smile, Mitch knew the war really had been won. Pulling Kate close, he hugged her as he never had; he finally cried burying his head on her shoulder. This was love, this was home, and these people were his family. In an instant they both had a future again. Life would go on as it always did --maybe a little different, but surely forward.

Mitch's dad, before his death had told him: "Change is always good." Only time would tell if he was right. Just maybe another story someday....

But as always, the town lived on.

CPSIA information can be obtained at www.ICGtesting.com
Printed in the USA
BVOW02s0305240815

414656BV00001B/1/P